Also by Susan Wiggs

Family Tree
Just Breathe
The Apple Orchard
The Beekeeper's Ball
Table for Five

THE LAKESHORE CHRONICLES

Starlight on Willow Lake
Candlelight Christmas
Return to Willow Lake

For a complete list please visit susanwiggs.com/books.

And from Sarah Morgan

FROM MANHATTAN WITH LOVE

Sleepless in Manhattan
Sunset in Central Park
Miracle on 5th Avenue
New York, Actually

PUFFIN ISLAND

First Time in Forever
Some Kind of Wonderful
One Enchanted Moment

For a complete list please visit sarahmorgan.com/books.

SUSAN WIGGS

SARAH MORGAN

A Summer *of* Firsts

mira

ISBN-13: 978-0-7783-1801-9

A Summer of Firsts

Copyright © 2017 by Harlequin Books S.A.

The publisher acknowledges the copyright holders of the individual works as follows:

The Goodbye Quilt
Copyright © 2011 by Susan Wiggs

First Time in Forever
Copyright © 2015 by Sarah Morgan

For questions and comments about the quality of this book, please contact us at CustomerService@Harlequin.com.

www.Harlequin.com

Printed in U.S.A.

CONTENTS

THE GOODBYE QUILT

Susan Wiggs

To my curly-headed daughter, Elizabeth—
you are my sunshine.

Odometer Reading 121,047

**Wanted: a needle swift enough
to sew this poem into a blanket.**

—Charles Simic,
Serbian-American poet, (1938-)

One

How do you say goodbye to a piece of your heart? If you're a quilter, you have a time-honored way to express yourself.

A quilt is an object of peculiar intimacy. By virtue of the way it is created, every inch of the fabric is touched. Each scrap absorbs the quilter's scent and the invisible oils of her skin, the smell of her household and, thanks to the constant pinning and stitching, her blood in the tiniest of quantities. And tears, though she might be loath to admit it.

My adult life has been a patchwork of projects, most of which were fleeting fancies of overreaching vision. I tend to seize on things, only to abandon them due to a lack of time, talent or inclination. There are a few things I'm truly good at—*Jeopardy!*, riding a bike, balancing a checkbook, orienteering, making balloon animals… and quilting.

I'm good at pulling together little bits and pieces of disparate objects. The process suits me. Each square captures my attention like a new landscape. Everything about quilting suits me, an occupation for hands and heart and imagination.

Other things didn't work out so well—Szechuan cooking, topiary gardening, video games and philately come to mind.

My main project, my ultimate work-in-progress, is Molly, of course. And today she's going away to college, clear across the country. Correction—I'm taking her away, delivering her like an insured parcel to a new life.

Hence the quilt. What better memento to give my daughter than a handmade quilt to keep in her dorm room, a comforter stitched with all the memories of her childhood? It'll be a tangible reminder of who she is, where she comes from…and maybe, if I'm lucky, it will offer a glimpse of her dreams.

All my quilting supplies come from a shop in town called Pins & Needles. The place occupies a vintage building on the main street. It's been in continuous operation for more than five decades. As a child, I passed its redbrick and figured concrete storefront on my way to school each day, and I still remember the kaleidoscope of fabrics in the window, flyers announcing classes and raffles, the rainbow array of rich-colored thread, the treasure trove of glittering notions. My first job as a teenager was at the shop, cutting fabric and ringing up purchases.

When Molly started school, I worked there part time, as much for the extra money as for the company of women who frequented Pins & Needles. Fall is wonderful at the fabric shop, a nesting time, when people are making Halloween costumes, Thanksgiving centerpieces and Christmas decorations. People are never in a hurry in a fabric shop. They browse. They talk about their projects, giving you a glimpse of their lives.

The shop is a natural gathering place for women. The people I've met there through the years have become my friends. Customers and staff members stand around the cutting tables to discuss projects, give demonstrations and workshops, offer advice on everything from quilting techniques to child rearing to marriage. The ladies there all know about my idea to make a quilt as a going-away gift for Molly. Some of them even created pieces for me to add, embroidered with messages of "Good Luck" and "Congratulations."

You can always tell what's going on in a woman's life based on the quilt she's working on. The new-baby quilts are always light and soft, the wedding quilts pure and clean, filled with tradition, as though a beautiful design might be an inoculation against future strife. Housewarming quilts tend to be artistic, suitable for hanging on an undecorated wall. The most lovingly created quilts of all are the memory quilts, often created as a group project to commemorate a significant event, help with healing or to celebrate a life.

I've always thought a quilt held together with a woman's tears to be the strongest of all.

Nonquilters have a hard time getting their heads around the time and trouble of a project like this. My friend Cherisse, who has three kids, said, "Linda, honey, I'm just glad to get them out of the house—up and running, with no criminal record." Another friend confessed, "My daughter would only ruin it. She's so careless with her things." My neighbor Erin, who started law school when her son entered first grade, now works long hours and makes a ton of money. "I wish I had the time," she said wistfully when I showed her my project.

What I've found is that you make time for the things that matter to you. Everyone *has* the time. It's just a question of deciding what to do with that time. For some people, it's providing for their family. For others, it's finding that precarious balance between taking care of business and the soul-work of being there for husband, children, friends and neighbors.

I'm supposed to be making the last-minute preparations before our departure on the epic road trip, but instead I find myself dithering over the quilt, contemplating sashing and borders and whether my color palette is strong and balanced. Although the top is pieced, the backing and batting in place, there is still much work to be done. Embellishments to add. It might not be proper quilting technique, but quilting is an art, not a science. My crafter's bag is filled with snippets of fabric culled from old, familiar clothes, fabric toys and textiles that have been outgrown, but were too dear or too damaged to take to the Goodwill bin. I'm a big believer in charity bins. Just because a garment is no longer suitable doesn't mean it couldn't be right for someone else. On the other hand, some things are not meant to be parted with.

I sift through the myriad moments of Molly's childhood, which I keep close to my heart, like flowers from a prized bouquet, carefully pressed between sheets of blotter paper. I fold the quilt and put it in the bag with all the bright bits and mementos—a tiny swatch of a babydoll's nightie, an official-looking Girl Scout badge, a precious button that is the only survivor of her first Christmas dress… So many memories lie mute within this long-handled bag, waiting for me to use them as the final embellishments on this work of art.

I'll never finish in time.

You can do this. I try to give myself a pep talk, but the words fall through my mind and trickle away. This is unexpected, this inability to focus. A panic I haven't been expecting rises up in me, grabbing invisibly at my chest. Breathe, I tell myself. Breathe.

The house already feels different; a heaviness hangs in the drapes over the old chintz sofa. Sounds echo on the wooden floors—a suitcase being rolled to the front porch, a set of keys dropped on the hall table. An air of change hovers over everything.

Dan has driven to the Chevron station to fill the Suburban's tank. He's not coming; this long drive without him will be a first for our family. Until now, every road trip has involved all three of us—Yellowstone, Bryce Canyon, Big Sur, speeding along endless highways with the music turned up loud. We did everything as a family. I can't even remember what Dan and I used to do before Molly. Those days seem like a life that happened to someone else. We were a couple, but Molly made us a family.

This time, Dan will stay home with Hoover, who is getting on in years and doesn't do well at the kennel anymore.

It's better this way. Dan was never fond of saying goodbye. Not that anybody enjoys it, but in our family, I'm always the stoic, the one who makes the emotional work look easy—on the outside, anyway. My solo drive back home will be another first for me. I hope I'll use the time well, getting to know myself again, maybe.

Scary thought—what if I get to know myself and I'm someone I don't want to be?

Now, as the heaviness of the impending departure presses down on me, I wonder if we should have planned things differently. Perhaps the three of us should have made this journey together, treating it as a family vacation, like a trip to Disney World or the Grand Canyon.

On the other hand, that's a bad idea. There can be no fooling ourselves into thinking this is something other than what it is—the willful ejection of Molly from our nest. It's too late for second thoughts, anyway. She has to be moved into her dorm in time for freshman orientation. It's been marked on the kitchen calendar for weeks—the expiration date on her childhood.

At the other end of the downstairs, a chord sounds on the piano. Molly tends to sit down and play when she has a lot on her mind. Maybe it's her way of sorting things out.

I'm grateful for the years of lessons she took, even when we could barely afford them. I wanted my daughter to have things I never had, and music lessons are one of them. She's turned into an expressive musician, transforming standard pieces into something heartfelt and mystical. Showy trills and glissandos sluice through the air, filling every empty space in the house. The piano will sit fallow and silent when she's away; neither Dan nor I play. He never had the time to learn; I never had the wherewithal or—I admit it—the patience. Ah, but Molly. She was fascinated with the instrument from the time she stretched up on toddler legs to reach the keys of the secondhand piano we bought at auction. She started lessons when she was only six.

All the hours of practice made up the sound track of

her growing years. "Bill Grogan's Goat" was an early favorite, leading to more challenging works, from "The Rainbow Connection" to "Für Elise," Bartok and beyond. Almost every evening for the past twelve years, Molly practiced while Dan and I cleaned up after dinner. This was her way of avoiding dish-washing duty, and we considered it a fair division of labor—I rinse, he loads, she serenades. She managed to make it to age eighteen without learning to properly load a dishwasher, yet she can play Rachmaninoff.

In the middle of a dramatic pause between chords, a car horn sounds.

The bag with the quilt falls, momentarily forgotten, to the floor. That innocent *yip* of the horn signals that summer has ended.

Molly stops playing, leaving a profound hollow of silence in the house. Seconds later, I can still feel the throb of the notes in the stillness. I go to the landing at the turn of the stairs in time to see her jump up, leaving the piano bench askew.

She runs outside, the screen door snapping shut behind her like a mousetrap. Watching through the window on the landing, I brace myself for another storm of emotion. She has been saying goodbye to Travis all summer long. Today, the farewell will be final.

Here is a picture of Molly: Curly hair wadded into a messy ponytail. Athletic shorts balanced on her hip bones, a T-shirt with a dead rock star on it. A body toned by youth, volleyball and weekend swims at the lake. A face that shows every emotion, even when she doesn't want it to.

Now she flings herself into her boyfriend's arms as a sob breaks from her, mingling with the sound of morning birdsong. Oh, that yearning, the piercing kind only love-dazed teenagers can feel. Hands holding for the last time. Grief written in their posture as their bodies melt together. Travis's arms encircle her with their ropy strength, and his long form bows protectively, walling her off from me.

This kid is both the best and worst kind of boyfriend a mother wants for her daughter. The best, because he's a safe driver and he respects her. The worst, because he incites a passion and loyalty in Molly that impairs her vision of the future.

Last spring, he won her heart like a carnival prize in a ring toss, and they've been inseparable ever since. He is impossibly, irresistibly good-looking, and there's no denying that he's been good to her. He makes no secret of the fact that he doesn't want her to go away. He wants her to feel as if *he* is her next step, not college.

All summer I've been trying to tell her that the right guy wouldn't stand in the way of her dreams. The right guy is going to look at her the way Dan once looked at me, as if he could see the whole world in my face. When Travis regards Molly, he's seeing…not the whole world. His next weekend, maybe.

Hoover lifts his leg and pees on the tire of Travis's Camaro, the guy's pride and joy. Travis and Molly don't notice.

I can't hear their conversation, but I can see his mouth shape the words: *Don't go.*

My heart echoes the sentiment. I want her to stay close, too. The difference is, I know she needs to leave.

Molly speaks; I hope she's telling him she has to go away, that this opportunity is too big to miss. She has won a scholarship to a world-class private university.

She's getting a chance at a life most people in our small western Wyoming town never dream of. Here in a part of the state that appears roadless and sparse on travel maps, life moves slowly. Our town is filled with good people, harsh weather and a sense that big dreams seem to come true only when you leave. The main industry here is a plant that makes prefab log homes.

I turn away from the window, giving Molly her private farewell. She is far more upset about leaving Travis than about leaving Dan and me, a fact that is hard to swallow.

Dan comes back from the service station. He visits with Travis briefly. I compare the two of them as they stand together talking. Dan is solidly built, his shoulders and arms sculpted by his years at the plant before he made supervisor. He looks as grounded and dependable as the pickup truck he drives. By contrast, Travis is tall and lithe with youth, his slender body curving into a question mark as he gestures with pride at his cherry-red car.

The two of them shake hands; then Dan heads inside. Our eyes meet and skate away; we're not ready to talk yet. In the kitchen, the two of us make a few final preparations—bundling road maps together, adding ice to the cooler of drinks.

Summer glares against the screen door, its hot scent a reminder that the day is already a few hours old. I think of a thousand other summer days, whiled away without a care for the slow passing of time. We built a tree house, went on bike rides, hung a rope swing over a swimming hole, made sno-cones, watched ants on the march. We lay faceup in the grass and stared at clouds until our eyes watered. We fought about curfews, shopped for back-to-school supplies, sang along with songs on the radio. We laughed at nothing until our sides ached, and cried at movies with sad endings.

I sneak a glance at Dan. I can't picture him crying at the movies with me. That was always Molly's role, the exclusive domain of females. Without really planning to, she and I created rituals and traditions, and these things formed a powerful bond.

There is a vehemence to the thoughts tearing through my head, a sense of rebellion—How can I just let her go? I didn't sign up for this—for creating my greatest work only to have to shove her away from me.

When I pushed her out into the world, she was handed immediately into my arms. I never thought of letting her go, only of holding her next to my heart, under which she'd grown, already adored by the time she made her appearance. The idea of her leaving was an abstraction, a nonspecified Someday. Now it's all happening, exactly as we planned. Except I didn't plan for it to throttle me.

Dan seems easy about the process. He's always accepted—even welcomed—life's movements from one phase to the next, like birthdays or promotions at work. He is the sort of person who makes life look effortless, a trait I admire and sometimes envy in him.

As for me, I find myself unable to move. I'm not ready. This wrenching grief has blindsided me. I didn't expect it to be this intense. All kids leave home. That's the way it works. If you do your job of parenting correctly, this is the end result. They leave. When it *doesn't* work that way, that's when a mother should worry. If the kid sticks around, takes up permanent residence in her childhood bedroom, you're considered a failure.

Ah, but the price of succeeding is a piece of your soul. I bite my lip to keep from trying to explain this to Dan. He would tell me I'm being overly dramatic. Maybe so, but everything about this process *feels* dramatic. This child has been the focus of every day of my life for the past eighteen years. After being a parent for so long, I am forced to surrender the role. Now, all of a sudden, a void has opened up.

Snap out of it, I tell myself. I have so much to be thankful for—this rich, full life. Health, husband and home. And lots to look forward to. It's wrong to mope and wallow in the tragedy of it all. What's the matter with me?

The matter is this—I'm facing a huge loss. The biggest part of my daughter's life is about to start, and it doesn't include me and Dan. Granted, we've had plenty of time to prepare, but now that the moment has arrived, it's as unexpectedly painful as a sudden accident.

Although greeting card companies have created themes around every possible life event, there's no ritual for this particular transition.

This is surprising, because when a child leaves for college, it is the end of something. Other than birth or death, leaving home for any reason is the most extreme of life transitions. One moment we're a family of three. The next, we've lost a vital member. It's a true loss, only people don't understand your grief. They don't send you sympathy cards or invite you to join a support group. They don't flock to comfort you. They don't come to your door bearing tuna casseroles and bottles of Cold Duck and platters of cookies on their good chintz china.

Instead, the journey to college is a rite of passage we mark as a joyous occasion, one we celebrate by buying luggage and books on how to build a fulfilling life. But really, if you ask any mother, she'll tell you that deep down, we want to mark it as a loss, a funeral of sorts. We never show our sorrow, though. Our sadness stays in the shadows like something slightly shameful.

Travis leaves, peeling himself away like a Band-Aid that's been stuck on too long. His union job at the plant keeps him on a strict schedule; he cannot linger. Molly stands on the front sidewalk and watches his Camaro growing smaller and smaller down the tree-lined street, flanked by timber frame houses from the 1920s, remnants of the days when this was a company town. Molly's face is stiff and pale, as if she's been shocked and disoriented by unexpected pain. Her arms are folded across her middle.

I hurry outside, wanting to comfort her. "I know it's hard," I say, giving her a hug.

She is stiff and unyielding, regarding me like an intruder. "You have no idea how this feels," she says. "You never had to leave Dad."

She's right. Dan and I met at a bar twenty-some years ago, and after our first dance together, we already knew we'd be a couple. If somebody had told me I had to leave him and head off to a world of strangers, would I have been willing to do that? Yes, shouts a seldom-heard voice inside me—oh, yes.

Molly waits for an answer.

"Aw, Moll. Your dad and I were in a much different place—"

"Nobody forced you two apart," she says, her voice rising.

"And nobody's forcing you and Travis apart."

"Then why am I leaving? Why am I going thousands of miles away?"

"Because it's what you've always wanted, Molly."

"Maybe I've changed my mind. Maybe I should stay and go to college in state."

"We need to finish loading the car," I tell her.

We argue. Loudly, in the driveway. About what won't fit in the car. About what is necessary, what Molly will not be able to do without. She flounces into the house and returns a few minutes later with a duffel bag and a green-shaded lamp.

"Sweetie, I don't think you need the lamp," I point out.

"I want to bring it. I've always liked this lamp." She crams the duffel bag in the back, using it to cushion the lamp.

It has shone over her desk while she worked diligently at connect-the-dots, a report on Edward Lear, a tear-stained journal, a labored-over college essay, a love letter to Travis Spellman. The lamp has been a silent sentinel through the years. Remembering this, I quickly surrender. I don't want to argue anymore, especially not today.

Like making the quilt, driving her to college seemed like a good idea at the time. She could have flown, and shipped her things separately, but I couldn't stand the thought of leaving her at the curb at the airport like a houseguest who's overstayed her welcome.

A road trip just seemed so appealing, a final adventure for the two of us to share. A farewell tour. All through the summer I've been picturing us in the old Suburban, stuffed to the top with things Molly will need in the freshman dorm, singing along with the radio and reminiscing about old times. Now as I face the sullen rebellion in Molly's face, the idyllic picture dissipates.

The trip is still a good idea, though. A long drive with no one but each other for company will give us a chance to talk about matters we've been avoiding all summer long, possibly her entire adolescence. When she was little, we discussed the great matters of her life at bedtime, lying together in the dark, watching the play of moon shadows on the ceiling. In high school, she stayed up later than I did, and our conversations shrank to sleepy utterances. Nighttime was punctuated by the creak of a floorboard under a furtive foot, the rasp of a toothbrush washing away the smell of a sneaked beer. Some days, we barely spoke a half-dozen words.

I want these long, empty hours with her on the road. I need them with an intensity that I hide from Molly, because I don't want her to worry that I'm getting desperate. She's a worrier, my Molly. A pleaser. She wants everyone to be happy, and if she had some inkling of how I'm feeling right now, she'd try to do something about it. I don't want her to feel as if she's responsible for my happiness. Good lord, who would wish that on a child?

We finish packing. Everything is in order, every checklist completed, our iPods organized with music and podcasts, every contact duly entered in our mobile phones. Finally, the moment has arrived.

"Well," says Dan. "I guess that's it."

What's it? I wonder. What? But I smile and say, "Yep. Ready, kiddo?"

"In a minute," she says, stooping and patting her leg to call the dog.

I am unprepared for the wrench as she says goodbye

to Hoover. We adopted the sweet-faced Lab mix as a pup when Molly was four. They grew up together—littermates, we used to call them, laughing at their rough-and-tumble antics. Since then, she has shared every important moment with the dog—holidays, neighborhood walks and summer campouts, fights with friends, Saturday morning cartoons, endless tosses of slimy tennis balls.

Through the years, Hoover has endured wearing doll clothes and sunglasses, being pushed in a stroller, taken to school for show-and-tell, and sneaked under the covers on cold winter nights. These days, he has slowed down, and is now as benign and endearing as a well-loved velveteen toy. None of us dares to acknowledge what we all know—that he will be gone by the time Molly finishes college.

She hunkers down in front of him, cradling his muzzle between her hands in the way I've seen her do ten thousand times before. She burrows her face into his neck and whispers something. Hoover gives a soft groan of contentment, loving the attention. When she draws away, he tries to reel her back in with a lifted front paw—*Shake, boy.* Molly rises slowly, grasps the paw for a moment, then gently sets it down.

Next, she turns to Dan. I notice the stiff set of his shoulders and the way he checks and rechecks everything—tires, cell phone batteries, wiper fluid. I can see him checking Molly, too, but she doesn't recognize the pain in his probing looks. He hides behind a mask of bravado, reassuring to his daughter but transparent to me.

Their goodbye mirrors their history together through the years—loving, a little awkward. He's never been one to show his emotions, but he was the one who taught her to swim, to laugh, to belch on command, to throw a baseball overhand, to pump up a bicycle tire, to eat smoked oysters straight out of the can, to flatten pennies on railroad tracks.

Their farewell is perfunctory, almost casual. They both seem to possess a quiet understanding that their lives are meant to intersect and diverge. "Call me tonight," he says. "Call me whenever you want."

"Sure, Dad. Love you."

They hug. He kisses her on the crown of her head. His hand lingers on her arm; she doesn't meet his eyes. Sunlight glances off the car window as she gets in.

Dan comes around to the other side and kisses me, his lips warm and familiar. "Take care, Linda," he says in a husky voice, the same thing he always says to me, but today the words carry extra weight.

"Of course," I say, holding him for an extra beat. Then I whisper in his ear, "How will I get through this?"

He pulls back, giving me a quizzical look. "Because you will," he says simply. "You can do anything, Lindy."

I smile to acknowledge the kind words, but I'm not certain I trust them.

The rearview mirror frames a view of our boxy, painted house, where we've lived since before Molly was born. Not for the first time, it hits me that I'll come home to an empty nest. People say this stage of life is a golden time, filled with possibility. Someone—probably a woman with too many kids and pets—once said the true definition of freedom is when the last child leaves home and the dog dies. At last, you get your life back. Your time is your own. The trouble is—and

I can't bear to admit this, even to Dan—I never said I wanted it back.

As we pull out onto the street, he stands and watches us go, the dog leaning against his leg. My husband braces an arm on the front gate and lowers his head. When I get back from this journey, he and I will be alone again, the way we were eighteen years ago, before the explosion of love that was Molly, before late-night feedings and bouts of the croup, before scary movies and argued-over curfews, before pranks and laughter, tempests and tears.

With Molly gone, we'll have all this extra space in our lives. I'll have to look him in the eye and ask, "Are you still the same person I married?" Or maybe the real question is, *Am I?*

I picture us seated across the dinner table from each other, night after night. What will we talk about? Do we know everything about each other, or is there still more to discover? I can't recall the last time I asked him about his dreams and desires, or the last time he asked me something more than "Did you feed the dog this morning?"

I invested so much more time in Molly over the years. When there's a daughter keeping us preoccupied, it's easy to slip away from each other.

With all my heart, I hope it's equally easy to reach across the divide. I suppose I'll find out soon enough.

Two

~~~

I don't even bother offering to drive. Molly insists on driving everywhere, and has done so ever since she turned sixteen. At the moment this is a convenient arrangement. I can use the time to work on the quilt. I'm picturing the completed piece at the other end of the journey—warm and soft, a tangible reminder of Molly's past. Each bit of fabric is a puzzle piece of her childhood, tessellating with the others around it. All that remains is to finish quilting the layers together, adding more embellishments along the way.

Working by hand rather than machine is soothing, and the pattern is free-form within the wooden hoop. On the solid pieces of fabric, words and messages can be embedded like secrets in code: *Courage. You're beautiful. Walk it off. Freud was wrong.* I should declare the thing finished by now but, like a nesting magpie, I keep adding bright trinkets—a button from a favorite sweater, a blue ribbon from a piano recital, a vintage handkerchief and a paste earring that belonged to her grandmother. There's some old, faded fabric from Molly's kindergarten apron, green with little laughing monkey heads. And a bow from her prom corsage, worn with shining pride just a few months ago.

Though it's impossible to be objective, I know this thing I have created is beautiful, even with all its flaws. Even though it's not finished. This is a record of her days with me, from the moment I realized I was pregnant—I was working in the garden, wearing a yellow dotted halter top, which is now part of the quilt—to today. Yes, even today I grabbed Hoover's favorite bandanna to incorporate.

Like so many projects I've tackled over the years—like parenting itself—the quilt is ambitious and unwieldy. But maybe the hours of enforced idleness in the car will be just what I need to add the final flourishes.

As we drive along the main street of our town, Molly looks out at the flower baskets on the streetlamp poles, the little coffee stands and cafés, the bank and bike shop and bookstore, the fashion boutiques and galleries advertising fall sales, the congregational church with its painted white spire. There's the stationery shop, advertising back-to-school specials, and of course, Pins & Needles, my favorite place in town. The charming old building stands shoulder-to-shoulder between a bakery and a boutique, sharing a concrete keystone that marks the year it was built—1902. Arched windows in the upper stories, which house an optometrist and a chiropractor, are decked with wrought-iron window boxes filled with asters and mums. On the street level is the abundant display window, replete with fabrics in the delicious colors of autumn—pumpkin and amber, flame red, magenta, shadowy purple.

A small, almost apologetic-looking sign in the window says "Business for sale." Minerva, the shop owner, is retiring and she's been looking for a buyer since the previous Christmas. She's told all her customers that if it's not sold by the new year, she'll simply close its doors. This option is looking more and more likely. It's hard to imagine someone with the kind of passion and energy it takes—not to mention the capital—to run a small shop. Once the store is cleared to the bare walls, it will look like a blight on our town's main street, a missing tooth in the middle of a smile. On top of Molly going away, it's another blow.

Across the street is a trendy clothing boutique where Molly has spent many an hour—and many a dollar— agonizing over just the right look. As she was trying on jeans the other day, a debate ensued. Do girls on the East Coast wear skinny jeans or boot cut? Do they even wear hoodies? As if I would know these things. When she began worrying about what to wear, I realized that everything was getting very real for Molly. For a girl who has never lived anywhere else, this is a huge step. Now that we're on the road, she is facing the reality that college is an actual place, not just a display of glossy pictures in a catalog. I want to tell her not to be afraid, but I suspect the advice wouldn't be welcome.

Navigating the ungainly Suburban up the ramp to the interstate, Molly fiddles with the radio, but it's all talk so she switches it off. We've got our iPods if we're desperate for music.

From the grim look on Molly's face as she cranes her neck to check the rearview mirror, it's clear that she knows I was right about the lamp taking up too much space. I can't help thinking what I won't allow myself to say: I told you so.

Agitated, I put on my discount-store reading glasses—

the ones that perch on my nose and make me look like a schoolmarm. Another visible rite of passage. For me, the moment occurred a few years back, when I turned thirty-nine-and-a-half. I was in a gift shop, trying to read a sale tag, and suddenly my arm wasn't quite long enough to make out the price.

A sales clerk offered me a pair of reading glasses, and the fine print came into focus. The fact that the glasses had cute faux-Burberry frames offered scant comfort. At first, I was a bit embarrassed to put them on around Dan and Molly, but when you love needlework and cross-word puzzles as much as I do, you swallow your pride.

I open the canvas quilt bag and the project spills across my lap. The oval hoop frames a section made of a calico maternity blouse I wore while carrying Molly. I stab the needle in, telling myself it'll be finished soon enough, one stitch after another. The needle flashes in and out like a little silver dart.

"Bad intersection up here," I say, glancing up when we reach the crossroads leading to the interstate. "Be sure you signal."

"Hel*lo*. I've only been through this intersection a zillion times. And did you know that at eighteen, a person's vision is performing at its peak?"

I adjust my glasses. "So is her smart mouth." My needle starts writing the words "be sweet," adding a curlicue at the end.

"I'm just saying, don't worry about my driving. I learned from the best."

This is true. Dan's an excellent driver, alert and confident, traits he passed along to our daughter. Most of her friends learned through Driver's Ed, but money was tight that year due to a layoff, and Dan did the honors. I used to wonder what they talked about during all those hours of practice, but when I asked, they both offered blank looks. "We didn't talk about anything."

What she means is, Dan has a way of communicating without talk. He can speak volumes with a glance, a chuckle or a shrug. The two of them are comfortable in their silence in the way Molly and I are comfortable nattering away at each other.

Sure enough, there's a small tangle of traffic at the intersection, but I bite my tongue. Literally, I press my teeth into my tongue. I will not speak up. The time is past for correcting my daughter, giving directives. These final days together should be special, sacred almost, the last slender thread of a bond that has endured for eighteen years and is about to be willfully severed.

Molly expertly accelerates up the on-ramp and merges smoothly with the flow of traffic. She keeps her eyes on the road, her profile delicate and clean-lined, startlingly adult.

It's a bright September morning, and the lingering heat of late summer shimmers, turning the asphalt into a river of mercury. With a flick of her little finger, Molly signals and moves into the swift current of the middle lane. She is a competent driver, skilled, even. She's competent and skilled at many things—water polo, trigonometry, getting rid of phone solicitors, being a good friend.

Her spirit, her self-assurance and independence, are the sort of wonderful qualities a mother wants in her daughter. My goal was always to raise a child capable of making judgments on her own. Teaching her has been a joyous process, while actually seeing her go off in her own direction is intensely bittersweet. Adulthood, I suppose, is the final exam to see which lessons she absorbed.

"What do you suppose your father's doing?" I ask, picturing Dan alone in the house. For the next several days, his diet will consist only of things that can be made from tortilla chips, cheese and cold cuts.

Molly shrugs. Her shiny dark curls spring with the motion. "He's probably breaking out the cigars."

I think of him standing on the driveway this morning, giving his daughter an awkward hug before stepping back, stiff-faced, his eyes shining. I wonder if she looked in the rearview mirror as we pulled away, if she saw her father bow his head, then lean down to pet the dog.

"Oh, come on," I chide her. "Is that what you really think?"

"I don't know. I figure he's been looking forward to this day for a long time. Dad's good with change."

Meaning I'm not. And although he might be good with this particular change, there's a part of him that has come unmoored. Dan loves Molly with both a consuming flame and a heart-pounding fear. Their complicated relationship has always been full of contradictions. Dan was in the delivery room when Molly was born on a cold February morning eighteen years ago, and the moment the baby appeared in all her pulsing, slippery, newborn glory, he wept, the tears soaking into the paper surgical mask they'd made him wear. The first time Molly was placed in his arms, he held the tiny bundle with the shocked immobility of abject terror. He hadn't smiled down into the red, wrinkled face, not the way I did, instantly a mother, with a mother's serene confidence and a sense of accomplishment so intense I was floating. He hadn't cooed and swayed to that universal internal lullaby all mothers begin to hear the moment the baby is laid in their arms. He had simply stood and looked as though someone had handed him a vial of nitroglycerin.

Yet last night, I awakened to find him crying. He was absolutely silent, but the bed quivered with his fight to keep from making a sound. I said nothing, but lay perfectly still, helplessly drifting. Have I lost the ability to comfort him? Maybe I just didn't want to intrude. We are each dealing with the departure of our only child in our own way. When you're married, you don't get to be let in, not to everything.

"Trust me," I assure Molly. "He's going to miss you like crazy."

"He never said so."

"He wouldn't. But that doesn't mean he won't be missing you every single second."

"I guess."

Too often, there's a disconnect between Dan and Molly, despite the undeniable fact that they love each other. I pause, frowning at a knot that has formed in my thread. "That's just the way he is," I tell Molly. This is my role—the go-between, translating for the two of them.

I tease the knot loose and go back to my stitching. The border abuts a trapezoid-shaped swatch of neutral-colored lawn, snipped from the dress she wore to the eighth-grade banquet, the first grown-up dance of her life. At age thirteen she was impossible, taking drama to new heights and sullenness to new depths. I used to try to turn our dirgelike family dinners into something a little more upbeat. "What's the highlight of your day?"

I used to ask my husband and daughter. "What's the one thing that makes it worth getting up in the morning?"

Dan had been grinding pepper on his salad in that deliberate way of his. Barely looking up, he said, "When Molly smiles at me."

He startled both Molly and me with that remark. And our sullen, teenage daughter had smiled at him.

Now Molly's phone rings with a familiar tone—an Eddie Vedder song called "The Face of Love." It's Travis's ringtone.

A heartbreaking softness suffuses her face as she picks up. "Hi," she says, her voice as intimate as a lover's. "I'm driving." She listens for a moment, then ends with a "Yeah, me, too," and closes the phone.

More silence. The needle darts. The day slides by the car windows. Prairie towns between endless grasslands. We make a pit stop, eat some junk food, talk about nothing. Same as we always do.

Day Two

Odometer Reading 121,633

"...it may have been some unconsciously craved compensation for the drab monotony of their days that caused the women...to evolve quilt patterns so intricate. Only a soul in desperate need of nervous outlet could have conceived and executed, for instance, the 'Full Blown Tulip...'"

—Ruth E. Finley,
Old Patchwork Quilts and the Women Who Made Them (1929)

Three

"Remember this one?" I ask, angling part of the quilt into Molly's line of vision.

"I guess."

"I bet you don't remember it."

"Then why did you ask? You always do that, Mom."

"Do I? I never noticed."

"You're always quizzing me about stuff you think should be important to me."

"Really? Yikes." I brush my hand over the piece of purple cotton, covered by lace.

"So what about that one?" She is instantly suspicious. All summer long, little "do-you-remembers" and "last times" have sneaked in—the last time we drove to the lake at the county line to set off fireworks, the last time Dan and I attended one of her piano recitals, the last time she went for a haircut at the Twirl & Curl.

"It's from a dress your father bought you," I say, needle pushing in and out, running a line of stitches to spell out *Daddy's girl*.

"Dad bought me a dress? No way."

"He did, at the Mexican Marketplace. I can't believe you forgot."

"Mom. What was I, three or four years old?"

"Four, I think."

"I rest my case."

In my mind's eye, I can still see her turning in front of the hall mirror, showing off the absurd confection of purple cotton and cheap lace. "It swirls," Molly had shouted, spinning madly. "It *swirls*!" I was less charmed when she insisted on wearing it to church for the next nine weeks. The dress fell apart years ago, but there was enough fabric left to work into the quilt.

Memories flow past in a swift smear of color, like the warehouses and billboards lining the interstate. When I shut my eyes, I can picture so many moments, frozen in time. So many details, sharp as a captured image— the wisp of my newborn baby's hair, the sweet curve of her cheek as she nurses. I can still imagine the drape of her christening gown, which is wrapped in tissue now, stored in the bottom of the painted cedar chest in the guestroom. I can clearly see myself poking a spoonful of white cereal into a round little birdlike mouth. I see Molly spring forward on chubby legs off the side of the pool, into my outstretched arms.

All those firsts. The first day of kindergarten: Molly wore her hair in two tight pigtails, her plaid jumper ironed in crisp pleats, her backpack filled with waxy-smelling new crayons, sharpened pencils, lined paper, a lunch I'd spent forty-five minutes preparing.

"Do you remember your first day of school?" I ask her now, flourishing the part of the quilt made of the uniform blouse.

"Sure. My teacher was Miss Robinson, and I carried

a Mulan lunch box." Molly changes lanes and eases past a poky hybrid car. "You put a note in my lunch. I always liked it when you did that."

I don't recall the teacher or the lunch box, but I definitely remember the note, the first of many I would tuck into Molly's lunch over the years. I always tried to write a few words on a paper napkin with a little smiling cartoon mommy, with squiggles to represent my hair, and the message "I ♥ U. Love, Mommy."

I tried to upgrade my wardrobe for the occasion, wearing slacks, Weejuns and coral lip gloss from a department store counter. I felt important, compelled by mission and duty, as Molly chattered gleefully in the back of my station wagon.

Stopping at the tree-shaded curb of the school, I pretended to be calm and cheerful as I kissed Molly's cheek, stroked her head and then smilingly waved goodbye. She met up with her friends Amber and Rani. The girls went inside together, giggling and skipping the whole way, into the redbrick institution that suddenly looked huge and forbidding to me.

There was a New Mothers' coffee in the library. At the meeting, we moms worked out party plans and car pool arrangements with the sober attention of battle commanders. I felt secretly intimidated—not by the working moms in their power suits and high heels. On some level I understood they were as scared and uncertain as I was, even with their advanced degrees and job titles.

No, I was overawed by the stay-at-home moms. They were the gold standard we all aspired to. They seemed so organized and poised, in khakis with earth-tone sweaters looped negligently over their shoulders, datebooks open in front of them, monogrammed pens poised to make notes. Independent yet obviously supported by the unseen infrastructure of husbands and homeowners' associations, they were eminently comfortable in their own skin.

To this day, I don't remember driving home after handing my child over to a new phase of life. All I remember is bursting into the house, sitting down at the breakfast counter with the view of the jungle gym Dan had built in the backyard, and shaking with a sense of emptiness I hadn't expected to feel. Even Hoover, huddled in confusion at my feet, couldn't cheer me up. But back then, hope had glimmered at the end of the day. Molly would come home, she'd eat pecan sandies and drink a glass of milk while chattering on about kindergarten, and all would be well.

Although years have passed since that bright August morning, I never quite mastered the put-together look or the air of confidence I observed in my peers. I didn't really fit in with the stay-at-homes, but I wasn't a career woman, either. A scattershot woman, you might call me, aiming myself in different directions, my only true calling that of loving my family.

I kept meaning to find something—a vocation, a passion, a marketable way to spend my time. But after Molly was born, the quest simply didn't seem to matter so much. Unconcerned with a career trajectory, I bounced around to a few different jobs, never quite finding the right fit. This didn't bother me, because without really planning it, I had lucked into a life I loved so much I never wanted it to change. The quilt shop became my second home. I loved the creative energy of the shop, the dry smell of the fabric, the crisp metallic bite of my super-sharp scissors on the cutting table. Working at Minerva's shop became more than a part-time job during the school year. It was a place of refuge from the empty hours of the school day.

Molly glances over; I see her watching my busy hands.

"What?" I ask.

"Did you know Athena is the goddess of quilting?"

"She's the Warrior Woman," I correct her. "It's one of the few things I remember from mythology."

"Most people don't know she's also the goddess of arts and crafts," Molly says, full of authority, the way she gets sometimes. "Domestic crafts require planning and strategy, too. That's how the logic goes, anyway."

"Athena was superwoman, then. Waging war and weaving baskets." I settle back with the quilt draped over my lap and try to focus on feeling like a goddess. My stitches meander into overlapping spirals. These will be a reminder of the cyclical nature of families, the comings and goings of generations. They say a child leaves home in phases. She is weaned: Molly weaned herself as soon as she learned to walk, preferring a binky she could carry around in her pocket. Then she starts school. Goes on her first sleepover. To sleep-away camp. A field trip to the state capitol. She learns to drive, and each time she heads out the door, it takes her out of reach, on her own. This is simply the next step in the process. She'll be fine. I'll be fine.

I swear.

"I spotted an *A*," Molly says abruptly, bringing me back to the present. "The Aladdin Motel. And there's a *B*—Uncle Porky's Burger Barn…."

The hunt is on—an old alphabet game we used to play on long car trips. We quickly find our way through

to the letter *J*, calling out names of towns and cafés,
cribbed from highway signs, billboards and truck stops.
The town of Jasper keeps the game moving. The *Q* is
found on a hand-lettered roadside "Bar-B-Q," and we
are grateful for colloquial spelling habits. We never get
stuck on *X*, thanks to the freeway exit signs, and *Z* is
found on a radio station billboard, KIZZ: Downhome
Country for Uptown Folks.

In a Big Boy restaurant in Franklin, a young mother
is trying to work the newspaper Sudoku puzzle while
her toddler, strapped into a little wooden high chair,
makes monkeyshines to get her attention. He leans
as far sideways as the high chair permits, makes a
sound like a cat, bangs his fork on the table, crams dry
Cheerios into his mouth and uses a chicken nugget to
smear ketchup on his tray like a baby Jackson Pollock.
The young mother tucks her hair behind her ear and
fills in another blank space on the puzzle.

I want to rush across the dining room and shake the
woman. Can't you see he needs you to look at him?
Play with him, will you, already? It'll be over before
you know it.

It's easy to recognize a little of myself in the weary,
distracted young mother. I used to be like her—preoccupied with matters of no importance, never seeing
the secretive, invisible passage of time slip by until it
was gone. Yet if someone had deigned to point this out,
I would have been baffled, maybe even indignant. Dis-
regard my child? What do you take me for?

However, when you're with a toddler who takes
forty-five minutes to eat a chicken nugget, the moments
drag. Or when your baby has the croup at 3:00 a.m. and

you're sitting in the bathroom with the steam on full blast, crying right along with her because you're both so tired and miserable—those nights seem to have no end.

From my perspective at the other end of childhood, I want to tell the young mother what I know now—that when a child is little, the days roll by at a leaden pace, blurring together. You're like a cartoon character, blithely oblivious while crossing a precarious wooden bridge, never knowing it's on fire behind you, burning away as you go. Sure, everybody says to enjoy your kids while they're little, because they'll be grown before you know it, but nobody ever really believes it. The woman at the next table simply wouldn't see the bridge, see time eating up the moments like a fire-breathing dragon.

Fortunately for everyone involved, even I'm not crazy enough to intrude. For all I know, she's got a load of worries on her mind, or maybe she just needs ten minutes to dream her own dreams. Maybe she craves the neat, precise order of a Sudoku puzzle as a reminder that everything has a solution. By the time she finishes her puzzle, the kid has given up on her and finished his Cheerios and nugget. She wipes his face and hands, scoops him up and plants a perfunctory kiss on his head as she goes to the register.

Molly has missed the exchange entirely. She is absorbed in paging through the college's glossy catalog. The booklet depicts an idyllic world where the grass is preternaturally green and weedless, buildings stand the test of time and students are eternally young, sitting around in earnest groups or laughing together over lattes. Professors look appropriately smart, many of them cultivating a kind of bohemian quirkiness that, in our hometown, would probably cause them to fall under suspicion.

"See anything you like?" I ask as she pauses on a page of course descriptions.

"Everything," she states, her eyes dancing. "There's a whole course called 'Special Topics in Women's Suffrage Music.' And 'Transgender Native American Art.' 'The Progressive Pottery Experience: Ideas in Transition.'" She struggles to keep a straight face. "I want it all."

We have a laugh, and I can feel her excitement. The catalog is a treasure trove of possibilities, new things for her to learn, ways to think, ideas about life, maybe even a way to change the world.

Though I'm thrilled for her, I feel a silly twinge of envy. There are matters Dan and I can't begin to teach her, I remind myself. That's what college is for.

"I have no clue how I'm going to pick," she says, her hand smoothing the pages.

"I wouldn't know where to begin." The admission masks an old ambivalence. I had always meant to finish college and even had a plan. For many people, this didn't seem particularly bold, but in my family, it was a big step. Neither of my parents had gone to college; their own parents were immigrants and higher education was simply out of reach for them. My folks regarded college as an unnecessary frill, an expensive four-year procrastination before you get to the real part of life.

My dad worked as a shift supervisor at the tile plant. My mom stayed home with us and ironed. Really, she did. She took in ironing. We saw nothing unusual about this. There was never any shame, no judgment. It was who we were, and we were perfectly happy together. The house often smelled of the dry warmth of a heated iron and spray starch. There was a little rate sheet posted behind the kitchen door. People would leave their stuff in a basket by the milk box on the back stoop in the morning; Mom would iron it and the next day, my big brother Jonas would deliver the items— crisply pressed dress shirts and knife-pleated slacks for the plant executives, party dresses and St. Cecilia's uniform blouses for their wives and kids.

I never really thought about what went through my mom's mind as she stood at the ironing board, perfecting the details of other people's clothing while Dire Straits played on the radio. Now I wonder if she was hot. Uncomfortable. Resigned. Or maybe she liked ironing and the work made her happy.

I wish I'd asked her. I wish she was still around, so I could ask her now.

Instead, eager for my independence, I planned my future. My dreams were nurtured by hours and hours in the library, reading books about women who created amazing lives for themselves, studying music and painting, science and business. I swore one day when I was a mother, I would instill these dreams in my children. I would be the mother I wanted my mother to be. And so I made a plan.

After high school, I would spend the summer working to save up money for tuition. Both my parents shook their heads, unable to fathom the idea of putting off work and life and independence for another four years, at the end of which there would be a massive debt and no guarantee of success. Besides, the closest university was nearly two hours away.

It was a powerful dream—maybe *too* powerful, because to someone raised the way I was, it seemed more like a fantasy. Particularly when I tallied up the cost of living without income for four years. Particularly when reality came crashing down on me, first semester. For monetary reasons, I had to live at home and quickly found the commute in my secondhand Gremlin to be almost unbearable. Later, I shared an apartment near campus with some friends, returning home each weekend with a sack of laundry. Worse, my classes were boring, keeping my grades decent was a struggle and dealing with a couple of bad professors nearly broke me.

Then Dan came along, Dan Davis with his incredible eyes, strong craftsman's hands, his sturdy work ethic and air of assuredness. In his arms, I realized the true meaning of happiness. My dreams of some nebulous *someday* stopped making sense in the face of such overwhelming happiness.

I once read in a book somewhere that the way you spend your day is the way you spend your life. Did I want a life of days filled with rushing back and forth on a commute, juggling coursework and having barely enough time for Dan? Or a life nurturing the love I'd found with him?

A no-brainer. We got married, Dan worked harder than ever so we could buy a house, and I got a job working retail. Don't ask me where. There are too many places to count. I put off returning to college; the plan kept being pushed back by the unending forward march of bills, and the sheer bliss of spending my time loving Dan, making a home, creating our life together.

After Dan and I married, I didn't exactly drop out of school, I just stopped going. There were a hundred rationalizations for this. Tuition was costly, and we wanted to save up for a house. The commute to campus took too much time and gas money. It seemed self-indulgent to spend our hard-earned money on classes like "Special Topics in Esoteric Cubism."

And then one day, after we'd been married a few years, the idea of getting a degree was taken off the table. We did use contraception, I swear we did, but mother nature and youthful zeal overrode the precautions. Along came Molly, the ultimate—and only truly valid—excuse for interrupting my education.

I always meant to go back. Early on, I told my friends and family I planned to finish my degree once Molly was in grade school. Of course, by then I knew what all mothers learn when their kids go to school. Those hours are spoken for, too. They're filled with everything else you put off when your child is young and at home, with that part-time job to give the bank account a much-needed boost. With Brownie projects and volunteer service. With taking care of that little female problem that's had you so worried for so long. With adding on an extra bathroom to the house—she's going to need that once she hits her teens, after all. Throwing in college-level courses simply seems impossible.

Nobody was surprised when I dropped the idea. My parents were simple, honest people who expected their kids to live a good life. I hope I didn't disappoint them.

My departure from the nest was not the dramatic, long-distance leap Molly is taking. My first home with Dan was only eight miles from my parents.

I wonder if they dreamed of a bigger life for me, if they wanted me to go further, do more. Probably not, I think, watching my needle flash through the fabric. I suspect they were perfectly content for their daughter to live close by.

My friend Erin wears her hard-earned law degree

like a badge of pride. I used to envy her—the big career, the big house, the big car, the big *life*. It all came at a price, though. There was a divorce; though she's remarried now and loving her empty nest, there were hard years when she'd come over and cry from the sheer exhaustion of juggling everything. I came to understand that there is no such thing as a perfect life, just a constant shifting, like the wind on the lake. You adjust your sails to catch the wind, not the other way around.

I often wonder, if I'd stuck with my degree program, would I have found my passion? That first semester, I floundered, unable make up my mind. I had friends who were so clear-eyed, wanting to be a kindergarten teacher. Or a CPA. Or a landscape designer. Not me. I never quite found the right fit. Skipping college, setting aside the thought of a professional career, turned out well for me. Life is good enough. We wanted more kids, but because of that female problem, which turned out to be not so little, it was not to be.

As each mile brings Molly and me closer to goodbye, I realize how little I know about this rarefied world she is about to enter. I wonder if it will drive a wedge between us, turn her into a stranger to me, a sophisticated stranger with a big vocabulary and bigger dreams. There won't be any three o'clock bell to start my world turning again. No swing to push in the backyard, no cookies to bake.

What there *will* be is time. So much of it. All the time in the world to figure out what to do with my life, now that I can do anything I want. This should not feel so fraught with uncertainty. Parents have done this since time immemorial. Fretting about it is silly.

I'm not fretting, that's the thing. I'm *afraid*.

* * *

We argue about where to spend the night. Should we stop on the west side of Omaha, or try to make it to the east side by nightfall, thus avoiding tomorrow's morning rush of inbound traffic?

"I'd just as soon stop now," I declare, checking the dashboard clock. "We're making good enough time."

Molly wants to keep driving. She has an adolescent's inexhaustible supply of late-night energy combined with an eagerness to get there. "Forget it," she says. "I'm going past the city for sure. No need to cut the day short."

"Come on, Moll—"

"I'm driving, Mom. You said I could. That means I get to pick where we stop. Find a stopping place in the Triple-A guide and pick a motel."

For a moment, I feel disoriented. Who is this person in the driver's seat, telling me what to do? A small laugh erupts from me.

"What's funny?" asks Molly.

"You sound like your mother."

"And that surprises you?"

"Yes. A little. I guess." Bemused, I take out the Triple-A guide. It is something I recall from my own childhood. We used to go on grim road trips each summer, with me and my three siblings fighting in the back seat, our dad hunched doggedly over the steering wheel and our mom flipping pages in the triptych while reciting facts and figures from the guidebook.

"Grady, Nebraska. Population 4,500," I tell Molly now. "There are four possible motels, two with two-diamond ratings and two with three."

"Go for the three."

Finally, something we agree on.

Four

We make our way to the Star Lite Motor Court and Coffee Shop. I'm not sure what the three diamonds in the auto guide signify. There's a pool, but a suspicious-looking green tinge stains the tiles, so Molly and I decide against taking a swim. The coffee shop looks promising; it's open late, and features a grill hissing with frying burgers, and a revolving glass case displaying pies of mythic proportions.

We let ourselves into our room, wondering what three-diamond amenities we'll find there. The carpet smells faintly of mildew and ancient cigarettes, so we open a window to let in fresh air. Ugh, I think with a twinge of disappointment. Given the nature of this journey, I'd hoped for better accommodations. I'd pictured the two of us sharing a charming suite in a B&B, or working out in the fitness room of a modern hotel. As usual, there's a gap between expectation and reality.

Molly flings herself on one of the beds, bouncing happily. "I love road trips," she crows. "I love staying in motels."

And with that, the disappointment is gone, lifted

away by the grin on her face. I am forced to notice this small but significant shift. Molly's mood has the power to determine my own. This was never apparent when she was at home, but once she's gone, where will the happiness come from? I need to make sure I remember how to find it.

"What's this?" She indicates the metal Magic Fingers box on the nightstand.

"You've never heard of Magic Fingers?"

"What?"

"Move over." I dig some quarters out of my jeans pocket, drop them in the slot and lie down next to Molly. "Your education's not complete until you've experienced Magic Fingers."

Nothing happens. "I guess it's broken," I say. "The thing is probably thirty years old if it's a day."

"Just because it's old doesn't mean it's broken." Determined, Molly reaches across me and gives the box a shake. Still nothing. She messes with the cord. And then: "Whoa. Did you feel that?"

I lie very still. There is a mechanical hum, then a faint vibration buzzes upward, penetrating through me and increasing in strength. Molly relaxes next to me, supine.

"Okay," she says. "This is weird."

"It'll stop in a few minutes."

"Weird in a good way," she amends.

"I can't believe you never tried this before." Through the years, we've stayed in dozens of motels together but this is the first time we've found Magic Fingers. "I guess they're a thing of the past," I tell her.

"Good thing we decided to stop here, huh?" She sighs with contentment.

A kinder way of saying "I told you so." We lie side by side, the bed humming beneath us for long minutes. When the vibrations stop, I am startled to feel more relaxed, the rigors of the long driving day eased from my muscles.

"What are you thinking about?" Molly asks.

The question catches me off guard. "You, I suppose. I've always liked doing new things with you, even little things."

"Like Magic Fingers."

"Exactly. Everything was new with you. That's what was so much fun about raising a child. I'd be in the middle of doing something—whipping egg whites into meringue or riding my bike with no hands or graphing a parabola—and you'd think I was amazing. A magician or something."

"You *were* amazing," Molly says quietly, turning on her side and tucking her hand under her cheek.

I must be hearing things. I consider asking her to say that again, but I doubt she will repeat it. "Who will I amaze now that you're leaving?"

Molly laughs. "Excuse me?"

"I'm losing my audience."

"You should have had more kids," she observes.

I hesitate, caught off guard by her words. Yet not off guard at all. It's an opening to a difficult conversation. I know this before either of us speaks again.

"Mom?"

I turn to her. "I couldn't have any more babies after…"

Her eyes widen. "After you had me?"

I gaze into her face, seeing maturity and wisdom there, trusting the compassion in her expression. When I first conceived of this cross-country adventure, I knew things would come up between us, difficult matters. And I knew this matter was the most difficult of all. Through the years, I had protected Molly from the most painful episode of my life. It wasn't fair to reveal a wound she didn't cause and couldn't heal. What would be the point of that?

Things are different now. She's a young woman. Another person's pain won't confuse or destroy her. Isn't that, after all, the essence of maturity?

Deep breath, I tell myself, gazing into her doe-soft eyes. "I had a baby boy named Bruce." Even after so much time has passed, I still feel the piercing loss. I was bleeding, drugged half out of my mind, but I can feel him even now, his slight, unmoving weight in my arms. Weeks premature, he was as pale and beautiful and silent as a fallen angel, having never drawn breath in this world.

Molly's eyes instantly fill with tears. "Mom, really? What happened? When?"

Pulling in a deep breath, I explain in a shaky voice. "You were just two years old at the time. He came too early, and I was bleeding. There was a tear in my uterus."

"Oh, Mom. Why didn't you ever tell me?"

I feel a tear slide over the bridge of my nose. Such an old, old wound, made fresh again by indelible memories. When it happened, it changed me in ways I am still discovering, even now. That kind of loss has the power to stop the world. My baby boy's tiny, otherworldly face will always haunt me. He looked so very much like my other newborn, Molly. "It was just so sad, honey."

She reaches for me and we're quiet together for a

long time, the moments slipping by, measured by our breathing.

"I don't know what to say," she whispers.

"You don't have to say anything." There are some things that simply can't be made better, not by talking or weeping or praying or pretending they didn't happen. Yet her reaction is exactly as I'd hoped it would be—compassionate without being pitying or obsessive.

"I wish…" Her voice trails off, but I understand exactly what she's saying.

"So do I."

More quiet moments. We turn on the Magic Fingers again to shake us out of the somber mood. "You're all the kid I need," I tell her. She's heard that from me before. Now she understands the hidden meaning behind the words.

"Well, I hope you know, I'm the one losing my audience," Molly insists. "When I'm away at college, who will *I* perform for?"

This surprises me. I know there are things she worries about, being so far from home in a strange world where no one knows her. Still, I thought her eagerness to go out and find her life had banished all her fears. Now I realize she's well aware of what she's leaving behind. And it's not just Travis Spellman. From her first smile to her last day of high school, and all the lost teeth, soccer trophies, piano recitals and Brownie badges in between, I've been there for her, cheering her on.

"I'll still be your number-one fan," I assure her.

"Sure, but it won't be the same." Then she smiles and bounces up off the bed.

I sit up and link my arms around my drawn-up knees. "You seem pretty okay with that."

"It's hard work, being your daughter."

"You're kidding, right?"

Now it's her turn to hesitate. "Right. Let's go check out the game room. I think I saw a ping-pong table."

Late at night, long after our dinner of iceberg lettuce salads and oyster crackers, Molly steals away to sit on the stoop in front of the motel room and call Travis on her cell phone. Although college beckons like a mysterious garden of rare delights, she has formed a deep bond with this boy, with his funny grin and Adam's apple, his appealing combination of cluelessness and charm.

A hometown boy at heart, he is causing her to have second thoughts about going to school so far away. For that, I could throttle him. At the same time, I feel an unexpected beat of empathy. I, too, would love to keep her close.

On their final night at home, Molly and Travis went out with a group of their friends, some college bound, others already immersed in jobs and responsibilities. They stayed out late, visiting all the places they knew they'd miss after dispersing like seeds to the wind. There were stops at the rusty-screened drive-in movie theater, the empty stadium, the all-night diner, the parking lot at the spillway below the lake. I don't doubt there were other stops as well, which were not revealed to me.

I can't be certain, but I suspect that Molly surrendered her virginity at the spillway at some point during the summer, in the secret place known to revved-up teenagers everywhere, tucked into the shadows of the sloping man-made bank. She didn't tell me so, but there have been subtle signs. I've watched her and Travis grow closer, their bond tightened by a private and impenetrable intimacy that is both invisible and obvious.

Sexually active. It's a clinical-sounding term. It's nothing a mother wants to think about with regard to her own child, but at some point, you have to take the blinders off. Or not, I suppose, thinking of Dan. Whenever I try to bring the subject up with him, he says, "They're good kids. They won't do anything stupid."

Pointing out that good kids who are not stupid get in trouble all the time doesn't seem to advance the conversation. I have given up on discussing it with Dan. Now and then, I try to broach the topic with Molly.

"I'm *fine.* Don't worry," she said when I got up the nerve to ask her.

It doesn't matter what century we're in. Parents and children were not meant to talk together in detail about sex. Nor should we pretend to be all-knowing experts on love, even if we are. I understand exactly what love feels like in a young girl's heart because I was that girl once, long ago. That's why the Travis situation worries me, because I understand. It has a power like the pull of the moon on the tides, overwhelming and inevitable. There is no antidote for the passion and certainty a girl feels for the boy she loves, and no end to the fantasies she spins about their future together.

I can explain convincingly that the emotions engulfing her and Travis are not likely to last. I can tell her they'll both grow and change, heading off in different directions. But then I would have to talk about my own choices, my own regrets, the many times I spent wondering about the life I would have had if I'd taken a different path.

For a brief moment, I consider telling Molly about Preston Warner, my first and, as far as I was concerned at the time, my only, forever and ever. Senior prom was the kind of magic-filled night every girl dreams about and, in my case, the dream came true. I wore something blue and silky; Preston was slicked-down, tux-clad and nervous. Not only did we consummate our relationship that night, we pledged to stay true forever, even though Preston was going far away to college.

That night, I surrendered not just my virginity but all my hopes and dreams, handing them over to a boy who—though I didn't realize it at the time—had no idea what to do with them. So he did what guys his age generally do. Three months into his first semester at a trendy private school a day's drive away, he started dating other people. When I found out, I wanted to die. I walked around like a zombie, every bit of happiness having bled from my broken heart.

I still remember the drama of our final confrontation—he came in person to tell me it was over. To this day, I can still feel the horror of facing a future without him. I raged, I wept until I was weak and drained, I swore I could not go on. It caused a pain I couldn't share with anyone. My mother brought me a pint of Cherry Garcia, but I promised her I'd never eat again. She said with utter confidence that I'd get over him. Then she went downstairs and ironed clothes, filling the house with the scent of lavender water. I ate the Cherry Garcia. Watched *Seinfeld* reruns and learned to laugh again. Somehow, one day dragged into the next…and eventually I realized that I didn't miss him.

Hearing a heartbroken sniffle and the murmur of Molly's voice drifting through the window screen of the motel, I decide not to tell her any of that. She and Travis will grow apart because that's the way it works. She will have to find this out for herself. The end of love has to be experienced firsthand, not explained by your mother.

I turn on the radio to give her more privacy. Even so, I can guess what they're saying. There are whispered promises of love-you-forever and we'll-stay-together, and no one knows as well as I do that they mean it— every word. Preston and I certainly meant it, all those years ago. We were going to travel the world and live a charmed life together.

These days, Preston owns the hardware store in town and has a cushy paunch around his middle, a receding hairline and four kids. When I drop in to buy upholstery tacks or a can of paint, I always think about that last summer after high school, the passionate hours in the back seat of his car, the vows we made to each other. I can look past his bifocals and graying temples, and still see a boy who was as handsome and romantic as a fairy-tale prince. As Preston rings up my purchases and we make small talk, I wonder if he thinks about the way we were, too, if he remembers. Does he look at me in my pull-on slacks and gardening clogs and re- call the girl I used to be?

Running into him is, weirdly enough, not awkward in the least. He's someone who came into my life for a brief time, and then stayed in the past. I feel no wistful- ness for him, no regrets. I do envy him those four kids, though. When one goes away, he still has the others to keep him company.

Or maybe saying goodbye four times is harder than saying it once.

When Molly comes back into the room, her eyes red and her chin trembling, I offer a smile, but I don't say anything. This is a volatile issue, and I don't want to push it. Travis is a boy of good looks and small ambition, one who regards his union job at the plant as a ticket to independence as well as an opportunity to work on his Camaro at his uncle's garage on the weekends.

Travis has a peculiar sweetness about him, a quality Molly finds irresistible. She loves him, and her love is as real as her grade point average. She trusts that love to endure, no matter what.

Molly expects so much of herself and wants so much from the world. At the moment, she is tender and lonely, missing him, her heart sore as it can only be for one's first love.

I have to wonder: Did I teach my daughter to love this hard and feel this deeply? Was I wrong to do so? On the other hand, maybe I shielded her too much from pain, and she never learned to deal with it. As more men loom in the future, a whole campus full of them, it makes me wonder if I've done enough to equip her to deal with love and heartache. My own mother never seemed comfortable discussing matters of the heart with me. That's what I used to think, anyway. Now I wonder if she simply knew I'd discover it all for myself.

"Hungry?" I ask Molly, after she's lain on the bed, staring at the ceiling for a while. "The coffee shop's still open."

"No," she says softly. "You?"

"No." This is a lie. The dinner salad was a disappointment. But I don't need to eat. I don't need that big, messy cheeseburger I've been fantasizing about since spotting it on the coffee-shop menu. I don't need the coconut cream pie I noticed in the revolving refrigerated case. Something my mother never told me—when you hit forty, not only does your vision start to go. Your body changes. Nowadays if I eat things like cheeseburgers and cream pie, the calories magically transform themselves into saddlebags on my hips. I don't feel any different than I did ten years ago, but boy, do my jeans fit differently.

My mind drifts. Maybe when I get home, I'll join the local gym, start a regular fitness routine. Running around with Molly has kept me reasonably fit all these years. Thanks to her, I've hiked miles with Brownie and Girl Scout troops, led field-trip expeditions to museums or nature preserves, ridden for hours on family bike trips. I suppose I could still hike and bike without Molly around, but why would I? Motivating myself is not going to be as easy as it used to be.

A quiet sniff brings me back to the present. I look over at Molly to see that she is still staring at the ceiling. Tears track sideways down her temples.

I don't say anything, because I know everything will come out sounding like empty platitudes. Instead, I find another quarter, drop it in the slot and start up the Magic Fingers once again.

DAY THREE

Odometer Reading 122,271

" It is not wise to be didactic about
the nomenclature of quilt patterns."
—Florence Peto, *American Quilts and Coverlets,* (1949)

"...it is unwise to be didactic
because the facts are very elusive.
I now realize that not every
pattern has a name, that there is
no correct name for any design."
—Barbara Brackman, *Encyclopedia of Pieced Quilt Patterns*

Five

The roadside is littered with last night's carnage, a raccoon here, a possum there, occasionally someone's household pet reduced to an unrecognizable smear. Neither Molly nor I say a word. I hate the idea of creatures suffering while people sleep, oblivious.

This morning's breakfast—the Bright Eyes Surprise, which I'd ordered solely because I liked the name— churns in my stomach. From the driver's seat, Molly reaches over and turns up the radio. She glides into the passing lane to get around a semi with a tweeting cartoon robin on the side.

I refold the map to encompass the day's journey. We plan to make tracks today, covering at least four hundred miles. The few towns along the way are no more than pinpricks with quirky names, like Nickel Box and Mulehorn and Futch's Corner. Mostly, it appears we'll be crossing uninhabited terrain, much of it protected by the Department of Natural Resources, shaded in green.

"Do we have plenty of gas?" I ask.

"Three quarters of a tank. Same amount we had the last time you asked, ten minutes ago."

The biggest of the pinpricks, Futch's Corner, lies at the halfway point. We'll get gas there.

"I can't decide whether to quilt or read," I tell Molly.

"Why don't you listen to music and look at the scenery?"

"I already did that."

She laughs a little, shakes her head. "You always have to be busy doing something."

"Nothing wrong with that."

"Except you might miss something. Chill, Mom."

"All right. I'll look out the window." The most interesting thing I spot is a red-winged blackbird in a thicket of cattails.

If I'm being honest with myself, there's a reason for staying busy. Being preoccupied with other things means I don't have to be preoccupied with my own baggage. I'm sick of myself, of my indecisiveness and mental whining. My daughter's leaving the nest, as all daughters eventually do, and my job is to let her go and move on with my life. It should be a simple matter to set a goal for myself, one that doesn't involve Molly, even indirectly. Maybe I don't have a college degree, but I'm not stupid.

I know I have to figure out who I am again, now that I'm not Molly's mom. Well-meaning friends tell me to go back to being the person I was before Molly. Am I that twentysomething woman who used to sleep late and smoke Virginia Slims and never felt the need to look at a clock?

That's not me anymore. It can never be me again. I don't want to go back to being that person who lived each day so thoughtlessly, spending the moments like nickels in a slot machine, as though she had an unending supply of time and could squander it any way she pleased.

Other friends remind me that my marriage moves to the front burner now. Dan and I will have to figure out how to be a childless couple again. What were we before we became Molly's parents? What did we used to talk about, dream about, laugh and cry about? A better stereo system, a bigger house, an extra week's vacation from work? How could those things matter now?

It was Molly who showed us the things that matter most. They're the moments that sneak up on you unexpectedly, when you're barely paying attention. You're going out to see if the mail has come, and you discover that your child has learned to ride a two-wheeler and is as thrilled about it as if she's learned to fly. Or you uncrate the new refrigerator you scrimped and saved for, and she shows you that the best thing about the new appliance is the empty box.

Before Molly, what was it that mattered to Dan and me? When we were first married, he'd grab me the second he woke up each morning and say, "You're here!" as if I were the answer to his dreams. I can't remember when he stopped doing that. Granted, it would seem tedious and downright weird if he kept it up indefinitely, but there was a clear appeal in knowing exactly where I stood with him.

Inside the oval hoop is a swatch of my mother's favorite cotton blouse, the one with tiny umbrellas printed all over it. For some reason, I'm inspired to stitch a message: "Do the thing you fear."

Not the thing your mother fears. The thing *you* fear. I hope Molly will understand the difference.

Something extraordinary flashes past my line of sight. "Molly, slow down," I say. "Look over there."

It's a turnoff marked Leaning Tower of Pisa, Iowa.

"Let's check it out," I say.

Molly looks dubious. Her gaze flicks to the dashboard clock. I feel a twinge of annoyance at her eagerness to reach our ultimate destination. Can't she slow down, just a little?

"You're the one who wanted me to watch the scenery and chill," I remind her. "We're making good time," I point out.

"All right. Let's do it."

We go take a look at the leaning tower, and it is exactly that. A water tower that has listed to one side. In the next big wind it could topple, explains a placard in the field beside it. We take pictures to email to Dan. We've been calling him to check in each day. The conversation is predictable—we're to keep the tank full and check the oil and tire pressure at least once a day. We're to take care of ourselves.

"See?" I try not to act too smug as we return to the car. "You learn something new every day."

Molly decides to give me a turn at the wheel. She wants to phone Travis and she's not allowed to do it while she's driving.

"No freakin' signal," she says, scowling at the screen of her cell phone. "That's lame."

"You'll just have to watch the scenery and chill."

She rummages in her bag and pulls out the folder of information sent to her by the college. "Kayla Jackson from Philadelphia," she says, referring to her roommate. "I wonder what she'll be like."

"Lucky," I say. "She was matched up with you, wasn't she?"

"Her mother's probably saying the same thing. Oh, man, what if we can't stand each other?"

"You said she sounded great in her email."

"Sex predators sound great in email, Mom."

My head whips in her direction. "How do you know that?"

"Everybody knows that. Geez, don't get your panties in a twist. I don't talk to perverts on email. I don't talk to perverts at all."

"Suddenly I feel as if we haven't discussed this topic enough."

"What, perverts? I'll talk about perverts anytime you want, Mom."

"All joking aside, honey—"

"Mom. We went through this a long time ago, the stuff about respecting myself and using my head. That women's self-defense class went on for twelve weeks and yes, I read *The Gift of Fear*. I'm as safe as it's possible to be."

"You have all the answers, don't you, Missy?"

"I'll have even more once I'm in college."

We stop for lunch and a fill-up in Futch's Corner, a town with four stoplights, a defunct train depot and a bus station. A row of storage silos covered in graffiti lines the main road. The lone café has a pictorial menu, which makes it easy to avoid the chopped salad, which in these parts appears to be coleslaw.

In the booth next to us, an elderly couple sits across from each other, slowly and methodically eating their cups of beef barley soup with soda crackers on the side. They manage to get through the entire meal without uttering a single word. The wife puts cream in both cups of coffee. When they get up after finishing their meal, the husband keeps one hand on the small of the wife's back.

"Old people are so cute, aren't they?" Molly remarks.

Old people are a nightmare. It's too easy for me to see myself and Dan in a couple like that, silent and companionable, with nothing to say to each other. I want so much more for us, laughter and interesting conversation, the richness of shared moments. I used to think I knew what my life would look like after Molly, but now I'm not so sure.

Once she's away at school, Dan and I are going to have to face each other once again with nothing between us, no sports matches to attend, no car pools to drive, no curfews to enforce, no school calendar to dictate our lives. To me, it looks like a void, a yawning breach. Empty space. It's supposed to be a good thing, but I've never been the sort to tolerate empty space. Maybe that's why I like quilting. Each piece fits perfectly against the others to fill the grid completely.

On the highway heading east again, we come upon a breakdown pulled off to the side of the road. I slow down but don't stop. The hood of the car is raised and there's a woman standing beside it. She has a baby on her hip and there's no one else in sight. I go even slower, checking the rearview mirror, hoping to see that she's on a cell phone, getting help.

She isn't. She's jiggling the baby and taking a diaper bag out of the car.

Someone else will come along and help her, I figure.

But this is a lonely stretch of highway and there's no one in sight in either direction.

"What are you doing?" Molly asks when I stop and make a U-turn.

"Making sure that woman back there is okay. Maybe she needs my cell phone."

"Mom. Aren't you the one with all the rules about not picking up strangers?"

"I didn't say anything about picking her up. But I'm not going to leave her stranded." I pass the breakdown, pull another U-turn and park on the shoulder in front of the woman's car, a dusty Chevy Vega with Nevada plates.

"Thanks for stopping," she says. "I blew a radiator hose." She doesn't appear to be much older than Molly. She's wearing a man's ribbed tank top under an open shirt, shorts and flip-flops. Her eyes are puffy and the baby is fussing.

"Have you called for help?"

"I don't have a phone and the last town's forty miles back."

"Let's try my cell phone," I offer, getting out of the car and handing it to her.

The baby glowers at me. It's a boy, maybe fourteen months, and he smells like ripe fruit. His nose is running green sludge, and he has a rattling cough. As his mother dials the phone, he pokes a grubby finger at the buttons.

"Nothing," she says after a moment. "No signal. Thanks anyway." She hands back the phone. I resist the urge to clean it off on my shirttail.

The baby barks out a cough. The woman looks around. A breeze shimmers through the silver maples and a few dry leaves fall off, scattering. There is a folded umbrella stroller and a car seat in the back of the car.

The silence stretches out. I take a deep breath, violating my own better judgment as I say, "We'll give you a ride."

"You don't have to do that." Despite her words, the woman looks as if she might melt with relief.

Molly gets out of the car, map in hand. The cranky baby glowers at her.

"Really, you don't," the woman persists.

"It's fine," I assure her. "Where are you headed?"

"Honeymoon," she says. "It's my hometown. I'm moving back there, but this piece of crap car doesn't want to cooperate."

Molly finds the town on the map. It's about fifty miles to the north on a road marked with a faint gray line, well out of our way. The smart thing to do would be to drive on until I get a cell phone signal and then call in the location of the breakdown.

Maybe I'm not so smart. I keep thinking if Molly were stranded, I'd want a nice woman to stop. "Molly, can you give me a hand with the baby's car seat?" I ask.

My daughter's eyebrows lift, but she instantly complies.

I introduce myself and learn that the woman's name is Eileen. Her baby is Josten. "His grandparents have never seen him," she says. "I sure appreciate this." Wrinkling her nose, she adds, "He needs a change." She lays him on the back seat of her car. The creases of the seat are filled with bits of broken cookies and dry cereal. "Last one," she says, extracting a diaper from the bag.

The little one yowls as she peels off his romper

and diaper. "Cut it out," she snaps as he kicks at her. "Josten—oh, Josten. What a mess." She digs in the diaper bag. "Shoot. I'm out of baby wipes."

Molly looks on in horror for a moment, then grabs something from the quilt bag. "Here, use this."

It's a piece of an old Christmas tree skirt from Dan's and my first Christmas together. You can't really tell it was ever a tree skirt; it just looks like a green tablecloth.

"Are you sure?" Eileen asks.

"No problem," I tell her.

"Thanks."

Molly's expression is priceless as she watches Eileen dry the kid's tears and wipe his nose, then clean his bottom. This is a better justification for birth control than any lecture from me, although it means a sad end for the old tree skirt. Eileen puts on a clean diaper, but the romper is soaked through. The baby starts wailing again.

"I don't have a change of clothes for him." Eileen looks like she's about to lose it, too.

I glance at the quilt bag, hesitating only a moment. At the bottom is a pair of Oshkosh overalls in candy pink. "This will probably work. It was Molly's when she was about his size. See if it fits." I answer the question in her expression. "I brought along a bag of old fabric scraps to add to the quilt I've been working on."

"Then I can't take this."

"Sure, go ahead. I've got plenty. I have enough."

She threads him into the overalls. The baby cries as she straps him into his car seat, the sobs punctuated with liquid coughs. Eileen gives him a plastic bottle of Gerber apple juice, but he flings it away. Molly is actively trying not to cringe; I can tell.

"Hush," Eileen says. "Please. Sorry about him."

"You don't need to apologize. Is he running a fever?"

"A little, I think. I gave him some Tylenol drops right before you stopped." She loads in the diaper bag and her purse, then locks her car, and we all take off.

Eventually, the storm of crying subsides as the monotony of the ride lulls the baby. The stretch of road that looked so innocent on the map is narrow and curving, with a posted speed limit of forty. It's too late to change our minds now, though. We're committed.

We learn that Eileen and her boyfriend went to Vegas together to get work. "My mother didn't want me to leave, but there was nothing for me in Honeymoon, except maybe some crap job at a fast-food place. Vegas was our best bet, especially since I wanted to be a dancer. I *was* a dancer, until I got pregnant."

"Onstage, in Vegas?" Molly turns to her in interest.

Eileen nods her head. "I was in the chorus line of a show at the Monte Carlo."

"That's so cool," Molly says.

"It was. But…harder than you'd think, especially with a kid and a lousy boyfriend. My mother danced, too, but never professionally. She always wanted to work onstage and didn't ever have the chance."

"Then it's great that you got the opportunity," I tell her, trying to say something positive.

Eileen gives a brief, humorless laugh. "I doubt my mother would think so. She was scared I might succeed at something she never got to do."

I have no idea what to say to this. I peek in the rearview mirror. Eileen is stroking the hair off Josten's forehead. "Mama tried like hell to talk me out of going, but I went anyway," she says. "Big mistake."

"What, leaving home?" Molly asks.

"Leaving with *him*. With my boyfriend, Mick. My ex, now."

There is no air of I-told-you-so when we stop at a modest clapboard house at the far side of a town called Honeymoon. Eileen's mother, who doesn't look a day over forty, gathers her into a hug that emanates relief and gratitude. She inspects the baby, now groggy and mellow from his nap, and holds him against her as if he's a missing piece of herself. "Look at this doll, baby," she whispers, shutting her eyes and inhaling. "Just look at him."

Through the lines of fatigue around her mouth, Eileen beams. "It's good to be home," she says.

"I'm glad you're here," the mother replies. "No idea what I did without you." Then she turns and thanks me in a trembling voice. "Would you like to stay for supper?" she asks. "I got some sweet corn from a neighbor. And I just made some lemonade, fresh."

"Thanks, but we have to keep going," I tell her.

Molly surprises me by saying, "Maybe a glass of lemonade…"

The woman, whose name is Shelley, serves it in mismatched glasses and asks us about our trip.

"My mom's dropping me off at college," Molly says.

"Goodness, college. That's exciting."

The baby starts fussing himself awake and Eileen turns away to tend to him. I admire the patchwork quilt draped over the back of the sofa, and Shelley tells me it's a family heirloom.

"I'm working on one myself," I say. "It's my biggest project to date."

"I like sewing," she says. "I made all of Eileen's costumes for her dance routines. I don't sew much anymore. The local fabric store folded, and the nearest superstore's thirty miles away. They got everything you need there, but I miss the shop. All the women were friends, you know?"

I think of the shop back home. Here in the middle of nowhere, this woman had nailed it—a community for women.

She gives us a local map that shows more detail than my Triple-A triptych. She indicates a route back to the highway that will put us a good eighty miles ahead of where we were.

Molly takes over driving again. I pick up my quilting. She says, "Dad's going to freak when you tell him we picked up a stranger."

"She needed a lift. We had no choice."

"I'm glad we helped her out. We're behind on our schedule now, though."

"We don't need to be anywhere specific," I note. "It was a goal, the four hundred miles."

We drive through a few towns fringed by strip malls or trailer parks. There is an air of exhaustion that seeps into the atmosphere of these places, and we're glad to leave them behind.

By the time we reach the highway, dusk has fallen and it's time to find food and a place to spend the night. An eerie emptiness hovers over the open road and few cars pass by.

"It's looking bleak," Molly says. "How far to the next city?"

"Almost a hundred miles. You up for it?"

"Looks like we don't have a choice."

She plugs an adaptor into her iPod so we can listen on the stereo speakers, and we get into a discussion about the stupidest lyrics ever written—"This Is Why I'm Hot" would be my pick. But Molly points out Van Morrison's "Ringworm" and then we dissect the lyrics of some old Yes songs.

"Anything sounds stupid if you listen too closely," I say.

Molly switches to a track that's in French. "Clearly, we've been in the car together too long."

A few minutes later, I spot a billboard rising from an alfalfa field, with a light shining on it. "Ramblers Rest, in Possum, Illinois. Want to check it out?"

She nods and drives another mile to the next sign. There's a red-neon light indicating Vacancy in the window of the office, which also contains a convenience store. The tires crackle over the gravel in the drive.

"What do you think?" Molly asks.

"It's worth a look. If it's horrible, we'll drive away."

It's not horrible, just a bit strange. Ramblers Rest consists of a group of small, self-contained wayfarers' cabins at the edge of a small trout pond. Our room is plain but clean, with walls of scrubbed pine, checkered curtains and an old-fashioned prayer posted above one of the beds.

The proprietor, a man in jeans and a plaid shirt, tells us there's a bonfire down by the pond where guests gather around to sing songs and toast marshmallows.

"Songs?" Molly mutters. "No way."

"We could harmonize 'You Are My Sunshine.'"

She cringes, and I send her a wicked grin. "Or 'Kumbaya'?"

The closest restaurant, our host says, is a place called Grumpy's, a few miles down the road.

"They're probably closed now," he warns.

Starving, we head up to the convenience shop adjacent to the office and buy hot dogs to roast over the fire, plus bright yellow mustard and squishy white buns—the kind of meal that is forbidden in a proper kitchen. On a whim, I buy the ingredients for a kind of dessert we haven't made since Molly's childhood camping trips. We hike down to the water's edge where a teepee-shaped bonfire roars at the night sky. There are at least three discrete groups here, but all share that sort of instant camaraderie that seems to crop up among strangers at campgrounds. They make room for us in the firelit circle and we roast hot dogs, sharing the extras.

It's amazingly tranquil around the pond, the sky intensely black in the absence of city lights. It's so dark you can make out the colors of the stars—red and violet, silver and the shimmering green of moss in shadow. Their reflections glow like coins on the surface of the water.

Molly and I sit shoulder-to-shoulder and make small talk with the other travelers. There's a young family from Cottage Grove, who just sold their house and are moving to Cleveland. A not-so-young family is there, too. The parents are about my age, but the kids are little, with Asian features, so I assume they're adopted. A retired couple, who seem self-contained and not as eager to mingle, tell us they're on a monthlong driving tour of the midwest. Molly, of course, gravitates toward two boys who seem to be about her age. They're juniors at Penn State, so leaving home is routine to them, and they're driving themselves.

She seems to have forgotten about dessert, but the younger kids eagerly gather around when I ask them if they want to help. I demonstrate how to put a little whipping cream and sugar into a small Ziploc bag. The sealed bag then goes into a larger plastic bag of ice and salt. This is the kids' favorite part—you shake until the cream and sugar in the sealed bag turns to ice cream.

"What a great trick," the young mother says to me, watching her little ones shiver and shake.

"I learned it from my mother." I look across at Molly, who is now explaining the process to the college boys, who are totally into it. Before long, everyone around the campfire is making ice cream in a bag, the kids turning it into a wild dance. Sparks land on someone's blanket, and a tiny flame ignites. Fortunately, it is spotted and beaten out. People tuck their loose blankets away from the fire, and we're more vigilant after that.

Everyone pronounces the ice cream delicious. In fact, it's a bit bland, but flavored by the fun we had making it. One of the college boys plays a harmonica. Then, possessed by the silliness of knowing we'll never see these people again, Molly and I sing "You Are My Sunshine" in perfect harmony, and our listeners are polite enough to clap. We stay by the fire way too late, until I feel the stiffness of the long day and the cold night at my back.

"I'm heading to bed," I tell Molly. I worry that she might want to linger here with the college boys. Her eyes glow when she talks to them. I battle the urge to remind her that these guys are strangers and we're in a strange place. Pretty soon, I won't be around to protect her at all, so I'd best get used to the churning nervousness in my gut.

She surprises me by getting up and helping collect the trash and leftovers. "I'm going to turn in, too. If we get an early start, we can make up for the time we lost today."

We didn't lose any time. I know exactly how and where we spent it, and I wouldn't change a thing.

As we walk together to our cabin, Molly says, "Those kids loved making the ice cream."

"Remember the first time I made it with you?"

"The Brownie campout at Lake Pegasus. I was— what—six years old? And I had the coolest mom."

What I remember about that campout was feeling inadequate. The professional moms, as I'd come to regard them, had remembered everything from bug spray to breakfast bars. They knew how to roast a whole meal in a foil packet, braid a lanyard into a friendship bracelet and name the constellations. My clever little ice cream trick didn't seem like much. Now I'm ridiculously pleased to know she thought I was the coolest.

Molly goes off to shower. I flip through the Triple-A book, wondering what tomorrow will bring. On the back cover is an ad I never noticed before, with a list of phone numbers—who to call in event of a breakdown.

DAY FOUR

Odometer Reading 122,639

"As her father and brother constructed the simple, sturdy shelter that might house generations after her, a young girl at her mother's knee would work her own Log Cabin. It became the quintessential American quilt."

—Sandi Fox,
Small Endearments, 19th Century Quilts for Children

Six

The next day we make tracks and we're curiously quiet with one another, both lost in our private worlds and lulled by the monotony of the road. We stop for the night at a far more conventional place, one with wireless internet and pay-per-view movies. We are not nearly as entertained by this as we were by last night's bungalows and campfire. The room smells of new carpet and cleaning solution. The beds are like two rectangular rafts, covered in beige spreads.

"Let's go out," I say, opening the door to the parking lot to scan the neon collage of signs along the main drag.

Molly looks at me as if I've sprouted horns. "What do you mean, out? We already had dinner."

"I mean out. To one of these clubs."

"And do what?"

I have to think for a minute. It's been a long time since I've gone to a club. "Get something to drink," I explain. "I'm sure bartenders still remember how to make a Shirley Temple. We can people-watch and listen to music."

"What if I get carded?"

"It's legal for you to be in a bar in Ohio so long as you aren't served."

"You checked?"

"I always check."

She looks so dubious that I feel vaguely insulted. "What?"

"It's just weird going clubbing with your mom."

"We're not going clubbing. We're going to a club, just to get out a little bit. Nothing else seems to be open."

"That's weird."

"Fine. Let's stay here. You can watch *Simpsons* reruns and I'll work on the quilt and reminisce about the past."

Fifteen minutes later, we're headed out the door. Molly spent the entire preparation time in front of the mirror. I have to admit, she has a knack for primping. Her eyes are now smoky around the edges, her hair glossy and her lips slick and pink. She gives me the once-over and frowns again.

"I've seen that shirt before, Mom."

"I never realized you *noticed* this shirt before." I smooth my hands down the polished cotton. Except it's not so polished anymore. I think the polish wore off some time ago.

"Isn't it kind of...old?"

"It still fits. It's in perfectly good shape."

"But you've had it forever. Those jeans, too, and the shoes. And the purse. You carried that purse when you drove first-grade car pool."

"I take care of my belongings," I explain. "It's a virtue."

"Sure, but...Mom? You keep things too long."

She speaks kindly, yet I know what she's saying. Although I've always been quick to get something new for Molly, I never paid much attention to my wardrobe.

Other than the occasional school event, I don't tend to need much in the way of clothes. I can sew like the wind, but I like doing costumes and crafts, not blouses and shifts. And I've never been much for shopping. I laugh at Molly as I grab a light jacket and my purse. "Trust me, the world is not interested in my lack of style sense. Especially not when I'm with a girl who's flaunting her midriff."

"I'm not flaunting." She checks out her cropped shirt in the mirror.

A year ago, she had begged us to let her get a tattoo and, of course, we refused. Once she turned eighteen, she didn't need our permission but, to my immense relief, she didn't run out to the tattoo parlor. Maybe she forgot it was the one thing that was going to make her life complete. I'm not about to remind her.

We walk out together into the twilight, and the breeze holds just the faintest hint of the coming fall. There's none of the coolness of autumn in it, but a nearly ineffable dry scent. The smell of something just past ripeness.

The main street is lined with mid-twentieth-century buildings of blond brick or cut stone. The shops and banks are closed, window shades pulled like half-lidded eyes, but in the center of the block, the sound of music and laughter streams from three different clubs.

One of them, called Grins, has a sandwich board out front boasting No Cover. Across the street is Tierra del Fuego, featuring unspecified live music, and two doors down is a place called Home Base. Twinkling lights surround a picture of Beulah Davis, and we choose that club because she has the same last name as us and because I like her picture. She's smiling, though there's a wistful look in her eyes. Her hands, draped over an acoustic guitar, look strong, capable of bearing the weight of a large talent.

We enter between sets. Canned music pulsates from hidden speakers. The place is crowded with people clustered around bar-height tables. The yeasty scent of beer hangs in the air. A group of guys is playing pool under a domed light with a Labatt insignia. In the corner, the musical set is dark and quiet, two guitars—acoustic and steel—poised in their holders like wallflowers waiting to be asked for a dance.

I pause, letting my eyes adjust to the dimness, and a wave of uncertainty hits me. I can feel Molly's hesitation, too, and unthinkingly I grab her hand, still the mom, leading her to a booth that has a view of the dance floor and stage. A good number of couples are swaying in the darkness, the women's bare, soft arms draped around men's shoulders.

I miss Dan. It hits me suddenly, a swell of nostalgia. He's not fond of dancing, but he's fond of me. Sometimes he has no choice but to sweep me into his arms and dance with me.

Molly orders a 7UP with lime, and I ask for a beer on tap.

"I'll need to see some ID," the waitress says.

"The beer's for me."

"ID, please," she says, bending toward me.

This is both startling and flattering. I readily show her my driver's license; she nods in satisfaction and heads for the bar. Molly samples the snack mix and scans the crowd. It's a diverse bunch, people of all ages relaxing and talking, some of them drinking too much and laughing too loudly. A couple in a booth across the room appears to be in an argument, leaning toward each other, their mouths twisted, ugly with over-enunciated insults.

The music stops and the dancing couples fall still. The singer appears on the corner stage, accompanied by a drummer, a bass player and a woman on keyboard. Applause greets them and we set aside our drinks to listen. She picks up the steel guitar and smiles as they tune up, then places her lips close to the speakers. "Here's something by a guy I once knew, Doug Sahm, from Kilgore, Texas." A ringing, sweet melody slides from the speakers as she strokes the guitar.

It's the kind of song that sounds fresh, even though we've heard it a hundred times before. There's something about good live music that does that to a person. I feel a sense of happiness sprouting from within, and when I look across at Molly, I can tell that she feels it, too. There are very few people you can talk to without words. The fact that my daughter has always been one of those people for me is beyond price.

I grab and hang on to this moment, because I learned long ago that happiness is not one long, continuous state of being. Like life itself, happiness is made up of moments. Some are fleeting, lasting no longer than the length of a sweet song, yet the sum total of those moments can create a glow that sustains you. Watching Molly, I wonder if she knows that, and if she doesn't, if it's something I can teach her.

Sensing the question in my look, she tilts her head to one side and mouths, "Something wrong?"

The singer is joined by other band members, and the set segues into a lively swing tune. The volume increases tenfold. I lean across the table. "Nothing's wrong. I'm just wondering if we've talked about what happiness is."

She cups her hand around her ear and her mouth moves again.

"Happiness," I say, nearly shouting. "Do you know how it works?"

She shakes her head, at a loss, then meets me halfway across the table. "Are you happy?" I ask in her ear.

She sits back down, laughing, and mouths the words, "I'm fine."

Her words remind me that there are some things I'm not meant to teach her. She'll only learn them by finding out for herself. I can hope and pray that I've raised a young woman who knows how to be happy, but I can't hand it to her like my mother's button collection, sealed in a mason jar. Starting now, she will have to be the steward of her own life.

After four songs, greeted with enthusiastic applause, the band takes a quick break and we buy a copy of their CD. The singer smiles a little bashfully and we smile back, two strangers who like the sound of her voice. She signs the case with an indelible marker. "Y'all enjoy that, now," she says.

"We will," I say.

The waitress reappears, another beer and another 7UP on her tray, even though we didn't ask for a second round.

"The gentlemen over there sent them," she explains, indicating with her thumb and a wink.

"Oh, uh…" My cheeks catch fire. I can't bring myself to look.

The waitress sets down the drinks and leaves.

"Get out of town," Molly says. "Mom, those guys sent us drinks."

"Don't make eye contact. And for heaven's sake, don't drink—"

She takes a sip of her fresh 7UP. Watching her expertly made-up eyes over the rim of the glass, I see a whole world of things I haven't told her, matters that need to be explained to someone who, in so many ways, is still only a child. I've had eighteen years to teach her not to accept gifts from strange men. I never got around to doing it. So much of this thing called parenting is a matter of waiting for a situation to arise and then addressing it. Just when you think you have all your bases covered, you—

"They're coming over," she says in a scandalized whisper.

I want to slither under the table. I've never been good in social situations, not with men, anyway. For Molly's sake I need to get over the urge to slither. This is a teachable moment.

"Thank you for the drinks," I tell the older one. He's maybe thirty, and the way he's looking at me makes me glad I'm wearing the mom clothes. "We were just leaving, though."

"I bet you have time for one dance," he says, smiling beneath a well-groomed mustache. He looks like the guy in that old TV series, *Magnum PI*. Magpie, Dan called it. I never did like that show.

His friend is clean-shaven, late twenties, checking out Molly with an expression that makes me want to call 911.

And here's the thing. I can't call 911. Nobody's doing anything illegal. It just feels that way to me.

"My mother and I really need to go," Molly says, polite but firm as she stands up. She tugs her shirt down, probably hoping they don't notice her midriff.

"Just trying to be friendly," the clean-shaven one said. His buddy seems to be having a delayed reaction to the word *mother*.

On the way out, I hand the waitress $20 and don't ask for change.

"Okay, that was weird," Molly says as we step out onto the street.

"Honey, when a guy approaches you—"

"I didn't mean it was weird that they approached me," she interrupts. "I'm just not too keen on guys hitting on my mom."

"Guys hit on women. It's what they do. They don't think about whether she's somebody's mother. Or daughter, or sister. And when we were in there, all I could think about was whether or not I've talked to you enough about staying safe around strange guys."

She laughs. "You're killing me, Mom."

"Oh, that's right. You know everything. Sorry, I forgot." She doesn't realize it now, but the older she gets, the wiser *I* get.

Something I probably won't share with her—the last time I met a man in a bar, I married him. Not right away, of course. But there are eerie similarities. The bar was dim, like the one we just left, and—in those days—smoky. Dan didn't send a waitress to do his work for him. He strode right over to me and said, "Let me buy you a drink."

I was too startled to say no. By the time the drink arrived, it was too late. I had noticed his lanky height and merry eyes, the heft of his biceps and the humor in his voice and his mouth, even when he wasn't smiling. I wouldn't go so far as to say it was love at first sight, but it was definitely something powerful and undeniable.

He was a guy with clear potential and big plans, and I was a mediocre student at the state college. Less than half a year later, we found ourselves standing face-to-face at the altar, with nothing between us but dreams and candlelight. I still remember our first lowly, unde-manding jobs and the way the days melted into a rhythm of partying every weekend, making love before dinner, staying up late and watching edgy movies.

Then Molly came along, and nothing was ever the same. We thought, at first, that nothing would change. Our denial ran deep; we walked around with her in a Snugli or stroller, pretending she was a fashion accessory.

Of course, she was so much more than that. She had the power to turn us into different people. We were no better and no worse, but different. She was our happi-est, most blessed accident.

All of which goes to show what can happen when you talk to strange men in bars.

In the middle of the night, I wake up and blink at my surroundings, my sleep-blurred gaze tracking the seam of the drapes, glowing amber from the lights of the motel parking lot. I hear Molly breathing evenly, sweetly, a sound that catches at my heart now as it did the first time I ever heard it and thought, *My God*.

Emotion and memory chase away sleep and I get up, shuffling over to the laptop computer. I touch the key-board and it wakes up, too. Little boxes tile the screen; Molly was IMing with Travis late into the night. I quickly close the IM windows without reading the text.

It's 3:00 a.m., and the internet is there, waiting for

me. Following the stream of my own thoughts, I click to site after site, surfing from link to link as though pulling myself along some invisible, unending chain. Ultimately, it's unsatisfying, filling my head with too much information. Yet it's given me a huge idea.

Slipping on a light jacket, I step out into the parking lot with my cell phone. The whole world is asleep. There are no cars on the street, no critters rooting in the trash, no breeze stirring the tops of the trees. I punch in our home number on the cell phone.

"It's me," I say when Dan picks up on the second ring.

"What?" he asks, grogginess burgeoning to panic. "Where the hell are you? Are you and Molly all right?"

"We're fine. We're in…" I think for a moment. "Ohio. She's sleeping."

"So what's the matter?" In Dan's book, if everything is fine with Molly, everything is fine, period. I can hear the bed creak, can picture him rolling over, pulling up the covers. "What time is it?"

I'm not about to tell him. "Late," I admit. "Sorry I woke you. I couldn't wait. Dan, I just thought of something."

"What did you think of, Lindy?" He never gets mad when I wake him up out of a sound sleep. I wonder how that can be. Suddenly I wish I was there with him, rubbing his warm shoulders with gentle persistence.

"We need to get an orphan."

"A what?"

"An orphan. You know, adopt a child."

"Huh?" Another creak of the bed, or maybe it's the sound of Dan, scowling.

"From Haiti."

"Linda, for Chrissake—"

"No, listen, I found this site on the internet. There

are thousands of them, waiting for families. We have so much, Dan. We're still young. We could give some poor child a chance.

"There's one I found named Gilbert. He's six. He lost his family in the earthquake."

"Go back to bed, Linda. It was hard enough raising our own healthy, well-adjusted child."

"It hasn't been hard at all."

"Speak for yourself."

His comment reminds me of their struggles. His frustration, Molly's tears, the long silences and the breakdowns I used to feel compelled to fix. "We did a great job."

"I'm not saying we didn't. But we're done. It's our time now, Linda."

"And I want to do something with it, something that matters. Think about it, Dan. These kids…they're not sick or abused. They didn't grow up in institutions. They're kids like Molly, except they had the bad luck to come home from school one day to find that their families were gone."

"I'll send a check to the Red Cross."

"They need *families*. We could—"

"We could do a lot of things, but adopting an orphan from Haiti isn't one of them." He must know how that sounds, because he takes a breath and adds, "Honey, you're in panic mode over Molly leaving. This is no time to be discussing such a huge undertaking."

I pull the jacket tighter around me. Panic mode. Am I panicking?

"I need a child who needs me," I blurt out.

"Lindy. Slow down. What you need is a life of your own."

The words fall like stones on my heart. He's right. *He's right.* "I'll work on that," I say, feeling a bleak sweep of exhaustion.

"Have fun on your trip," Dan says, a yawn in his voice. "I love you both."

"Love you, too." After we hang up, I sit for a while and look at the stars. It's so quiet I can hear a train whistle blow, miles away.

Day Five

Odometer Reading 123,277

—

"From the manner in which a woman
draws her thread at every stitch
of her needlework, any other woman
can surmise her thoughts."

—Honoré de Balzac

Seven

"I'm running out of thread," I tell Molly.

"We can stop somewhere in the next town," she says, unconcerned. She is more interested in finding a radio station. We have a rule. Driver gets to pick the music. We're already bored with our playlists and she's hungry for something new.

"This is mercerized thread spun from Sea Isle cotton," I explain. "It doesn't grow on trees, you know."

"I know how cotton is grown, Mom."

In quilting, the type and quality of thread you use matters greatly. Just think of all the stitches that go into a quilt. You need the kind of thread that pulls through smoothly, that is strong despite repeated tugging, that will never fray or pill.

To people who don't practice the craft of hand-sewing, thread is thread. Therefore, this is far less of a concern than the dearth of radio stations. The FM band yields too much static, and the AM stations are crammed with crop reports or the phony sentiment of country tunes.

"In pioneer days, mothers and daughters worked on their quilts together," I tell her.

"Good thing we're not pioneers." A soybean rust update comes on the radio, and she groans in exasperation.

I tried to get her interested in quilting a time or two, to no avail. She was impatient with the detail and repetition. Our few "lessons" ended with her pricking herself with a needle and sighing loudly with boredom. She usually wound up shooting baskets in the driveway with her dad.

She fiddles with the dial a bit more, and hits paydirt. The announcer's voice says, "Settle back and enjoy this local favorite, from Beulah Davis and the Strivers."

"Hey, isn't that the group we heard last night?" asks Molly. "Cool."

The melody and words are soothing and emotional, and I pause in the quilting to look out the window. It's a sea of grass, rolling out on both sides, and I imagine Molly and me as pioneers, setting off on a journey into the great, wide unknown.

I wonder what it was like for those women and their daughters, when their lives took them in different directions. They weren't able to pick up the phone or log onto the internet and get in touch. Separation meant the possibility of never seeing each other again. I should count my blessings.

The quilt section in my lap is made of cornflower blue fabric sprigged with tiny daisies. It was a dress I made for Molly to wear to her very first piano recital, back when she was just eight years old. Her first public performance. What a nerve-wracking day that was. I recall her practicing Bach's "Minuet in G Major" over and over again until it drove Dan out into the yard with the weed-whacker. And I, of course, couldn't help tuning in on every note. I adjusted my breathing to the rhythm of her playing and when she hesitated—the long, agonizing pause in the fifth bar as she spread her tiny hand over the keys of a big chord—it made me hold my breath until she found the right notes. When she hit the wrong note I would wince and then remind myself not to do that at the recital.

The dress was meticulously put together, every stitch in place with hand-smocking across the bodice, the full skirt crisply ironed. She wore white ankle socks and Mary Janes, her hair held back in a blue band, and she looked like a dark-haired version of Alice in Wonderland.

"I'm not going in." I can still recall the exact sound of her little-girl voice as she balked at the door to the recital hall. It was an intimidating auditorium, filled with echoes. On the stage, the Steinway crouched like a slumbering black dragon.

"Okay," Dan said, immediately agreeable. "Let's go home." He had come under duress to begin with and was already chafing in his good shoes and starched shirt. He reached up to adjust the bill of the baseball cap that wasn't there. "Better yet, let's go for ice cream."

"We can't leave," I said, shooting daggers at him with my eyes. "Look, Moll, your name's already on the program." I showed her the printed sheet the piano teacher's son had given us at the door.

She refused to let go of Dan's hand. He was her ally and suddenly I was the enemy. We stood on either side of her, locked in a silent tug-of-war.

Not for the first time, it occurs to me that he was always quick to back off while I played the ogre, pushing her into new situations, sometimes against her will. I wonder if I'm doing that now, pushing her across the country to college. Dan, like Travis, would prefer for her to go to the state school.

Elsewhere on the quilt is a rosette of red stretchy fabric from the swimsuit she wore when I delivered her to her first swim lesson. At the YMCA pool, she had clung to me like a remora. Her howl of panic ricocheted around the pool deck, and her slippery, strong little body strained toward the locker room. Dan had rescued her that day, coming out on deck in his board shorts, looking like a hunk on *Baywatch* as he snatched her up. I was furious with him, but didn't want to make even more of a scene, so I bit my tongue. He took her by the hand and led her away from the noisy echo chamber of shrieks, punctuated by coaches' whistles.

An hour later, I found them both in the rec pool. "Watch me, Mommy, watch!" Molly yelled, and leaped off the side, disappearing under the surface. She sprang up and swam, struggling like a puppy, straight to her waiting father. "See?" she said, her wide eyes starred by wet lashes, "I don't need lessons."

This is different, I thought at the recital. He can't save her from the piano. He can only help her run away.

In the end, the decision was taken from all of us. "There you are," said Mrs. Dashwood, the piano teacher, bustling forward. "Let's go backstage and get some lipstick on." The teacher, who had an MFA and the face of a pageant winner, was idolized by her little-girl students. Mrs. Dashwood was wise, too, understanding the power of the promise of stage makeup to distract a kid from fear. She took Molly by the hand and walked her down the sloping aisle of the auditorium.

Molly glanced back once, her eyes filled with uncertainty, yet she was unresisting as Mrs. Dashwood led her away. I watched the teacher stop at the edge of the stage to point something out. By the time Molly disappeared behind the curtain, there was a discernible spring of excitement in her step.

I found myself clutching Dan's hand. I didn't even remember grabbing it, but I would never forget what he said. Leaning down to kiss my cheek, he said, "Relax. She's in good hands."

"Hey, if it were up to you, she'd be at the ice-cream parlor."

"And guess what—the world wouldn't come to an end."

As the youngest on the program, Molly went first. Mrs. Dashwood welcomed everyone, then introduced her. A smattering of applause and a few adoring "Awws" came from the audience, which consisted of carefully dressed parents, grandparents and the occasional doting aunt or restless sibling.

Molly walked slowly with a curious dignity, her full skirt tolling like a bell with each step she took. So tiny, I thought. A porcelain doll, all alone up there. She didn't look at the audience, didn't try to find me with her eyes. She stood still, and my heart skipped a beat. But Molly knew what she was doing. She jacked up the stool to its highest level so she could reach the keyboard.

We had practiced how to smooth the full skirt in order to sit down properly. She remembered every unhurried move. Her patent leather shoes glittered in the stage lights, dangling above the pedals. Mrs. Dashwood said she wouldn't use the pedals until she was tall enough to reach them.

She rested her little hands on the keyboard. This was it, I thought. This was her moment. I took in a breath, ready to be dazzled.

It was a disaster from the first chord. Wrong notes, hesitation, whole measures forgotten. It was the longest ninety seconds of my life.

When it was over, I had aged a decade. Molly barely made it through the adorable curtsy we'd rehearsed. She fled into the wings and we found her in the stage hallway, a crushed flower surrounded by blue petals.

"This is the worst thing that ever happened to me," she sobbed, going limp against Dan when he picked her up. "This is worse than missing *larynx* in the spelling bee."

"I still can't spell *larynx*," I murmured.

"We should have gone for ice cream," Dan said.

In the passenger seat of the Suburban, I dart my needle into the heart of the fabric, quilting it with the words, "Be audacious." The cornflower blue fabric is like new. Molly never wore the dress again.

She didn't give up piano, though. Following the recital, she walked into the house, went straight to the piano and played the Bach flawlessly, every note ringing sweet and true through the empty rooms. "Just to make sure I could," she said.

Glancing over from the driver's seat now, Molly notices me working the blue piece. "What's that one?" she asked.

I angle it toward her. "Your first piano recital."

"I don't remember that dress."

"Bach's 'Minuet in G Major.'" The name of the piece usually jogged her memory.

"I'm blanking. Cute fabric, though."

Funny how the heart holds its memories, or lets them go. Each detail of that day is etched into me. I can even remember the flavor of ice cream we got afterward— maple walnut with chocolate sprinkles. Yet Molly has cast the nerves and trauma of that day from her mind. They are not important to her.

"Remember that red silk charmeuse you wore to your senior adjudication last January?" I ask her.

"Of course. I brought it along to keep you from cutting it up," she says, her urgency making me smile. "I love that dress."

"I know. I figured you'd want to wear it again." Unlike the flounces and sashes of her childhood, the red dress makes her look truly grown-up, slender and elegant. Maybe even sexy, with its clinging shape and single bare shoulder. In the same auditorium where she'd once stumbled through a minuet, she had performed last on the program. Supple as a ribbon of scarlet silk in a breeze, she had swayed through a grand, emotional rendition of Chopin's "Nocturne in C Minor," a piece he composed when he was seventeen, the same age Molly was.

Mrs. Dashwood, scarcely changed from the no-nonsense teacher we'd known for years, had handed her a tube of Chanel lipstick and declared her one of her most accomplished students ever.

The adjudicator gave Molly the highest possible marks and pronounced her the winner of the competition. Had she played better than the other students? It was hard to say. The adjudicator was Italian, a retired professor from the state college. All the other competitors were boys. It was hard not to miss the professor's enthusiasm for a pretty, talented girl in a red dress.

Still, I believed she had outdone the others in more than just looks. She had a gift. That nocturne sang with feeling. She knew how to take a heartfelt emotion and fling it wide for all to hear.

I'm kind of glad she doesn't remember the first disastrous recital. But I'm also glad I pushed her to do it. It occurs to me how much simpler it is to push your child in the right direction rather than yourself.

Molly flicks on the turn signal and drifts over to the right lane.

"What are you doing?" I ask.

"Thread, remember? You need thread."

The Suburban glides down the exit ramp and she takes a right, following a sign that points to "City Center."

Before too long, we find one of those chain craft and fabric stores. "They won't have the right kind," I lament.

"Then get another kind. No biggie." She catches the look on my face. "You should have brought more of the magical thread, if it's so important."

We step into the bright commercial glare of the craft shop. "You're right," I admit, "but Minerva's ran out and won't be getting in any more. She's closing the shop, you know."

"Nope, I didn't know. I thought it was for sale."

"It is. She's retiring and selling the place, but I doubt she'll find a buyer in this economy. I'll miss it. All her customers will. The idea of driving all the way to Rock Springs has no appeal to me at all."

"Bummer," Molly says, tucking her thumbs in her back pockets as she regards a display of notions.

As always, beautiful fabrics draw my eye. A few impossible-to-resist fat quarters make it into my shopping basket. The lure of a new project beckons. This happens a lot; I get close to the end of one thing and another pops into mind, seductive and infinitely more alluring than the project at hand.

At the end of a multitiered aisle, Molly fingers a green glass suncatcher marked Special of the Week. "Can I get this?"

My knee-jerk reaction is, *You don't need more junk.* But she takes after me, a magpie drawn to every glittering object that catches her eye. She's always been this way. Besides, it's in the shape of a music note, and it's only five bucks.

"One more pit stop," Molly says. Instead of going to the car, she heads into the shop across the way, a department store named Bradner's.

I happily follow her. It's fun shopping with someone who has her figure; everything looks good on her. But when I step into the store, I catch a whiff of White Shoulders perfume. This doesn't seem like Molly's kind of shop.

"What do you need, sweetie?"

"Come on," she says, her eyes sparkling. "We're going to pick out some new clothes for you."

"But…"

"But *what*, Mom?" Her excitement flashes to annoyance.

The usual litany of excuses piles up: I don't need new clothes. I don't have time. I don't want to spend the money. I want to lose some weight before I buy a bunch of things. *I'm not important enough.*

I look at Molly and grin. "Let's do it."

She did not inherit her fashion smarts from me. Must be all those style blogs and glossy magazines she loves to read. When she teams up with a salesgirl named Darcy, there is no stopping the two of them. I surrender to their superior savvy and wait in a big double dressing room in a bra and panties that have seen better days, bare feet in need of a pedicure.

The glaring fluorescent lights and full-length, three-way mirror have no mercy. I stare at myself in triplicate, the images growing smaller and smaller into infinity. Molly and Darcy bring in tops, slacks and jeans, silky cardigans and jackets nipped in at the waist, belts and low-heeled pumps. They can't resist accessorizing with statement jewelry, bright scarves, slender hoop earrings. The attention feels good—and the clothes look good on me.

Molly hands me a cream leather hobo bag. "You are so pretty, Mom. Wait until Dad sees you. Wait until everyone sees you."

In the end, I buy about half of what she wants me to get. Even that seems excessive to me, but with all the nice things to choose from, it was hard to narrow them down. We walk out of the store with a parcel as big as the quilt bag. It's filled with new jeans and shoes, a top and sweater and skirt, a wrap dress and hoop earrings, and a melon-colored paisley scarf I couldn't bear to leave behind. Molly and Darcy made me keep the new undergarments on, leaving my elastic-less ones in the trash. "When you start with a good foundation," Darcy pointed out, "everything looks better."

"Well," I say, setting the shopping bag on the back seat next to the quilt. "That was unexpected."

"That was fun," Molly said. "Way more fun than a fabric shop."

"A different kind of fun than the fabric shop."

She's not done, and her enthusiasm is infectious. On Darcy's recommendation, we go to a nearby salon for a shampoo and style. We have our toenails polished candy pink and emerge from the salon flipping our hair around and giggling.

"Look at us," Molly says, primping in the Suburban's visor mirror. "We're new women."

Eight

The next day, the sheen is off our hair. Molly urges me to wear something new but I decline, not wanting to wrinkle the clothes, sitting in the car all day. The bag with the beautiful new things stays on the back seat. The outfits are too nice for a car trip. I want to save them for something special.

According to the peeling roadside billboards, we have two choices for lunch—a Stuckey's that has ninety-nine-cent burgers, or Bubba's Beach Shack, on the scenic shores of Lake Ontario.

"It's a lake," Molly says. "How can it have a beach?"

"It's one of the Great Lakes." I am nearly cross-eyed from sewing. The end of our journey looms closer, an outcome I can see and practically touch. I stayed up late last night, working on the quilt. Working is, of course, an elastic concept. I can be staring out at the night sky and call it "working" if I'm planning the next quilt.

"I never thought about a lake having a beach. Back home it's just…a shore, I guess."

"We should have taken you to see the Great Lakes when you were little." And here it is again, that sense of things left undone, unfinished. What else have I forgotten to show her, to teach her?

She glances over at me. "You took me to Mount Rushmore and Yosemite and the Grand Canyon and the Everglades. You can't show me everything."

"I wish I had, though. We always had such fun on those summer driving trips, didn't we?"

There is a heartbeat of hesitation. And in that heartbeat, I hear a contradiction. Could be, she has memories of being hot, carsick, bored. Sometimes Dan and I were short-tempered and we were terrible at picking out places to stay. Bad motel karma became a family joke. Remembrances of summers past are marred by nonfunctioning swimming pools, moldy smells, shag carpets.

"Sure," Molly says. "We had a blast."

"But the Great Lakes—I remember going to Mackinac Island on my high school senior trip. I saved up for months in order to go. It was so beautiful, like stepping back in time. I wish we'd taken you there."

"You can't take me everywhere," she repeats.

New adventures lie ahead of her, a vast stretch of unexplored terrain. She'll be taking trips without me, seeing and experiencing things I'll never share. Which is as it should be, I remind myself.

Without further debate, she takes the next exit and wends her way through a threadbare town of redbrick buildings and convenience stores plastered with fading advertising posters. The route to Bubba's is well-marked, and within a few minutes we enter Tanaka State Park in western New York, a quiet oasis on a weekday afternoon. As we head toward the water, I notice that the colors of summer are fading here, the greens subtly shifting to yellow, the wildflowers casting their petals to the breeze.

The beach shack is adorable, and I'm instantly glad we've come. It has a huge deck with picnic tables covered in red-and-white-checkered oilcloth, and a long dock reaching out to the deep, wind-crested waters of the lake. And it truly is a beach, fringed by sand and weathered by wave action. From this perspective, the lake looks as infinite as the sea itself. There are even herring gulls here, and I wonder if they lost their way and became landlocked, and if that would matter to a bird.

The waiter is the sort of gorgeous teenage boy who makes me feel like an urban cougar as I check him out. I can check him out as much as I want, because he has not even noticed me. He's eyeing Molly. Who wouldn't? Boys have always been drawn in by her pretty eyes, her smile that hints that she knows a secret.

We order the fish fry lunch, and it arrives in paper-lined baskets with French fries and coleslaw. It's beautiful here, and graceful boats skim across the water in the distance, the sails puffed out in the breeze.

"Check that out," Molly says, indicating a parasail kite flying from the back of a speedboat.

"Yikes, looks scary."

"Looks awesome." She dips a French fry in her coleslaw, a habit she acquired from Dan ages ago. She gazes dreamily at the sky, studying the little sailing man with stick legs, like a paratrooper GI Joe.

As we watch, the parasail is reeled into the back of the boat, and they tie up at the dock right below the restaurant.

"It's definitely awesome," the cute waiter says, coming to refill our iced tea glasses. From the pocket of his half apron, he hands her a card. "Here's a coupon for $5 off a ride."

I shake my head. "We won't be needing—"

"Thanks." Molly snatches the card. "Thanks a lot."

"We're not doing it." I dole out cash to cover our tab, leaving a generous tip even though I wish he hadn't put ideas in Molly's head.

"Come on, Mom. We've got time." Ignoring my protests, she heads down the stairs to the dock, her steps light with excitement. When I get to her side, she's already talking with the guys in the speedboat.

"It takes fifteen minutes," she says, "and we won't even get wet, except maybe our feet."

"We're not doing it."

"Ma'am, it's very safe. I've been doing this for years," the boat driver assures me.

I hate looking like a stick-in-the-mud. But I also hate the idea of dangling several hundred feet above the lake, tethered to the world by a rope no bigger than my finger.

Molly has that expression on her face. I don't see it often, but when I do, I know she means business. The stubborn jaw, the fire in her eye. A minute later, she's signing a faded pink form on a clipboard without reading it, and asking if I'll pay the fee. I haven't read the disclaimer, either, but I'm sure it absolves the boat guys of any liability if we happen to wind up at the bottom of Lake Ontario.

Studying the form over her shoulder, I point out one line. "It says here you need to weigh at least a hundred pounds. Last I knew, you were just under that."

She shrugs it off. "After this summer, I'm well over a hundred."

The boat guys seem to believe her. They put her in a high-tech life vest and helmet and she kicks off her shoes.

"A helmet?" I ask.

"Just a safety precaution," the man says.

I want to ask how a helmet is going to keep her safe if she plummets into the lake. I want to say that she's never tipped the scale past a hundred pounds, but I stop myself. It's my nature to cite the potential disaster in every situation. I recognize that. So, apparently, does Molly, because she learned to dismiss my fears years ago. She has gone mountain biking, horseback riding, scuba diving. A spirit of adventure is good, I remind myself. It's small and mean of me to dampen it.

Just the other day, I was thinking about what a pushy mother I've been. But the things I pushed her to do didn't place life and limb at risk. Especially pointless risk.

She's grinning ear-to-ear as they harness her to the sail. "'Bye, Mom," she says. "See you when I come back around."

"Be careful," I can't help saying, and now there's a fire in *my* eye as I send out warning signals to the boat driver and his helper.

Then there is nothing more to say as they head away from the dock, the big engine cutting a V-shaped wake behind the boat. My heart is in my throat as they reach open water, and the rainbow-colored sail fills with wind. Then, a moment later, Molly is aloft, a tiny doll tethered by a slender cord. She flies like a kite tail, higher and higher until they run out of rope. I shade my eyes and look at her, silhouetted by the sun.

Then my heart settles and I wave both arms wildly

over my head. "Go, Molly!" I shout, jumping up and down on the dock. "Go, Molly!"

Watching her fly is incredibly gratifying. I fumble with my mobile phone, try to get a picture to send to Dan. She'll probably look like no more than a speck against the sky, but he'll get the idea.

A gust of wind ripples across the water in a discernible path. I can actually see the gust filling the sail and then turning it sideways. Molly's stick figure legs swing to and fro like a pendulum.

"Omigod," I say. "Omigod, she's going to fall."

Apparently the boat driver knows something isn't right. His partner starts cranking in the cord, his movements fast, maybe frantic. I stand motionless on the dock, my feet riveted to the planks, my stomach a ball of ice. Here is the definition of hell—knowing something terrible is happening to your child and being completely powerless to stop it.

If she dies, I think with grim clarity, so will I.

The wind whips her like a rag doll. Her screams sound faint. I wonder if she's calling my name. I send up a prayer, pushing it out with every cell of my body and soul.

The screams grow louder, and then I realize she's not screaming at all. She's laughing.

Nine

"You should try it," Molly says, combing back her wind-tossed hair and pulling it into a bun. She is still shivering from the lake, her lips tinged a subtle blue. With her hair pulled back, she looks sophisticated, older. We return to the beach shack to get her something warm to drink. The hunky waiter hovers, bringing her hot tea in a small stainless steel pot.

"In my next life, maybe."

"Seriously, Mom, you'd love it."

"I'm too chicken to love something like that." Still, I feel a slight twinge. What would it be like, dangling in midair like the tail of a giant kite? But no. That is so far out of my comfort zone I can't even imagine myself doing it.

"What's that piece of fabric?" Molly asks, indicating the dotted Swiss. She's been enjoying my stories about the pieces in the quilt.

"This is from your grandmother's square-dancing skirt. There's plenty of fabric, yards and yards of it, so I used it for sashing. Do you remember how she and Grandpa used to go square dancing?"

"Sort of. Maybe just from looking at old pictures, though."

My parents were avid square dancers. They belonged to a club that held a dance the first Saturday of every month. I can still see them in my mind's eye, my dad trim and dapper in a Western-cut shirt, with mother-of-pearl snap buttons, and a string tie. My mother's dresses were outrageous confections. She made them herself, with yards of ruched calico or dotted Swiss draped over a pinwheel froth of crinolines. The dresses had puffy sleeves that sat like weightless balls on her shoulders, and she always wore these horrible little one-strap dancing shoes.

The sight of my folks in their square-dancing getup might have made me squirm, except that they were so damn happy to be going out to the dance hall together, to laugh with their friends and drink sticky fruit punch.

"They loved those dances so much," I tell Molly, drawing a stitch through the sashing. "Grandma more than Grandpa, but he was a good sport about it."

"I never saw them dance," Molly says.

"Every once in a while, they'd have family night and we'd go." Of course she wouldn't remember that; she was in a stroller at the time. Still, I could see her swinging her tiny feet and clapping, mesmerized by the noise and the movements.

When Molly was in the second grade, my mother suffered a massive stroke. She was just sixty-four; it shouldn't have happened. I took Molly to see her, praying my child wouldn't act frightened when she saw Mom's altered face, the left side slack and unresponsive, her neck encased in a cervical collar.

I needn't have worried. Molly had happily rolled an

ergonomic table in front of my mother and said, "Now you can play cards with me."

The funny, sewing, square-dancing mom I knew vanished that day, even though she lived for two more years. Her personality changed, and dark anger emerged from a place we never knew was inside her. It was as if the stroke awakened a slumbering dragon inside her. She raged at how hard she had worked, and how frustrated she was that she hadn't given her kids more. I constantly reassured her that what she'd given her family was enough. She always liked it when I brought Molly to visit her, though. Seeing her only granddaughter quieted the angry sadness.

She was supposed to get better with a long and rigorous course of physical and occupational therapy. She hated the therapy, though—squeezing a hard blue rubber ball, poking a thick shoelace through holes on a board to form the shape of a spider, walking back and forth between parallel bars. Most days, she refused to do any of it, preferring to let my dad tie her shoes and push her wheelchair. Her hands, which used to effortlessly knit Fair Isle sweaters and mittens and hats, closed around some invisible object and refused to open. Once or twice, she tried knitting again, but the yarn wound up in knots of frustration on the floor. The physical therapists told my father that in the long run, she'd be better off dressing herself and learning to walk on her own, but Dad didn't listen. It was more important to him to do what my mom wanted.

"I wish I could remember the square dancing," Molly says. "Not the assisted living place."

I wish that, too. Even though I know it's irrational, I feel irritated at Molly because she doesn't remember my mother the way I want her to. I want her to recall the funny singing voice, the strong hands with their faint smell of onion, the perfect bulb of hair held slick with Aqua-Net. I want Molly to miss *that* woman, even though I understand it's impossible.

"How did she die?" Molly asks. "You never talk about that."

"Ask me how she lived. After all, that's what she spent most of her life doing."

"You talk about that all the time," Molly notes. "And I do love hearing the stories, Mom. But you've made her into this Disney grandma who's barely real to me."

"She got pneumonia and was too weak to fight it." I smooth my hand over the fading calico. "She died early one morning when you were in fourth grade. I didn't tell you right away because you had a school party that day. I didn't want to ruin it for you. So I waited until you got home."

Molly is quiet for a minute, sipping her tea, staring out across the lake, where the wind whips up white tufts in the water. Wrapped in a blanket someone at the restaurant gave her, she looks little and lost. But there is a sharpness in her eyes. "You were always cushioning me, Mom."

"It's what mothers do." I wish my own mother could see this young woman now, vibrant and excited about her future. My dad, who has grown quiet and slow with age and loneliness, often tells me he wishes that, too.

"It didn't work," she says, not looking at me. "I knew, anyway. I could tell from the way you rushed me off to car pool. I was scared to say anything because I didn't want to see you cry."

This shocks me. Dan and I had been prepared;

Mom's doctors had let us know her death was imminent, even offering signs and markers to watch for. For me, the sense of loss was so overwhelming that I hadn't been able to talk about it.

Even now, years later, it's still hard. There is something about losing your mother that is permanent and inexpressible—a wound that will never quite heal.

"I had a rotten day at school that day," Molly explains. "Hated the party. There were these awful cupcakes, and the games were lame. So it's not like you spared me anything."

"Moll, I never realized you knew what was going on that day."

"Nope. You didn't. I didn't say anything because I didn't want to upset you. We were both trying to protect each other, and it didn't work."

I draw the thread to the end and make a tiny, invisible knot before cutting it free. "How did you get so smart?"

"Must've inherited it from my mother. We'd better get going." She drinks the last of her tea, combs her hair again. The breeze is reviving her curls. She stands up and folds the blanket. She waves a thank-you to the waiter and he hurries over to our table.

I put my things into the crafter's bag and head back to the car while she lingers to talk to the waiter. Looking back, I feel a jab of annoyance. I don't like the way he stands so close to her, checking her out. It's on the tip of my tongue to call out, to remind them both that I'm standing here. Then I think about what Molly said about me always stepping in, trying to smooth things over for her, to absorb the body blows life tends to deal out from time to time.

The afternoon at the lake caused an almost imperceptible shift in our mood. We're more on edge. Our silences are longer, corresponding to the flat, boring stretches of highway.

How do long-haul truck drivers handle the tedium? How will I handle it, driving back alone, the Suburban emptied of Molly's things, devoid of her fruity-smelling hair products and her lively chatter?

What's really eating me is this. We're almost there.

Odometer Reading 123,597

"No other border was applied with
greater ingenuity and diversity
than the Sawtooth. It could be applied
in one of three methods to a perfect
turn and direction, but it is in its less
precise applications that it often assumed
its greatest charm."

—Sandi Fox,
Small Endearments, 19th Century Quilts for Children

Ten

There is a change in Molly's phone calls with Travis. Pacing back and forth, the tiny silver phone glued to her ear, she talks to him at every rest stop, it seems. The shift in tone and emphasis is subtle but palpable. She is both more animated and more intense.

I don't say anything, of course. What is there to say? They're eighteen, and in love.

Give it time, I remind myself. The drifting-apart is not going to happen overnight. I picture the two of them like the huge layers of ice we get on the lake back home. All winter long, the frozen surface is strong and impermeable; the skating goes on for weeks. Yet in spring, the ice cracks apart, and once that happens, the pieces never fit together properly again. Even if the temperature drops sufficiently at night to refreeze the ice, it's not the same; it's rough and chunky, prone to breaking. The skaters all go home for the season.

Separation is rough on any relationship. On a pair who have barely dipped a toe into adulthood, it's usually a death knell. They just don't have the emotional hardware to sustain a love that depends on physical closeness. And I won't kid myself. Those two were close. They were physical.

I can't imagine Travis Spellman going dateless for movie nights or football games, not for long. Likewise, I don't want Molly to be like a war widow at college, holding back from the social scene because of her hometown boyfriend.

That lack of availability, physical and emotional, is undoubtedly what will cause them to go their separate ways, as they must. Molly has a future ahead of her filled with brand-new people, challenging studies, a city she's never seen before. Settling into college will take all her time and energy. Nurturing a long-distance relationship is simply not feasible.

Except, of course, that she believes it is. And here's the thing about my daughter. If she believes in something with her whole heart, no one can tell her otherwise.

At a rest stop where we park to stretch our legs and use the facilities, she is pacing back and forth on the sere, dun-colored grass that has gone dormant from drought. The phone is still glued to her ear and her flip-flops kick up dust in her wake.

I wander along the walkway of the rest stop. It's a pleasant spot, insulated from the noise of the interstate by a stand of thick trees, evergreens and sugar maples that are just getting ready to take on their fall colors.

The local historical society in this area has a craft booth set up at the rest stop, and I buy a bottle of amber maple syrup from a woman in a homespun apron and—I kid you not—a poke bonnet. The clear glass bottle is in the shape of a maple leaf, and when I hold it up to the sun, it sparkles like a jewel.

According to the information flyer that came with

the syrup, the maple trees will put on a dazzling display of fall color. These country roads will soon be crowded with RVs and busloads of leaf-lookers, coming to enjoy the scenery so beautiful that it attracts tourists from the world over to view them each year. After the riot of color, the trees lose all their leaves and appear to die.

Yet it is then, in the dead of winter, that the maples are most productive. If you tap deep enough into the tree, sinking a metal tube into its most hidden heart, you'll discover a gush of life.

The sap is drained through the tube, collected in covered buckets and boiled in huge vats to make maple syrup.

Who the heck thought of that? I wonder. At some moment in the unremembered past, someone walked up to a leafless maple tree, hammered a tube into its center, harvested the sap and rendered it into sweet syrup. What a random thing to do.

One thing I'd guess—whoever thought it up wasn't a college graduate. She—I'm quite certain it was a *she*— was probably a mother. An ancient Algonquin desperate housewife. At the end of a long winter, her kids were probably bored and cranky from being cooped up in the longhouse, chasing each other and driving her crazy with their noise. They had no idea supplies had run low, that the men hadn't done too well on the latest hunt. Pretty soon, the kids' war whoops and giggles would turn to whining. Yelling at the older kids to keep the younger ones away from the fire, the woman strapped on snowshoes made of hide, with gut laces, and trudged out into the deadening cold to look for food.

How did she know about the secret inside the maple tree? Maybe the deer clued her in. During the starving season, the hungry animals stripped the bark from the trees as high as they could reach. Maybe the woman, her vision sharpened by desperation, noticed the glistening ooze from the flesh of the trees. Maybe she touched a finger to the sticky dampness, tasted a faint sweetness on her tongue. And the rest was history. An industry was born. The hunting party came home with their limp, skinny rabbit to find the women and children feasting on boiled cornmeal, magically sweetened with an elixir from the sugar maples.

I reach the end of the walkway and wander back. The woman in the poke bonnet is standing behind her booth, furtively smoking a cigarette.

Still on the phone, Molly notices me watching her and wanders over to an information board covered with maps and tourist brochures. She tucks one hand into the back pocket of her shorts and keeps talking.

Her face is bright with love.

Seeing her like this conjures up mixed emotions. On the one hand, I am proud and gratified that my daughter has a great heart, that she can give it away with joy and sincerity. Yet on the other, I wish she understood the difference between the passionate heat of first love and the deep security of a lasting commitment.

But there is no difference, not in Molly's mind, and no amount of discussion—lecturing, she would call it—on my part will change her mind about that. Love is love, she'd tell me, and who am I to say she's wrong? I can't claim to be an expert. There is a part of me—and it's not even a small part—that keeps wondering what my marriage will be like when I get home and it's just Dan and me.

Agitated, I take a seat at an empty picnic table, which faces a lovely marsh fringed by cattails, the reeds clacking in the light breeze. The distant hiss of truck brakes joins the singing of frogs from the marsh.

I pull out the quilt, thinking I'll add a stitch or two. The feel of the age-softened fabrics is oddly soothing. Yet at the same time, I am nagged by the sense that I wish I'd never started this thing. What a crazy notion, to think I could actually put the final touches in place in time for the journey's end.

"That's a beautiful piece," someone says, and I look up to see a woman about my age, walking a scruffy little dog on a retractable leash. The dog ranges out to the end of the leash and then comes reeling back toward her, like a yo-yo on a string. The woman is checking out the quilt with a practiced eye.

"Thanks," I say, recognizing the expertise with which she studies the project. It's gratifying to realize quilters are everywhere. It's such a universal art, beloved by so many women. "I'm making this for my daughter's dorm room."

She nods appreciatively. "What a great idea. Wow, are you hand quilting?"

"More portable that way. More variety." This morning I stitched the word *Remember* across a piece made from my mom's square-dancing dress.

"I've always thought crazy quilting was much more challenging than a regular pattern," the stranger remarks.

"You might be right. At first, I thought it would make the work to go faster. Instead, I keep trying to force things together and changing my mind."

"I like going slowly when I quilt," she comments. "It keeps me in the moment, you know?"

I do know. And here's what happens when quilting women meet. When one quilter encounters another, there's always something to talk about. We go from being strangers to friends in about three seconds. I've seen this happen again and again, back home at the shop. It's like the fabric itself is common ground, the pattern a secret handshake. Quilting women already know so much about each other. We get to skip over the petty details.

Within moments, I am giving her a guided tour of Molly's quilt—the snippet of fabric from the tooth fairy pillow, upon which she placed her first lost tooth. The blue ribbon she won at the seventh-grade science fair, for her pond water display. A Girl Scout badge she earned delivering Christmas cookies to a nursing home. One square is decorated with pink loops of ribbon in honor of the time she raised a thousand dollars in a Race for the Cure.

Sometimes I wonder if I'm being fair with the milestones and memories I'm stitching into this quilt. It's easy to block out a square to celebrate her little victories and happy times. But what about a square to commemorate her detention notes for skipping school, or the time she pierced her own navel and it got infected, or the night the local police brought her home, reeking of peach-flavored wine cooler? Why not remember those times? They're part of her history, too.

"You're making a family heirloom," the woman remarks.

Ha, I think, vindicated. That's why I don't need those reminders in the quilt. "It's not going to be finished in time."

The woman smiles, leans back against the picnic table. "In time for what?"

"Move-in day at the dorm."

"I have a rule. If it's not falling apart, it's finished."

She is about my age, I surmise, yet she seems wiser, and I'm not sure why. Her posture is relaxed, and she appears to be in no hurry.

I tell her about the shop back home, how I'll miss it when it's gone, how it won't be the same, buying my fabric somewhere else.

"Maybe someone will take over," the woman suggests.

"I sure hope so. I'm not optimistic, though. Most of the women I know who'd be capable already have other jobs, or they're retired, or too busy with their families. It's a huge risk and a huge commitment."

"I hear you," the woman says. The dog has finished its business in the reeds, and she calls out to a little girl who is playing on the swing set. "Amanda, we'd better get going."

The dark-haired child runs over on chubby legs. "Five more minutes," she begs in a voice every woman within earshot recognizes.

"One more," my companion says, and we both know it will stretch out to five.

"Your daughter's adorable," I tell her.

"Thanks, but she's not my daughter." The woman glances over at Molly, her fleeting look filled with insight. "Amanda's my granddaughter."

Oh, man. She's a grandmother. I don't want to be a grandmother. I'm not finished being a mother.

Yet when she finally reels in her dog and calls to the dark-haired little girl, and Amanda runs into her arms, there is a magical joy in their bond. It's sweeter, somehow, than motherhood, probably because it's simpler.

"Drive safely," I tell them.

"You do the same," she says, "and good luck with the quilt."

Eleven

On the final leg of our journey, the landscape is a patchwork of forest, field, stream and village, stitched together at the seams by country roads and rock or whitewashed fences.

"God, do people actually live here?" Molly wonders aloud, taking it slow as she navigates the Suburban down a hill to an old-fashioned town, complete with white church spire and village green. "It looks like a movie set."

She's right. It's a strange and beautiful land, innocent and pristine, yet with a faint air of danger that comes with alien territory. As a girl, I dreamed of traveling far, but I never did. In my family, vacations were few and far between, and when we went somewhere, it was usually a car trip to a state park. For my parents, life at home was enough.

My mother had a favorite escape, and it was as simple as turning on the TV. She was fanatical about the TV soap *Dallas*, about a family like none we'd ever known. In my head, I hear the brassy theme song that heralded the start of the show. It's one of the most vivid memories of my childhood. The churning melody signaled my dad's bowling night and my mother's sacrosanct program. On Sunday nights, the routine never varied. She would shoo him out the door, then fix an Appian Way pizza out of the box, oiling her hands with Wesson and expertly spreading the dough in a thin circle on a round baking sheet. A splash of canned tomato sauce, a sprinkle of questionable-looking cheese, and heaven was only minutes away.

Unlike any other day of the week, we didn't have a proper, sit-down family dinner on Sundays. No salad or side dishes, no pretense of a token vegetable. Just slices of hot pizza and glasses of cold milk. Maybe a Little Debbie for dessert.

Then, despite my deeply resentful protests and martyr-like sighs, I was sent to bed. Even in the summer, when the light lingered for an extra hour, Mom made me de-camp upstairs to my room, because Sunday nights were sacred. They were *Dallas* nights.

Mom wanted no interruptions. I suppose she would have taken the phone off the hook, but she didn't have to, because all her friends were doing the same thing— hastening their children off to bed, urging their hus-bands out the door—so they could spend an hour in that fabled living-color world of millionaire matrons and the scoundrels who loved them.

I wasn't allowed to watch and wouldn't have wanted to, anyway. To a kid, the endless adult conversations, high-stakes oil deals and secret affairs were deadly.

Sequestered in my room, I always knew when the show started. First, there would be the clink of a glass. On Sunday nights, Mom opened the wicker-clad bottle of jug wine we kept in the cupboard and poured herself exactly one round-bellied, stemmed glass, full to the brim. Next, a curl of cigarette smoke would snake its way upstairs, emanating from a Parliament 100 with recessed filter, whatever that meant. It was all part of Mom's curious ritual of self-indulgence. I wonder if she ever imagined Southfork Ranch as a real place, tucked into the green folds of the Texas countryside, with skyscrapers in the distance.

The high-octane music would swell, the sound boiling up the stairs to my resentful ears. Mom loved the theme from that show so much that she bought the sheet music. Even though we didn't have a piano, she learned to hum the notes. A few years ago, Molly found the music in the piano bench and picked it out while I was working in the kitchen. I felt the same curious shiver of resentment and intrigue I'd felt as a child.

Nowadays, women escape by running away to urban spas, yoga retreats or wild-woman weekends of paintball drills and primal screams. Others frequent male strip clubs or dress to the nines for high tea. Back then, women like my mom didn't have to go any farther than their living rooms.

We stop at a deli for a take-away lunch, and Molly is drawn to the counter girl's flat New England accent, which skips blithely over the *r* and elongates the vowels.

The sub sandwiches are called "grinders," and the milkshakes are "frappes." The word feels awkward and foreign in my mouth, and when we place our order, Molly and I don't look at each other because we'll start giggling.

We take our lunch to a roadside park with a scenic

overlook. There is a sign pointing the way to the Norman Rockwell home.

"I can see where he got his inspiration," I tell Molly, gesturing at the spill of rounded mountains below us.

"Who?"

"Norman Rockwell." I indicate the signpost.

"Who's that?"

Not again. This is crazy. Is it possible that she isn't familiar with the quintessential American artist of the twentieth century?

"You know, the one who did all the illustrations of kids fishing and families praying," I say. "He did the cover of the *Saturday Evening Post* for years. That was even before my time, but you saw those illustrations everywhere—calendars, greeting cards, posters, dentist's offices."

"I guess."

"Maybe we could drive over there, check out the place where he created his art."

"Let's not." She speaks quickly. Maybe there's an edge of urgency in her voice.

I let the topic go. "I've got one thing to say about grinders and frappes, or frapp-ays, however you say it."

"What's that?"

"They rock."

She nods in agreement. The homemade bread and exotic cold cuts—olive loaf, dry salami, maple-smoked ham—and tart dressing and relish are delicious. I tell myself I can start my diet when I get home.

It's too nice a day to hurry. Molly decides to take a walk, her euphemism for going somewhere private in order to call Travis. I doubt she'll get a cell phone signal here, but I don't say anything. Instead, I pull out the quilt and jab my needle into the fabric, piercing through all the layers. The quick silver flash travels fast, but not fast enough. Bit by bit, I am coming to realize that I have failed. By the time we get to the college, the quilt still won't be finished.

Feeling unsettled, I watch Molly walking down the road, hands in her back pockets. Suddenly she looks very small and alone to me, and the urge to protect her—from what? Who knows?—rises up strong in me. Soon I won't be around to protect her. But she has to go.

And as for me, I have to let her. After that, I have to figure out how to be my own person again.

"What's that look?" Molly asks, returning from her walk and sitting beside me at the picnic table.

"I don't have a look."

"Come on. Spill."

"Just thinking of this huge change. It feels so sudden."

"It's not like we didn't see it coming."

"I know. And this is what I wanted. I wanted to raise a child. And I did, I raised a wonderful child. But now you're leaving."

"Mom." She offers a sweet, ironic smile. "That's the whole point."

"Well, I just wish someone had told me how hard it is to let go."

"Did you think it would be easy?"

"Of course not." The needle darts again, in and out of the quilt.

"A little bird once told me you shouldn't avoid doing something just because it's hard."

My exact words, only I'd probably said them to her

in order to get her to go off the diving board or eat a portobello mushroom.

"If you go away and screw up," I blurt out, "how will I help you fix it?" I am instantly horrified. What a stupid thing to say. An apology rushes up through me. It came out all wrong. I shouldn't have said that.

Before I can babble out *I'm sorry, I didn't mean it*, Molly bursts out laughing. "News flash, Mom. It's not your job to fix it."

I laugh with her, but I can't help the next thought that pops into my head: Then what *is* my job?

We spend longer than we intended at the roadside park. It's so pretty and the air feels so good. When the breeze shifts just so, I can sense the forward march of the season, and I can see it in the crowns of the distant trees in the high elevations, which are starting to turn.

Molly seems preoccupied. I wonder if she's thinking about what lies ahead—or what she left behind. Her phone calls and text messaging with Travis have decreased in frequency, which I take to be a good sign. She is driving while I keep doggedly working on the quilt, and she is fixated on the posted distance to the city. "Only forty more miles," she says. "Hard to believe we're finally that close."

My needle slides through the fabric, paying homage to a swatch of old flannel from Dan's pajamas, something she probably doesn't even remember. But I do and suddenly I miss the feel of his arms around me, the sound of his breathing, calm and steady. I think about his warmth and his scent as he sleeps beside me. I miss him. If he were here, he'd make me say exactly what's on my mind. No use bottling it up.

"I suppose we could go all the way right now," I say, "instead of finding a place to stay way out in the suburbs." We had planned for a noon arrival on orientation day, so she would have time to organize her dorm room before heading into the maze of new student activities.

"No." Her reply is surprisingly swift and firm. "That's not the plan. We don't want to get to the city after dark. And I bet there won't be any vacancies near the school, anyway, and even if we found a place to stay, the hotels are massively overpriced and the residence halls don't open to new students until tomorrow at noon."

Her barrage of protests is a bit mystifying. She couldn't wait to get to college but now, the night before her new life is set to begin, she seems to have all the time in the world. I'm gratified that she wants to extend our time together.

"You're right," I agree, and I watch out the window for the exit sign to the town we'd picked out as our final stop. "We should stick to the plan."

She nods and glances at her cell phone, lying on the seat beside her. Travis hasn't called all day, which I suspect is the cause of the prolonged silences that stretch between us. I, with a terrible and dark sense of satisfaction, find myself hoping this is the beginning of the end for them, that his failure to call is not due to the lack of a signal, but to the lack of commitment.

My own thoughts make me feel horrible. She adores Travis, and he makes her happy. Isn't that what I want for her, to be happy? Still, I don't want my daughter's future to belong to him, a charming local boy who has spent the entire summer trying to convince her that there is no better life than the one our small Western town has to offer.

It was enough for me, I realize with a surge of guilt, and I swiftly glance at her. There in that same small town she's been forced to leave, I've found all of life's happiness. Suppose I'm robbing her of the chance to do the same?

And why do I hope her dreams are bigger than mine ever were? What is it that I want for her that I never wanted for myself?

The onslaught of second thoughts assaults me. Molly flips on the turn signal. "This will do."

We have a club card for Travelers Rest, a chain of midrange hotels, and so I nod in agreement. The room is predictable, clean and bland, a faint whiff of stale air blowing from the register vent. We are plenty early, with a large portion of the afternoon ahead of us. Maybe I'll finish Molly's quilt after all.

Instead, I am possessed by restlessness. I take the Suburban to a nearby station and fill it with gas, asking the attendant to check the oil, the tires, the wiper fluid. I use the squeegee to clear the squished bugs from the windshield and grill. It occurs to me that I performed this same routine the day I went into labor with Molly. In childbirth class, we'd been told that a woman on the brink of labor often experiences a burst of energy—the nesting instinct kicking in. I cleaned and scrubbed the house and car all day and was just settling down for a good night's sleep when my water broke.

So what is this, the *de*-nesting instinct? Simple common sense, I tell myself. Tomorrow, I don't want to be distracted by the menial tasks of checking gauges and tires. I want everything to go smoothly, with the Suburban as ready as a criminal's getaway car.

When I return to the motel, Molly is at the pool, a turquoise oval set in an apron of groomed grass. It's not exactly swimming weather, but this might be the last swim of the summer. So, despite the hint of a nip in the air, I decide to join her. I duck into the room, don my swimsuit, one of those figure-flattering jobs with hidden panels designed to suck everything in. Of course, it can't suck in what it doesn't cover, so I slip on the secret weapon of the forty-year-old woman—the cover-up.

My flip-flops slap against the sun-softened asphalt of the parking lot as I approach the pool. Molly is wearing the yellow-and-white bikini we picked out in the end-of-season sale at the mall back home, and her hair is slicked back, her skin dewy from swimming. She sits at the edge of the shallow end, watching two little kids, a boy and a girl who are maybe four and six.

I take in the sight of her, wondering when we'll travel together again, when we'll pick a motel because of its pool, when we'll eat junk food and watch TV together late into the night. Everything on this journey is more significant and intense because it's the last time.

The kids are laughing and splashing under the watchful eye of their mother, who turns occasionally to make conversation with Molly. As I watch, Molly wades in to help the little girl adjust her water wing, then holds her hand and turns her in a circle while making a motorboat sound. The little girl giggles and flails while I stand off to the side, watching. And suddenly I am seeing Molly and me, hearing our laughter echo across the water, feeling her tiny hand in mine as I lead the way.

I'm struck by how like me she is right now, angling

her arm just so, making certain she's not going too fast or too deep for the small, trusting child. Where did she learn her gentleness with children, her humor? I don't remember teaching it, yet here she is, replicating a moment I didn't recall until just now. Suddenly, the memory is as clear to me as if it had happened the day before yesterday. One long-ago summer day, we looked exactly like this, a young woman and a little girl, sharing a small moment together.

Except I am not in the picture. This is Molly's moment, one that has nothing to do with me. And it's weirdly okay with me. She is her own person and I don't feel the need to insert myself into any of this.

Her cell phone, which is lying on a metal poolside table, suddenly goes off. Travis's ring sounds like a fire alarm.

Molly rushes to hand the little girl off to her mother, then leaps out of the pool, swift as a trained dolphin. She dabs her hand on a towel, then snatches up the phone. At the same moment, she sees me coming toward her.

Her face lights up with a glow of pure joy, a clear echo of the look she used to give me when she was tiny and I'd say, "Let's go for a swim, Moll."

She's lighting up for someone else now. She acknowledges me with a wave, then says into the phone, "Omigod. Omigod, really? I don't believe you!" She is jumping up and down now, a young adult no longer but a child bouncing with excitement. "Where?" she asks, and then, *"Now?"*

The settled feeling that had enveloped me only moments ago now swirls away. I set my towel on the chaise next to Molly's, wondering what's got her so excited. Here I thought she was uncoupling herself from Travis, their calls growing fewer and shorter as our journey progressed. Now she is as excited as she was when he asked her to prom.

Watching her, listening to the sparkle in her voice, I realize that I miss this Molly. Throughout this journey, she has been pleasant but guarded. Even soaring over Lake Ontario or watching line dancers at a honky tonk, she has been entertained, but not exuberant. Not until now.

What's he saying to her that causes the air to slip under her feet and lift her up?

And then with a laugh of joy, she drops the phone onto the table. "I don't believe it," she keeps saying and then she scoops up her flip-flops and runs. I am slow, not really hooked into this reality, not really believing it, either.

In slow motion I stand up and walk to the chainlink safety fence that surrounds the pool. Her bikini flashing in the sunlight, Molly races across the parking lot, shooting straight up in the air when the asphalt burns her feet, then hopping up and down as she throws her flip-flops to the ground and jiggles into them. Then she resumes running but she doesn't have to go much farther, just across to the porte cochere, straight and true as an arrow shot from a bow, into Travis's waiting arms.

Twelve

Travis catches her in his embrace, and my mind races with panic. What the hell is this kid doing, stalking her across the country?

With an effort of will, I restrain myself. For now. He's come all this way. The least I can do is give them a little privacy.

I offer Travis a greeting that is brief but not unkind. "I'm going for a swim," I tell Molly. "I'll see you in a little bit."

Yes, a swim in the pool. I need to cool off, calm down, clear my head. I don't want to go off halfcocked, say things in haste, jump to conclusions.

When it comes to pools, I'm usually a toe-dipper, getting wet gradually, inch by careful inch. Today I peel off my cover-up and dive off the edge in one swift motion, surrounding myself with a storm of bubbles, hands brushing the gunite bottom. The water is cold but I'm glad for that. Every nerve ending is wide awake, as I imagine a soldier's would be on the eve of battle.

For me, this is a nightmare—to bring my daughter to

the brink of a brand-new, exciting future, only to have the past reach out and pull her back.

Yet for Molly, it's a dream come true. What girl doesn't romanticize about a love so strong, it makes a guy fly across the country just to see her? And in my heart of hearts, I can understand this. We teach our daughters to dream of love. We read them stories of damsels in distress and the knights in shining armor who rescue them, laying happiness at their feet like a carpet of roses.

Of course, in this day and age, we also read about enlightened princesses who do just fine without a man, but those are not the stories that stick with our girls. For some deep-seated, primal reason, the politically correct tales lack appeal. The stories that stay with them always seem to involve a big-shouldered alpha male, sweeping them off their feet.

After a long, vigorous swim, I shower and dress, trying to compose myself. Flying off the handle, yelling, getting mad won't help the situation in the least. I try calling Dan but get voice mail, and hang up without leaving a message. If I try telling his voice mail what's going on I'll use up all our free minutes.

Instead, I head outside to find Molly. She and Travis have been in the shady garden of the motor court, talking and holding each other for a good half hour.

"What's going on?" I ask them. Molly's hair has dried stiff with chlorine, the curls out of control, her eyes red from crying.

"I had to see Molly," Travis says. His ears are scarlet. I can tell it's hard for him to talk to me.

I struggle to erase all anger and judgment from my

stance. "Travis, I understand it was hard to say goodbye. I know you guys miss each other a lot. But it's time—"

"Okay, don't freak out," Molly says. "I have a plan."

To screw up your life. I bite my lip to keep from saying it.

"I'm listening."

"I changed my mind about college," she says, in one short phrase bringing my most negative fantasies out into the open. "I mean, I'll still go. Just not so far away."

"Whoa, hang on. This is a big decision." Brilliant, I tell myself. You're a real rocket scientist.

"It's the right decision." She is instantly defensive. "What I realized this week is that it's too hard, being apart from Travis. I'll be happier at UW."

"Aw, Molly. I know you think that now, but remember, you always wanted—"

"This has never been about what I want," she says, each word slashing like an finely-honed blade. "It's about what you want for me."

"We want the same thing."

"Do we? When was the last time you checked, Mom? This train started out of the station as soon as I got the acceptance letter. It was never, *Do you want this?*"

"I didn't think I had to ask. Forgive me for assuming you wanted to study at one of the best schools in the country and see where it takes you. Forgive me for assuming you worked so hard in high school so you could explore a future beyond the boundaries of a small town."

"I've been thinking about it all week long. We never talked about other options, Mom. We never talked about the fact that one of those options is that I can say, 'Thanks very much, but I have other plans.'"

Travis, never a kid of many words, simply stands there, stalwart and—I can't deny it—impossibly handsome. He shuffles his feet, looks at the message window of his phone as though someone has sent him an answer through the digital ether.

"Tell me about these other plans, Moll. I really want to know."

"The state school makes perfect sense," she insists, her voice as intent and convincing as a trial lawyer's. "It's way cheaper."

"You have a scholarship. One you earned, I might add, all on your own. I didn't make you. This is something you went after because you wanted it."

"And now I want something else." She sends Travis an adoring look, but he's still studying his phone.

The state university is filled with commuter students juggling marriage, motherhood and work in addition to their courseload. No doubt they're gifted, hard-working people who are doing it all, succeeding, living happy and fulfilling lives. Of course the state school is a good option.

Still. It's not the same as the rarefied world of students hand-selected from a pool of the best and brightest, with an endowment big enough to give scholarships to kids like Molly. There will be none of the things we've heard about, no bonfires or late-night study sessions or elaborate pranks, no students from Ghana or visiting lecturers from the UN, no Nobel laureates, no dorm hall dramas or campus productions of *The Vagina Monologues*, no Parents' Weekend or commencement addresses in Latin.

"I'll get to have what you and I both want," Molly continued. "An education, and Travis."

"There's so much more for you to discover," I tell her, knowing she doesn't believe me.

"Trav and I will discover it together."

I grit my teeth, refusing to let myself explode. "Travis," I say to him, "could Molly and I have a minute?"

"He should stay," she says, clinging to his hand.

"Er, that's okay." He disengages his hand. "Go ahead and talk stuff over with your mom." He steps aside with a conciliatory smile, barely concealing his relief. I almost feel sorry for him, knowing the tension between Molly and me is stretched to its limit, and very palpable. He walks over by the pool and plugs some change into a vending machine.

"Oh, Molly." I pause, trying to find a way to persuade her. "Look how far you've come. Don't give up on something you've been dreaming of for years."

"It's my decision," she says, her eyes welling with tears. "I'm the one who has to go through the next four years. I can either spend them with strangers, struggling to keep up and trying to fit in, thousands of miles from home, or I can be near the people who love me, getting good grades and an education without sacrificing four years of my life."

This sudden streak of practicality is something new. But I can be practical, too. "Most people wouldn't regard a scholarship to a top university as a sacrifice."

"For me it would be. Even this week has been torture," she says. "I *love* him."

Her stark passion gives me pause. What if Travis *is* the one? What if he's the love of her life? It's not as if love comes along every day. Do I have the right to turn her away from him? Suppose she does it my way and tells him goodbye, and something terrible happens? How would I ever forgive myself?

If turning around and going home with Travis is a mistake, it's hers to make, not mine. If it's the right thing to do, then it's only right that she gets to choose.

I can't deny that this unexpected new plan has its appeal. The thought of Molly living in state, coming home with her laundry on weekends, having Sunday dinner with us, draws me in. Yes, I think, yes, that could work, after all.

Still…

Over at the vending machines, Travis has scored a Coke and a bag of Cheetos. He's chatting up the young mom with the two little kids.

Molly sees me rallying a defense. "A college degree… I can get that anytime—anywhere—I want."

"That's what I used to think."

"But Travis. There's only one of him. There are a lot of ways to get a college degree but there's only one Travis."

"And if he loves you, he'll love the dream you're going after."

"If he loves me, he can't stand to be without me. He spent a whole week's pay to fly out here, even."

I bite my tongue to keep from expressing my opinion of *that*. Long ago, I had rationalizations of my own that sounded eerily similar to Molly's. What if she makes the choice I made? "Sweetie, you're so young. Let yourself *be* young instead of closing all those doors."

"I can be young with Travis." As though reading my mind, she adds, "It's exactly what you did, Mom. You went for love and look how your life turned out. It's wonderful. You and Dad are wonderful. You focused on what's important."

This is what I've taught her. I've modeled it for her. Go for the love, every time. It's surprising—and admittedly gratifying—that she looks at Dan and me and thinks we're wonderful together. I hope like hell we are.

Yet her insistence on choosing this path still sits poorly with me. Travis is…just so damn young. He's a good enough kid, from a nice enough family, but he can be careless with Molly's feelings, though I've never pointed that out for fear of starting an argument.

Maybe Dan was that way, too, and I never noticed because I was crazy about him. Now, years later, I sometimes catch myself wondering, what could I have done, who could I have been, if I'd gone for the big life instead of the big love?

Am I making Molly live the life I missed out on? Is that fair to her?

I gather in a deep breath of courage. "I don't want to force you into a decision. If you stick to the original plan and it turns out badly, you'll never forgive me. I'll never forgive myself. You call the shots, Moll. I'll support you, no matter what."

"Really? You're not just saying that?"

Maybe. No, I mean it. Molly's life is her own now. "I mean it."

I feel her strength and determination. She goes to find Travis.

And just like that, that world shifts. The dream changes. Love has transformed her life. Love has a way of doing that.

I call Dan and give him the news. Travis has come for her. He has convinced her to change her mind about going to college so far away. The rundown of Molly's rationalizations spills from me—she claims she can still enroll in the honors program at UW. We won't really forfeit all that much, just this past roller coaster of a week and a percentage of the first tuition payment.

"Says something for the kid, traveling all that way to make his case," Dan tells me.

"What?" I ask, exasperated. "What does it say, Dan? That he's got nothing better to do? That he's ready to take responsibility for her, to hold her heart and her dreams and keep them safe? Or that the plant had a temporary layoff and he got bored hanging out with his friends?"

"Maybe he'll surprise you."

"This is not helping. We need to be on the same page."

"No, we don't. We're two completely different people, and Molly's her own person, too. She's old enough to understand we can have differing points of view."

As we talk, I move around the room, needing an outlet for my agitation. I seize on the bag of quilting supplies. There's a piece made from a pocket with a little embroidered dog on it. This was from the pedal-pushers Molly had worn the day she learned to ride a two-wheeler.

By five years of age, she had worn her training wheels down to the rims and I insisted it was time to take them off. She had balked, arguing to the point of tears.

She agreed only when Dan promised he would run alongside her, holding her up.

"I won't let go until you say," he vowed.

I was certain she'd never get to the letting-go phase, so I went about my business. I was in the kitchen, trying a new recipe, when I heard shouting and the faint *brrring brrring* of the bell on Molly's bike. I went out to see her cruising on two wheels, Dan standing in the middle of the street and grinning from ear to ear.

"They're young," Dan is saying, "but they're still adults."

"If he was thinking of Molly, then he wouldn't take this opportunity away from her."

"The thing is, it's not up to us—not anymore. Back off, honey. Let Molly work on this herself."

Back off. I can hear Molly's voice—*Oh, like* that's *going to happen.*

I hang up the phone. Something has happened to me over the days of our journey, a subtle shift in the way I see my daughter. She is smart, genuine and more mature than I've given her credit for. Trying to bend her to my will won't work on her any more than it would have worked on me when I was her age. Dan tells me to back off. He has no idea how hard that is. With a heavy sigh, I pick up the quilt where I left off. My needle easily pierces through the layers of cloth and batting, soft beneath the pads of my thumbs. I work in a phrase my mother loved to quote: *To thine own self be true.*

There's a dot of blood on the white underside of the quilt. I didn't notice I'd pricked my finger. I grab an ice cube from the bucket I'd filled earlier and try to get the stain out. It dissolves to a faint rusty shadow but doesn't disappear completely. A bloodstain never does.

After blotting the stain, I set the quilt aside. I don't feel like quilting. I don't feel like anything.

I lie on the bed, staring up at the pockmarked tiles on the ceiling. It's getting late, but I'm not sleepy in the least. Is it my job as a mother to convince her to stay on track for college? No. It's not. It's my job to raise a daughter with an open heart and a good head on her shoulders.

It's a balancing act. Love and dreams and duty. I pick up the quilt again, filled with the softness of memories. All the wisdom in the world is in this quilt.

I stare at it for a long time, wondering if there's anything in it for me.

I wake up in the morning to discover a warm lump of girl curled up against me, under the quilt. She stirs and snuggles closer.

Other memories—all the mornings I awakened her, doing my best to soften the ordeal of getting up for school. I'd lie down next to her on the bed and rub her back until she surrendered to the day. Then I think about all the late nights lying awake, listening for the reassuring rumble of her car engine. We used to have long, whispered conversations when she came in moments after curfew, sitting on the side of the bed to tell me about her date.

Now I marvel at how tender I still feel toward this fully grown creature.

Oh, baby. I used to be responsible for drawing the boundaries around your world. Now you're on a path that leads you over the boundaries and away from me. I'll always cherish our time together. Always. But you'll never be my baby again.

She curls closer, a subtle natural movement, a drawing in. I tuck my arm around her. After a while, she pulls away as though preparing herself for her departure.

"Moll?"

She sighs herself awake. "Yes," she whispers, turning away from me. "This means what you think it means."

"Where's Travis?"

"Where do you think? He went standby on the next flight home."

I exhale a cautious breath of relief. It doesn't last long. Molly comes fully awake, crying with the kind of sobs that shake the whole bed. She's crying too hard to speak, so I just wrap myself around her and hold on for a while, silently willing her to stop. As an infant, she'd been fretful, and I spent many midnight hours walking the floor with her, making mindless shushing sounds, just as I do now.

Eventually, the storm subsides. She is still tearful, her voice shaky. "He was so mad at me, Mom. He was so mad. He might never speak to me again. I hurt him that bad."

"I'm sorry, Moll. I know you can't stand hurting anyone."

"Why couldn't you just let me go home? Why did you have to make a federal case out of it?"

"I left it up to you," I reminded her.

"But it was the *way* you did it. It made me feel like an idiot." Agitated now, she blots her tears with a corner of the quilt and sits up.

"I never meant to do that." But wow, is she right. I want her to have the life I passed up in order to be a wife and mom. She is my road not taken. And it's not fair to put that burden on her. "I'm sorry," I tell her. "If you want to turn around now, we'll do it. No hard feelings, no recriminations."

She's quiet for a long time. "I'd hate myself if I didn't go for this. But I need for you to listen, Mom. This is my choice. I'm not doing it because you never had the chance. I'm doing it because I want the chance for me."

DAY SEVEN

Odometer Reading 123,937

Take your needle, my child,
and work at your pattern;
it will come out a rose by and by.
Life is like that–one stitch at a
time taken patiently and the
pattern will come out all right
like the embroidery.

—Oliver Wendell Holmes

Thirteen

I hold the map, with the route to the city highlighted. "I think our turn-off is coming up." We pass through suburbs filled with crackerbox houses, small businesses, big-box stores. I notice a fabric shop with a nice window display; maybe I'll stop in on my way back home. There's a charmless strip center with a beauty salon called the Crowning Glory and a charitable organization called New Beginnings, apparently dedicated to providing clothing and supplies for a local women's shelter. There's also a bakery that fills the air with a smell so delicious, it brings tears to my eyes.

We treat ourselves to butterhorns and insulated cups of strong coffee. Molly, always a compulsive reader of free literature, grabs a flyer with a hair salon coupon and a rundown of the women's shelter services: "Help someone make a New Beginning. Career clothes needed." We try to imagine what it might be like, running for shelter with nothing but the clothes on our backs. It puts our own issues into perspective, for sure, and I keep the flyer, vowing to send a check. We don't linger, though. The destination we've been driving toward for days now lies just a few miles ahead.

We haven't said much about yesterday. Finally, Molly says, "So Travis is home now. He just sent me a text."

I brace myself. She might still want to turn around. "I know you're hurting and I hate that. Everything that happens to you goes straight through my heart."

"Then you know how it feels."

In the beat of hesitation, I hold my breath and wait for her to speak again.

"I have to do this," she says. "I want it, I really do."

"I'm proud of you, Moll. You're going to do great."

We take the interstate to the multilane bridge. Like thick arteries, ramps delve down toward the heart of the city.

An official green-and-white sign marks the city limits. Elevation 40 Feet. Population 101,347.

Molly whips her head toward me. "Which way, left or right?"

"Left."

My thumb traces the route, inching forward as each side street flips past. This place has no grid, just densely aligned roads, some only a block long, others leading nowhere. It's like a web or a net. How will Molly get around in this strange, busy city? How is she going to find her way?

"You have to go left here. Can you make a left from this lane?"

A sense of change takes hold as the city rises around us; I am delivering my only child into uncharted territory. We're here. Our arrival seems abrupt, even though the drive lasted for days. We go from one world to another in a matter of steps. One moment, we're wending our way through a tangle of turnpikes and traffic jams, and the next, we find ourselves in a placid oasis of calm.

The quiet brick street looks like a movie set: trees gracefully shedding the first of their leaves, green rectangular yards crisscrossed by footpaths, colonial-style redbrick buildings with small-paned windows, their frames painted a fresh white. Gaslight fixtures line the sidewalks. The brick walkways bear generations of pockmarks and dents.

We stop and purchase a one-day parking permit. Cars and minivans and SUVs are parked along the curbs on both sides of the roadway. Shiny vehicles disgorge long-legged, laughing girls, slender boys staggering under boxes and cartons, mothers consulting lists, a father or two, standing around talking on cell phones or looking lost.

It's a good thing Dan's not here, after all. He hates feeling like a misfit.

Upperclassmen, facing their orientation groups and talking constantly, are showing the new students around. The tour guides walk backward with impressive confidence, certain they won't stumble.

Molly maneuvers the rumbling old SUV into the narrow street. It's easily the largest noncommercial vehicle in sight. She pulls into a gap at the curbside, her mouth grim as she tries to align the big truck along the curb. "I won't miss parking this beast," she grumbles.

She switches off the engine. It dies with a shudder. I turn to find her looking at me, and for a moment, the two of us just sit, staring into each other's eyes, not smiling, not talking, just…looking.

It's amazing how much you can see in a face you love, all the layers of years, still visible in the present moment. The infant Molly, her eyes as blue now as they were then, round and open wide, staring upward at me. And my face, eighteen years ago, had filled the baby's whole world.

"Okay," Molly says suddenly, unbuckling her seat belt with a decisive click. "We're here." The car inhales the belt as she jumps out and slams the door.

A black Lexus trolls along the street, headed straight for Molly. *Watch out.* I nearly scream the warning, but the moment passes before I open my mouth. She steps up onto the curb, the car whizzes by and I sit alone in the passenger seat, my heartbeat a stampede of anxiety.

"Okay," I mutter, echoing Molly. "We're here." The breeze carries a subtle chill, a whiff of dry leaves, the tang of autumn. If we were back home, I'd be posting the high school football schedule on the fridge and paging through bulb catalogs.

Molly has the cargo doors open and is staring at the lopsided stacks and bundles. Uncertainty creases her brow.

I offer a suggestion. "Maybe you'd better—"

"—check in first," Molly finishes for me. "I was *so* going to do that."

"You want me to come in with you?"

"That's okay, Mom. It'll probably only take a few minutes."

"I'll wait out here, then."

The Suburban huddles in a rusty heap, disreputable, inferior compared to the gleaming, late-model cars with plates from Massachusetts, Connecticut, New York, Virginia. In contrast to the forest-green and burgundy imports, the old Chevy, with its flaking paint job, is as garish and ungainly as a parade float left out in the rain.

The Joads go to college, I'm thinking, certain everyone is staring at me. Glancing in the rearview mirror,

I focus on the shopping bag filled with my brand-new, never-worn clothes. I should have worn something special for today, comes the belated thought.

Old worries surface. I still find myself feeling inferior, the misfit, the one who gets picked last. Oh God. Does Molly feel inferior, or did I teach her better? I check her out to see if she's self-conscious about the car. But no. Molly's oblivious as she makes her way inside. She couldn't care less what the car looks like, what state is on the license plate.

I call Dan. I've never been a big fan of mobile phones, but right now, I love my cell phone so much I would marry it. It's proof that someone wants to talk to you. It saves you from having to loiter in a strange place, trying to appear as though you belong.

Molly called him this morning to talk about Travis. He doesn't sound surprised. We backed off and she made her own choice.

"We're here," I tell Dan. "It's amazing."

"How's our girl doing?"

"She didn't have much to say about Travis. We're not talking about it yet. I'm hoping she'll just focus on getting settled here." My gaze skips over the quad, currently an anthill of activity as students move in en masse. "Looks like there's plenty to keep her busy." I take a breath. "Speaking of which, I had a thought."

"Lindy, not another orphan."

"No. Not now, anyway. Saying goodbye to Molly is making me crazy, I admit it. What I've been thinking about is that I need a new life when I get back."

"Something wrong with your old life?"

"Not at all, but without Molly there, I need a plan. So I thought… Don't freak out."

"I'm listening."

"I'm going to talk to Minerva about the shop."

"What do you mean, talk to her?"

"About taking over the shop. She's retiring, and I thought maybe… I could see if I can qualify for a small-business loan and…" I falter. Spoken aloud, it sounds silly. "Anyway, maybe it's a crazy idea, but I think I can make it work."

Silence.

"Dan?" I wait for him to tell me how foolish I'm being, especially now, with a kid in college.

"You can make anything work, Linda."

It's the last thing I expected to hear from him. "Really?"

"Hell, yeah. Don't sound so surprised."

"But…you never… I never knew you felt that way."

"Sweetheart, I've always felt that way about you. Just because I didn't say it every day doesn't mean the sentiment's not there."

"You were such a skeptic about my last idea—"

"Adopting an orphan? Come on, Linda. This is hardly the same. This is something you want for you, not to fill some void left by Molly."

I shut my eyes, catch my breath. When did I stop knowing this man? I never did; I just let the busy part of life get in the way. *"Thank you."*

"I miss you," he says. "I can't wait to see you."

His words ignite a rush of passion in me, an emotion as strong and fresh as the first time I felt it. "Same here," I say, smiling.

Carrying a thick manila envelope, Molly comes out of the dorm, talking to a woman with a clipboard. The woman is about my age, early forties, but she wears her hair in a sleekly careless ponytail and sports an ethnic-print skirt, a trendy blouse and a tooled silver thumb ring. Molly looks enchanted with her.

Acutely aware of my lap-creased jeans and the mustard stain on my sweatshirt, I chastise myself again for not wearing a selection from my new clothes. Then I put on my best smile, walk over to the sandstone steps and introduce myself.

"Linda," the woman says. "I'm Ceci Gamble. The residential facilitator." She has a slightly nasal voice and a distinctive, East Coast boarding-school accent.

The theme music of the Wicked Witch of the West buzzes in my head. Who is this exotic new mentor, poised to supplant me? "Nice to meet you. So is Molly all set to move in?"

"Absolutely. Everything's in the information packet. Let me know if you need anything, anything at all."

I smile in gratitude, quashing the sudden resentment, but Ceci Gamble is already turning away, her glossy ponytail flying. She greets another mother who is busy unloading a Mercedes station wagon with a Choate sticker on the back. They crow at each other, embrace, old chums from prep school or the country club. Girls stream past in groups, all talking, the autumn sun strong on their silky, straight hair as they mount the stairs to the freshman dorm.

For a fraction of a second, Molly looks uncertain, her full lower lip soft and vulnerable. She scrunches a hand into her hair. The beautiful corkscrew curls have been the bane of her existence for years, no matter how much her friends claim to covet them. She wishes for straight hair. Prep school hair. East Coast hair.

She's the outsider here, after fitting in so comfortably

in high school, playing varsity sports, winning music competitions, laughing on the phone, never at a loss for a friend or a date. She looks lost in the moment now, uncertain. Hesitation is written in her stance, though I'm the only one who can see it. I see the tiny girl afraid to take off her training wheels, jump into a pool, recite a poem for the class, endure her first piano recital, taste an oyster for the first time.

I was always the one pushing her to get past the fear and do it anyway. Dan tended to want to whisk her away from it all. Now I wonder if she felt the constant push-pull of our warring need to protect and promote. Then I remember her confidence in sports, in music, in academics. The gift of her hard work is that self-confidence. She's going to be fine.

I can see her rally in the determined set of her chin. We head inside, to a building that once housed future scientists, jurists, artists and world leaders. Following the directions in the packet, we find a bare room, hung with the smell of Pine-Sol and airless summerlong neglect. Molly heads straight for the window and opens it wide.

The roommate hasn't arrived. Kayla from Philadelphia is nowhere in sight. The barren room contains two phone jacks and wireless modem setups, two desks, twin consoles of drawers and shelves and the requisite two beds. We climb up and down the worn concrete stairs, bringing stuff from the truck to the room. "Want some help unpacking?" I ask.

"That's all right. I'll do it myself. That way, I'll know where everything is." She is clear on not wanting me to linger, to tuck shirts away in drawers, stack office supplies, stand in registration lines with her.

She tackles the first box—towels and toiletries. Then she opens another. Her face looks tense.

"Did you remember your alarm clock?" I ask a mundane question to distract her, but it doesn't work. "Moll?" I ask, tentative, not pushing at all now. "What's up?"

She pulls out the green-shaded desk lamp. "It's broken. I wonder when it broke. Maybe when I slammed on the brakes to miss that deer."

"It can be fixed. We could find a store, look for a replacement for the shade."

"I don't need it."

"You're the one who insisted on bringing it."

"And I was wrong. So sue me. Geez, I can't believe you're still doing this," she snaps.

"Doing what?"

"This… I don't even know what to call it. You want me to be here, to have the whole college experience, but at the same time, you keep acting like I'll fall apart any second. You don't need to fix everything. You don't need to be my human shield anymore. I'm not that fragile. I won't break, I swear. Don't feel like you have to protect me."

"It's my job to protect you."

"Well, congrats. You're finished. Now you can do something else."

The breeze through the open window is reviving her curls.

"Why are you acting so annoyed?" I ask her. I'm getting annoyed, too.

"You always try to make everything easier for me. It's like I live inside this artificial bubble you created. That's what's annoying. It's my time. My life. My turn to screw up and suffer the consequences."

"Your turn to succeed and be amazing."

"Whatever. The point is, it's my turn, Mom. What happened with Travis—just to remind you again, it was my decision. Not yours or Dad's or even Travis's. Mine, a hundred percent. Right or wrong, I own it, okay?"

"Of course."

"So quit worrying." She's close to tears, her expression taut with suppressed panic.

My Molly is terrified. She's afraid she'll be lonely. Afraid she'll fail. Afraid she won't measure up.

"Aw, Moll."

Her shoulders hunch. "What if I blow it? What if I disappoint you?"

Finally, I know what she needs. Maybe this is the whole point of the past week. She needs to be free of the weight of her parents' expectations. "That will never happen."

With a decisive air, she shoves the lamp into a trash can. She looks at me for a long time, her stare penetrating. I try to offer a reassuring smile. She doesn't smile back. Instead, she says, "I'm worried about you, Mom."

It's the last thing I expected to hear. "Worrying is my job."

"No, I mean it. We've had our moments, but you know I think you're great. The thing that worries me is what you're going to do now that I'm gone."

"Don't be silly. I'll do what I've always done."

"What you've always done is be my mom. You need to figure out something else now."

"There's nothing to figure," I say reassuringly. "I have a fulfilling life, great friends, a loving husband. I never defined myself as a mother and nothing else. I have other roles to play."

"Really? Like what?"

"Lots of things. I just have to figure out which roles to pursue. I've been thinking of doing more volunteer work."

Molly clearly notices my lack of enthusiasm. "You should do something you love."

What I love is being your mom. I bite my tongue. I will not lay that on her. Setting my jaw until my back teeth ache, I take out her alarm clock and set it to local time.

Soon we'll be living in different time zones.

"Mom, didn't you used to say you wanted to finish your degree?"

"Yes, but I put it off when I—"

"You put it off," Molly prods.

"I was so busy with everything else, it just wasn't practical. Now it's not important."

"Are you sure? When was the last time you thought about it?"

"Say, I've got an idea—I could get my degree here, while you're here. We could even get an apart—"

"Very funny." Molly's face flashes panic—no doubt she senses I'm only half joking. "Anyway, what's stopping you now?"

"I'm not sure. Lack of ambition, maybe." But there is something I do want, something I have only begun to believe in. "Your dad liked the idea of me taking over Pins & Needles."

"Of course he liked it. It's a perfect idea, are you kidding? You can do anything, Mom. I love the thought of you running the fabric store. I totally love it. I hope you go for it."

Fear and uncertainty turn to something else—Hope. Excitement.

She takes out a small stack of framed pictures, gazes at a shot of her dad with Hoover.

"I know he wishes he could be here," I tell her.

"No, he doesn't. You think I don't know why Dad didn't come?" Molly is incredulous. "You think he stayed home because he doesn't care? He's my father. He didn't come for the same reason he didn't go to the vet with you last spring when Hoover was so sick. It's not weakness or that he doesn't care. It's that he cares too much."

"You know your father well."

"You don't need a college degree to figure Dad out." She sets the photograph on a shelf in her dorm room and her gaze lingers on it. "Look what you're going back to, Mom. How can you not be happy?"

The tension in my chest unfurls on a wave of lightness. I am married to a man with a great heart. My daughter and I both know it.

"Where are you going to eat tonight?" I page through the orientation booklet. "The freshman dining room's in Memorial Hall—"

"Don't worry, Mom. I won't starve. I'm still full from lunch. I might just settle for granola bars and juice."

"You should go to the dining hall, even if you're not hungry." I bite my tongue. I have to stop with the you-shoulds.

I take out the quilt, which I've carefully folded and tied with a ribbon in her high school's colors. "I want you to have this, a reminder of home. It's not really finished, though," I point out. "There's a lot more I wanted to do to it."

"It's great." She unties the ribbon and wafts the quilt

over the bed. Sunlight falls across the crazy patchwork, the loopy quilting with its hidden messages.

"It's not finished," I say again, feeling a thrum of panic all out of proportion with the situation. "I thought I would finish it during the trip, and we're here and it's still not done."

"It's beautiful, Mom. I love it."

"I still have to—"

"No, you don't."

"Maybe you could bring it home at Christmas break and I'll work on it some more then."

"Mom, would you stop?" Her sharp tone brings me up short. Out in the hallway of the dorm, we hear a clatter. Then someone shouts, "We need a cleanup on aisle one! I just dropped a blue raspberry slushie." More noise and laughter ensue.

Very slowly and carefully, her hands brushing over the fabric, Molly folds the quilt in half, and half again. And again, revealing the soft, faded underside. She makes a perfect bow with the colored ribbon. "Listen, Mom, don't freak out, okay? But this doesn't belong here, in a dorm room."

"What?"

"I mean, I appreciate it and all, but this is a dorm room. And the quilt is a wonderful, one-of-a-kind work of art. I don't want it to get damaged. I don't want it being used to mop up spilled beer or whatever, not that I would do that but who knows about other kids?"

"You should have it, Moll. See, all the fabric comes from things that are familiar to you, stuff I've saved over the years. It's a keepsake. A picture of your life so far."

"I know, Mom. Believe me, I know. And I love it for that reason," she says. "I love you for making it. That quilt is incredible." She takes a breath, regards me with a wisdom I never knew she possessed. "But it's not my story, Mom. It's yours."

The clarity and wisdom of her words fills me up completely. She's looked at the big picture and seen what I never could. I was so focused on each tiny stitch and detail that I didn't realize what I was creating. What a nutty idea, thinking I could stitch together some kind of patchwork picture of Molly's life so far. It's arrogant, too, to presume to tell her story. Because like she says—it's not a picture of her life. It's a picture of mine. The best part of mine.

"What do you want me to do with it?" I ask her.

"Just don't leave it here where it could get ruined or lost. Keep it for you and Dad... I don't know. Mom, it's so beautiful. It doesn't belong here. Seriously, you know I'm right." She holds the folded quilt out to me, handling it with reverence and respect. "You decide."

I hesitate, then take the quilt from her, holding it against me, knowing my heart is stitched into every square inch of the piece. Each bit of fabric comes from a vanished but fondly remembered moment in time. All along, I thought it was about Molly, but ultimately, it is about me—the mother I was, the moments I remember, the hopes and dreams in my heart.

But bring it home? What will I do with it then? It'll just end up in the old cedar chest, stale and forgotten. For me, the joy of the quilt was in its creation, not in *having* it. But that doesn't mean Molly's obligated to drag it around.

The last thing she needs is the smothering burden of this blanket I've patched together, covered with messages from the past. She wants to create her own story, in her own way, on her own blank canvas.

That's the daughter I raised.

Fourteen

"Then..." I shove my hands into the back pockets of my jeans. "I guess I'd better hit the road."

Alarm flashes in Molly's eyes. It's finally real to her. I'm leaving, and she'll soon be all by herself. But she visibly conquers her fear, squelching panic with steely resolve, evident in her posture and the set of her jaw. "Okay," she says. "I'll walk you downstairs."

I turn to conduct one last survey of the place that will be her home for the next year. The room isn't ready. The furniture arrangement isn't ideal. The bookcase is too close to the radiator, and there aren't enough outlets. With every fiber of my being, I want to stay here and fix things, make adjustments, improvements. I force myself to turn away.

The hallway smells of bleach and fresh paint. Someone is mopping up a spill on the floor. Other parents and kids are moving in, some in weighty silence, others with caffeinated chattiness, a few engaged in low-voiced arguments.

"You're not going to lose it, are you, Mom?" Molly asks.

"Yes," I say. "I might."

Molly looks startled. She's used to being protected, shielded, having troubles glossed over and smoothed out so they don't snag on her. But as she pointed out to me earlier, she is a young adult now, old enough to know her mother is not infallible. She swore she didn't need me running interference for her at every turn.

"Check it out," she says, bracing her hands on the windowsill. A cluster of students has gathered in the old yard below. "I think that's the meeting point for the orientation groups. It's geeky, but I kind of want to go."

We step out into the sunny afternoon. I feel a piercing sweetness deep in my heart. A barely dammed river of tears pushes against my chest.

"If you cry," Molly warns, "I'll cry, too."

"Then we'll both cry." And we do, but somehow we manage to stop, regaining control by focusing on the long line of departing cars.

"I've got that orientation meeting," she says, pressing her sleeve across her eyes.

"And I need to get going, too. Maybe miss the traffic heading out of the city."

"That information packet lists some local places to stay," Molly points out. "I mean, if you don't feel like a big drive today…"

"I'm kind of eager to head back to your dad and Hoover," I tell her. What I don't tell her is that I can't face a night at the Colonial Inn with its stupid plaster lamplighters in three-corner hats, knowing Molly is only a short walk away. The temptation to go check on her would be too great and prolong the pain of separation. I plan to drive a couple hundred miles, take a long soak in the hotel hot tub, then phone Molly from a safe distance.

The breeze that sweeps through the quadrangle smells of autumn. A few yellow leaves flutter down with lazy grace. Students and statues populate the ancient, broad lawns laid out centuries before by idealists who embraced order and harmony.

The grassy yard is crisscrossed by walkways littered with new-fallen leaves. Long-bodied boys lie with their heads cushioned on overstuffed backpacks, their noses poked into dog-eared novels. Girls with sweaters draped over their shoulders sit cross-legged in small groups, engaged in earnest debate.

All up and down the street, there is the sound of car doors slamming shut, farewells being called out.

Molly and I walk to the SUV, which is now as empty as an abandoned campsite. My lone suitcase lies in the back alongside the parcel filled with my new clothes. I place the quilt back in its bag and set it down next to the glossy sack from the department store. The thing is coming home with me after all, it seems. Maybe I'll finish it this fall.

"So, okay," Molly says uncertainly. Her eyes dart here and there; she does not look at me. "Thanks for driving with me, Mom. Thanks for everything."

"Sure, honey. Promise you'll call if you need anything, anything at all. I'll have my cell phone on, 24/7." I touch her arm, feeling its shape beneath my fingers. Then I give up pretending to be casual. No point trying to minimize the moment. "Oh, baby. I'm going to miss you so much."

"Me, too, Mom."

Everything I need to say crowds into my throat— eighteen years of advice, guidance, warning, teaching. And it overwhelms me. It is too much…and not enough. Have I forgotten something important? Have I taught her to do laundry and balance her checkbook? To write thank-you notes by hand? Turn off the coffee maker when it's done? To fend off a horny guy and to contest an unfair grade? To look in the mirror and like what she sees?

There is so much to say. And so I say nothing. There was a time when eighteen years felt like forever, or at least more than enough time to cover every possible topic, but I was wrong about that. I can only hope Dan and I equipped her to make the right choices.

I am amazed to feel something new. I don't want to spout out any more advice or commentary. I want life to happen for Molly in all its pain and joy and richness, revealing itself moment by moment, unfiltered by a mother's intervention. An unexpected, settled feeling creeps in. There are things she knows that will hold and keep her, whether or not I am there. Finally, I'm starting to trust that.

I want her to be on her own. This is what she is supposed to do. It's the natural progression of things. Dan and I have given her everything we have. Now it is time for her to fly, seek new mentors, find her place in the world. I think about all the things that will happen to Molly. Things that will bring her joy and break her heart, make her laugh, cry, rage, exult. I wish I could protect her from the rough parts, but I know I can't. And really, I shouldn't.

The essence of life is the journey, unblunted by an overprotective parent. There is a richness Molly will find even in the deepest sadness. She has a beautiful future ahead of her. Sticking around, interfering and shielding her will rob her of something she needs to figure out on her own. I don't want to stand in the way. Life as it unfolds is just too incredible.

She knows we will always be here for her. Our lives are forever entwined. And yes, she's going to suffer a broken heart and face disappointment and make bad decisions and do all those other things we humans do, but she'll survive them. She's smart and big-hearted and deeply resourceful, probably more than I know, though on this trip I've seen glimpses.

"You're going to be incredible," I finally say. "I'm so happy for you." I am, but I had no idea happiness could hurt so much.

This is it. This is really it. This is goodbye. Suddenly I don't care that there are people all over the place, people who are going to be Molly's friends and neighbors for the next four years. I take my daughter's face between my hands and stare into the eyes I know so well, into a soul that is as bright and clear as the September sky.

She's going to soar, I'm certain of it. Higher than she or I can ever imagine. "Goodbye, Molly," I say. "Goodbye, my precious girl."

Smiling mouth. Trembling chin. "'Bye, Mom."

I kiss her soft cheek, and we embrace, a long strong hug, filled with the wistful scent of autumn and of herbal shampoo. "You are golden," I whisper to my daughter, quoting one of our favorite songs. "You are sunshine." We pull back, smiling, eyes shining.

"I'll call you tonight, okay?" I tell her.

"That'd be great, Mom."

One more kiss. A squeeze of the hands. With slow deliberation, I climb into the truck, roll down the window. We hold hands again while I start the engine. Then

I put the car in Drive and let go. Our fingers cling for a heartbeat, then slide apart.

In the rearview mirror I can see Molly standing on the sidewalk, as slender and graceful as the turning trees of the old college yard. Golden leaves fly upward on a gust of wind, swirling around her lone form. My daughter stands very still, and just as the truck turns the corner onto the busy avenue, she raises one hand, waving goodbye.

Tapping the horn to acknowledge the wave, I let out a breath I didn't realize I was holding.

I set the iPod to a mix of quiet songs. The first one is a classic, from my dating days with Dan. As the music plays, I head for the interstate, tears still escaping to soak into the neckline of my sweatshirt. I flex my hands on the steering wheel, set my jaw. So what if I'm crying. I'm the mother. I get to cry if I want to.

The traffic flows like a viscous liquid, undemanding, carrying me swiftly away from the city, the car a fallen leaf in a rushing stream.

As the city fades away behind me, I picture Molly in her freshly painted dorm room, unpacking her belongings, putting her new sheets on the narrow iron-frame bed, propping up snapshots of her friends and family, her dog and Travis, shelving books and supplies, plugging in the computer, organizing her things. Eventually she will come across the covered plastic box I filled with her favorite snacks— microwave popcorn, granola bars, Life-savers, pecan sandies, canned juices, cinnamon-flavored gum. Inside she will find a familiar note scribbled on a paper napkin: a little smiling cartoon mommy, with squiggles to represent the hair, and a message that will remind her of all the homemade lunches of her childhood: "I ♥ U. Love, Mommy."

I think about giving Dan a call and I will, but not just yet. This moment is too raw, but it's mine to feel—the bittersweet triumph, the sadness, the hope. On this leg of the journey, there will be no detour or scenic route as I make my way home.

Home, to Dan, who said he can't wait to see me. Home, to a life that is open like the pages of an unread book. *Yes*.

I'm ready to live my life. Okay, maybe I'm a little scared, but in a good way. I want to discover who I am on my own, what I love beyond the obvious, and what I really want for the rest of my life.

At the west end of the city, I pass a suburban strip mall I remember from the day before, with the Crowning Glory Salon, the delicious-smelling Sweet Dreams bakery and the charity called New Beginnings. The charity is closed for the day but there's a big metal donation box in the front. Under the web address for the charity is its slogan: "Comforting women and children in need."

On impulse, I turn into the parking lot, go around to the back of the Suburban and open the gate. Molly's observation drifts back to me: This is about *your* life, Mom.

I stand there for a minute, thinking about the woman I've been for the past eighteen years and wondering who I'll be for the next eighteen. It's a bit scary to contemplate, but exciting, too.

When I grab the parcel, my resolve wavers. Then I think, go for it. The true meaning of charity is to give freely, no strings attached. I have to let go, only trusting that my gift will be out there in the world somewhere, doing whatever it's bound to do.

And then I push the bag into the drop box, having to shove its soft bulk inch by inch through the narrow slot. At first I worry that it won't go down the chute, and I have to push hard. Then the last bit slips through easily and disappears.

Stenciled under the chute are the words, "Thank you for your donation."

I return to the still-running car. Something stirs inside me, a sensation as empty and light as the curling, cup-shaped leaves lifted by the autumn wind.

Stopping at the last red light before the on-ramp to the interstate, I catch the blinding beam of the late-afternoon sun in my eye. The days of summer have grown shorter. The year is getting old already.

I flip down the sun visor, and a stray slip of paper drifts into my lap. Picking it up, I unfold it and see a little smiling cartoon face, corkscrew squiggles for hair, and a note that says, "I ♥ U. Love, Molly."

Epilogue

The shop called Pins & Needles looks the way it always has, since its founding decades ago. Its brick and concrete façade glows in the evening light, the windows framed with swaths of fabric. The holidays are past and winter has settled in. The air is sweet and dry with the peculiar clarity that the winter cold brings. The shop is open late tonight, but there is no business to be done.

In the window is a hand-lettered sign: "Retirement party. Come celebrate with us."

Standing behind the counter, I feel as if I'm glowing, too, with a sense of happiness and fulfillment. All around me are my customers, the women who frequent the shop, talking together and sharing all the events of their lives. They've brought platters of cookies and a crystal bowl filled with punch. Minerva, now in a wheelchair, beams at me. "It's a good time to move on, eh?"

"I can't believe it's been twenty-five years," says my best friend, Erin, as she gives me a hug. "Happy retirement, Linda."

I can't believe it either, sometimes. All those years

ago, when I struggled with myself after taking Molly to college, the answer was staring me in the face. I didn't need a bag full of gorgeous new clothes to find my new life. They did more good giving someone else a fresh start; donating the brand-new things to the women's shelter was the right thing to do. Dan loves me as I am. The women at Pins & Needles do, too. I just needed to be the person I've always been—a wife, a friend and neighbor, a needleworker, a dabbler.

The proof is here before me now, a warmhearted shop filled with women I've come to know like sisters through the years. Minerva, who celebrated her ninetieth last year, has been my mentor. As the festivities go on, Molly and her husband arrive, their three kids in tow, and suddenly my arms are filled with grandchildren. The sweetness of this moment makes my heart expand with joy. Dan comes over, laughing about being outnumbered by females. He's as strong and handsome as the day I met him nearly fifty years ago, wearing his age like a fine patina. He raises a cup of punch to me. "I knew you could do it, but now I can't wait to have you all to myself." Still a man of few words, he retreats with our son-in-law to forage for snacks and to escape the chattering women.

After Molly left for college, I missed her terribly, but my life took a new turn and opened up in new ways. I found a dream of my own and went for it. Running the quilt shop didn't make me a rich woman, not in the financial sense. But it enriched my life beyond measure, and I can see that so clearly now, looking around at the faces of my family and friends, customers and well-wishers. The big changes can't be seen, only felt.

Molly gives me a hug and steps back, her eyes shining. "Happy retirement, Mom. I'm really proud of you."

Her words light me up like sunshine, as they always have. We turn together to the display wall behind the counter, regarding the quilt, the one I was making for Molly so long ago. She had it right all along—it *was* my story, and it wasn't finished.

Family. History. Love and loss. I've touched every inch of this fabric. It's absorbed my scent and the invisible oils of my skin, the smell of our household, the occasional drop of blood, and sometimes my tears. I've added to the piece through the years; it's an ever-expanding record of our days as a family. There's a swatch from Molly's graduation gown, and a ribbon from the table decorations on her wedding day. There's a piece from her husband's desert fatigues, and little precious bits from my grandchildren. A tiny silver bell marks our twenty-fifth wedding anniversary. I'm already wondering what little symbol will commemorate our golden anniversary. I try not to plan ahead. Why rob life of its surprises?

I plan to take the quilt home with me tonight, and no doubt more keepsakes will make their way into the design. Life has taught me not to be afraid of starting something new.

How do you say goodbye to a piece of your heart? You don't ever have to. There's always a way to keep the things we hold most dear.

* * * * *

Acknowledgments

I'm very fortunate to have a publisher that allows me to put my heart on paper. Many thanks to my editor and great friend, Margaret O'Neill Marbury, and to everyone at MIRA Books. As always, I'm indebted to Meg Ruley, Annelise Robey and their associates at the Jane Rotrosen Agency—your wisdom, patience and friendship mean the world to me.

To my fellow writers—Anjali Banerjee, Kate Breslin, Carol Cassella, Sheila Roberts and Suzanne Selfors—thank you so much for reading multiple drafts and helping me pull this patchwork of emotion together.

I'm grateful to master quilter Marybeth O'Halloran for the insights and expertise into her colorful world—any liberties and errors in the text are my own. A very special thank-you to my dear friend, Joan Vassiliadis, for creating the original Goodbye Quilt and for sharing her talent in the pages of this book.

The Goodbye Quilt Pattern

by Joan Vassiliadis

www.joanofcards.blogspot.com

Pattern copyright © 2011 by Joan Vassiliadis

Finished size is approximately 45" x 56"
Instructions based on 42" wide fabric
All seams are ¼"

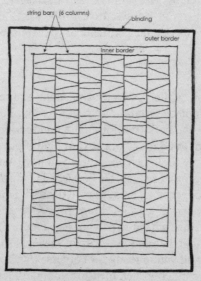

string bars (6 columns)

binding

outer border

inner border

Figure 1

Fabric Requirements

Collect 100% cotton fabric scraps that have special meaning to you. Don't be afraid to cut into old things. You will be able to enjoy them much more in a quilt that will be seen and touched every day. Make sure your scraps are at least 7" wide and total approximately 2½ yards. Inner border: ½ yard solid color to frame the string bars. Outer border: 5/8 yard. Backing: 3¼ yards. Binding: ½ yard.

Cutting Instructions

Cut approximately 220 strings all 7" in length—cut uneven widths ranging between 1" and 3". Inner solid border: cut 4 strips crosswise (from selvage to selvage) 2½" wide. Outer border: Cut 4 strips crosswise 4" wide. Binding: Cut 2½" strips to total the perimeter of your finished quilt.

Sewing Instructions

Play music while you work, sing along and remember why each piece of fabric is special to you. Begin constructing the bars first into pairs and then into fours and so on. Put dark colors next to light if possible, but don't worry too much about it if you have more darks than lights or vice versa. Do be careful to pin and press. Whenever possible, press toward the dark fabric. Construct six bars at least 44" long. Your edges will be uneven so trim each bar to 6" wide (see Figure 2). Sew all six bars together and press. Trim the ends so they are all even and you're ready for borders.

For the inner border, measure your quilt lengthwise first, and construct two strips 2½" wide to this length.

Sew to the sides of the quilt and press. Next, measure the width of your quilt. Construct two strips 2 ½" wide to this measurement. Sew to the top and bottom of the quilt and press. Now for the outer border: Measure the sides of your quilt and construct two strips 4" wide to this length. Next, measure the width of your quilt. Construct two strips 4" side to this measurement. Sew to the top and bottom of the quilt and press. Your top is now complete! Think about all of the memories sewn into this quilt...remember the sweetest moments of life.

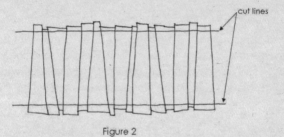

Figure 2

Finishing the Quilt

Linda finished her quilt on the drive with Molly. You can finish yours in the car, in a comfy chair, with your quilting friends at the dining-room table...any way and anywhere you please! If tying your quilt, you can embellish with more memories: buttons, ribbons, badges. Do think about how often your quilt will be washed and how your embellishments will endure. If you make your quilt an art piece, then you can incorporate almost anything. After quilting, measure the perimeter and sew binding strips together to total this measurement. Attach binding.

FIRST TIME IN FOREVER

Sarah Morgan

For Laura Reeth,
makeup expert, style guru and dear friend.

"We must free ourselves of the hope that the sea will ever rest. We must learn to sail in high winds."

Aristotle Onassis

One

It was the perfect place for someone who didn't want to be found. A dream destination for people who loved the sea.

Emily Donovan hated the sea.

She stopped the car at the top of the hill and turned off the headlights. Darkness wrapped itself around her, smothering her like a heavy blanket. She was used to the city, with its shimmering skyline and the dazzle of lights that turned night into day. Here, on this craggy island in coastal Maine, there was only the moon and the stars. No crowds, no car horns, no high-rise buildings. Nothing but wave-pounded cliffs, the shriek of gulls and the smell of the ocean.

She would have drugged herself on the short ferry crossing if it hadn't been for the child strapped into the seat in the back of the car.

The little girl's eyes were still closed, her head tilted to one side and her arms locked in a stranglehold around a battered teddy bear. Emily retrieved her phone and opened the car door quietly.

Please don't wake up.

She walked a few steps away from the car and dialed. The call went to voice mail.

"Brittany? Hope you're having a good time in Greece. Just wanted to let you know I've arrived. Thanks again for letting me use the cottage. I'm really... I'm—" *Grateful.* That was the word she was looking for. Grateful. She took a deep breath and closed her eyes. "I'm panicking. What the hell am I doing here? There's water everywhere and I hate water. This is—well, it's hard." She glanced toward the sleeping child and lowered her voice. "She wanted to get out of the car on the ferry, but I kept her strapped in because there was *no way* I was doing that. That scary harbor guy with the big eyebrows probably thinks I'm insane, by the way, so you'd better pretend you don't know me next time you're home. I'll stay until tomorrow because there's no choice, but then I'm taking the first ferry out of here. I'm going somewhere else. Somewhere land-locked like...like...Wyoming or Nebraska."

As she ended the call the breeze lifted her hair, and she could smell salt and sea in the air.

She dialed again, a different number this time, and felt a rush of relief as the call was answered and she heard Skylar's breathy voice.

"Skylar Tempest."

"Sky? It's me."

"Em? What's happening? This isn't your number."

"I changed my cell phone."

"You're worried someone might trace the call? Holy crap, this is exciting."

"It's not exciting. It's a nightmare."

"How are you feeling?"

"Like I want to throw up, but I know I won't because

I haven't eaten for two days. The only thing in my stomach is a knot of nervous tension."

"Have the press tracked you down?"

"I don't think so. I paid cash for everything and drove from New York." She glanced back at the road, but there was only darkness. "How do people live like this? I feel like a criminal. I've never hidden from anyone in my life before."

"Have you been switching cars to confuse them? Did you dye your hair purple and buy a pair of glasses?"

"No. Have you been drinking?"

"I watch a lot of movies. You can't trust anyone. You need a disguise. Something that will help you blend in."

"I will never blend in anywhere with a coastline. I'll be the one wearing a life jacket in the middle of Main Street."

"You're going to be fine." Skylar's extrafirm tone suggested she wasn't at all convinced by what she was saying.

"I'm leaving first thing tomorrow."

"You can't do that! We agreed the cottage would be the safest place to hide. No one is going to notice you on an island crowded with tourists. It's a dream place for a vacation."

"It's not a dream place when the sight of water makes you hyperventilate."

"You're not going to do that. You're going to breathe in the sea air and relax."

"I don't need to be here. This whole thing is an overreaction. No one is looking for me."

"You're the half sister of one of the biggest movie stars in Hollywood, and you're guardian to her child. If that little fact gets out, the whole press pack will be hunting you. You need somewhere to hide, and Puffin Island is perfect."

Emily shivered under a cold drench of panic. "Why would they know about me? Lana spent her entire life pretending I don't exist." And that had suited her perfectly. At no point had she aspired to be caught in the beam of Lana's spotlight. Emily was fiercely private. Lana, on the other hand, had demanded attention from the day she was born.

It occurred to Emily that her half sister would have enjoyed the fact she was still making headlines even though it had been over a month since the plane crash that had killed her and the man reputed to have been her lover.

"Journalists can find out anything. This is like a plot for a movie."

"No, it isn't! It's my *life*. I don't want it ripped open and exposed for the world to see and I don't—" Emily broke off and then said the words aloud for the first time. "I don't want to be responsible for a child." Memories from the past drifted from the dark corners of her brain like smoke under a closed door. "I can't be."

It wasn't fair to the girl.

And it wasn't fair to her.

Why had Lana done this to her? Was it malice? Lack of thought? Some twisted desire to seek revenge for a childhood where they'd shared nothing except living space?

"I know you think that, and I understand your reasons, but you can do this. You have to. Right now you're all she has."

"I shouldn't be all anyone has. That's a raw deal. I

shouldn't be looking after a child for five minutes, let alone the whole summer."

No matter that in her old life people deferred to her, recognized her expertise and valued her judgment; in this she was incompetent. She had no qualifications that equipped her for this role. Her childhood had been about surviving. About learning to nurture herself and protect herself while she lived with a mother who was mostly absent—sometimes physically, always emotionally. And after she'd left home, her life had been about studying and working long, punishing hours to silence men determined to prove she was less than they were.

And now here she was, thrown into a life where what she'd learned counted for nothing. A life that required the one set of skills she *knew* she didn't possess. She didn't know how to be this. She didn't know how to *do* this. And she'd never had ambitions to do it. It felt like an injustice to find herself in a situation she'd worked hard to avoid all her life.

Beads of sweat formed on her forehead, and she heard Skylar's voice through a mist of anxiety.

"If having her stops you thinking that, this will turn out to be the best thing that ever happened to you. You weren't to blame for what happened when you were a child, Em."

"I don't want to talk about it."

"Doesn't change the fact you weren't to blame. And you don't need to talk about it because the way you feel is evident in the way you've chosen to live your life."

Emily glanced back at the child sleeping in the car. "I can't take care of her. I can't be what she needs."

"You mean you don't want to be."

"My life is adult-focused. I work sixteen-hour days and have business lunches."

"Your life sucks. I've been telling you that for a long time."

"I liked my life! I want it back."

"That was the life where you were working like a machine and living with a man with the emotional compass of a rock?"

"I liked my job. I knew what I was doing. I was competent. And Neil and I may not have had a grand passion, but we shared a lot of interests."

"Name one."

"I—we liked eating out."

"That's not an interest. That's an indication that you were both too tired to cook."

"We both enjoyed reading."

"Wow, that must have made the bedroom an exciting place."

Emily struggled to come up with something else and failed. "Why are we talking about Neil? That's over. My whole life now revolves around a six-year-old girl. There is a pair of fairy wings in her bag. I don't know anything about fairy wings."

Her childhood had been a barren desert, an exercise in endurance rather than growth, with no room for anything as fragile and destructible as gossamer-thin fairy wings.

"I have a vivid memory of being six. I wanted to be a ballerina."

Emily stared straight ahead, remembering how she'd felt at the age of six. Broken. Even after she'd eventually stuck herself back together, she'd known she wasn't the same.

"I'm mad at Lana. I'm mad at her for dying and for putting me in this position. How screwed up is that?"

"It's not screwed up. It's human. What do you expect, Em? You haven't spoken to Lana in over a decade—" Skylar broke off, and Emily heard voices in the background.

"Do you have company? Did I catch you at a bad time?"

"Richard and I are off to a fund-raiser at The Plaza, but he can wait."

From what she knew of Richard's ruthless political ambitions and impatient nature, Emily doubted he'd be prepared to wait. She could imagine Skylar, her blond hair secured in an elegant twist on top of her head, her narrow body sheathed in a breathtaking designer creation. She suspected Richard's attraction to Sky lay in her family's powerful connections rather than her sunny optimism or her beauty. "I shouldn't have called you. I tried Brittany, but she's not answering. She's still on that archaeological dig in Crete. I guess it's the middle of the night over there."

"She seems to be having a good time. Did you see her Facebook update? She's up to her elbows in dirt and hot Greek men. She's working with that lovely ceramics expert, Lily, who gave me all those ideas for my latest collection. And if you hadn't called me I would have called you. I've been so worried. First Neil dumped you, then you had to leave your job, and now this! They say trouble comes in threes."

Emily eyed the child, still sleeping in the car. "I wish the third thing had been a broken toaster."

"You're going through a bad time, but you have to remember that everything happens for a reason. For a start, it has stopped you wallowing in bed, eating cereal from the box. You needed a focus and now you have one."

"I didn't need a dependent six-year-old who dresses in pink and wears fairy wings."

"Wait a minute—" There was a pause and then the sound of a door clicking. "Richard is talking to his campaign manager, and I don't want them listening. I'm hiding in the bathroom. The things I do in the name of friendship. You still there, Em?"

"Where would I go? I'm surrounded by water." She shuddered. "I'm trapped."

"Honey, people pay good money to be 'trapped' on Puffin Island."

"I'm not one of them. What if I can't keep her safe, Sky?"

There was a brief silence. "Are we talking about safe from the press or safe from other stuff?"

Her mouth felt dry. "All of it. I don't want the responsibility. I don't want children."

"Because you're afraid to give anything of yourself."

There was no point in arguing with the truth.

"That's why Neil ended it. He said he was tired of living with a robot."

"I guess he used his own antennae to work that out. Bastard. Are you brokenhearted?"

"No. I'm not as emotional as you and Brittany. I don't feel deeply." But she should feel *something*, shouldn't she? The truth was that after two years of living with a man, she'd felt no closer to him than she had the day she'd moved in. Love wrecked people, and she didn't want to be wrecked. And now she had a child. "Why do you think Lana did it?"

"Made you guardian? God knows. But knowing Lana, it was because there wasn't anyone else. She'd pissed off half of Hollywood and slept with the other half, so I guess she didn't have any friends who would help. Just you."

"But she and I—"

"I know. Look, if you want my honest opinion, it was probably because she knew you would put your life on hold and do the best for her child despite the way she treated you. Whatever you think about yourself, you have a deep sense of responsibility. She took advantage of the fact you're a good, decent person. Em, I am *so* sorry, but I have to go. The car is outside and Richard is pacing. Patience isn't one of his good qualities and he has to watch his blood pressure."

"Of course." Privately Emily thought if Richard worked harder at controlling his temper, his blood pressure might follow, but she didn't say anything. She wasn't in a position to give relationship advice to anyone. "Thanks for listening. Have fun tonight."

"I'll call you later. No, wait—I have a better idea. Richard is busy this weekend, and I was going to escape to my studio, but why don't I come to you instead?"

"Here? To Puffin Island?"

"Why not? We can have some serious girl time. Hang out in our pajamas and watch movies like we did when Kathleen was alive. We can talk through everything and make a plan. I'll bring everything I can find that is pink. Get through to the weekend. Take this a day at a time."

"I am not qualified to take care of a child for five minutes, let alone five days." But the thought of getting back on that ferry in the morning made her feel almost as sick as the thought of being responsible for another human being.

"Listen to me." Skylar lowered her voice. "I feel bad speaking ill of the dead, but you know a lot more than Lana did. She left the kid alone in a house the size of France and hardly ever saw her. Just be there. Seeing the same person for two consecutive days will be a novelty. How is she, anyway? Does she understand what has happened? Is she traumatized?"

Emily thought about the child, silent and solemn-eyed. Trauma, she knew, wore different faces. "She's quiet. Scared of anyone with a camera."

"Probably overwhelmed by the crowds of paparazzi outside the house."

"The psychologist said the most important thing is to show her she's secure."

"You need to cut off her hair and change her name or something. A six-year-old girl with long blond hair called Juliet is a giveaway. You might as well hang a sign on her saying 'Made in Hollywood.'"

"You think so?" Panic sank sharp claws into her flesh. "I thought coming out here to the middle of nowhere would be enough. The name isn't that unusual."

"Maybe not in isolation, but attached to a six-year-old everyone is talking about? Trust me, you need to change it. Puffin Island may be remote geographically, but it has the internet. Now, go and hide out and I'll see you Friday night. Do you still have your key to the cottage?"

"Yes." She'd felt the weight of it in her pocket all the way from New York. Brittany had presented them both with a key on their last day of college. "And thanks."

"Hey." Sky's voice softened. "We made a promise,

remember? We are always here for each other. Speak to you later!"

In the moment before she hung up, Emily heard a hard male voice in the background and wondered again what free-spirited Skylar saw in Richard Everson.

As she slid back into the car the child stirred. "Are we there yet?"

Emily turned to look at her. She had Lana's eyes, that beautiful rain-washed green that had captivated movie audiences everywhere. "Almost there." She tightened her grip on the wheel and felt the past rush at her like a rogue wave threatening to swamp a vulnerable boat.

She wasn't the right person for this. The right person would be soothing the girl and producing endless supplies of age-appropriate entertainment, healthy drinks and nutritious food. Emily wanted to open the car door and bolt into that soupy darkness, but she could feel those eyes fixed on her.

Wounded. Lost. Trusting.

And she knew she wasn't worthy of that trust.

And Lana had known it, too. So why had she done this?

"Have you always been my aunt?" The sleepy voice dragged her back into the present, and she remembered that this *was* her future. It didn't matter that she wasn't equipped for it, that she didn't have a clue—she had to do it. There was no one else.

"Always."

"So why didn't I know?"

"I—your mom probably forgot to mention it. And we lived on opposite sides of the country. You lived in LA and I lived in New York." Somehow she formed the words, although she knew the tone wasn't right.

Adults used different voices when they talked to children, didn't they? Soft, soothing voices. Emily didn't know how to soothe. She knew numbers. Shapes. Patterns. Numbers were controllable and logical, unlike emotions. "We'll be able to see the cottage soon. Just one more bend in the road."

There was always one more bend in the road. Just when you thought life had hit a safe, straight section and you could hit "cruise," you ended up steering around a hairpin with a lethal tumble into a dark void as your reward for complacency.

The little girl shifted in her seat, craning her neck to see in the dark. "I don't see the sea. You said we'd be living in a cottage on a beach. You promised." The sleepy voice wobbled, and Emily felt her head throb.

Please, don't cry.

Tears hadn't featured in her life for twenty years. She'd made sure she didn't care about anything enough to cry about it. "You can't see it, but it's there. The sea is everywhere." Hands shaking, she fumbled with the buttons, and the windows slid down with a soft purr. "Close your eyes and listen. Tell me what you hear."

The child screwed up her face and held her breath as the cool night air seeped into the car. "I hear crashing."

"The crashing is the sound of the waves on the rocks." She managed to subdue the urge to put her hands over her ears. "The sea has been pounding away at those rocks for centuries."

"Is the beach sandy?"

"I don't remember. It's a beach." And she couldn't imagine herself going there. She hadn't set foot on a beach since that day when her life had changed.

Nothing short of deep friendship would have brought

her to this island in the first place, and even when she'd come she'd stayed indoors, curled up on Brittany's colorful patchwork bedcover with her friends, keeping her back to the ocean.

Kathleen, Brittany's grandmother, had known something was wrong, and when her friends had sprinted down the sandy path to the beach to swim, she'd invited Emily to help her in the sunny country kitchen that overlooked the tumbling color of the garden. There, with the gentle hiss of the kettle drowning out the sound of waves, it had been possible to pretend the sea wasn't almost lapping at the porch.

They'd made pancakes and cooked them on the skillet that had once belonged to Kathleen's mother. By the time her friends returned, trailing sand and laughter, the pancakes had been piled on a plate in the center of the table—mounds of fluffy deliciousness with raggedy edges and golden warmth. They'd eaten them drizzled with maple syrup and fresh blueberries harvested from the bushes in Kathleen's pretty coastal garden.

Emily could still remember the tangy sweet flavor as they'd burst in her mouth.

"Will I have to hide indoors?" The little girl's voice cut through the memories.

"I—no. I don't think so." The questions were never-ending, feeding her own sense of inadequacy until, bloated with doubt, she could no longer find her confident self.

She wanted to run, but she couldn't.

There was no one else.

She fumbled in her bag for a bottle of water, but it made no difference. Her mouth was still dry. It had been dry since the moment the phone on her desk had rung with the news that had changed her life. "We'll have to think about school."

"I've never been to school."

Emily reminded herself that this child's life had never been close to normal. She was the daughter of a movie star, conceived during an acclaimed Broadway production of *Romeo and Juliet*. There had been rumors that the father was Lana's co-star, but as he'd been married with two children at the time, that had been vehemently denied by all concerned. They'd recently been reunited on their latest project, and now he was dead, too, killed in the same crash that had taken Lana, along with the director and members of the production team.

Juliet.

Emily closed her eyes. *Thanks, Lana.* Sky was right. She was going to have to do something about the name. "We're just going to take this a day at a time."

"Will he find us?"

"He?"

"The man with the camera. The tall one who follows me everywhere. I don't like him."

Cold oozed through the open windows, and Emily closed them quickly, checking that the doors were locked.

"He won't find us here. None of them will."

"They climbed into my house."

Emily felt a rush of outrage. "That won't happen again. They don't know where you live."

"What if they find out?"

"I'll protect you."

"Do you promise?" The childish request made her think of Skylar and Brittany.

Let's make a promise. When one of us is in trouble, the others help, no questions.

Friendship.

For Emily, friendship had proven the one unbreakable bond in her life.

Panic was replaced by another emotion so powerful it shook her. "I promise." She might not know anything about being a mother and she might not be able to love, but she *could* stand between this child and the rest of the world.

She'd keep that promise, even if it meant dyeing her hair purple.

"I saw lights in Castaway Cottage." Ryan pulled the bow line tight to prevent the boat moving backward in the slip. From up above, the lights from the Ocean Club sent fingers of gold dancing across the surface of the water. Strains of laughter and music floated on the wind, mingling with the call of seagulls. "Know anything about that?"

"No, but I don't pay attention to my neighbors the way you do. I mind my own business. Did you try calling Brittany?"

"Voice mail. She's somewhere in Greece on an archaeological dig. I'm guessing the sun isn't even up there yet."

The sea slapped the sides of the boat as Alec set the inshore stern line. "Probably a summer rental."

"Brittany doesn't usually rent the cottage." Together they finished securing the boat, and Ryan winced as his shoulder protested.

Alec glanced at him. "Bad day?"

"No worse than usual." The pain reminded him he

was alive and should make the most of every moment. A piece of his past that forced him to pay attention to the present. "I'll go over to the cottage in the morning and check it out."

"Or you could mind your own business."

Ryan shrugged. "Small island. I like to know what's going on."

"You can't help yourself, can you?"

"Just being friendly."

"You're like Brittany, always digging."

"Except she digs in the past, and I dig in the present. Are you in a rush to get back to sanding planks of wood or do you want a beer?"

"I could force one down if you're paying."

"You should be the one paying. You're the rich Brit."

"That was before my divorce. And you're the one who owns a bar."

"I'm living the dream." Ryan paused to greet one of the sailing club coaches, glanced at the times for high and low tides scrawled on the whiteboard by the dockside and then walked with Alec up the ramp that led from the marina to the bar and restaurant. Despite the fact it was only early summer, it was alive with activity. Ryan absorbed the lights and the crowds, remembering how the old disused boatyard had looked three years earlier. "So, how is the book going? It's unlike you to stay in one place this long. Those muscles will waste away if you spend too much time staring at computer screens and flicking through dusty books. You're looking puny."

"Puny?" Alec rolled powerful shoulders. "Do I need to remind you who stepped in to help you finish off the Ocean Club when your shoulder was bothering you?

And I spent last summer building a replica Viking ship in Denmark and then sailing it to Scotland, which involved more rowing hours than I want to remember. So you can keep your judgmental comments about dusty books to yourself."

"You do know you're sounding defensive? Like I said. Puny." Ryan's phone beeped, and he pulled it out of his pocket and checked the text. "Interesting."

"If you're waiting for me to ask, you'll wait forever."

"It's Brittany. She's loaned Castaway Cottage to a friend in trouble, which explains the lights. She wants me to watch over her."

"You?" Alec doubled up with soundless laughter. "That's like giving a lamb to a wolf and saying 'Don't eat this.'"

"Thank you. And who says she's a lamb? If the friend is anything like Brittany, she might be a wolf, too. I still have a scar where Brittany shot me in the butt with one of her arrows two summers ago."

"I thought she had perfect aim. She missed her target?"

"No. I *was* her target." Ryan texted a reply.

"You're telling her you have better things to do than babysit the friend."

"I'm telling her I'll do it. How hard can it be? I drop by, offer a shoulder to cry on, comfort her—"

"—take advantage of a vulnerable woman."

"No, because I don't want to be shot in the butt a second time."

"Why don't you say no?"

"Because I owe Brit, and this is payback." He thought about their history and felt a twinge of guilt. "She's calling it in."

Alec shook his head. "Again, I'm not asking."

"Good." Pocketing the phone, Ryan took the steps to the club two at a time. "So again, how's your book going? Have you reached the exciting part? Anyone died yet?"

"I'm writing a naval history of the American Revolution. Plenty of people die."

"Any sex in it?"

"Of course. They regularly stopped in the middle of a battle to have sex with each other." Alec stepped to one side as a group of women approached, arm in arm. "I'm flying back to London next week, so you're going to have to find a new drinking partner."

"Business or pleasure?"

"Both. I need to pay a visit to the Caird Library in Greenwich."

"Why would anyone need to go *there*?"

"It has the most extensive maritime archive in the world."

One of the women glanced at Alec idly and then stopped, her eyes widening. "I know you." She gave a delighted smile. "You're the *Shipwreck Hunter*. I've watched every series you've made, and I have the latest one on preorder. This is *so* cool. The crazy thing is, history was my least favorite subject in school, but you actually manage to make it sexy. Loads of us follow you on Twitter, not that you'd notice us because I know you have, like, one hundred thousand followers."

Alec answered politely, and when they finally walked away, Ryan slapped him on the shoulder.

"Hey, that should be your tag line. *I make history sexy.*"

"Do you want to end up in the water?"

"Do you seriously have a hundred thousand followers? I guess that's what happens when you kayak half-naked through the Amazon jungle. Someone saw your anaconda."

Alec rolled his eyes. "Remind me why I spend time with you?"

"I own a bar. And on top of that, I keep you grounded and protect you from the droves of adoring females. So—you were telling me you're flying across the ocean to visit a library." Ryan walked through the bar, exchanging greetings as he went. "What's the pleasure part of the trip?"

"The library is the pleasure. Business is my ex-wife."

"Ouch. I'm beginning to see why a library might look like a party."

"It will happen to you one day."

"Never. To be divorced you have to be married, and I was inoculated against that at an early age. A white picket fence can look a lot like a prison when you're trapped behind it."

"You looked after your siblings. That's different."

"Trust me, there is no better lesson in contraception to a thirteen-year-old boy than looking after his four-year-old sister."

"If you've avoided all ties, why are you back home on the island where you grew up?"

Because he'd stared death in the face and crawled back home to heal.

"I'm here through choice, not obligation. And that choice was driven by lobster and the three and a half thousand miles of coastline. I can leave anytime it suits me."

"I promise not to repeat that to your sister."

"Good. Because if there is one thing scarier than an ex-wife, it's having a sister who teaches first grade. What is it about teachers? They perfect a look that can freeze bad behavior at a thousand paces." Ryan picked a table that looked over the water. Even though it was dark, he liked knowing it was close by. He reached for a menu and raised his brows as Tom, the barman, walked past with two large cocktails complete with sparklers. "Do you want one of those?"

"No, thanks. I prefer my drinks unadorned. Fireworks remind me of my marriage, and umbrellas remind me of the weather in London." Alec braced himself as a young woman bounced across the bar, blond hair flying, but this time it was Ryan who was the focus of attention.

She kissed him soundly on both cheeks. "Good to see you. Today was amazing. We saw seals. Will you be at the lobster bake?"

They exchanged light banter until her friends at the bar called her over, and she vanished in a cloud of fresh, lemony-scented perfume.

Alec stirred. "Who was that?"

"Her name is Anna Gibson. When she isn't helping out as a deckhand on the *Alice Rose*, she's working as an intern for the puffin conservation project. Why? Are you interested?" Ryan gestured to Tom behind the bar.

"I haven't finished paying off the last woman yet, and anyway, I'm not the one she was smiling at. From the way she was looking at you, I'd say she's setting her sat nav for the end of the rainbow. Never forget that the end of the rainbow leads to marriage, and marriage is the first step to divorce."

"We've established that I'm the last person who

needs that lecture." Ryan slung his jacket over the back of the chair.

"So, what's a girl like that doing so far from civilization?"

"Apart from the fact that the *Alice Rose* is one of the most beautiful schooners in the whole of Maine? She probably heard the rumor that only real men can survive here." Ryan stretched out his legs. "And do I need to remind you that my marina has full hookups including phone, electricity, water, cable and Wi-Fi? I'm introducing civilization to Puffin Island."

"Most people come to a place like this to avoid those things. Including me."

"You're wrong. They like the illusion of escaping, but not the reality. The commercial world being what it is, they need to be able to stay in touch. If they can't, they'll go elsewhere, and this island can't afford to let them go elsewhere. That's my business model. We get them here, we charm them, we give them Wi-Fi."

"There's more to life than Wi-Fi, and there's a lot to be said for not being able to receive emails."

"Just because you receive them doesn't mean you have to reply. That's why spam filters were invented." Ryan glanced up as Tom delivered a couple of beers. He pushed one across the table to Alec. "Unless this is too civilized for you?"

"There are written records of beer being used by the Ancient Egyptians."

"Which proves man has always had his priorities right."

"And talking of priorities, this place is busy." Alec reached for the beer. "So you don't miss your old life? You're not bored, living in one place?"

Ryan's old life was something he tried not to think about.

The ache in his shoulder had faded to a dull throb, but other wounds, darker and deeper, would never heal. And perhaps that was a good thing. It reminded him to drag the most from every moment. "I'm here to stay. It's my civic duty to drag Puffin Island into the twenty-first century."

"Mommy, Mommy."

The next morning, devoured by the dream, Emily rolled over and buried her face in the pillow. The scent was unfamiliar, and through her half-open eyes she saw a strange pattern of tiny roses woven into white linen. This wasn't her bed. Her bed linen was crisp, contemporary and plain. This was like falling asleep with her face in a garden.

Through the fog of slumber she could hear a child's voice calling, but she knew it wasn't calling her, because she wasn't anyone's mommy. She would never be anyone's mommy. She'd made that decision a long time ago when her heart had been ripped from her chest.

"Aunt Emily?" The voice was closer this time. In the same room. And it was real. "There's a man at the door."

Not a dream.

It was like being woken by a shower of icy water.

Emily was out of bed in a flash, heart pounding. It was only when she went to pull on a robe that she realized she'd fallen asleep on top of the bed in her clothes, something she'd never done in her life before. She'd been afraid to sleep. Too overwhelmed by the responsibility to take her eyes off the child even for a moment. She'd lain on top of the bed and kept both doors open so that she'd hear any sounds; but at some point exhaustion had clearly defeated anxiety and she'd slept. As a result, her pristine black pants were no longer pristine, her businesslike shirt was creased, and her hair had escaped from its restraining clip.

But it wasn't her appearance that worried her.

"A man?" She slid her feet into her shoes, comfortable flats purchased to negotiate street and subway. "Did he see you? Is he on his own or are there lots of them?"

"I saw him from my bedroom. It isn't the man with the camera." The little girl's eyes were wide and frightened, and Emily felt a flash of guilt. She was meant to be calm and dependable. A parent figure, not a walking ball of hysteria.

She stared down at green eyes and innocence. At golden hair, tumbled and curling like a fairy-tale princess.

Get me out of here.

"It won't be him. He doesn't know we're here. Everything is going to be fine." She recited the words without feeling them and tried not to remember that if everything were fine they wouldn't be here. "Hide in the bedroom. I'll handle it."

"Why do I have to hide?"

"Because I need to see who it is." They'd caught the last ferry from the mainland and arrived late. The cottage was on the far side of the island, nestled on the edge of Shell Bay. A beach hideaway. A haven from the pressures of life. Except that in her case she'd brought the pressures with her.

No one should know they were here.

She contemplated peeping out of the window,

through those filmy romantic curtains that had no place
in a life as practical as hers, but decided that would
raise suspicions.

Grabbing her phone and preparing herself to draw
blood if necessary, Emily dragged open the heavy door
of the cottage and immediately smelled the sea. The
salty freshness of the air knocked her off balance, as
did her first glimpse of their visitor.

To describe him as striking would have been an
understatement. She recognized the type immediately.
His masculinity was welded deep into his DNA, his
strength and physical appeal part of nature's master plan
to ensure the earth remained populated. The running
shoes, black sweat pants and soft T-shirt proclaimed
him as the outdoor type, capable of dealing with whatever physical challenge the elements presented, but she
knew it wouldn't have made a difference if he were
naked or dressed in a killer suit. The clothing didn't
change the facts. And the facts were that he was the
sort of man who could tempt a sensible woman to do
stupid things.

His gaze swept over her in an unapologetically male
appraisal, and she found herself thinking about Neil,
who believed strongly that men should cultivate their
feminine side.

This man didn't have a feminine side.

He stood in the doorway, all pumped muscle and
hard strength, dominating her with both his height and
the width of his shoulders. His jaw was dark with stubble and his throat gleamed with the healthy sweat of
physical exertion.

Not even under the threat of torture would Neil have
presented himself in public without shaving.

A strange sensation spread over her skin and burrowed deep in her body.

"Is something wrong?" She could have answered her own question.

There was plenty wrong, and that was without even beginning to interpret her physical reaction.

A stranger was standing at her door only a few hours after she'd arrived, which could surely only mean one thing.

They'd found her.

She'd been warned about the press. Journalists were like rain on a roof. They found every crack, every weakness. But how had they done it so quickly? The authorities and the lawyers handling Lana's affairs had assured her that no one knew of her existence. The plan had been to keep it quiet and hope the story died.

"I was about to ask you the same question." His voice was a low, deep drawl, perfectly matched to the man. "You have a look of panic on your face. Things are mostly slow around here. We don't see much panic on Puffin Island."

He was a local?

Not in a million years would she have expected a man like him to be satisfied with life on a rural island. Despite the casual clothes there was an air of sophistication about him that suggested a life experience that extended well beyond the Maine coast.

His hair was dark and ruffled by the wind, and his eyes were sharply intelligent. He watched her for a moment, as if making up his mind about something, before his gaze shifted over her shoulder. Instinctively she closed the door slightly, blocking his view, hoping Juliet stayed out of sight.

If she hadn't felt so sick she would have laughed.

Was she really going to live like this?

She was the sober, sensible one. This was the sort of drama she would have expected from Lana.

"You live here?" she asked.

"Does that surprise you?"

It did, but she reminded herself that all that mattered was that he wasn't one of the media pack. He couldn't be. Apart from an island newsletter and a few closed Facebook groups, there was no media on Puffin Island.

Emily decided she was jumpy because of the briefing she'd had from Lana's lawyers. She was seeing journalists in her sleep. She was forgetting there were normal people out there. People whose job wasn't to delve into the business of others.

"I wasn't expecting visitors. But I appreciate you checking on us. Me. I mean me." She could see from the faint narrowing of those eyes that her slip hadn't gone unnoticed, and she wondered if he'd seen the little girl peeping from the window. "It's a lovely island."

"It is. Which makes me wonder why you're viewing it around a half-closed door. Unless you're Red Riding Hood." The amusement in his eyes was unsettling.

Looking at that wide, sensual mouth, she had no doubt he could be a wolf when it suited him. In fact, she was willing to bet that if you laid down the hearts he'd broken end-to-end across the bay, you'd be able to walk the fourteen miles to the mainland without getting your feet wet.

"Tell me what's wrong."

His question confirmed that she didn't share Lana's acting ability.

His gaze lingered on hers, and her heart rate jumped

another level. She reminded herself that a stressed out ex-management consultant who could freeze water without the help of an electrical appliance was unlikely to be to his taste.

"There's nothing wrong."

"Are you sure? Because I can slay a dragon if that would help."

The warmth and the humor shook her more than the lazy, speculative look.

"This cottage is isolated, and I wasn't expecting visitors, that's all. I have a cautious nature." Especially since she'd inherited her half sister's child.

"Brittany asked me to check on you. She didn't tell you?"

"You're a friend of Brittany's?" That knowledge added intimacy to a situation that should have had none. Now, instead of being strangers, they were connected. She wondered why Brittany would have made that request, and then remembered the panicky message she'd left on her friend's voice mail the night before. She obviously hadn't wasted a moment before calling in help.

Her heart lurched and then settled because she knew Brittany would never expose her secret. If she'd involved this man, then it was because she trusted him.

"We both grew up here. She was at school with one of my sisters. They used to spend their summers at Camp Puffin—sailing, kayaking and roasting marshmallows."

It sounded both blissful and alien. She tried to imagine a childhood that had included summer camp.

"It was kind of you to drop by. I'll let Brittany know you called and fulfilled your duty."

His smile was slow and sexy. "Believe me, duty has never looked so good."

Something about the way he said it stirred her senses, as did his wholly appreciative glance. Brief but thorough enough to give her the feeling he could have confirmed every one of her measurements if pressed to do so.

It surprised her.

Men usually found her unapproachable. Neil had once accused her of being like the polar ice cap without the global warming.

"If I married you I'd spend my whole life shivering and wearing thermal underwear."

He thought her problem lay in her inability to show emotion.

To Emily it wasn't a problem. It was an active decision. Love terrified her. It terrified her so much she'd decided at an early age that she'd rather live without it than put herself through the pain. She couldn't understand why people craved it. She now lived a safe protected life. A life in which she could exist secure in the knowledge that no one was going to explode a bomb inside her heart.

She didn't want the things most people wanted.

Flustered by the look in his eyes, she pushed her hair back from her face in a self-conscious gesture. "I'm sure you have a million things you could be doing with your day. I'm also sure babysitting isn't on your list of desirable activities."

"I'll have you know I'm an accomplished babysitter. Tell me how you know Brittany. College friend? You don't look like an archaeologist." He had the innate self-confidence of someone who had never met a situation he couldn't handle, and now he was handling *her*, teasing out information she didn't want to give.

"Yes, we met in college."

"So, how is she doing?"

"She didn't tell you that when she called to ask you to babysit?"

"It was a text, and, no, she didn't tell me anything. Is she still digging in Corfu?"

"Crete." Emily's mouth felt dry. "She's in Western Crete." There was something about those hooded dark eyes that encouraged a woman to part with confidences. "So you've known Brittany all your life?"

"I rescued her from a fight when she was in first grade. She'd brought a piece of Kathleen's sea glass into school for show-and-tell and some kid stole it. She exploded like a human firecracker. I'm willing to bet they could see the sparks as far south as Port Elizabeth."

It sounded so much like Brittany, she didn't bother questioning the veracity of his story.

Relaxing slightly, she took a deep breath and saw his gaze drop fleetingly to her chest.

Brittany had once teased her that God had taken six inches off her height and added it to her breasts. Given the choice, Emily would have chosen height.

"You knew Kathleen?"

"Yeah, I knew Kathleen. Does that mean you're going to open the door to me?" His voice was husky and amused. "Puffin Island is a close community. Islanders don't just know each other, we rely on each other. Especially in winter after the summer tourists have gone. A place like this brings people together. Added to that, Kathleen was a close friend of my grandmother."

"You have a grandmother?" She tried to imagine him being young and vulnerable, and failed.

"I do. She's a fine woman who hasn't given up hope of curing me of my wicked ways. So, how long are you staying?" His question caught her off guard. It made her realize how unprepared she was. She had no story. No explanation for her presence.

"I haven't decided. Look Mr.—"

"Ryan Cooper." He stepped forward and held out his hand, giving her no choice but to take it.

Warm strong fingers closed around hers, and she felt something shoot through her. The intense sexual charge was new to her, but that didn't mean she didn't recognize it for what it was. It shimmered in the air, spread along her skin and sank into her bones. She imagined those hands on her body and that mouth on hers. Unsettled, she snatched her hand away, but the low hum of awareness remained. It was as if touching him had triggered something she had no idea how to switch off.

Shaken by a connection she hadn't expected, she stepped back. "I'm sure Brittany will appreciate you dropping by to check on the cottage, but as you can see, everything is fine, so—"

"I wasn't checking on the cottage. I was checking on you. I'm guessing Eleanor. Or maybe, Alison." He stood without budging an inch, legs spread. It was obvious he wasn't going to move until he was ready. "Rebecca?"

"What?"

"Your name. Puffin Island is a friendly place. Around here the name is the first thing we learn about someone. Then we go deeper."

Her breath caught. Was that sexual innuendo? Something in that dark, velvety voice made her think it might have been, except that she didn't need to look in the mirror to know that a man like him was unlikely to waste time on someone like her. He was the type who liked his women thawed, not deep-frozen. "I don't think I'll be seeing much of people."

"You won't be able to help it. It's a small island. You'll need to shop, eat and play, and doing those things will mean meeting people. Stay for a winter, and you'll really learn the meaning of community. There's nothing like enduring hurricane-force winds and smothering fog to bring you close to your neighbors. If you're going to be living here, you'll have to get used to it."

She couldn't get used to it. She was responsible for the safety of a child, and no matter how much she doubted she was up to the task, she took that responsibility seriously.

"Mr. Cooper—"

"Ryan. Maybe your mother ignored the traditional and went for something more exotic. Amber? Arabella?"

Should she give him a false name? But what was the point of that if he already knew Brittany so well? She was out of her depth. Her life was about order, and suddenly all around her was chaos. Instead of being safe and predictable, the future suddenly seemed filled with deep holes just waiting to swallow her.

And now she didn't only have herself to worry about.

"Emily," she said finally. "I'm Emily."

"Emily." He said it slowly and then gave a smile that seemed to elevate the temperature of the air by a couple of degrees. "Welcome to Puffin Island."

Two

Secrets and fear. He'd sensed both the moment she'd opened the door, just enough for conversation but not enough for the gesture to be construed as welcome.

He knew when a person had something to hide.

It was in his nature to want to unwrap secrets and take a closer look. He'd tried to switch that side of himself off, but still the instinct to ask questions, to dig and delve, persisted.

There were days when it drove him crazy.

To distract himself, he thought about the woman.

He'd woken her. One glance had told him she was the type who liked to be prepared for everything, and his visit had caught her unprepared. A few strands of silky hair had escaped from the clip on the back of her head and floated around smooth cheeks flushed from sleep. She'd been deliciously flustered, those green eyes focused on him with fierce suspicion.

She'd looked as if she were ready to defend someone or something.

Maybe that body.

Holy hell.

Ryan was proud that he hadn't swallowed his tongue or stammered. He'd even managed to keep his eyes on her face. Most of the time. Then she'd taken a deep breath that had challenged the buttons on her sober shirt, and those full breasts had risen up as if hopeful of escape. The resulting jolt of sexual hunger had been powerful enough to make him lose the thread of the conversation.

It had been a struggle to keep his mouth from dropping open. Even more of a struggle not to press her back against the wall and prove that, even though they had Wi-Fi, not everything on Puffin Island was civilized.

If he was lucky, she hadn't guessed how shallow he was.

Picking up the pace, he ran back along the coastal trail, dropped down to the rocky shoreline and then climbed up again, pushing hard until his lungs screamed for air and his muscles ached. No one looking at him now would be able to guess that four years earlier he'd died in a pool of his own blood. It was thanks to the skill of medics he hadn't stayed dead.

He paused at the top because one of the promises he'd made to himself was to take time to appreciate being alive. Of all the places he'd traveled in his life he considered Penobscot Bay, Maine, to be the most beautiful. Forty miles long and ten miles wide, it stretched from Rockland on the western shore up around the Blue Hill peninsula to Mount Desert. The scenery ranged from wave-soaked rocky islands to lush national park. To a waterman it was heaven, to an outdoorsman a playground. To him, it was home.

On a day like today he wondered why it had taken him so long to come back. Why he'd had to hit the bottom before making that decision. He'd stared into the mouth of hell and might have fallen, had it not been for this place.

He'd swapped stress for sandy shores and rocky tidal pools, the smells and sounds of foreign cities for the crash of the sea and the call of the gulls, food he couldn't identify and didn't have time to eat for lobster bakes and hand-cranked ice cream. Instead of chasing the truth, he chased the wind and the tides.

He was smart enough to appreciate the irony of the situation. As a teenager he'd been so desperate to escape he'd fantasized about swimming the bay in the dead of night to get the hell off this island. He'd been trapped, imprisoned by circumstances, his cell mate the heavy burden of responsibility that had clung to him since the death of his parents. To keep himself sane, he'd dreamed about other places and other lands. Most of all he'd dreamed about being anonymous, of living in a place where the only thing people knew about you was what you chose to show them.

Taking a mouthful of water from the bottle in his hand, he watched a schooner glide across the bay, its sails plump with the wind.

On impulse, he pulled his phone out of his pocket and called Brittany. By his calculations it should be afternoon in Greece.

She answered immediately. "You're calling to tell me you messed with my friend?"

"I offered the hand of friendship as requested." He waited a beat. "You didn't tell me there was a child."

"It slipped my memory."

Knowing that nothing slipped her memory, Ryan wondered why she'd chosen not to tell him. "I was starting to think you'd done me a favor. I might have known there would be a catch."

"A kid isn't a catch. You treat children like viruses, Ryan. Man up."

He smiled. "So what's the story? You said she was in trouble. Am I to expect a visit from an abusive ex-husband?"

"Why does it matter? You'd handle him with one hand behind your back."

"I like to know what I'm dealing with, that's all."

"You're dealing with my stressed friend. Keep her safe."

Ryan thought about the fierce look in her eyes. "She's not exactly embracing my offer of help."

"No, she wouldn't." There was a pause. "Let's just say it wouldn't hurt for her to have another layer of protection."

"It would be helpful to know what I'm protecting her from."

"She'll tell you that when she's ready." The line crackled, and in the background he could hear Brittany having a conversation with someone called Spyros.

"Who is Spyros? Are you planning on marrying a Greek man and moving to Crete permanently?"

"I'm not marrying anyone. Been there, done that." Her flippant tone didn't fool him. He knew how deeply she'd been hurt in the past.

"Listen, Brit—"

"I have to go. I'll talk to you soon, Ryan." She broke the connection and he stared out to sea.

People fascinated him. The choices they made and the stories that lay behind those choices.

He knew Brittany's story. He wanted to know Emily's, and he thought about it now, his mind sifting through possible scenarios as he watched the waves rolling in.

He could have watched the ocean until the sun set, but he was needed back at the Ocean Club. They had to drain every drop out of the summer business to see them through the long Maine winter. He'd plowed all his money into the business and he was determined to make it pay, and not just because living here required him to earn money.

The island had given to him, and now he was giving back.

He had people depending on him.

Driving would have saved time, but choosing to live on this island had been about saving his sanity, not saving time, so he ran instead.

He ran down to the waterfront, past the old fisherman's cottage where Alec was no doubt absorbed in his research, and then took a shortcut inland.

The scent of the sea mingled with the smell of freshly mown grass and spring flowers.

This was his favorite time of year, before the flood of summer visitors swelled the population of the island, clogging roads and spreading across the beaches in a sprawl of people and picnic baskets.

Tourism poured welcome funds into the island's economy, but still there were moments when he resented the intrusion. It was like having guests in your home, and even welcome guests came with an expiration date.

Alec teased him that he couldn't give up those links to civilization—high-speed internet, phone signal—and it was true, but that didn't alter the fact that his choice to move here had been driven by a desire to change his life.

He wondered what had brought Emily to this place. There had to be a reason. There was always a reason.

She had a city look about her. Pale and pinched.

On Puffin Island doors swung open for visitors.

Hers had almost closed in his face.

He took a detour to the school, ran in through the gates and pressed the buzzer. "It's Ryan."

The door opened, and he strode through the cheerful foyer, past walls lined with brightly colored artwork.

His sister bounced out of the classroom, a vision of curls and color. Her dress sense had always been eclectic, and today she'd chosen an eye-popping combination of red and purple. She claimed that color made her happy, but Ryan knew she just had a happy disposition. She saw light where others saw dark and found exciting possibilities in small, daily tasks that to others appeared boring.

If he'd had to pick the perfect teacher for first graders, he would have picked Rachel.

Looking at her, he thought that maybe, just maybe, he hadn't entirely screwed up her childhood.

"Something wrong?" The concern in her eyes made him wonder when his family was going to stop worrying about him.

He was used to being the one in the role of protector, and the reversal made him uncomfortable. Presumably this was the price he paid for frightening them to death.

"Can't a man drop in to say hello to his baby sister? Why does something have to be wrong?"

"Because school starts in less than thirty minutes, you're sweaty and you only ever come and see me when you want something or you want to lecture me."

"That's harsh."

"It's true. And if you call me your 'baby sister' again, something *will* be wrong."

He looked at those bouncy curls and remembered spending impatient minutes trying to drag a hairbrush through the tangles when she was young. On more than one occasion he'd had to choose between dealing with the hair and being late for school, so he'd given up and bunched it back in a ribbon. It was lucky for him the kids at school hadn't known about his stock of ribbons.

Eventually she'd learned to do it for herself, but not before he'd learned far more than he ever wanted to know about braids and bows and girls' hair.

"You *are* my baby sister. And you still look as if you should be sitting in class, not teaching it."

She gave him the stare she used to silence over-excited children. "Not funny, Ryan. It was even less funny when you made the same joke last week when I was on a date with Jared Peters."

"I wanted to shake him up a little. The guy has a reputation."

"That's why I'm dating him."

Ryan reined in the urge to seek out Jared Peters and make sure he couldn't walk to his next date with Rachel. "That guy is all about having a good time and nothing else."

"Oh, please, and you're not?"

"He's too old for you."

"He's the same age as you."

"That's what I mean."

"Is there some reason I shouldn't have a good time as well or is this a 'man only' thing? Last time I checked, women were allowed to have orgasms."

Ryan swore under his breath and ran his hand over

his face. "I can't believe you used that word in this class-room. You look so wholesome."

"I'm not going to dignify that with a response."

"I'm looking out for you." For some reason an image of Emily's anxious face was wedged in his brain. She'd looked wholesome, too. And out of her depth. "That's my job."

"When I was four years old, maybe, but I'm all grown up. Your job is to let me make my own choices and live my life the way I want to live it."

Ryan wondered how parents did it. Wondered how they stood back and let their kids walk slap into a big mistake without trying to cushion it. "I can still step into the parent role when I need to."

She grinned. "Okay, Daddy."

"Don't even joke about it."

"We both know that raising us, me in particular, was the equivalent of being injected with a lifelong contraceptive."

"It wasn't that bad." It had been exactly that bad, to the point where there had never been a time in his life when he hadn't carried condoms. "I care about you. I don't want to see you hurt."

"Do you think you have a monopoly on that feeling? Do you think I enjoyed seeing you leave for all those dangerous places? It killed me, Ryan. Every time you left I wanted to beg you not to go, and then when I got that phone call—" Her voice broke. "I thought I'd lost you."

"Hey—" He frowned, unsettled by the emotion in her voice. "I'm still here."

"I know. And I love you. But you don't get to tell

me how to live my life any more than I get to tell you how to live yours. You're my brother, not my keeper."

He held up his hands. "You're right and I'm wrong. You want to date Jared, then go ahead." But he made a mental note to have a deep and meaningful conversation with Jared next time he saw him.

Not that he had anything against him. Jared was a skilled boat builder who was also a paramedic. Because of the rural nature of the community, most of the emergency care provision came from trained volunteers, and they played a vital role in island life.

"I don't need your permission, Ryan." There was a glint in her eyes. "Do I interfere with your love life? Do I tell you it's time you stopped thinking a relationship is all about sex and settled down? No, I don't. I love you, and I believe that eventually you'll figure out for yourself what you really want."

He raised his eyebrows. "You think I don't know what I want?"

She gave him a pointed look. "I have no comment on the way you live your life."

"Point taken."

Relenting, she stood on tiptoe and hugged him. "I'm glad you're alive. I'm even glad you're living here, but I look out for myself."

She'd been demonstrative and affectionate as a toddler, and she hadn't changed. She held nothing back. She didn't guard herself or search for the truth behind the surface people presented. She took them at face value. She trusted. She gave love freely and asked for nothing in return.

It frightened the shit out of him.

"Just don't say 'I love you' to Jared. Those words

either encourage a guy to take advantage, or they send him running."

"You mean send *you* running. Not all men are like you."

"Hey, I used to cut up your food and walk you to school. You can't blame me for being protective."

"I'm protective, too. How's your shoulder?"

"It's fine." Dismissing it, he glanced at the walls of her classroom, pasted with the colorful artwork. "There's a woman staying in Brittany's cottage. I wondered if you knew anything about her."

"Ah, so now we're getting to the reason for the visit. A woman." There was a gleam of interest in her eyes. "Why would I know anything?"

"Because there's a child." Ryan thought about the little face he'd seen peeping around the filmy white curtains in the upstairs bedroom. Was the child the reason Emily hadn't opened the door fully? That didn't make sense to him. In his experience children made people eager to connect, especially when they were new to a place. "I thought maybe you had a new pupil starting."

"Not before summer. There's just two weeks of school left." Rachel turned away to finish preparing for her lesson. "Why would you be interested in a woman with a child? We both know you've had enough of child rearing, and yes, I might just feel a tiny bit guilty about that, given that I'm the reason you can't stand the thought of settling down and having kids."

"Not true."

"Yes, it is. You were stuck looking after three little kids when you were a teenager. You couldn't wait to get away."

"Not because I didn't love you."

"I know that. All I'm saying is that I'm the reason you run from the idea of settling down. When we lost Mom and Dad, you had to do the serious stuff without any of the fun, so now you're having the fun. It's part of the reason you used to keep your bag packed, so you could run at a moment's notice."

He looked at her, his sweet-natured sister who had been orphaned at such a young age. "Hey, I've been living here for four years. That's stability."

She placed a large sheet of paper on the center of each low table. "There are still times I wonder if one day I'm going to wake up and find you gone. Not that it would matter if that's what you wanted," she said quickly. "You paid your dues."

He discovered that guilt could feel like sandpaper on a raw wound. "I didn't 'pay' anything. I did what needed to be done and I was happy to do it." If you ignored all the times he hadn't been happy and had complained like hell at the world for putting him in that situation. "And I'm not going anywhere. How could I after all the effort you put into saving me? I owe you."

"No one owes anyone anything, Ryan. We're a family. We help each other when we're in trouble. That's what family does. You taught me that." She walked across the classroom and picked up a bucket of seashells.

Even as a very young child she'd loved everything about the sea.

He'd spent hours with her on the beach, hunting for sea glass and building castles out of sand.

Ryan had always envied her calm contentment, a direct contrast to his own restless energy and burning desire to escape.

"What are you doing with those?"

"We're making a collage using things we found from the seashore on our trip last week. I still don't understand why you'd be interested in a woman renting the cottage, especially if there's a child in tow." She added paints and glue to each table. "Why the mystery?"

The mystery was that she'd been scared.

"I'm curious."

She flicked him a look. "Curiosity killed the cat, Ryan."

"If you can't come up with something more original than that, then there is no hope for the younger generation."

But he understood the reason for the tension. She was worried this wouldn't be enough for him. That he'd wake up one morning and decide to go back to his old life.

Since she'd been the one to clear up the mess last time, he couldn't blame her for hoping that didn't happen.

"Miss Cooper?" A small voice came from the doorway, and Ryan turned to see the Butler twins, Summer and Harry, hovering with their mother. Lisa Butler had moved to Puffin Island the summer before and had taken over the ice cream parlor, Summer Scoop, near the harbor.

While his sister worked her magic on two excited children, Ryan smiled at Lisa. "Gearing up for the summer rush? How is everything?"

"Everything is good." Her expression told him everything was far from good, and instantly he wanted to know why. He couldn't help himself. Some might have said it was his passion, but he knew it was closer to an addiction, this need to find the truth buried beneath the surface. He wanted to know who, what, why, when. In this case he suspected the "what" was the state of the business. After a harsh Maine winter when the mention of ice cream was a joke not a temptation, Summer Scoop had to be suffering. The business had been limping along for years before Lisa Butler had decided to sink her life savings into it.

"I'll leave you to mold young minds, Miss Cooper." He nodded to his sister. "Talk to you later."

And in the meantime he was going to find out more about the woman in Castaway Cottage.

"Has the man gone?"

"He's gone." But his face was still in her head. Remembering the encounter, Emily felt heat rush through her body. "I'm sorry he woke you."

"He didn't." Those pale green eyes were ringed by tiredness, and Juliet's long hair fell in tangled curls of gold past narrow shoulders.

Emily looked for signs of tears, but there were none. The girl seemed remote. Self-contained.

That was good, wasn't it?

She tried to ignore the simmer of unease in her belly that told her it wasn't good.

"Was the bed uncomfortable?" Emily had tucked the girl up in Brittany's old room the night before, covered with the patchwork quilt.

"It was noisy."

"That's the sea. You can sleep in a different room tonight if you like."

"Can I sleep with you?"

Emily swallowed. "Sure."

The little girl stood, staring up at the shelf in the kitchen. "Why are there jewels in a jar?"

"It's sea glass." Emily reached and picked up the jar. "It washes up on the beach. Sometimes it gets trapped in the pebbles and rocks. Kathleen used to collect it. Every time she went to the beach she came back with her pockets stuffed. She liked the colors, the fact that each piece has its own story." Relieved to have something to take her mind of Ryan Cooper, Emily handed Juliet the jar and watched as the girl turned it in her hands, studying each piece of glass closely, absorbed by color and shape.

"It's like a rainbow in a bottle."

"Kathleen kept it by the window so it caught the sunlight. She called it treasure."

"Does she live here?"

"Not anymore. She died a few years ago." Emily wondered if she should have used a different choice of words. Maybe she should have talked vaguely about heaven and stars in the sky. "She left this cottage to my friend, and sometimes, when one of us has a problem, we come here."

"Do you have a problem?"

Looking down at the problem, Emily felt compassion mingle with panic.

She didn't know anything about children, but she knew how it felt to have something you loved snatched from you. She knew how it felt to learn, at a far too young age, that life was cruel and unpredictable. That it could take as quickly as it gave, and with no warning.

"No. There's no problem now that we're here."

"Was she your family?"

"Kathleen? No. She was my friend's grandmother,

but she was like a grandmother to me, too." And then she remembered "grandmother" probably meant nothing to a child whose short life had been spent among people paid to care for her and keep her away from a prying world. "Sometimes the people who are closest to you aren't the ones you're related to."

Let's make a promise. When one of us is in trouble, the others help, no questions.

The little girl held the jar to her chest. "You're my family."

"That's right." Her stomach lurched. Panic rose like the sea at high tide, swamping the deep fissures created by a lifetime of insecurities. She didn't want that responsibility. She'd never wanted it. "Why don't we explore the house? It was dark when we arrived last night."

Nestled in the curve of Shell Bay, Castaway Cottage had ocean views from all the front rooms. It was easy to see why Kathleen had never wanted to leave, despite the relative isolation and the long winters. She'd made sure that whatever the weather, there was warmth in the house. Wooden beams and hardwood floors formed a backdrop for furniture carefully chosen to reflect a nautical theme. A striped wingbacked chair, a textured rug, framed photos of the seabirds that nested around the rocky coast.

Still holding the jar, Juliet went straight to the window and clambered onto a chair. "Can we go to the beach?"

Emily felt a pressure in her chest.

Soon, she'd have to work out how she was going to handle that inevitable request, but she didn't have the energy for it now. "We need to settle in first. I have to unload our cases and unpack."

"I'm hungry."

Emily, whose usual caffeine-infused breakfast came in the form of strong coffee, realized she hadn't given any thought to feeding the girl. "I packed a few things in the car, but this afternoon we're going to need to go to the harbor and pick up some food."

Which presented her with another problem.

"I was thinking—" They walked back into the kitchen, and Emily opened cupboards, hunting for food that Brittany might have left on her last visit. "Juliet is a pretty name, but how would you feel about being called something else?"

"Juliet is from Shakespeare."

"I know, but—" *Everyone else knows, too.* "Do you have another name? I'm Emily Jane."

"I'm Juliet Elizabeth."

"Elizabeth. How about Lizzy? That's pretty."

"Why do I need a different name? So the men with cameras don't find me?"

Emily favored honesty and saw no reason to alter that approach in this instance. "Yes." She opened a cupboard and pulled out a bowl in a pretty shade of cornflower blue. "That's part of the reason. I don't want people asking you questions. It will be like a game."

"I used to play games with Mellie."

"Mellie?"

"She cooks. Sometimes she looks after me when Paula is in the bedroom kissing her boyfriend."

"P—what? Who is Paula?"

"She's one of my nannies."

One of them? Still, at least Lana had arranged child care, which was more than their mother ever had. "So Paula looked after you?"

"Yes. And sometimes we watched my mom on TV." Lizzy was still holding the jar clutched against her chest. "Paula says people take pictures because she was famous and beautiful."

"Yes, she was."

People will pay money to see my face. You'll never be as pretty as me, and that's why people don't love you.

She tried to wipe the memory from her mind. "No one will take pictures of you here. People are friendly."

That much was true. She, Skylar and Brittany had spent plenty of happy evenings laughing and drinking in the Shipwreck Inn, and Brittany was well-known and loved on the island. Too well-known.

She tried to remember whether her friend had ever mentioned a Ryan Cooper.

She was certain she hadn't met him before.

His wasn't a face that was easy to forget.

That face was in her head as she pulled open cupboards, looking through tins and dried pasta that Brittany left as emergency food. She found cereal, tipped it into the bowl along with the milk she'd bought and settled the child at the table. "We'll finish unpacking and then explore the island." Unpacking wasn't going to take long. Should she be depressed that everything she valued from her old life had fit into two small suitcases? A few clothes and her precious first editions. "We can have lunch by the harbor. You can pick anything you like from the menu. It will be fun."

"Can I bring my bear?"

Emily looked at the battered bear and decided its chances of surviving the trip were slim. There was a rip in its neck, and it had lost an eye. "Why don't we leave him here? We don't want to lose him." Or parts of him.

"I want him to come."

Concerned that half the bear might fall into the harbor, Emily was tempted to argue, but she was more afraid of doing something that might destabilize an already fragile situation. "We'll take the bear."

"Can I wear my fairy wings?"

Because fairy wings weren't conspicuous at all. She closed her eyes and told herself that no one would be looking for the child of a Hollywood actress on an island off the coast of Maine. And if Skylar was right, then Lizzy wouldn't be the only six-year-old wearing fairy wings. "If that's what you want." She stiffened as the child slid off her chair and walked across to her.

A small hand slid into hers. "Will they find us?"

The feel of that hand made the pressure in her chest worsen. "No." She croaked out the word. "We're safe here."

Or at least, she hoped they were.

Picking up her phone, she found Brittany's name in her contacts and sent a text.

Who is Ryan Cooper?

Because it was still early in the summer, she managed to park near the harbor. The busy working waterfront was a popular spot for tourists keen to experience all Puffin Island had to offer. Lobster boats, the lifeblood of the local community, bobbed alongside yachts, and fishermen rubbed shoulders with locals, tourists and sailing enthusiasts. The ferry that connected the island to the mainland ran three times a day when weather permitted. John Harris, the harbormaster, had been in charge of the service for as long as anyone could remember, terrifying everyone with his white shock of hair and heavy eyebrows.

From a distance, Emily recognized Dave Brown, who had been lobstering the waters around Puffin Island for three decades. She remembered standing with her friends, watching as he'd brought in the catch of the day, standing a safe distance from the deep waters of the harbor while Brittany and Kathleen had bought fish straight from the boat. They'd cooked it fresh and eaten it in the garden with butter dripping down chins and eager fingers.

"Can I see the boats?" Curious, Lizzy wandered toward the edge of the harbor, and Emily grabbed her shoulder and hauled her back.

Her heart was thudding and her palms were clammy. Why had she parked by the harbor? She should have found a side street and stayed as far from the water as possible.

John Harris walked across to them, a frown turning his eyebrows into a single shaggy line. "Careful. The water is deep here."

While Emily waited for her heart to slow down, she kept a grip on Lizzy. Brittany had once confessed the harbormaster had terrified her as a child, and Emily and Skylar had laughed, both unable to imagine Brittany being terrified of anything.

Lizzy didn't seem to share that fear. She looked from him to the ferry that was just leaving the harbor. "Is that the same ferry we came on last night?"

"It's the same. *The Captain Hook*."

"Like in *Peter Pan*?"

John Harris studied the child. "It's named for Dan

Hook, who donated the money for a ferry service fifty years ago. Is this your first visit to Puffin Island?"

"They're Brittany's friends." The male voice came from behind her, and Emily turned to find Ryan standing there. He nodded to John. "Busy ferry this morning."

"Full load. We're adding an extra crossing from next week as the summer season heats up." The introduction seemed to soften John Harris's mood a little because he nodded to Lizzy. "So, you're staying in Castaway Cottage. Best view on the island. Be careful by the water." He strode off, and Ryan shook his head.

"Don't let him scare you. A kid fell in once, and he's been nervous ever since. Summer is a busy time for him. So, you found your way to the harbor and Main Street. This is the closest thing we have to civilization. Can I direct you anywhere?"

He'd showered and changed since their encounter earlier that morning. He wore a pair of light-colored trousers and a dark blue shirt with the sleeves rolled up to the elbows. The addition of tailoring did nothing to disguise his powerful build.

Skylar would have observed that he was well put together.

Brittany would have described him as "smoking hot."

Emily found him unsettling. Not because he was so sure of himself—she was used to confident men, so that wasn't the reason—and not even because of the unexpected scorch of sexual awareness, although that was new to her. No, what frightened her was that those dark eyes seemed to see right through the invisible aura Neil had claimed made her unapproachable.

It suited her to be unapproachable. "I appreciate your concern, Mr. Cooper—"

"Ryan."

"Ryan, but we're fine."

"I didn't know you had a daughter."

She didn't correct him. "She's very shy. We were just—"

"I'm Lizzy."

Emily sighed. Right now shyness would have been preferable.

She waited for Ryan to make polite noises and back away. She was sure a man like him lived an adult-only life, free from the responsibility of children. Surprising her, he dropped into a crouch. The movement molded the fabric of his trousers to his thighs and pulled his shirt tight over broad, muscular shoulders.

"Hi, Lizzy. Nice bear."

Everything about him told her that he was a man's man, a person who could have been dropped in the wilderness with nothing but a knife and survived. Nothing had prepared her for the ease with which he handled Lizzy.

Watching him simply intensified her own feelings of inadequacy.

He took the bear and made admiring noises, his hands gentle as he handled the damaged toy. "What's his name?"

Name?

Not in a million years would she have thought to ask if the bear had a name, but apparently it did.

"Andrew." Lizzy's reply was hesitant, but Ryan nodded, as if the name made perfect sense to him.

"So, how are you and Andrew liking Puffin Island?"

Emily was grateful that the bear couldn't talk; otherwise he'd no doubt be reporting the fact that so far he'd been well and truly ignored.

If there was a Stuffed Bear Protection League, she was about to be reported for neglect.

She watched as Ryan handed the bear back carefully, envying the ease with which he talked to the child. He didn't use baby talk, nor was he patronizing or condescending. He behaved as if Lizzy had something to say that he was interested in hearing. As if the answers she gave were important to him. Some of the tension in Lizzy's shoulders melted away.

"I like the boats."

Why did it have to be the boats that had caught her attention?

Emily wondered what had possessed her to think coming to the island would be a good idea. She should have picked Wyoming or another state with no coastline.

"I like boats, too." Ryan rose to his feet. "What's your favorite food?"

This time Lizzy didn't hesitate. "Waffles. And chocolate milk."

"That's a lucky thing, because I happen to know somewhere that sells the best waffles you have ever tasted. And it has tables overlooking the sea so you can watch the boats at the same time. It will be my treat."

"Thank you, but we're fine." Emily found herself staring at him. He was at least a head taller than her. The casual attire did nothing to diminish the overwhelming sense of presence.

"You don't like waffles and chocolate milk?" There was humor in his eyes and something else. A sexy, lazy gleam that flustered her. He was the sort of man who made most women lose their heads and throw caution away with their underwear.

Emily had never lost her head or her underwear. Relationships were something to be thought through, measured and calculated, like every other important decision in life. She'd never found that difficult. But nor had she ever met anyone who made her feel the way Ryan Cooper did.

She'd spent three years with Neil and not once had he left her with this sense of breathless awareness. When he'd walked into a room, her heart rate hadn't altered.

"I appreciate the offer, but Lizzy and I have things we need to do before we have lunch."

Lizzy clutched the bear to her chest. "I'd like waffles."

To please her niece, she had to sit at a table with a man who made her feel as if she was naked?

He smiled. "Seems to me that what you need to do most of all is relax. You look as if you're about to explode."

"I've been driving for two days, and—"

"So a cool drink on the deck is just what you need to help you unwind."

"I don't need to unwind."

His gaze slid over her face. "There is more tension in your spine than in the mast of that yacht over there."

"I appreciate your concern, but if I'm stressed, then it's because I don't appreciate being stalked, Mr. Cooper."

"Stalked?"

"It seems as if every time I turn around, you're standing there."

"Welcome to island living, Emily. Chances are you're going to be bumping into me several times a day. And then there's the fact I promised Brittany I'd keep an eye on you."

"I appreciate your concern, but I'm absolving you of that duty."

"She told me you might need someone you could trust. She asked me to watch out for you. So, here I am, watching out for you."

Emily met that lazy, interested gaze and decided no normal, sane woman would be foolish enough to put her trust in a man like him. You might as well hand over your heart and say "stomp on this."

"I appreciate the offer, but I don't need anyone to keep an eye on me." In fact, people keeping an eye on them was the last thing she needed.

She was all that stood between Lizzy and a media hungry for a story at any cost.

They reminded her of vultures, swooping down to strip the last pieces of flesh from a carcass.

Lana was dead.

Surely that should be enough for them. Why did they need to unpick her life? There had been a constant parade of stories in the press. A catalog of salacious details that one day Lizzy might read.

If Emily could have found a way of destroying all of it, she would have done so.

Ryan stepped closer, his voice low. "Tell me what the trouble is, and I'll fix it."

She wondered how it felt to be that confident. It didn't seem to occur to him that there might be something he couldn't fix.

"It isn't trouble as much as a change in circumstances. Brittany was exaggerating."

And she was going to kill her.

"She said you'd push me away."

She wasn't just going to kill her; she was going to kill her slowly. "It was wrong of her to put you in this position. I'm sure you're a busy man, so you should get on and do whatever it is you do, and I'll—" She'd what? Carry on messing up parenthood? "I'll be fine."

"I made her a promise. I keep my promises." He gave a disarming smile. "And on top of that, I'm scared of Brittany. Apart from the fact she's an expert in Bronze Age weaponry and has an unnerving fascination for re-creating daggers and arrowheads, I remember what happened when someone stole her sea glass. I don't want to be on the wrong side of her temper."

She eyed those broad, powerful shoulders, noticing that his biceps filled out the arms of his shirt. She was willing to bet there wasn't much that scared him.

"Aunt Emily?" Lizzy tugged at her hand. "I'm hungry."

She saw Ryan lift an eyebrow and knew he'd filed the information that she was an aunt, not a mother.

"We'll buy some food. You can choose the things you like." Because she had no idea what the girl liked.

"Harbor Stores is the best place for that. And don't miss the bakery next door. They sell the best cheesecake I've tasted outside New York." He broke off as an elderly lady crossed the street toward him. The face was lined and the hair was white, but there was no missing the twinkle in her eyes.

"Ryan Cooper, the most eligible man on the island. I was hoping I might bump into you."

"I was hoping the same thing." He was all charm as he reached out and took her arm. "All ready for tonight, Hilda?"

"I might have a problem with transportation because the doctor told Bill he shouldn't be driving for a few weeks." She looked at him hopefully, and Ryan didn't disappoint.

"What time are you planning on leaving? Seven?"

"Perfect. Will you drop me home afterward?"

He laughed. "You think I'm in the habit of leaving my date stranded?"

"You're a good boy, despite all the rumors." She patted his arm. "I hear all sorts of stories about all-night parties at the Ocean Club, but I try not to listen."

Boy? Startled, Emily looked at the stubble that darkened Ryan's jaw and the lazy, sleepy eyes. She saw nothing of the boy in him, only the man. She wondered what the rumors were.

Women, no doubt.

With a man who looked like that, it had to be women.

"You're talking about Daisy's twenty-first birthday party. It didn't last all night, but it's true that the sun was coming up."

"I heard she was wrapped like seaweed around the Allen boy."

"Is that right?" It was clear that if he knew, he wasn't telling. "If anyone else needs a lift tonight, let me know."

Emily liked the fact he wasn't prepared to reveal someone else's secrets.

As someone currently guarding a big secret, it reassured her.

Hilda glanced around and then stepped closer to

him. "This month's book was a shocker. It was Agnes's choice."

He looked amused. "You don't surprise me. My grandmother enjoys shocking people."

"True. I still remember the time she hired a nude model for our drawing class." The woman's face wrinkled into a smile. "We had better attendance that night than any other night in the history of our group. We had to paper over the windows to stop people peeping through the glass. This book was a step up from that." She noticed Lizzy and lowered her voice. "There were naked people *and* spanking." She gave him a knowing look, and Ryan's eyes gleamed.

"Now I'm thinking I should join the group."

"You can't do that. No testosterone allowed."

That would rule out Ryan Cooper, Emily thought. He was surrounded by a force field of testosterone.

"This is Brittany's friend Emily," Ryan said easily. "She's staying at Castaway Cottage, and this is her niece, Lizzy."

Hilda studied Emily closely. "I remember you. You're one of Kathleen's girls. You used to spend the summer here. You and the pretty blonde girl."

Emily hadn't expected anyone to recognize her. "Skylar."

"Kathleen talked about the three of you all the time. 'Hilda,' she said, 'those three are as close as sisters. They'd do anything for each other.' You were the quiet one." Hilda transferred her attention to Lizzy. "You're going to love Puffin Island. You should take a boat trip to see the seals and the puffins. And don't forget to visit Summer Scoop. Best ice cream in Maine and all organic. What's your favorite flavor?"

Lizzy considered. "Chocolate."

Emily felt something stir inside her.

Everyone knew the right way to talk to a child except her. They were easy and natural, whereas she used the same tone she used when presenting to a board of directors.

Miserably aware that she was only a few hours in to a responsibility that was going to last a lifetime, she watched as Ryan helped Hilda back across the street. If they were going to escape, this would be the perfect time.

She could walk to the store and do what she'd planned to do, stock up the cottage.

"Aunt Emily?" Lizzy was clutching the bear so tightly it seemed unlikely the stitching would survive.

Emily looked at the white knuckles and the lost expression on the child's face.

She didn't know anything about fairy wings or teddy bears, but she knew this.

She crouched down in front of Lizzy. "It must feel strange for you, being here without your—" *cook, nanny, cleaner, mother?* "—the people you know around you. It's strange for me, too. It's a new life for both of us, and it's going to take a little while before it feels normal." She didn't admit how afraid she was that it would never feel normal for her. "We don't know each other very well yet, so I won't always know what you want unless you tell me. It's important that you know you can ask me anything. Talk to me about anything. And if there's anything you want, you just have to ask."

Lizzy looked at her for a long moment. "I want waffles and chocolate milk."

Three

 ───❧❧❧───

Ryan ordered at the bar and exchanged a few words with Kirsti, who ran the Ocean Club and had made herself indispensable in the short time she'd been with them.

"Who is she?" Kirsti passed the order through to the kitchen and then glanced across to the deck, where tables had views across the bay. "She's pretty. Not in an obvious way, but in an interesting way. A little too innocent-looking for you, but it's time you mended your wicked ways, so that could be good. I think she could be The One."

Kirsti was obsessed with finding The One. It drove some people crazy. It made Ryan smile.

"It's a big world out there. If there really was only one person for everyone, we'd all be single."

"You are single. And you're mixing up sex with relationships." She selected a tall blue glass from the shelf. "A common mistake, particularly among the male sex, and the reason so many partnerships fail. You don't only need someone who can rock your body, you need someone who can rock your mind."

Ryan was fairly sure Emily would be able to do both, but Kirsti didn't need encouragement, so he kept that thought to himself. "Sometimes sex *is* the relationship."

"With you, sex is *always* the relationship. I bet you slap a page of terms and conditions in front of every woman you date."

"I don't, but it's a good idea. I'll run it past my lawyer."

She gave him a reproving look. "You're not funny."

"I'm hilarious. You just don't share my sense of humor."

"Does anyone? But this is my point! You need someone who is going to hold your attention. Your eye might be caught by a double-D cup, but your cynical heart will be caught by something more complex."

He glanced across at Emily's eye-popping curves. "My attention is caught. There's just one thing wrong. One thing that makes me completely sure she's not The One."

"Don't tell me—the child." With a sigh, Kirsti whipped up chocolate milk, added a straw and put the glass on the tray. "What do you have against children?"

"Nothing. I like children. I just don't want to be responsible for one."

"A bit of responsibility would do you good. Who is she, anyway?"

He knew all about responsibility, the sort that made you sweat and kept you awake at night. But Kirsti wasn't an islander, so she wouldn't know the details of his past.

"Friend of Brittany's. She's staying in Castaway Cottage."

"I love that place. The garden is like something from

a fairy tale." Her eyes narrowed. "I think you might marry her."

"Jesus, Kirsti, keep your voice down." He was torn between exasperation and amusement. "For all you know, she's already married."

"She isn't. And the child isn't hers."

"How can you possibly know that?"

"The way she behaves. She isn't comfortable. It's as if this whole thing is new to her, as if they barely know each other and she isn't quite sure what her role is."

Ryan thought about the text Brittany had sent.
She's in trouble.

He wanted to know what the trouble was.

"There's no such thing as The One. Love is like Russian roulette. You have no idea what the outcome is going to be."

"You're such a cynic. Why do I work for you?"

"Because I pay better than anyone else on Puffin Island, and I don't fire you when you try to run a dating business on the side." Having successfully diverted the conversation, he strolled toward Emily. Kirsti was right. She looked uncomfortable. No, he corrected himself. Not uncomfortable. Shell-shocked. Dazed. Gazing at her, he had the sense she was on the verge of snapping.

He tried to avoid women with baggage, and he suspected she had more baggage than an airline.

The baggage that really put the brakes on his libido was sitting with her legs swinging, waiting for chocolate milk.

He wove his way through crowded tables, noticing with satisfaction that very few were empty. He'd settled them at a table overlooking the beach, knowing that the view was the best on the island. From here you could watch the boats sailing between the island and the mainland. If you were lucky, you caught the occasional glimpse of seals on the rocky headland in the distance. So far they'd had three proposals on this deck, and one sunset wedding.

Almost everyone he knew chose a seat facing the water. He'd had to mediate between couples arguing with other couples over the tables with the best water-front view.

Emily sat with her back to the water and her eyes on Lizzy as if she were afraid she might disappear in front of her. It only took a glance to see she was fiercely protective.

Keep an eye on her, Brittany had said.

He intended to do just that. Not just because a friend had asked him to, or because it was part of island culture to watch out for each other, but because he wanted to know the story. Kirsti was right that Lizzy and Emily didn't have the easy relationship of people who knew each other, and yet Lizzy had called her "aunt."

He wondered where Lizzy's mother was.

Was there a family crisis and she was filling in?

"One chocolate milk, extra large, two of the best-tasting coffees you'll find anywhere and a plate of our homemade waffles. They look so good I want to sit down and eat them with you." Kirsti placed everything on the table with a flourish and the smile that guaranteed her large tips and endless inappropriate invitations. "Enjoy. If you need anything else, let me know."

"Nothing else for me, thank you." Emily sent her a grateful glance. She had the air of someone who was improvising madly, feeling her way in the dark with no idea what she was meant to do next.

The breeze lifted a strand of her hair and blew it across her face. And her face fascinated him. Her eyes were the same green as the child's, her mouth soft and full, hinting at a sensuality hidden behind the tailored clothes. His mind leaped ahead, and he imagined her hair tumbling loose after a night of crazy sex. Given a couple of hours and a babysitter, he was fairly sure he could do something about her tension. Disturbed by how badly he wanted to put that thought into action, he lifted his hand to brush the strand of hair away at the same time as she did, and their fingers tangled. Heat ripped through his body.

"Sorry." He murmured the word and let his hand drop, watching while she anchored the offending locks with slender fingers. It was a blur of rich caramel and sunshine gold. He wanted to toss that damn clip into the water where she wouldn't be able to find it.

Because he didn't trust himself not to do that, he turned his attention to the child. The waffles had gone, the only evidence of their existence a pale smear of maple syrup over the center of the plate. "How is your chocolate milk?"

Lizzy sat on the chair, legs dangling, as she watched the boats glide across the bay, their sails curved by the wind. She'd needed two hands to manage the tall glass, so she'd put the bear down on the seat next to her. "It was good, thank you." She was stiff and polite, and it occurred to him he'd never seen a more uncomfortable pair.

He remembered Rachel at the same age, lighthearted and playful. She, too, had refused to be separated from her favorite toy, only in her case, the toy had been a puffin and she'd had a habit of leaving it everywhere.

He'd chased around the island more times than he cared to remember hunting for that damn puffin. On one occasion Scott Rowland, the island fire chief, had delivered it to the house after someone in the library had found it and recognized it as belonging to Rachel. Anticipating the day the puffin would be found by a tourist, not a local, Ryan had persuaded his grandmother to buy a spare, and he'd hidden it in his room as a precaution. His closest friend, Zach, had found it when they'd been sprawled in his room one day playing video games. It had taken Ryan six months to live down the fact he'd had a stuffed puffin in his room. Every week when he'd played football there had been a puffin in his locker. He'd dragged his skateboard out of the garage one morning only to find someone had painted a puffin on it. That had been the summer Ryan had given up skateboarding and taken up basketball. For one whole semester, the team had adopted the puffin as their mascot. By the time Zach had gotten bored with the joke, Ryan had enough stuffed puffins to give Rachel a whole colony of the things.

He'd gone to bed at night dreaming of living somewhere that didn't have Puffin in the name.

"So, Brittany is in Greece." He kept the conversation neutral, avoiding any topics that were likely to make her jumpy. Since he didn't know what those were, he figured it was best to stick to talking about her friend. "I remember when she was ten years old, she was playing at being an archaeologist, and she dug a deep hole in Kathleen's garden. When Kathleen asked what had happened to her flowers, Brit told her it was what was underneath the soil that was important."

Emily reached for her coffee. "You knew Kathleen well?"

"Very well. There is a group of women on the island, including Hilda, who you met earlier, who have been friends forever. They grew up here, went to school together and then married and had their children around the same time. They've seen each other through triumph and tragedy. Island life fosters friendships. They were as close as family." He saw her expression change. "You don't believe friends can be like family?"

"Oh, yes." There was a faraway look in her eyes. "I do believe that. Sometimes they can be better than family."

So, her own family had let her down.

He filed that fact away. "Over the years their meetings changed. When they had young children, it was a toddler group, a way of getting out of the house and breaking up the Maine winter. When the children were older, they turned it into a hiking club for a short time, and there was one summer when they took up kayaking. In the winter there was yoga, art—that was when the episode of the nude life drawing happened—and right now it's a book group." After he'd left home he'd stopped reading for a while. He put it down to all the times he'd read *Green Eggs and Ham* to Rachel.

"Where do they meet?"

"They used to meet in each other's houses, but now that's too much work for one person to cope with, so I let them use one of our function rooms, and provide the food."

"You own this place?" Curious, she glanced around. "It's busy. You're obviously doing something right."

"Took a lot of effort to design something that satisfied everyone. We needed it to work for the community." And he'd needed it to work for him. "The buildings and the marina were already here, but we made improvements, increased the number of member moorings and guest moorings, offered boat maintenance and a valet service. The first thing I did was employ a club manager. We had this huge building that was basically unused, so I converted it into apartments and kept the top one for myself. Then we developed this place and called the whole thing the Ocean Club. I worked on the principle that people who have just spent time at sea are happy to crash at the first decent place they find. We're full most nights in the summer."

"You've lived here all your life?"

"No. Like most people, I moved away, just to check there wasn't anything better out there."

"And was there?"

He thought about what he'd seen. The life he'd led. His shoulder throbbed, and he forced himself to relax because tension made it worse. "It was different. I grew up on this island. My grandfather was a lobsterman. My father took a different route. He spent time in the merchant marine and then joined the crew of the schooner *Alice Rose*, sailing around the coast."

"I don't know anything about boats."

Ryan wondered once again what she was doing on this island, where sailing was the main preoccupation. "That's a schooner." He pointed, and she turned her head reluctantly, leaving him with the feeling that if she could have found somewhere else to look she would have done so. "See the two masts? Some have more, but two is common. They have shallower drafts, perfect for coastal waters, and the way they're rigged makes them easier to handle in the changing winds along the coast, so they need a smaller crew."

Lizzy craned her neck. "It looks like a pirate ship."

Remembering Rachel saying the same, Ryan smiled. "My father became captain. He taught seamanship and navigation and then decided the teamwork needed to sail the *Alice Rose* should be transferable to the corporate world, so he persuaded a few of the big companies in Boston to send their executives up here. The rest of the time he offered coastal cruises to tourists and twice a year he ran bird-watching trips around the islands. He believed that the best way to see the sea, the islands and the wildlife was from the deck of the *Alice Rose*."

Lizzy put down her empty glass. She had a ring of chocolate milk around her lips, and the breeze had whipped color into her cheeks. "Was he a pirate?"

"No. The opposite. He was a pioneer of sustainable ecotourism, which basically means he loved nature and tried to make sure that everything he did helped the island. He donated part of his profits to local conservation projects, particularly the protection of the puffins."

"What's a puffin?"

"It's a seabird. They used to nest on these islands a long time ago. Conservation experts have been finding ways to bring them back."

"This is their home? That's why it's called Puffin Island?"

"Yes, although now the puffin colony is on Puffin Rock." He pointed to the small uninhabited island just visible in the distance. "They lay one egg a year, and young puffins usually return to breed on the same island where they hatched."

"That's fascinating." Emily glanced at him, curious,

and he noticed the dark flecks in her green eyes. The dark smudges under those eyes told him that whatever her trouble was, it was keeping her awake. Presumably it was also affecting her appetite given that all she'd ordered was coffee.

"I guess they have a sort of homing instinct." He'd done the same, hadn't he? In the end he'd dragged himself back here, to the place where he'd been born.

Lizzy's eyes were huge. "Can we see them?"

"You can take a boat trip. Humans can't get too close because otherwise they scare the puffins. Where is home to you?"

"New York." It was Emily who spoke, and he noticed she glanced at Lizzy and gave a brief shake of her head. He wondered what the child would have said without that warning glance to silence her.

Without looking at him, Emily reached for a napkin and carefully wiped the milk from Lizzy's mouth. It was a natural response, something he'd done himself when his sister was very young, but something about the way she did it made him think it was new to her.

"You said you met Brittany at college. What were you studying?"

"Applied math and economics. We had rooms next door to each other."

"You, Brittany and—" he searched for the name "—Skylar."

"You know Sky?"

"No. But I've heard Brittany talk about her.

"So did Brit fill her room with skulls and old coins she'd dug up from the ground?"

Her brief smile was cut off by the sudden burst of loud laughter from a group behind them. She turned her head quickly, and her gaze was caught by something. A glance became a stare, and whatever it was that had drawn her attention unsettled her because her face lost color. Her smile gone, she fumbled blindly for her bag and stood up. "We should go. Thank you for the drink."

Ryan rose, too, and caught her arm. "Why the rush?" Standing this close, he caught the scent of her hair, saw the unusual blend of colors up close and acknowledged that his interest in her stemmed from something deeper than the desire to keep a promise made to a friend.

There was a cool breeze, but all he could feel was heat, and the strength of the attraction almost rocked him off his feet.

Her mouth was right there, and he knew if it hadn't been for Lizzy he would have kissed her. Maybe she would have slapped his face, but he would have been willing to take that chance.

The few relationships he'd had since his return to the island had been brief. His choice. A marine biologist who had spent a summer working in the research lab at the north of the island, a nurse who came from the mainland to help out at the medical center occasionally. He didn't know if they'd hoped for more because he hadn't asked. He lived his life in the moment.

"We have things to do." There was panic in her voice. "Thank you for the waffles and chocolate milk." She kept her back to the group and kept the child in front of her, shielding her from a threat invisible to Ryan.

"Goodbye, Ryan." Without waiting for a reply, she took Lizzy's hand and hurried her out of the café, keeping her head down and not looking back.

"Good to meet you, too," he murmured to himself, quashing the urge to stride after her and protect her from whatever perceived threat had sent her running from the table.

Sudden illness? She'd certainly been pale enough; but she'd been just fine moments earlier, so her health couldn't be responsible for the sudden shift in her attitude.

Hunting for clues, he rewound events in his head and remembered that she'd looked over her shoulder.

A swift glance revealed nothing but a group of young people who were spending the summer at the marine center on the north side of the island. Linked to the university, the floating laboratory ensured a steady stream of customers for the Ocean Club. They were loud, enthusiastic, in love with life and harmless. And untidy. They'd strewn their belongings over the table and vacant chairs. Backpacks, water bottles, leaflets detailing boat trips, a scientific magazine and a newspaper. They were deeply involved in a discussion about ecosystem-based fisheries management. He knew that at least a couple of them had the right to use "Dr." in front of their names. They were absorbed and argumentative and passionate. Not one of them had glanced over at their table.

There was no visible reason to justify Emily's abrupt departure.

"So you scared her away." Kirsti was back, clearing the plates. "You must be losing your touch. Still, at least you have a reason to chase after her."

Ryan lifted an eyebrow. "I do?"

"Sure." Kirsti put down the loaded tray and picked up the bear. "She's not going to want to be without this. Unless she has a spare. When I'm a mom, I'm going to buy spares of everything."

Ryan took the bear. "She'll be back for it when she realizes she left it."

"Or you could take it to her." Kirsti added an empty glass to the tray. "You shouldn't let The One get away. That bear is the equivalent of Cinderella's slipper. Except that you know it fits."

Ryan rolled his eyes. "I changed my mind. You're fired."

"You can't fire me. I make great coffee, and I never complain when we're busy. And it's my moral duty to make sure people don't choose the wrong partners. Talking of which, those two at the table by the door are totally wrong for each other. I might have to interfere." She strolled off carrying the tray, Cupid in disguise.

Still holding the bear, Ryan started to follow her but accidentally knocked the chair behind him.

A bag and the newspaper fell to the floor, and he stooped to retrieve both with a murmur of apology.

Without thinking, he scanned the headline, something about health care reforms.

Returning the newspaper to the chair, he was about to walk back to the bar when something else caught his eye.

Juliet, Juliet, wherefore art thou, Juliet?

It wasn't the misquote of Shakespeare that caught his attention, it was the picture beneath it.

The media was still focused on the plane crash that had killed actress Lana Fox and her much older lover. There had been endless speculation about the whereabouts of her little girl.

Ryan grabbed the newspaper and took a closer look at the photograph, and in that single moment he had the answers he'd been looking for.

He no longer needed to speculate as to why Emily had run. He didn't need to wonder why she'd almost closed the door in his face or even why someone who knew nothing about boats had come to Puffin Island.

He knew.

And he knew why the child looked familiar.

Four

"We have to go back." Lizzy refused to move from the front door. "I left Andrew."

"It's late, Lizzy. Almost time for bed. We can't go back now. I'll phone the Ocean Club and explain. They'll keep Andrew safe."

"Nooo. I can't sleep without him. Someone might take him."

Emily didn't think a battered bear with one eye missing and a slit throat would fit most people's idea of a dream toy, but she kept that thought to herself. She was too busy beating herself up for making such a basic mistake. How could she have left the bear? And why hadn't she noticed sooner? It proved what she already knew—that she was the wrong person for this task. "Most people don't take things that belong to other people." Hoping her faith in human nature wasn't misplaced, she fumbled for her phone. "I'm going to call and ask them to keep Andrew. We'll pick him up tomorrow." By then the newspaper would have been thrown away, hopefully by someone more interested in tidying it up than reading it.

If she was lucky, no one would make the connection, but the incident had shaken her.

All thoughts of leaving the island faded. She needed to hide away, and there was no better place for that than Castaway Cottage.

Lizzy's face crumpled. "I want Andrew."

Emily's hands shook on the phone. "I'm going to make the call right now. Remember that nice girl, Kirsti? We're going to ask her to take care of Andrew until tomorrow."

Lizzy didn't answer. Instead, she ran into the living room and flopped down on the sofa with her face turned away.

Emily couldn't help thinking a tantrum would have been easier to handle, but she was learning that Lizzy's way of handling stress was to lock herself away.

She was looking up the number for the Ocean Club when there was a knock at the door.

What now?

Had someone recognized them?

Was this the moment she'd been dreading?

Braced for defensive action, she opened the door. She'd call the police. She'd sneak away in the night. She'd—

Ryan stood there, the bear in his hands. "I thought you might be missing this. I would have brought it over sooner but we've been insanely busy."

Emily sagged against the door frame. She'd never been so pleased to see anyone in her life. "You're a lifesaver. She adores that bear." She took it from him, wondering how to clone the battered bear. "I should have been more careful." She felt like hugging him but decided hugging Ryan Cooper probably qualified as a dangerous sport.

"Don't be hard on yourself. When my sister was Lizzy's age she was always losing toys. And you left in a hurry."

"We had things to do." Relief was tempered by caution. "It was kind of you to drive over. I don't know how to thank you. You're obviously busy, so—"

"It calms down around this time. The lull before the storm. Can I come in?"

Only minutes earlier she'd been wishing she wasn't on her own with this. Now she was wishing the bear's rescuer had been anyone but him.

She wanted to close the door on all that raw masculinity, but he'd brought the bear and saved her life. She couldn't be rude to him simply because he made her feel things she didn't have time to feel right now.

Reluctantly, she opened the door wider. "I'll give Lizzy the bear."

She found the little girl exactly where she'd left her, lying listlessly on the sofa, staring at the wall.

"Ryan brought Andrew back." Dropping to her knees in front of the sofa, Emily tucked the battered bear into Lizzy's arms. "I promise we'll never leave him again."

Lizzy squeezed the bear so tightly Emily was afraid it might lose its head permanently.

Ryan watched from the doorway. "I love a happy ending." He glanced around the living room. "It's been a while since I've been here. You have no idea how many offers Kathleen had for this piece of land."

"It doesn't surprise me. But Brittany will never sell." She stood up. "Can I fetch you a drink? We haven't had time to stock up properly yet, but I have juice or soda. Or coffee?"

He followed her into the kitchen and scanned the bags on the table she hadn't yet unpacked. "That's not going to keep you going for long."

"It will do for now." Pulling milk out of the bag, she stowed it in the fridge. She had a carton of eggs in her hand when he spoke.

"Emily, I know."

"Sorry?"

He glanced over his shoulder, checking Lizzy was still in the living room. "I know why you ran."

She forced herself to keep breathing. "I don't know what you mean."

"The world is speculating on the whereabouts of Juliet Fox, six-year-old daughter of troubled Hollywood actress Lana Fox, who died a month ago in a plane crash along with the man everyone assumes was one of her lovers. Rumor has it the child is staying with a friend or relative in an unknown location."

The carton of eggs slipped from her fingers and crashed onto the floor, spreading the contents in a sticky mess. "You saw the newspaper."

"I was looking for a reason for your abrupt departure."

Trying to think through the panic, she sank onto the nearest chair, ignoring the puddle of eggs congealing on the floor. "I came here because I thought we'd be safe."

"Safe from what? I assume you're her guardian."

"Yes, although as you can see, I'm not the right person for the job." She gripped her knees until her knuckles were white, and Ryan dropped to his haunches in front of her so they were eye level.

"Why aren't you the right person?"

"Do you want a list? First, I lose the bear, then, I risk exposing her by taking her out in public. I shouldn't have said yes to the drink." There was another reason why she knew she wasn't the right person, the most important reason of all, but that wasn't something she intended to share.

"I was the one who invited you for a drink."

"The responsibility was mine. You didn't know."

His eyes were dark velvet, his voice calm. "Are you seriously planning to hide away?"

"What choice do I have? I don't want the press to know we're here." She took a deep breath and tried to steady herself. "I talked to a bunch of people who have been with her since the accident. Lawyers, case workers, grief counselors. *My* head was spinning, so goodness knows what hers was doing. But the message I took from it all was that she needs to live as normal a life as possible. No media attention. No cameras. It freaks her out. There were great packs of them outside the house. One of them even got inside and cornered her, trying to get information about her mother. He's the one that scared her the most. Can you believe someone would actually do that? She's six years old. Six. I have to protect her from that."

His expression unreadable, he rose to his feet. "They told you her life needs to be as normal as possible. Not going out isn't normal. A child can't live her life trapped in a house and neither can you."

"I think she used to spend a lot of time in her old house, although of course, it was more of a palace than a house, and she had everything she needed within those walls and staff."

"You think? So you don't know her that well?"

"I don't know her at all." She reasoned that he already knew the part that could hurt them, so revealing detail wouldn't make a difference.

"Whatever her old life was like, it's gone. She needs to rebuild a life. And it needs to be a normal life. She doesn't need staff, she needs security."

"That's why I've already decided that from now on I'm only leaving the cottage when we need food."

"I don't mean that sort of security. I mean the sort that comes from knowing there are people around you who care about you and have your back. You can't keep her hidden in the cottage, Emily. Both of you will go crazy. She's a kid. She needs to explore and play. She needs to meet other kids. And what about you? Are you going to spend the next twelve years shut away here with no adult company?"

"I'm planning the next twelve hours. I can't think further ahead than that." Twelve years? The thought made her want to hyperventilate. "I'm going to need to make trips into town. She's too young to be left alone and I don't have anyone here I can trust."

"Hey, let's take this a step at a time." He sat down in the chair opposite her. "This is why Brittany said you were panicking."

There was much more to her panic and feelings of inadequacy than her ability to keep Lizzy's identity a secret. Eventually, she knew, media attention would move to other things, other lives, but she'd still be the child's guardian, and she knew she wasn't equipped for that monumental task. "When I told her what happened, she suggested I use the cottage. Kathleen left it to Brittany because she wanted her to have somewhere that was hers, somewhere she could go when life was tough. On our last day together at college Brittany gave us both a key."

"You and Skylar?"

"Yes. She said Kathleen would have wanted it. We were moving to different sides of the country. In Brittany's case, to a different continent half the time. It was somewhere we could come if we ever needed it."

"And you needed it."

"It seemed like a perfect place to hide while I worked out what to do."

For Lizzy it was perfect. For her, it was a nightmare. The crash of the waves kept her awake, churning up memories like the ocean churned sand on the seabed.

"What's your connection to Lana Fox?"

Emily was filled with a ridiculous desire to lean on all that hard strength, an impulse that made no sense because she'd been taking care of herself since she was younger than Lizzy.

"She was my sister." She saw his expression shift from concern to surprise. "I hadn't seen Lana since I left to go to college, and I met her child for the first time three days ago. We have no relationship. Lizzy has lost her mother and everything familiar and all she has is me." Panic bubbled up inside her. "That isn't good."

"Yeah, that must feel like a hell of a responsibility to shoulder alone. Is someone contesting the guardianship? Another relative?"

"There are no other relatives."

"Do you know the identity of the father?"

"Lana never told anyone. I'm all she has." Saying it aloud made it seem all the more terrifying.

"I didn't know Lana Fox had a sister."

"Half sister. We had the same mother. Different fathers." Nameless, faceless men whom her mother had taken home after one of her nights of endless drinking.

"I saw mention of her mother once. She was an alcoholic…" His voice tailed off as he saw her expression change. "I apologize. She was your mother, too."

"I'm not afraid of facts, and the facts were that my mother used to sleep with men when she was drunk and then face the consequences sober. She died a couple of years ago. Her liver decided it had been to one party too many."

"I don't remember Lana Fox ever talking about her family in the press."

"She reinvented herself. We didn't exactly have a fairy-tale childhood."

"Some fairy tales are pretty bad." He stretched out his legs. "That woman in *Cinderella* was a real bitch."

It lightened the atmosphere, and a laugh bubbled up from her throat. "Yes. And then there was the queen in *Snow White*. She was a classic case of narcissistic personality disorder."

"Cruella de Vil was a serial killer."

"—of Dalmatians."

"True, but she demonstrated the same psychotic tendencies seen in other murderers. Lack of compassion and lack of remorse."

"Maybe my childhood was closer to a fairy tale than I thought."

"Too many elements missing. For a start, you didn't find your prince." He glanced at her left hand. "You're single."

"Whenever I saw him climbing up the tower to my bedroom I gave him a push."

"Yeah? Just for my own interest and research, what was it that put you off?"

"He was creepy."

"Right." His smile faded. "So you and Lana weren't close as children?"

"I was the ugly sister."

"Given how manifestly wrong that description is, I assume it was hers."

"It wasn't wrong. She was very beautiful." Emily thought about the reality of her childhood. "And, no, we weren't close. We were just people living under the same roof for a little while. It was a shock when they called me to say she'd named me guardian, but then I thought about it and realized there wasn't anyone else. It was a decision made out of necessity, not choice."

"Did she leave you a letter?"

"Nothing."

"So one minute you were living your life, a life in which you'd had no contact with your half sister since you were a teenager, and the next you were guardian to her child. That is a major life change. Were you working? What did you do with the math and economics you studied?"

"Up until last month I was a management consultant. I worked for Taylor Hammond in New York."

He looked impressed. "That's the big-time."

"They had a reorganization and there was no job for me in the new structure. I was interviewing for new jobs when I found out about Lizzy." She clenched her hands in her lap. "Skylar would make some observation about how that was an indication that this was meant to be. How one day I'll look back and be pleased this happened."

Ryan gave a low laugh. "Kirsti would probably say the same thing. She believes in fate. So, are you missing New York? You had a life there."

Emily wondered if what she'd had could really be described as a life. "I had a job and a boyfriend."

"So there *was* a prince. You pushed him down the tower with the others?"

"He jumped. He got a look at the princess, decided she didn't look like a good deal and got the hell out." It helped to make a joke of it. "He dumped me a month ago."

"Not very princely behavior. And that was before Lizzy was on the scene. So it wasn't because of the child?"

"No." She stared at the mess on the floor. "Not because of that."

"How long were you together?"

"Three years. Two of which we lived together."

"Life really has dealt you a hand." His gaze was steady. Sympathetic. "I just want you to know I'm here for rebound sex or revenge sex whenever you need it. Just say the word. Or just grab me and explain afterward, whatever works for you."

She wouldn't have thought it possible to want to laugh at that moment, but she did. "Did you really just say that?"

"I really did. Want to think about it?"

The crazy thing was she had thought about it. What woman wouldn't? Ryan Cooper was insanely attractive. If all you were looking for was a night you'd never forget, he'd be the perfect choice. "I'm trying to be a responsible parent figure. I've already lost the bear.

I think being caught having sex on the kitchen table would be a major fail."

"Possibly. So, just to clarify—the only thing that's stopping you is that your niece is asleep in the living room?"

"I can't believe I'm laughing. What is there to laugh about?"

"In my experience laughing always helps. So, what's your plan?"

"I got myself here. So far, that's it. I need to lie low while I work out what is best for Lizzy."

"And what about you?"

Her mouth was dry. "What about me?"

"You didn't sign on for this. It wasn't your choice." Something about the way he said it made her wonder if there was more to his comment than an astute observation.

"It wasn't a choice for either of us."

"I presume you chose the name 'Lizzy' because you're worried Juliet might draw attention."

"It's not a common name, and right now it's in the press a lot, so I thought it safer not to use it."

"Good decision. While the story is hot, the fewer people who make the connection, the better."

"But you know." As the implications of that struck her, she had to force herself to breathe. "What are you going to do with the information? The media would pay good money for a photo of Lana's child."

"Do I look like I need to sell a story to the media?" His mild tone coated layers of steel, and she squirmed because it seemed an uncharitable accusation, given he'd been nothing but helpful.

"I'm sorry. That was inexcusable. But I don't know you. And I don't know her, either."

"You know she likes chocolate milk and waffles."

She gave a wan smile. "Small steps."

He stood up. "Life is made of small steps. Let's start by clearing up the eggs before you slip. Breaking both your legs and knocking yourself unconscious isn't going to make the future easier."

"The eggs were for tomorrow's breakfast."

"I'll bring you breakfast. I'll be around at nine. Don't leave the cottage until I get here. That's the next twelve hours sorted. After that, we'll plan the next twelve hours. You can get through a life like that." With an efficiency that surprised her, he cleaned up the mess and stowed the contents of the bags while Emily went to check on Lizzy.

She found her asleep, still clutching Andrew.

"She's exhausted. I should put her to bed."

"I'll carry her upstairs." Ryan was behind her, and she shook her head.

"I can do it."

"Are you sure?" He eyed her frame. "You don't look strong enough."

"Careful. You're starting to sound like a fairy-tale prince. Just for the record, I'm capable of storming my own castle." She scooped Lizzy up in her arms and headed upstairs. She weighed more than Emily had expected, but she would rather have sprained her back than admit it to Ryan Cooper.

She lowered Lizzy to the bed, pulled off the little girl's shoes, tucked Andrew next to her and covered child and bear with the quilt. Then she stood, looking down at the feathery lashes brushing pale cheeks, and felt overwhelmed by the responsibility.

This wasn't temporary. This wasn't just for a few days or even the summer.

This was forever.

Subduing the panic, she stepped away from the bed. She couldn't think about forever.

She returned to the kitchen to find Ryan opening cupboards. "What are you looking for?"

"Wine?" He paused. "Or maybe you don't drink."

She knew he was thinking of her mother. "I drink. But I stop. Unfortunately wine wasn't one of the things I grabbed in my two-minute raid of Harbor Stores."

"Will coffee keep you awake?"

"I don't sleep, anyway." She was afraid to close her eyes in case something happened.

And now she had Lizzy in the bed with her.

"So, which is the worst part of all this? The boyfriend, the job or the kid?" He reached for a coffeepot while she found two mugs and put them down on the counter.

"Definitely the child."

"Not the boyfriend?"

"It would have ended eventually."

"Commitment phobia?"

"In a way."

"Plenty of men suffer from the same affliction."

"I was talking about me. I end all my relationships."

He gave her a curious look. "I would never have cast you in the role of serial heartbreaker."

"I try and disguise it. I sand the bedpost to hide the notches."

"So, what do you want out of a relationship?"

She watched as he moved around the kitchen and poured coffee into the two mugs, handing one to her. He looked competent and relaxed. "I don't want a traditional happy ending if that's what you're asking. Two children and a dog have never interested me."

"Which bit of that scenario bothers you most? The dog?"

She knew he was teasing, but this time she couldn't smile. "All of it bothers me."

"But you've ended up with a child, anyway."

"Yes." She walked to the window, trying to steady herself. "My favorite part of this house is the garden. We used to pick blueberries and eat them for breakfast."

"The climate and the soil are perfect here. You should try the blueberry ice cream at Summer Scoop on the harbor. It's delicious." Ryan paused. "What will you do about a job? Puffin Island isn't exactly a hub of activity for management consultancy firms."

"I'm not thinking about that right now." She sipped her coffee, thinking how strange it was having a man in her kitchen. "I'm still adjusting to being responsible for a child. I have some money saved up. I'll worry about the rest of it later."

"Does your ex-boyfriend know what happened?"

"No."

His eyes narrowed. "Let me get this straight. You were together for three years, and he hasn't once checked to see how you're doing?"

"The only people who know are Brittany and Skylar. And the lawyers, obviously. Even Lana's staff weren't told, for obvious reasons, since at least one of them let a journalist into the house. Who does that? Who stalks a child?" She put the mug down and stared over the garden. "I'm not going to be able to keep it a secret, am I? This place is going to be crowded with tourists in the summer. Someone is going to recognize her."

"Not necessarily. You forget that they're not looking. This isn't Hollywood. People come here to spend time away from the busy crush of their lives. They come here for the coast and the sea air."

"One of the locals will say something, then. Her picture was on the front page of the newspaper. They shouldn't be allowed to do that."

"The community is very protective of its own."

"But I'm not a member of the community."

"You're Brittany's friend, living in Brittany's cottage. That makes you a local."

"All it takes is one person. One call to the press and suddenly the island is flooded with them, like ants finding sugar to feed on."

He finished his coffee. "You're safe here tonight. Tomorrow we'll formulate a plan."

She knew a plan wasn't going to change the basic facts.

Like it or not, she was responsible for a child.

He drove home along the coast road, saw a light burning in Alec's house, considered stopping in and then decided he'd end up fielding questions he didn't want to answer.

He avoided the bustle of the bar and went straight to his apartment. The building that now housed the Ocean Club Apartments had originally been a boatyard. It had stood empty for over three decades, battered by storms and winter weather, which was why he'd managed to buy the land for a ridiculously low price. He'd seen potential where others hadn't.

It had been a labor of love converting it, but his reward had been a profitable rental business and a premium apartment he could have sold a hundred times over. It stretched the length of the building and had a large glass-fronted open-plan living space that was always flooded with light regardless of season or weather.

At night he liked to sprawl on one of the sofas and watch the sun melt into the sea. Tonight he made straight for the office area in the corner and flipped open his laptop.

He hit the power switch and grabbed a beer from the fridge while he waited for it to boot up. Sprawling in the chair, he thought about the woman.

Those green eyes had been the first thing he'd noticed about her when she'd opened the door to him that day, closely followed by those delicious curves that no amount of discreet clothing could conceal.

The fact she'd put her life on hold to care for her orphaned niece was laudable, but at the same time put her strictly out of bounds.

Ryan wasn't looking for that level of complexity or intimacy in his relationships.

He'd had his fill of parenthood at an age when most kids had barely discovered the meaning of sex.

Without the plea from Brittany asking him to check on her friend, he would have stayed the hell away from her, and now that he had the facts, he was starting to wish he had.

He understood her situation better than she could possibly have imagined, which made the power of the sexual connection an inconvenience he was determined to ignore.

A woman with a child was not part of his game plan, and the fact that the child wasn't biologically hers made no difference. White knight was a role he avoided, right along with women who made noises about weddings and settling down.

Juliet Fox.

Brittany obviously hadn't mentioned his past. If Emily had known the truth, she definitely would have closed the door in his face.

With a soft curse he turned to his laptop and hit a couple of keys.

He started by searching the internet. He knew where to look to get the information he needed, and once he'd found everything he could without going deeper he reached for his phone and made one call.

"Larry?"

"Hey, stranger."

He could imagine his old colleague and adversary hunched over his untidy desk with papers overflowing over every square inch of space. "Slow news day?"

"Why would you care about the news? I thought you'd retired, yacht boy."

"I have, but the paper I saw today was enough to send a person to sleep. Lana Fox on the front page. What's that about?"

"Why do you care? Not exactly your area of interest, and anyway, last time I heard, all you read was tide tables. Are you thinking of coming back to the real world?"

"No. I'm just curious."

"Curious is one step from coming out of retirement."

"I'm not retired. I changed direction." Ryan picked up his beer, blocked out images that still kept him awake at night and stared at the information on his computer screen. "Tell me what you know about her."

"Lana Fox? She's dead."

"Yeah, I got that part. I was hoping for a little more depth."

"Depth and Lana Fox aren't words that sit comfortably together. What do I know? Total wacko. How she managed to hold it together in front of a camera, no one knows. Rumor has it they were threatening to fire her from her last film because she lost so many days on set."

Ryan stretched out his legs and stared out to sea. "The paper mentioned a kid." A kid she'd left in the care of an aunt she'd never met.

"Why would you be interested in that?"

"Can't imagine Lana as a mother, that's all. Didn't seem the type."

"Well, she wasn't Mary Poppins, if that's what you're asking me. I think she forgot she had a kid except for the few occasions when it suited her to show her off to the cameras. If you ask me, that child was a publicity stunt. Maybe she wanted the attention. She certainly had everyone speculating about the father. Who knows? Maybe she was going to reveal it at some point. Use it in some way. Casting couch in reverse. Woman on top."

Ryan thought about what Emily had told him about Lizzy being scared of cameras and photographers.

Mind working, he watched the lights from a yacht winking in the darkness. "Any idea what happened to her?"

"The kid? That's a mystery. There was some talk of family, but I always thought Lana invented herself with some pixie dust and a fairy wand. No one has been able to find out details. There's probably a story there if anyone can be bothered to look."

Ryan thought about the child fast asleep just a couple of miles away.

"Doesn't sound like much of a story to me."

"Me neither, but that's because I prefer something more challenging than trapping first-graders. So, why all the questions? You're tired of lounging around with lobsters and want to come back to the bright lights of the city?"

"That won't be happening anytime soon."

"Are you bored with being a tycoon? You thinking of starting up a newspaper? *The Puffin Post?*" Larry laughed at his own joke. *"The Crab Chronicle."*

"You are hilarious."

"No, you're the one who is hilarious burying yourself in the freezing wastes of rural Maine when you could have been here at the sharp end. You don't have to travel if you've lost the taste for it. You could pick your job. That's what happens when you were the best of the best. Come back. Dust off that Pulitzer Prize. Return to the dark side."

"No." Ryan watched as the lights of a boat blinked in the bay. "Those days are over."

"They'll never be over. You're a born journalist. You can't help yourself. You smell blood and you hunt. So, is something going on there? Is that nose of yours on the scent of something?"

Ryan thought about Juliet Fox. About how much the media would love to get their hands on that juicy piece of information.

He thought about how Emily would react if she found

out what his career had been before he'd moved back to the island.

"No," he said slowly. "I don't have anything. I'm living in the freezing wastes of rural Maine, remember? Nothing ever happens here."

Five

Emily rose to sunshine and blue skies after another night where sleep had barely paid a visit. Switching on her phone, she found a voice mail from Skylar asking how she was.

Ryan Cooper's dark, handsome features swam into her vision. Last night her anxieties about being responsible for Lizzy had been punctuated by thoughts of the calm way he'd dealt with her mini meltdown.

Pushing those thoughts aside, she texted Skylar, doing okay, thanks. She knew better than to mention Ryan to her friend, an incurable romantic. She sent a similar message to Brittany, who had asked the same question in a text sent in the early hours, and then slid out of bed.

Lizzy was still asleep, so she took a quick shower in Kathleen's pretty bathroom. Afterward she secured her hair on top of her head and reached for another pair of black tailored pants that were the staple of her wardrobe.

Sooner or later she was going to have to do something about that. She didn't own clothes suitable for casual beach living.

It felt strange not to be living her life checking the time and syncing calendars.

In New York her working day would have started hours ago. If she'd been in the office she would have been at her desk by six in the morning. If seeing clients, she would probably have been thirty thousand feet up in the air flying between meetings. Her life had been a series of stays in faceless hotel rooms and endless work on projects that would never be remembered by anyone. There had been no time to stand still, and she realized that the furious pace of her life had stopped the past settling on her.

Neil had wanted her to slow down and invest in their relationship.

She'd had nothing to invest. Emotionally, she was bankrupt.

She took nothing and had nothing to give. Which was presumably why she had felt nothing when he'd ended it.

Wondering how her carefully ordered life could have spun so wildly out of control, she walked downstairs, brewed coffee and unlocked the door to the garden. She stood, breathing in the aroma of good coffee, absorbing the warmth. Here, the sound of the birds almost drowned out the sound of the sea.

It was a sun trap, sheltered from the whip of the wind and designed as a sanctuary for nature. Kathleen had planted carefully, perennials clustered together in a haze of purples, blues and yellows to attract the bees. Wildflowers, moss and fern grew between rocks, and butterflies danced across petals dappled by sunlight.

It was a perfect peaceful spot. There had been summers when she'd spent hours curled up on one of the chairs reading, lost in worlds that weren't her own.

"Aunt Emily?"

She turned to see Lizzy standing there, eyes sleepy, her hands holding tightly around the bear.

"Hi." Emily softened her voice. "You slept?"

"Can we go to the beach?"

The fleeting calm left her. "Not today." Sooner or later she was going to have to face that challenge, but not yet. Braced for an argument, she was relieved to hear the sound of a car. "That will be Ryan. He's bringing breakfast."

"Waffles?"

"Let's find out." She should probably have been pushing healthy food, but she told herself there was plenty of time for that. Reluctantly she left the tumbling tranquility of the coastal garden and walked to the front door.

Ryan stood there, one large hand holding several bags stuffed with groceries, the other holding the lead of a thoroughly overexcited dog, a spaniel with eager eyes and soft floppy ears. "Sit. *Sit!* Do not run into the house. Do not jump up—" He broke off as the dog sprang at Emily and planted his paws on her thighs. "Sorry. I think you can see who is in charge." He dumped the bags on the porch, reached out and hauled the excited dog away from her, but Emily dropped to her knees, unable to resist those hopeful eyes and wagging tail.

"You're gorgeous." She crooned, talked nonsense, smoothed satiny soft fur with her hand and was rewarded with more affection than she could ever remember receiving in her life before. When the dog planted its paws on her lap and tried to lick her face, she put her hands on all that scrabbling warmth and laughed. "He's yours?"

"It's a she and, no, not mine. A dog is a responsibility, and I'm not interested in anything that dictates the way I live my life." But his hand was gentle as he removed the wriggling animal from Emily's lap. "Calm down. She doesn't recognize either of those words, by the way. Her vocabulary is a work in progress. So far *food* is the only word she's sure about."

"Who does she belong to?"

"My grandmother. Unfortunately she had her hip done last winter and hasn't fully recovered her mobility, so walking Cocoa is now my job. I try and delegate, but we're busy at the Ocean Club today, so she had to come with me. I thought she could play in the garden while we have breakfast."

A week ago she'd had neither dog nor child in her life. Now she had both. "We're keeping you from your work."

"My staff will thank you. They have more fun when I'm not there."

Taking advantage of his lapse in concentration, the dog darted into the cottage, paws sliding on the floor, and cannoned into Lizzy who was standing in the hallway holding her bear.

Unsure how Lizzy felt around dogs, Emily reached her in two strides and scooped her up. "Her name is Cocoa and she won't hurt you." The child was rigid in her arms, and she wondered if lifting her had been a mistake. Should she have lifted Cocoa instead? She was about to lower her when she felt those skinny arms slide around her neck and tighten. Silken curls brushed against her cheek, and she felt warm breath brush against her neck as Lizzy burrowed into her shoulder in an achingly familiar gesture. Something woke and stirred deep inside her, and Emily closed her eyes.

Not now.

This wasn't the time to start remembering.

"Is she all right?" Ryan made a grab for the dog. "You are a bundle of trouble. My grandmother thought a dog would keep her youthful, but this animal has put ten years on me."

Dragging her mind back to the present, Emily lowered Lizzy gently, and dog and child stared at one another.

The dog whined and lay down on her belly at the little girl's feet.

Ryan's eyebrows lifted. "I guess we know who wields the power. Nice work, Lizzy. She likes you. From now on, you're in charge. Put your hand out and let her sniff you."

The dog stood up, tail wagging, and thrust her damp nose into the child's palm.

Lizzy smiled. The first smile Emily had seen since she'd picked her up at the airport along with a suitcase. One suitcase, but more baggage than one small person should have to carry alone.

Emily licked dry lips. Right now it was her own baggage that was troubling her.

Grateful for the distraction provided by the dog, she retrieved the bags Ryan had abandoned on the step and carried them through to the kitchen.

He followed her. "You didn't sleep."

"How do you know that?"

"Pale face. Dark circles. It's a dead giveaway. Don't worry, I have the perfect gift for you." He dipped his hand into one of the bags and pulled out two tall cups stamped with the swirling logo of the Ocean Club. "Iced cappuccino with an extra shot made by Kirsti's fair hand."

Emily reached for the cup gratefully. "I might love you."

He grinned. "Don't threaten me so early in the morning." He sprawled in the nearest chair, coffee in his hand, the bags abandoned on the table. "So, you were awake all night wondering how many people saw that newspaper."

"Not just that. I'm used to city noises. I can't sleep here." She hadn't slept a full night since the phone call that had given her a child she wasn't qualified to raise.

"Most people find the sound of the sea soothing."

She wasn't most people. "What else is in the bags? Please, tell me it's a month's supply of iced cappuccino."

"Better. You said you didn't have time to stock up, so I thought I'd help. Here—" he pushed a bag toward her "—start with that one." He glanced over his shoulder as Lizzy came into the room with Cocoa. "What's your favorite color, Lizzy?"

"Pink."

"Then this is your lucky day." He pulled something pink from another bag and handed it to her. "It's a hat. I thought when you were out in town, you might like to wear it." His gaze flickered to Emily. "To keep the sun out of your eyes."

And prying eyes away from her face, Emily thought, as she loaded the fridge and cupboards. Smart thinking. She wished she'd thought of it herself.

"What would you have done if she'd said blue was her favorite color?"

Ryan dipped his hand back in the bag and produced a blue one.

Lizzy clutched the pink one possessively. "I like this one. What do the words say?"

"Do you recognize any of the letters?"

"The writing is curly." Lizzy stared hard and spelled out a few letters. "It says something *Cl-ub*."

"Ocean. It says Ocean Club." Ryan traced the words with his finger. "It's a very special hat. Only people who have eaten waffles on the terrace can have one."

Emily was touched. "Thank you. That was thoughtful."

His gaze connected briefly with hers, and she felt that same ripple of awareness she'd felt on the first day. For a moment she stood, mesmerized by the unapologetic interest in those dark eyes. She had no idea how to respond. Her relationship with Neil had been comfortable, her emotions and feelings around him safely predictable. He'd never threatened her heart rate or her equilibrium. Ryan threatened both, and he knew it.

He turned his attention back to Lizzy. "Keep the brim pulled low, and it will keep the sun off her face. Not that I think there's much risk of exposure."

Emily understood that the "exposure" he referred to wasn't solar driven.

Lizzy tugged it onto her head. "I like it."

"Do you know Cocoa's favorite game?" He dipped his hand into another bag and pulled out a ball. "Fetch. Take her into the garden and throw the ball. She'll bring it back to you."

Child, ball and dog tumbled into the garden to play while Emily stared dizzily at the image of her new life.

A month earlier she'd been living in Manhattan. Jobless, admittedly, but with plans and ambitions. At least two companies had made positive noises about employing her. When she'd thought about the future, it hadn't looked like this.

It was like booking a flight to Europe and finding yourself in the middle of the African desert, unprepared and unequipped.

"I didn't know she couldn't read fluently. I don't even know what age most children start to read."

"It varies. Rachel was reading by four. Others take longer, but as long as they get there in the end, I don't see why it matters."

"You know a lot about children." And she hadn't expected that. He seemed like the type of man who saw children as nothing more than an inconvenient by-product of sex. And then something occurred to her, something that made her stomach lurch. "Are you divorced? Married?"

"You think I left my wife in bed to come here and eat breakfast with you? You have a low expectation of relationships, Emily. And I'm not married." He looked at her in a way that made her heart beat faster and her insides melt, but what really worried her was the sudden and unexpected lift of her mood that came from the knowledge he was single.

Why should she care that he was single?

Her life was already complicated enough, and when she eventually got around to thinking about relationships again, it wouldn't be with a man like him.

"You're comfortable with young children. The sort of comfortable that usually comes from having them."

"So now you're asking if I spent my wild youth populating Maine?"

He was attractive and charming. She had little trouble believing he'd had a wild youth.

She watched as he unpacked the last of the bags. She was aware of every tiny detail of him, from the flex of shoulder muscle to the scar visible on the bronzed skin above his collarbone.

Feeling her scrutiny, he turned his head, and his gaze met hers. Slowly, he put the bag down, as if he could no longer remember why he was holding it.

Heat rushed through her, infusing her cheeks with livid color.

Oh, God, she was having sex thoughts about a man she barely even knew.

She felt as if she'd been caught watching porn.

"Did you ask me a question?" His voice was roughened, his eyes fixed on hers, and she knew he'd forgotten the conversation.

She'd forgotten it, too. "Sex. I mean, populating Maine," she stammered. "Children, yes, that was it. Children."

His gaze held hers steadily. "Children have never been on my wish list."

"So you don't have experience?"

"I have tons of experience."

"Nieces? Nephews?"

"Siblings. Three of them. All younger." He reached for the bottle of maple syrup he'd brought with him. "I was thirteen when my parents were killed. The twins, Sam and Helen, were nine, and Rachel was four. It was a typical Maine winter. Snow, ice and no power. They collided with a tree. It was all over before anyone could get to them." He spoke in a modulated tone that revealed all of the facts and none of the feelings.

She didn't know what she'd expected to hear, but it hadn't been that.

The story saddened her on so many levels. It proved that even happy families weren't immune to tragedy.

"I'm sorry."

"My grandmother moved in and took over parenting, but three kids were a challenge, and her health has never been good."

"Four." Emily put down the loaf of bread she'd unpacked. "You were a child, too."

"I left childhood behind the day my parents were killed." His face was expressionless. "I remember the police coming to the door and the look on my grandmother's face when she told me what had happened. The others were asleep, and we decided not to wake them. It was the worst night of my life."

She knew exactly how he would have felt because she'd felt it, too, that brutal loss of someone who was part of you. Like ripping away flesh and muscle down to the bone, the wound going so deep it never really healed. Eventually it closed over the surface, leaving bruises and scars invisible to the naked eye.

"How did you cope?"

"I don't know if you'd describe it as coping. I just got up every day and did what needed to be done. I helped get them up in the morning before I went to school and came home at lunchtime to give my grandmother some respite. Bedtime was fun. The twins slept in bed with my grandmother for months, which left me with Rachel. She clung to me like a monkey for the first two years after our parents were killed. In the end I dragged her bed into my room because I was getting no sleep, and my grades were dropping."

She studied those broad shoulders, her mind trying to construct the boy he was then from the man he was now. She imagined him cradling his little sister while struggling with his own loss. "Lizzy has been sleeping in the bed with me."

His glance flickered to hers. "Yeah, she probably feels safer that way. She's afraid you might disappear, too."

Emily didn't say that she felt like a fraud. Unworthy of the trust Lizzy had placed in her.

"But you had three siblings—so much for you to manage."

"We weren't on our own with it. The islanders pulled together. We didn't cook a meal for the first year. They set up a rotation, and every day something would appear. Things got easier once Rachel started school and the twins were teenagers. Thanks to our background, they were pretty independent, and there was always someone to turn to if they had problems."

He'd had a web of support. He'd suffered, but he hadn't been alone.

Her first experience of loss had been suffered alone.

Disturbed by her own feelings, she took her cappuccino to the French doors that opened from the kitchen on to the pretty garden. Lizzy was chasing around the grass with the dog.

Not in a million years would she have thought to give Lizzy a pet. The grief counselor had advised her not to make any changes, to allow Lizzy time to adjust, but watching child and dog rolling around the garden simply proved there were no rules for handling grief. You did whatever helped you get through another day.

She turned and looked at Ryan. "Where are they now? Your siblings?"

"Rachel is a teacher at Puffin Elementary. She loves island life. Loves the water and loves kids. In the summer she works at Camp Puffin on the south of the island. She teaches kayaking. Sam is a doctor in Boston, and Helen works as a translator for the United Nations in New York. They turned out okay, considering all the mistakes I made." He said it with humor, but everything he told her somehow served to underpin her own sense of inadequacy.

"Did you read a lot of parenting books?"

"None. I relied on intuition and, as a result, screwed up repeatedly."

And yet it had been intuition that had driven him to return the bear and bring the dog for a visit, something she was sure would never have occurred to her. There had never been a place for animals in her life.

"Did you ever think you couldn't do it?" The words tumbled out, revealing more than she'd intended to reveal, and Ryan gave her a long, steady look.

"Is this about me or you?"

Her hand shook on the cup, and she put it on the nearest countertop. "Did you ever worry that you wouldn't be able to keep them safe?"

"Safe from what?"

"Everything." Her mouth felt as if she'd run a marathon through the desert. "There are dangers everywhere."

"I made plenty of mistakes, if that's what you're asking. Fortunately, kids are resilient. They survived the culinary disasters, the laundry mistakes, the fact I couldn't sew and didn't have a clue about child development. Rachel followed me everywhere. I think she was afraid I might disappear like our parents."

She tried to imagine it. The teenage boy and the little girl. "It must have been a wrench when you left to go to college."

"Are you kidding?" He gave a short laugh. "After spending my teenage years with three kids crawling all over me, I was so desperate to escape this place I would have swum to the mainland if that was the only way to leave the island. By then I had my bedroom back, but I was looking forward to a night that didn't start with reading *Green Eggs and Ham*."

"You didn't miss them?"

It was a moment before he answered. "I loved them, but, no, I didn't miss them. I badly needed to get away and have a life that didn't include school plays and parent-teacher conferences. My grandmother had help from the other women in her group and several of the islanders. In a way, they were an extended family. They had rotations for babysitting, collecting from school. When there were school events, Rachel had all of them in the front row."

It made her smile. "This was the same group who were meeting for book club the other night?"

"Yeah. And Kathleen, of course."

"You had a great deal of responsibility at a young age. That's why you're not married?"

He laughed. "Let's just say I value my independence. The ability to come and go as I please. I don't plan on giving that up anytime soon."

Emily picked up her coffee, pulled out one of the pretty blue kitchen chairs and sat down. Through the open door she could see Lizzy throwing the ball over and over again while the dog bounded after it, tail wagging. "The first time I met Kathleen, I couldn't believe she was real. I'd never met anyone like her. She was so kind and genuine and interested. She never expected anyone to conform. She truly valued individuality."

"Yes. She was a special woman with a gift for reading people."

"I barely spoke on my first visit." Emily took a sip of coffee. "I was overwhelmed by everything. The exchange of ideas. Laughter. It was alien to me because my home life was nothing like that."

If he was wondering how her home life was, he kept the questions to himself. "You came often?"

"Every summer. I had nowhere else to go, and Skylar would do just about anything to avoid going home, so Brittany invited us here."

"It wasn't enough to be together at college?"

Emily finished her coffee and put the cup down. "When Brittany invited me into her room on that first day, I wondered how on earth I'd survive living next to someone as volatile as her. Skylar arrived a couple of minutes later, dropped off by the family chauffeur rather than her parents because they thought she was throwing away her life studying art when she could have been a lawyer. I took one look at her clothes and assumed we'd have nothing in common. I admired her dress, trying to be polite, and she told me she'd made it herself for less than ten dollars. Then Brittany took a call from her lawyer about her divorce while we sat open-mouthed. I assume you know all about that as you're friends?"

He didn't look at her. "Yeah, I know."

"She was a mess, but in a way it broke the ice. Right

from the start there were no barriers. We talked until we couldn't keep our eyes open. At the beginning, all we had in common was that we'd been let down by the people closest to us. Maybe it was a sense of isolation that brought us together. I don't know, but we understood each other. Our friendship grew from there."

"I can't believe our visits didn't overlap."

"Maybe we didn't notice each other." Her heart thudded uncomfortably as his gaze locked on hers.

"I would have noticed you."

"Ryan—"

"I would have noticed you." His voice was soft, his eyes fixed on her face with such unwavering attention that she felt something uncurl deep inside her.

Most people looked at another person and saw the surface. Ryan ignored the surface and looked deeper, as if he'd learned that the face someone presented to the world had no more substance than a picture.

He hadn't touched her, and yet her skin tingled and her body heated.

The tense, delicious silence was broken by Lizzy, who came back into the kitchen, the dog at her ankles. "Can she stay with us?"

With visible effort Ryan transferred his gaze from Emily to the child.

"I have to take her back to my grandmother, but I'll bring her to see you again soon." He leaned forward and picked up the final bag. "I've brought you some things to keep you busy." He pulled out a bucket and spade in bright sparkly pink. "You are living next to one of the best beaches on the island. You're going to want to make the most of that."

And just like that, the mood was shattered.

Emily stared at the bucket, numb, while Lizzy reached for it.

"Emily doesn't like the beach."

Pulling herself together, Emily stood up. "We've been busy, that's all. Maybe in a few days."

"I could go by myself."

"No. You mustn't go near the water." The words came out in a rush and she saw Ryan's eyes narrow. "I… We… Let's take a few more days to settle in and then we'll see. The bucket is a thoughtful gift, Ryan. And the hat was a great idea."

What wasn't a great idea was a trip to the beach.

She knew she wasn't ready for that.

She wasn't sure she ever would be.

Skylar arrived late Friday afternoon, bringing an explosion of color and city sophistication to their peaceful existence. "I've brought provisions." She winked at Emily, delved into the bag and pulled out a parcel that she handed to the child.

Lizzy looked at her, dazzled by the halo of golden hair and the bright smile. Skylar wore a cluster of silver bangles on her wrists, and they clinked together as she moved her arms. Lizzy lasted five minutes before climbing onto a chair to take a closer look.

"They're shiny."

"They're silver. Want to try one on?" Sky slid one off her arm. "I made them."

Lizzy was wide-eyed with awe. "How?"

"It's what I do. I make jewelry." She made it sound like a fun hobby, but Emily knew Skylar was starting to make ripples, not just in the jewelry world but also with her glass. She'd recently had a small exhibition in

New York, showing not only glass and jewelry, but also ceramics and some of her artwork.

Lizzy fingered the bracelets. "Could I make them?"

"Yes. Not silver, but there are other types of jewelry that are just as pretty. We'll make something tomorrow. The first stage is always design. Do you have paper and coloring pens?"

Lizzy shook her head and Sky smiled. "Look in the white bag. There are glitter pens underneath the fairy wings and tiara."

Emily rolled her eyes. "Why not a cowboy outfit?"

"Wanting to be a fairy princess is a perfectly reasonable ambition when you're six." Skylar thrust a bulging bag toward her. "This is for you."

"You bought me fairy wings and a tiara?"

"I bought you the adult equivalent. Something suitable for a summer at the beach, so you don't have to walk around looking as if you're taking a lunch break from running a prison. You're welcome." Sky leaned forward and hugged her tightly. "Stop wearing black and undo a few buttons. Let the sunshine in. If you won't do it for me, do it for your health. Maine has over forty-five identified species of mosquitoes, and black just happens to be their favorite color. Right now you are an insect banquet."

Later, much later, after a supper of pizza and ice cream followed by a girlie movie marathon, they waited for Lizzy to fall asleep and then curled up on Kathleen's sofas and shared a bottle of wine.

"I'd give anything for a slice of Kathleen's apple-topped ginger cake." Skylar stretched her arms in a long, languid movement that reminded Emily of a contented cat. "With maple cream."

"It would cost you around a week pounding on the treadmill."

"It would be worth every stride and every bead of sweat."

"I don't know how you can keep such terrible eating habits and stay so slim."

"It's nervous energy. So, how has it been?" Settling into the sofa, Sky curled her legs under her, her waterfall of white-blond hair flowing over her shoulder. "I didn't see anyone with cameras when I arrived."

"No. I'm starting to think I overreacted. If they're looking, they're not looking here. Ryan thinks they'll be bored with it soon."

"Ryan? You met a man?" Skylar looked interested. "Tell me more."

"He's a local businessman. He owns the Ocean Club. Friend of Brittany's."

"Friend? Friend, as in someone she knows, or someone she's had sex with?"

"I haven't asked." And she wasn't sure she wanted to know the answer.

"That's the difference between us. It would have been my first question. Let's ask her, although I'm pretty sure she would have told us if there was something to tell." Sky reached for her phone. "Is he sexy?" She tapped at the keys and pressed Send.

Emily thought about the hard planes of his handsome face and the power of that body. *Oh, yes.* "Why is that relevant?"

"Because you need some light relief after Neil. You'll have lines on your forehead before your time, and no man should ever do that to a woman." Putting her phone down, Skylar leaned forward and topped up her wine-glass. "Do you trust him?"

"Ryan? Yes." It surprised her to discover that she did. "Tell me about you. How is Richard?"

"Busy. Running for senate means he isn't home much. He wants me to give up my business and travel around the state with him. He says he needs my support." She talked quickly and Emily listened, dismissing the nagging voice in her head that told her Skylar wasn't suited to that life.

Who was she to give advice?

What did she know about long-term, functioning relationships?

"Do you want to give up your business?"

"No. I love what I'm doing and it's going well. A new store in Brooklyn has just agreed to stock my jewelry, and a gallery in London is hosting an exhibition for my new collection *Ocean Blue*, so I'm crazy busy getting ready for that."

"You have an exhibition in London? Skylar, that's wonderful!" Emily reached across and hugged her friend. "I'm so proud of you. Wow. Richard must be proud, too. And your parents? Surely now they can see this is right for you."

Skylar took another gulp of wine. "My choice of career is something my parents don't mention. And Richard doesn't want me to go to London."

"He doesn't—" Emily was thrown. "But this is *huge*. Why wouldn't he want you to go? He should be so proud of you."

"The timing is bad. If he wins in November, he'll want me by his side for all the Christmas functions." Skylar put her glass down, her eyes miserable. "And I hate the way things are right now, Em. I bump into my parents and it's as if we're strangers. The only thing I've ever done right in their eyes is date Richard Everson. They want me to go home to Long Island for the holidays."

"You said you weren't putting yourself through that again."

"I know what I said. They want me to bring Richard. And he wants to go, of course, because he needs my father's support. So I'm facing a miserable Christmas with my parents, being held up as an example of a daughter who wasted her life. My younger brother passed the bar exam by the way, so I'm now officially the only non-lawyer in the family." The smile stayed on her face, but her voice was thickened. "Whatever happened to the fairy-tale Christmas we used to dream about, Em? What happened to ice-skating, roasting chestnuts and family fun? Christmas in my house is about as much fun as a day in the Supreme Court."

"You can't give up your exhibition, Sky. They should be excited for you! They should—on second thought, don't get me started on that one." Emily flopped back against the sofa. "Can you believe this? On the outside you have the perfect family, but you're no better off than I am."

"I know. My friendship with you and Brit has been stronger than anything I've had with my family." Sky stared down into her glass. "The other reason I don't want to go home for the holidays is that I'm afraid Richard is going to make some dramatic gesture."

"Like what?"

"I don't know. He's hinting at marriage again. He thinks it will help his image."

Emily almost spilled her wine. "He wants to marry you because he thinks it will garner him public approval? What about what you want? And, more to the point, what about love?"

"I asked that exact same question."

"And?"

Skylar took a mouthful of wine. "He told me not to be ridiculous. Said that of course he loves me. That goes without saying."

"Love should never go without saying." Emily felt a flicker of unease. "You did tell him how you feel about marriage?"

"Of course. I've always been honest about it. He knows it isn't what I want. For me a relationship should be held together by strong emotions, not a piece of paper." Some of the sparkle in her eyes dimmed. "Do you think I'm too romantic?"

"For believing in love? No, but that isn't what matters. What matters is finding a man who understands and respects your views, whatever they are." And she was fairly sure Richard wasn't that person. Emily found his charm superficial and manipulative rather than genuine. She would never have put him with someone as creative and sensitive as Sky. It was like sending an armored tank to catch a butterfly. "Relationships are hard. Finding someone who wants the same things as you is rare. Finding someone who understands you, even rarer."

"Are you about to tell me you had that with Neil? Because I won't believe you."

What had she had with Neil? She wasn't sure she could put a name to it. "It was an easy relationship."

"Is easy another word for boring?"

"Maybe. It was safe. I was with him for three years and not once did I ever feel confused about my feelings." She'd known Ryan two days, and her feelings had been all over the place.

"It was your lucky day when he dumped you. The only thing I don't understand is why you didn't dump him first. You deserve so much better. All you need to do now is throw out everything black in your wardrobe."

"I like black."

"It makes you fade into the background."

"That's exactly where I want my body to be. In the background. You have no idea how many men have had conversations with my chest."

"And I bet you managed to get them to look into your eyes two seconds after you opened your mouth. You're bright and witty, Emily. Your body is your body. It's the only one you have, and you shouldn't feel you need to hide it."

"You don't understand. Even Neil agreed that my breasts, if not exactly my worst feature, were unfortunate."

"He said that? I'm glad you told me because now if I ever get the chance to kill him, I'm going to make sure it's a slow death. Why do you think he said that, Em? Because underneath the surface he was a jealous creep, and he didn't want other men looking at you."

Emily tried to picture Neil jealous. "I want people to take me seriously."

"I understand. Look at this blond hair—" Skylar lifted a handful of pale silk "—do you think people don't prejudice me? Of course they do, but I don't care. I love my hair, and if they want to take it as a sign that my brain is minuscule, then it will give me all the more pleasure to prove them wrong. This isn't about the way you relate to men. It's to do with your mother."

Emily examined her nails. "Maybe."

"Not maybe. She used her body because she had a pathological need for attention and didn't know any other way to get it. You're nothing like her."

"Sometimes when I look in the mirror, I see similarities."

"Change your mirror. I am going to take a pair of scissors to your clothes. It's time you stopped hiding. You deserve a grand passion, and your breasts deserve to have a life outside the rigid confines of corsetry."

Emily stared wistfully into her wineglass. "I've never had a grand passion. I've never felt that strongly about anyone. I'm not sure I want to."

"That's because you associate passion with the sleazy encounters your mother had. But that wasn't passion. That was opportunistic sex."

Emily thought about the constant parade of men when she was growing up. The cramped apartment had been busier than Times Square in July. The walls had been paper thin, the lack of air-conditioning adding to the oppressive atmosphere of the place. She was fairly sure her mother hadn't been a passion addict, just an attention addict. "Lana inherited some of her traits. She had that same desperate need to be the focus of attention."

She'd worked hard to be the opposite, but in doing so she'd put a label on passion as something to avoid, which had proven to be easy enough until now.

She thought about Ryan and the way he made her feel. Of the sexual awareness simmering beneath the surface of every interaction. "Do you see a future with Richard?"

Skylar lay back on the sofa. "He has many qualities that I admire. He knows what he wants and he's determined to do what he has to do to get there."

"And he wants you." She didn't voice her uneasy suspicion that Richard saw Skylar as an acquisition, a tool to enhance his political appeal.

"Yes, but there's no escaping the fact that we're different. He has a five-year plan. I have a five-minute plan."

"I love that about you."

Sky finished her wine and put her glass down. "How is it going with Lizzy?"

"It's tough. I feel like I want to tie her to me so that nothing bad can happen." Emily toyed with her glass. "I don't trust my ability to keep her safe. I don't have the skills for this."

"Yes, you do, but you're scared." Sky took her hand. "It's understandable after what happened. You're an intelligent woman, you should understand that."

"What I know intellectually doesn't change how I feel emotionally." She stared down at Skylar's slender fingers, relieved to be able to talk about it. "When I got that phone call, I thought Puffin Island was the perfect place to bring Lizzy. Secluded, miles away from her home, but I didn't think about the other things."

"You mean the sea?"

"Yes. I couldn't have brought her to a worse place. All my phobias are concentrated in this one small island."

"You love this island. We spent every summer here when we were in college."

"That was different. I didn't have a child to care for. I could think about myself. I helped Kathleen in the garden, I walked up through the woods, I spent time in the kitchen with her learning to bake—"

"So, you can still do those things." Skylar put her glass down. "You don't have to go to the beach, Em."

"It's right outside the door and she keeps asking." She took a deep breath. "And I feel like a coward."

"You're not a coward. You had a terrible experience. And you've only been back on the island for a week. Give yourself time. There's no shortage of things to do here. We just need to get her interested in things that don't involve the sea." Skylar suppressed a yawn. "I haven't been to the harbor for ages. We'll do that tomorrow. We'll eat ice cream and you can take me to the Ocean Club. I want to try the chocolate milk Lizzy keeps talking about. And I want to meet Ryan."

Ryan was seated at a table by the water talking to Alec when Kirsti strolled over to them.

"She's back. I told you she was The One. She can't stay away from you. And she brought a hot blonde for Alec."

Alec didn't lift his gaze from the book he'd been reading before Ryan had joined him. "I'm allergic to hot blondes."

Ryan glanced over to the doorway, saw Emily and Lizzy and, behind them, another woman he assumed to be Skylar.

She was tall, her almost ethereal beauty emphasized by the dress she wore. A mixture of green and blue, it floated round her slim frame as she walked.

"She looks like a mermaid," Kirsti muttered. "Alec, you are going to want to look at this."

"In Greek mythology mermaids summon men to their doom."

"You read too much. You need to watch more TV and play some video games. Rot your brain a bit like normal folk."

Ryan's gaze was fixed on Emily. It had been two days since he'd seen her, and he'd had to force himself to stay away and give her space. He saw her smile at something her friend said and felt something clench in his gut. There, right there, was the real Emily. He wanted to capture that smile and follow it to see where it led, but it vanished quickly, and she was watching the child again, as if she were afraid she might blow away in the breeze. He understood that the responsibility was new to her, but he sensed there was more to her overly protective attitude than the unfamiliarity of unplanned parenthood. "Give them the same table as last time."

"It's reserved for the couple sailing that racing sloop. There will be pistols at dawn."

"I'll handle them. Give it to Emily."

"You're the boss." With a shrug Kirsti moved away to welcome her new customers.

Convenience should have made Emily take the seat with the best view of the water, but instead she switched with her friend so that she once again sat with her back to it.

Pondering the possible reasons for that, Ryan tried to focus on the conversation with Alec. "So, you're planning to see Selina while you're in London?"

Alec wrapped his hand around the beer. "Yes, but that's one encounter that will be as brief as possible."

"I don't understand how the two of you ever got together."

"Never underestimate the mind-distorting power of great sex." Alec stared broodingly over the ocean. "Before me, she dated bankers and mega-rich city types. She wanted adventure and thought I was a sea-loving version of Indiana Jones. I took her kayaking on our honeymoon."

Ryan raised his eyebrows. "White water kayaking?"

"No, just plain old sea kayaking. Her hair got wet. Let's talk about something else."

"I've got a better idea." Ryan stood up. "Put your book away. We're moving tables. You're going to talk to a live human instead of reading about dead ones."

"Dead ones are more interesting, and they don't bleed you dry. And I am not moving tables. I like this table. It seats two people which means no one can join us."

"I own this place," Ryan murmured. "If you don't move, I'll physically eject you."

With a sigh, Alec looked up. "Are you meddling with my sex life? Because I have enough of that from Kirsti."

"No. I'm meddling with my own, and you're my wingman."

"I'm not a good wingman."

"You're the perfect wingman. You're so bitter and twisted, you make me look good. Stand up. We're going to join them for lunch."

Alec's gaze flickered to Skylar, and just for a moment he stared. "Women like her don't eat lunch. They order it, make you pay and then push it round their plates."

"Every time you think like that, you're letting your ex-wife win."

"She has won. She has a large chunk of my income and my house in London."

"You have plenty of income left, you can stay in a hotel when you travel to London and you have your freedom. Seems like a good deal to me." Ryan gave him a slap on the shoulder and strolled across to the group on the other side of the terrace. Lizzy sat, swinging her legs, and she reminded him so much of Rachel at the same age, he smiled. "Cute hat."

Her face brightened. "Ryan! Can I play with Cocoa?"

"And there I was thinking you were pleased to see me, but it's all about the dog." He winked at her. "She's with my grandmother, but you can visit anytime. They live in the big white house with the wraparound deck just up from the harbor. If you wanted to walk Cocoa, you'd be her favorite person."

Lizzy instantly turned to Emily. "Can we?"

"Sure." Her gaze flickered to his, and he saw color warm her cheeks in the moment before she turned to introduce her friend. "This is Skylar."

He was tempted to ask Skylar if she'd babysit while he took Emily for a long walk along the beach followed by sunset-watching from the king-size bed in his apartment, but instead he reached across and extended his hand.

"I've heard about you from my grandmother." He took the chair next to Emily, leaving Alec no choice but to sit next to Skylar. "This is Alec Hunter. You have to excuse him. He's half British, but their weather isn't bad enough for him, so he spends most of his time here with us in Maine. He's a historian."

Alec's greeting was little more than a curt nod, and

Skylar's gaze flickered to Alec's rough, handsome features and lingered for a moment before returning to Ryan.

"What was your grandmother's name?"

"Agnes Cooper. You gave her friends a jewelry class once."

"I did. I remember her well. She was wonderful." A smile spread across her face, and Ryan saw warmth and humanity beneath the surface beauty.

"She'd love to see you again."

"We should call on her. Em, do you remember her?"

Next to him, Emily stirred. "I wasn't there."

"You must have been." Skylar frowned. "We made necklaces. Brittany helped. Why wouldn't you have been there? We spent the morning on the beach searching for sea glass and then—" She broke off and sent an agonized look of apology toward her friend. "I remember now. You stayed in the cottage. You had a headache."

It was obvious to Ryan it hadn't been a headache that had kept Emily in the cottage, but Skylar's protectiveness made it clear the subject was not up for further discussion.

Emily sat still, but Ryan could feel the tension emanating from her. Her hand rested close to his on the table, and he wanted to slide his fingers over hers and demand that she tell him what was wrong so he could fix it. He wanted to know everything about her. He wanted to know why she'd stayed in the cottage all those years before and not joined her friends on their expedition through the tide pools. He wanted to know why she'd spent three years of her life with a guy who clearly didn't appreciate her and why she'd filled every hour of her day with a job when there were so many more appealing ways of living. And he wanted to rip all the concealing black from her body and explore every inch of her until there wasn't a single part of her he didn't know.

He shifted, distracted by the brutal power of arousal.

And then he saw Lizzy, her hands clasped around a glass, her tumbling hair tucked under the pink baseball cap, and remembered the reason he couldn't follow up on his impulses.

Instead of taking Emily's hand, he picked up his beer, relieved when Kirsti came over to take their order.

Kirsti chatted to Emily, admired Lizzy's hat and tried to draw Alec into conversation with Skylar, an endeavor that earned her a black look.

Skylar ignored it and glanced at the menu. "So what do you recommend?"

Kirsti looked thoughtful. "Depends. Are you hungry?"

"Starving."

Ryan saw the faint gleam of cynical disbelief light Alec's eyes. He'd never met Alec's ex-wife, but the few reports he'd read in the press had given him the impression of a woman for whom the phrase *high maintenance* had probably been invented.

Kirsti leaned forward and pointed. "The clams are good, but my favorite are the homemade crab cakes with dipping sauce. We serve that with French fries and coleslaw but you can switch the fries for a salad if you prefer."

"No way!" Skylar looked horrified. "Fries, please. Lizzy? What do you like?"

"Try the chicken fingers," Kirsti advised. "They are the *best*."

While they waited for the food to arrive, Skylar did most of the talking, her vibrant energy flowing over the group, filling awkward silences, while Lizzy sat watching, her eyes fixed to the gleaming silver bangles that jangled on Skylar's slender arms.

Ryan noticed Lizzy was wearing one, too. It was too big, so she held it with her other hand, as if it were something precious she was determined not to lose.

Emily sat quietly; her eyes were trained on the restaurant, and every time someone new walked through the door she fixed them with her gaze, apparently assessing the threat level. He knew it was no coincidence that she'd given Lizzy the chair facing the water so that her back was to the other diners.

Whatever her feelings about her situation, it was obvious that she took the responsibility seriously.

He suspected she took everything seriously.

He glanced at her profile, taking in the fine bones of her face and the smooth caramel silk of her hair. At first glance it was impossible to believe she was related in any way to Lana Fox. Lana had been fully aware of her assets and prepared to put each and every one on public display in order to guarantee herself a place in the limelight. By contrast, Emily's was a quiet beauty, understated, her discreet manner the very antithesis of her half sister's apparent thirst for attention. From what he'd read, Lana had been addicted to a life of high drama. It seemed to him that Emily had done everything she could to remove drama from her life.

How must it feel for someone who avoided drama like that to assume responsibility for a child she'd never even met?

At least he'd had a close relationship with his siblings. Whatever his feelings on the situation, they'd stuck together as a family.

What Emily had described sounded less like a family and more like a disconnected group of individuals living at the same address.

Kirsti brought lunch, plates heaped high with crab cakes, bowls heaped high with crisp, golden fries.

Fitting five of them around a table intended for four was a squash, and Ryan's knee brushed against Emily's as they shifted to accommodate people and food.

He reached for the salt at the same time as she did, and their fingers tangled.

"Sorry." He murmured the word and disengaged his fingers from hers, but not before several volts of sexual electricity had traveled from her fingers to his.

The salt ended up on the floor.

Across the table, he met Sky's curious gaze.

"So, Ryan—" she sliced into the crab cake on her plate "—what do you do when you're not running this place?"

"I spend time on the water. Isn't that the point of living in Maine?"

Alec finally looked at Skylar. "Where do you live?"

"Manhattan."

Alec's face was blank of expression. "Of course you do."

"Wow." Skylar sat back in her chair and looked at him with a mixture of fascination and indignation. "Do you stereotype everyone you meet?"

Ryan retrieved the salt and handed it to Alec. "He does. You have to forgive him. He's lost his social skills since moving to a remote island. His research means he spends most of his time in the past. I have to force him to interact with live people occasionally."

"Research?"

"The good doctor is writing a naval history. He's much in demand around the world as a lecturer and TV presenter, although I've never understood why the public would want to look at anything that ugly." As expected, Alec didn't rise, but Skylar looked interested.

"Doctor?"

"PhD, so don't show him your war wounds. He only likes blood in the context of history."

Alec put down his fork. "Last time I looked, I was actually sitting here at the table with you. You could include me in the conversation."

"I could, but I'm worried you might lower the mood." Marriage wasn't something Ryan gave much thought to, but spending time with Alec had convinced him that it was better to be single than married to the wrong person. By all accounts his short relationship had more in common with cage fighting than romance.

Skylar pushed her bowl of fries toward Alec. "Help yourself."

"You can't finish them?" Alec threw Ryan a brief "I told you so" look that Skylar intercepted.

"Of course I can finish them, but you look cross, and I'm wondering if your bad mood is because you're hungry. I'm evil when I'm hungry."

Alec tightened his mouth. "I'm not in a bad mood."

Ryan stole one of Skylar's fries. "You should eat your food, Alec. It's good advice."

"If you don't want them, then I'll eat them." Sky pulled the bowl back and ate as if it were her last meal. "These are delicious. How do you make them?"

Ryan thought about the oil. "You probably don't want to know."

"If I didn't want to know I wouldn't have asked."

"They're double fried. It makes the outside extra crispy."

"Full of calories," Alec said pointedly, and Ryan saw Skylar smile.

"That explains why they're so good. You haven't eaten yours. You should. They're incredible."

Alec finally looked properly at Skylar. His gaze traveled from the top of her shiny, glossy hair, down her slender frame and lingered on her fingers, still dipping into her bowl of fries.

She licked her fingers, not provocatively but unselfconsciously, and Ryan felt Alec tense beside him.

"I don't stereotype people. I'm a good judge of character."

"You think you can judge character on external appearance?" Skylar reached for a napkin, her blue eyes cool and her voice low. "Personally I find it dangerous to make assumptions until you've spent time with a person. Take you, for example. If I went on appearances, I'd say you were rude, but you're best friends with Ryan, who is charming, so I'm guessing there's more to you than bad manners. I'm guessing you were hurt in the past, and now you're doing that thing of assuming all women are like the woman who hurt you. That's a way of making sure you live life alone."

A muscle flickered in Alec's jaw. "I'm working on it."

Ryan knew that in Alec's case, the wounds were just too raw for him to be able to see a time when Selina would be nothing more than a mistake in his past.

Alec and Skylar stared at each other, gazes locked in silent battle, and Emily cleared her throat.

"So, you're a maritime historian?"

"He's also a marine archaeologist," Ryan said, "which means we can push him under the water any time we've had enough of him on dry land. Which might be soon, Al."

"Archaeologist?" Emily poured herself a glass of water. "Do you know Brittany?"

Dragging his gaze from Skylar, Alec gave a brief nod. "Yes."

"Don't ever get them together," Ryan advised. "I remember a tedious evening when the two of them talked about nothing but the seafaring history of ancient Minoans. I wanted to drown myself."

Alec pushed his plate away, leaving most of his food untouched. "Is she coming back this summer or is she spending the whole time in Crete?"

"How do you know she's in Crete?"

"We exchange emails. And I read her blog. Her expertise is Bronze Age weaponry, and there was talk of an exciting find at one of the excavation sites." Alec frowned. "Daggers? Arrowheads?"

Skylar finished her fries. "I've always said that Brittany is the original Lara Croft."

"Does that mean she wears those cute tiny shorts when she's digging?" Ryan leaned forward and stole one of Alec's fries. "I always thought archaeology was boring, but maybe not. I still haven't forgiven her for shooting me in the butt, though, when I was running along the coast path. She'd spent the summer making Cretan arrowheads in Kathleen's garden and decided to test one as I passed."

"Wait a minute—" Emily put her fork down and focused on Alec. "I recognize you, now. You're the Shipwreck Hunter. You made a documentary on the shipwrecks of Maine, and you kayaked the Colorado River with a geologist. I can't remember what it was called. *Adventures through Time* or something. Did you see it, Sky?"

Ryan smiled. "That's the one that got him one hundred thousand female followers on Twitter. Or was that the one when you kayaked a section of the Amazon with your shirt off?"

Alec didn't smile, but fortunately Kirsti chose that moment to arrive, clearing plates and offering dessert menus, with a recommendation of warm blueberry pie.

"Did you say blueberry pie?" Skylar sighed wistfully. "Kathleen made the *best* blueberry pie."

"In that case, you should order it, because it's her recipe." Kirsti caught a napkin before it could blow away in the breeze, and the same breeze picked up a strand of Skylar's hair and blew it into Alec's face.

It wrapped itself around him like a golden tentacle, and he jerked away as if he'd been stung.

"Oops, sorry." Skylar scooped her hair over the opposite shoulder and gave Alec a conciliatory smile. "Breezy here. Let me buy you dessert to make up for that moment of unsolicited hair bondage."

The two of them stared at each other, cynic and beauty, violet blue locked with smoldering black.

Feeling as if he were trespassing on an intimate moment, Ryan was about to speak when Alec stood up abruptly.

"Not for me. I have work to do. I'm off to London

at the end of the week." He nodded to Emily. "Good to meet you."

To Skylar he said nothing, and Ryan watched as his friend walked out through the restaurant without a backward glance.

Skylar handed the menu back to Kirsti. "I guess he hates dessert." Her voice was calm, but Ryan could see she was upset.

"He hates a lot of things right now. He's going through a rough time. Bad divorce."

"We understand. It's not a problem." It was Emily who spoke, but Ryan noticed that she reached across and squeezed her friend's hand, the bond between the two girls visible to the naked eye.

Skylar gave a quick smile intended to indicate she was fine, and then stared out to sea.

As Kirsti disappeared to the kitchen on a mission to find blueberry pie, Ryan tried to resurrect the conversation.

"So, what are your plans for the afternoon?"

It was Lizzy who answered. "We're going to make jewelry."

For the first time Ryan noticed the pasta necklace around Lizzy's neck. Each piece was painted a different shade of purple and pink and sprinkled with glitter.

"Sounds like fun."

"Can we go on a boat trip?" The innocent question sent a ripple of tension around the table that Ryan detected but didn't understand.

In the end it was Skylar who spoke. "You'll be too busy making jewelry for me to wear next time I visit."

Lizzy wasn't so easily deterred. "I'd like to go on a boat and see the puffins."

"Boats rock and mess up your hair. Maybe we'll go on it next time I'm here," Skylar said quickly. "I'll take you."

Lizzy looked at Emily. "Do boats make you sick?"

"A little." Emily's face was as white as new snow-fall, and Ryan knew beyond a shadow of a doubt there was a reason she kept her back to the water.

They shared blueberry pie, and then Kirsti interrupted with a call for Ryan.

He excused himself and walked through to his office, but Kirsti stopped him as he was about to close the door.

"I think Skylar might be The One for Alec." She spoke in a whisper so that whoever was on the phone couldn't hear her.

Ryan laughed. "You have to be kidding me. They almost killed each other."

"I know. I've never seen Alec like that. The chemistry was electric."

"She almost blacked his eye."

"Because he was rude to her and she wasn't having it! Most people are daunted by Alec's intellectual superiority. She squashed him like a bug."

"And that's a good thing?" Baffled, Ryan shook his head. "Skylar isn't his type."

"Ryan, how can such an intelligent guy be so clueless when it comes to relationships? She's *exactly* his type. That's why he was in such a filthy mood. He's used to winning, and he didn't win." She turned away with an exasperated sigh, and Ryan stared after her, trying to picture brooding Alec with free-spirited Skylar.

Exactly his type?

He thought about Emily.

She was responsible for a child, which meant she wasn't his type at all.

Six

"Call me. I want to know how you're both doing."
Skylar pulled her case out of the car and took a last
breath of sea air. "There are days when I think I could
live here. It would be a simpler life. The air is fresh and
the light is wonderful. I'd find myself a little studio by
the sea where I could paint and make jewelry."

They were standing near the tiny runway, waiting for
the Cessna 206 owned by Maine Island Air. The business was the lifeline for islanders needing rapid, easy
access to the mainland. It delivered the mail, people
and occasionally medical supplies.

Today, Sky was the only passenger.

"Just me and the mail," she said cheerfully, leaning
forward to hug Emily. "Ryan is hot by the way, and by
hot I am talking weapons-grade sex appeal. And I'm
willing to bet he doesn't think your breasts are unfortunate. You really should use him to get over Boring Neil."

Emily didn't mention that Ryan had suggested the
same thing. Or that, for one crazy minute, she'd actually
considered it. "My life is already complicated enough."

Sky checked to see that Lizzy was still safely in the

car out of earshot. "Not all complications are bad. Ryan is the whole deal. Those shoulders. That smile. I wanted to crawl onto his lap and see if he's as good a kisser as I think he'd be."

"So why didn't you?"

"Because he's interested in you, and anyway, I'm with Richard."

"He isn't interested in me. He's a player, the sort who can't let a woman walk past without making a move."

"Honey, he could hardly keep his hands off you at the lunch table. He almost burst a blood vessel holding back the caveman inside. You should think about it." Sky spoke in a soft voice. "It's time you went to bed with something other than a good book."

She had thought about it, and thinking about it had caused a thrill of excitement low in her belly. "Thinking about it is all I intend to do."

"At least you've thought about it. If you hadn't admitted that, I would have phoned for medical help. Why aren't you going to do anything about it?"

"Because everything about this situation is unreal."

"He looked pretty real to me."

"I have to think of Lizzy."

"Having Lizzy doesn't mean giving up sex. You can't live in isolation, especially in a place like this. You need adult company. For what it's worth, I like him. I think you can trust him."

"I hope so, since he knows the truth." She'd told Sky what had happened. "Did Alec upset you?"

"A little." Skylar slid sunglasses onto her nose. "Personality clash. No biggie."

"I thought you and he seemed—"

"What?"

"Nothing. Ignore me."

"Like I said, I'm with Richard. And even if I wasn't, I don't have a thing for damaged men, and Alec Hunter is definitely damaged, not to mention rude." Her friend stared into the distance. "Insanely good-looking, of course, but that's not enough to compensate for his other deficiencies."

"Ryan mentioned that he's coming out of a bad divorce."

"If yesterday was an indication of his usual level of charm, the surprise is that someone married him in the first place, not that they divorced him."

"He's very successful. And he makes history accessible. I've watched him in a few different things. Type 'Shipwreck Hunter' into a search engine and you can find a video of him in action, kayaking the Colorado River. And last year he helped build and sail a Viking ship. Don't you watch TV?"

"Not much." Skylar watched as the plane approached. "I wish I didn't have to leave. I love this place. All I want to do is curl up here for the summer, walk on the cliffs and make jewelry, instead of which I have to smile and make polite small talk with people who bore me. My feet are going to be screaming by the weekend, and then we're going to The Hamptons to see Richard's family. Pity me."

"You're staying with his family? Are you being vetted?"

"I've already been vetted. Richard never wastes time dating anyone who doesn't have the right credentials. Just in case the relationship goes somewhere. My bloodline has been studied along with anything in my past that might cause embarrassment."

It sounded so unlike free-spirited Skylar that Emily felt another ripple of concern. "Do you want the relationship to go somewhere?"

"You know me. I think about the journey, not the destination. You can waste your whole life thinking about where you're going, and then one day you wake up and realize you missed today because you were thinking about tomorrow. I like to live in the moment."

And yet Richard was the opposite of that. As far as Emily could see, he'd spent his life working toward a single destination, and everything he did was designed to turbo-boost him along that path. "What are you doing with him, Sky?"

"When he isn't focused on the future, he can be charming. And he genuinely wants to do good and change the world. He knows what he wants. He has a goal. That's why he gets frustrated when things don't go the way he wants them to, and people don't feel the same way he does."

Emily felt another flicker of unease. "Be careful." She didn't know why she said it, except that something didn't feel right. "And don't forget I'm here if you need me."

"Hey, I'm the one supporting you." Skylar watched as the plane executed a perfect landing. "One day they'll arrange a direct flight to New York."

"Then this place would lose its charm."

"Maybe. I wish I'd bought one of those blueberry pies to take home. I could really—" Skylar's jaw dropped as the pilot emerged from the plane. "Holy crap, is that—? Tell me I'm hallucinating."

Emily squinted into the sun. "You're not hallucinating. It's Zach."

"What the hell is he doing here? Do you think Brittany knows?"

"I doubt it."

"Should we tell her?"

Emily thought about it. "No. She's in Crete. She's happy. He might be gone by the time she gets back."

"You're right. I can't remember the last time she even mentioned her ex-husband. Did you know he was here?"

"No. Last thing I heard, he was working as a pilot in Alaska. Should we kill him for her?"

"No. It was years ago, and she wouldn't want him to know he hurt her that badly."

"She hasn't been serious about a man since."

"I know. Apparently ten days of marriage to him cured her of commitment forever." Skylar stared at the man standing on the tarmac. Even from this distance there was no missing the power of his physique. He stood, legs spread, eyes hidden behind shades as he talked to an official. "It's wrong that he should look so attractive. It distracts from the fact he's a bastard. I hope he's as good a pilot as that arrogant smile suggests, given that he's going to be responsible for my life. How do I play this? Do I pretend I don't know he broke Brittany's heart?"

"That's probably best as he's in charge of the aircraft. I don't want him to dump you in the ocean."

"Good point. Instead of wanting to kill him, I'll be grateful. After all, if he hadn't acted the way he did, we never would have bonded that first night at college. Do you remember?"

"Of course. I remember all of it."

"I remember Brittany sticking a photo of him on the wall so that we could draw on it. I gave him a nose ring and pink hair." Skylar walked back to the car and hugged Lizzy. "See you soon, Tinker Bell. Make me a necklace. And make Emily throw out everything she owns that is black."

Emily watched her friend leave and then slid back into the car.

She wondered briefly why Zach would be flying for Island Air, and then decided that as Brittany wasn't here anyway, it didn't matter. Neither of them stayed in the same place for long. He'd be gone long before Brittany returned.

Keen to get home as fast as possible, she drove back along the coast road to Castaway Cottage. Today there was no blue sky, and the wind whipped the sea into a foaming, boiling cauldron, toying with boats and keeping swimmers out of the water. Surf crashed over the rocks, exploding in a burst of white froth.

Emily kept her eyes on the road.

If she worked really hard at it, she could just about pretend the sea wasn't there.

Two decades had passed, but she could still remember the moment when the water had closed over her head and dragged her down, hungry for an innocent victim.

Sweat formed on her brow.

Pulling up outside the cottage, she saw that Lizzy had fallen asleep.

Absolved of responsibility for a brief, blissful moment, she closed her eyes.

Only when the child slept did she manage to shake off the tension.

Out in the bay, Ryan made use of that wind as he hauled the sail and turned the boat. "So, your charm with women is something I aspire to emulate."

Alec ducked under the boom. "I wasn't trying to charm anyone."

"That's good to know." But he could tell that his friend's black mood had lifted and was glad he'd suggested making the most of the wind and the tide.

Work could wait until darkness fell over the water.

In the meantime, he was going to make the most of living next to some of the best sailing waters on the planet.

Penobscot Bay was peppered with hundreds of small uninhabited islands, many with secluded anchorages. A few of the larger islands, like Puffin, had working harbors and communities that swelled to ten times the size during the summer months.

They sailed along the coast, past beautiful old estates of weathered clapboard and wooded enclaves, rocky coves where forest met the sea, inlets, harbors and fishing villages dependent on lobstering and commercial fishing. Ducks and gulls bobbed on the surface of the water, and in the distance he could see the ferry making one of its three times a day trips back to the mainland.

With the wind in their sails, they sped across the water to Fisherman's Creek, past rocky outcrops, nesting birds and seal colonies, finally returning to the island as the sun set.

Ryan pulled his hat low over his eyes as they approached the harbor. "So, what did you think of her?"

"She should come with a warning. Marry this woman and your investments could go down as well as up."

"I was talking about Emily."

"Oh," Alec shrugged. "She looked tense. Jumpy. And she has a kid. Kids mean responsibility. Never mess with a single mother. There is never any question of a casual relationship. They're testing you out to see if you're marriage material."

Ryan decided not to disclose Lizzy's parentage. Not because he didn't trust Alec, but because he respected Emily too much to reveal her secrets. "Did you notice she sat with her back to the water?"

"She had no choice. You picked a table that wasn't big enough for five. I notice you squashed yourself next to her."

"She picked the same seat the day before, and the table was plenty big enough."

"What are you saying? That she doesn't like water?"

"I don't know what I'm saying, but there's something there." Ryan gauged the distance and guided the yacht skillfully against the dock.

"You're showing a lot of interest in her."

"Just being supportive. That's what we islanders do."

"How supportive? Are you planning on tucking her in and kissing her good-night?"

Ryan thought about it. "I might, except I have a feeling I wouldn't be welcome."

"Women always welcome you."

"I think there's more to her than meets the eye."

"There's more to every woman than meets the eye." Alec sprang off the boat. "That's the problem."

Responsibility shared the bed with her and kept her awake.

She'd locked the doors and checked the windows, but still the endless possibility for risk swirled through Emily's brain, tormenting her. Next to her, Lizzy slept deeply, curled under the pretty patchwork quilt, her arms clutching the bear.

It was a sight to soften the hardest heart, except that Emily had locked hers away years before and had no idea how to access it. And she didn't want to.

Numb, she closed her eyes and rolled over, but still sleep stayed just out of her reach.

She thought about Ryan, about the way his fingers had felt brushing over hers, the way he'd looked at her with that intense focus that caused the world around them to melt away. Her relationship with Neil had been comfortable and nonthreatening. He'd done nothing to disturb her equilibrium or threaten her sense of safety.

Ryan did both. He made her feel things she'd never felt before. But she had no intention of allowing herself to explore those feelings in greater depth.

She knew she had issues with attachment, and she was perfectly fine with that.

For all his sophisticated charm, Ryan Cooper represented danger. The kind of danger she was keen to avoid.

She finally succumbed to exhaustion as dawn sent sunlight pouring through the window and then woke later, much later, knowing she'd slept too long. The sun beamed strong rays through the glass, adding a warm glow to the white and muted blues of the bedroom.

Daylight and silence made an uneasy combination.

Feeling a powerful sense that something wasn't right, Emily turned her head to check on Lizzy and saw she was alone in the bed.

"Lizzy?" Her stomach cramped, and panic mingled with self-recrimination.

She should have stayed awake.

She shouldn't have taken her eyes off her for a moment.

Telling herself that the girl had probably gone to find

breakfast, she sprinted downstairs on legs that felt as useless as cooked spaghetti.

"Lizzy?" The kitchen was empty, but a chair had been dragged in front of the shelves.

Something about the position of that chair seemed all wrong, and Emily looked up and saw the glittery pink bucket was missing.

Her stomach dropped away. It was like losing your footing and tumbling into a dark chasm.

She shot into the hallway and saw that the front door was open.

Please, no, not that. Anything but that.

She should have been more careful. She should have hidden the key. She should have—

Her heart stopped because as she looked past the porch she saw the child on her knees on the beach shoveling sand into the pink bucket.

Her heart crashed against her ribs like waves on the rocks.

"Lizzy!" Forgetting that she was dressed only in flimsy pajamas, she ran. She ran faster than should have been physically possible, but it seemed the body was capable of unusual feats when driven by fear. Stones and tiny pieces of shell ripped at her bare feet, but she didn't even notice, and then she hit the soft sand and it acted like brakes, slowing her strides and throwing her off balance.

She stumbled, regained her balance, dragging air into her screaming lungs as she tried to reach Lizzy. She could smell the sea, hear the crash of the surf and the shriek of gulls, all of it combining to unleash dark memories that merged the past with the present.

The world closed in. She saw the child through a tunnel and knew she had to reach her.

And then she grabbed her, holding her tightly, vowing that this time nothing was going to make her let go. "Don't ever, *ever* do that again." Her legs shaking, she dropped to her knees in the sand with the child against her. "Never, do you hear me? Tell me you hear me. *Tell me!*"

"I hear you. I wanted to see the sea." Lizzy's voice was muffled, and Emily squeezed her eyes shut because she wouldn't care if she never saw the sea again.

Her limbs were shaking, and a horrible queasy feeling gnawed at her stomach.

"You must *never* go to the beach without asking me."

"You didn't want to."

"Beaches are dangerous places, do you understand me?" She released Lizzy enough to look into her face, and it was only when she saw the girl's eyes widen and fill with tears that she realized she was shouting.

Shouting and shaking.

Oh, God, she was losing it.

She should never have come to Puffin Island. She could have been anonymous in a city. A city would have been a better choice.

"Emily." Through a mist of panic she heard Ryan's deep baritone, calm and steady. "Emily? What happened?"

She couldn't answer. There was a weight on her chest, and she couldn't breathe. Was she having a heart attack? Something terrible was happening to her. Through the mists of panic she felt his hand, firm and reassuring on her shoulder, and he was easing her away from Lizzy, telling her that everything was fine, that everything was going to be all right, that she had nothing to worry about.

Which showed how little he knew.

She had everything to worry about.

She shouldn't be here, doing this. She was the wrong person.

Now that she was sure Lizzy was safe, she tried to stand up, but her legs were wobbly and unfit for their purpose. Fortunately Ryan must have realized because he drew her into his arms and held her, enveloping her with his strength as his body absorbed her shudders.

"She's safe. Everything is fine." It was all about the tone, not the words. His voice was deep and level, designed to reduce her panic. Except that her panic had gone too far to be reduced so easily. Her heart was pounding, and her breaths were coming in ragged gasps. She felt dizzy and detached, as if she were falling into a deep, dark hole. The loss of control terrified her.

"Ryan—"

"I know. I want you to stop taking those big gulping breaths because they're making you dizzy. Close your mouth, pretend you're blowing out a candle. That's it. Just like that." His hand moved up and down her spine, long, slow gentle strokes that soothed and calmed. "I'm here. I won't let anything happen to you."

She clung to his shoulders, to hard muscle and warm strength. He was the only solid, safe thing in her world, and she held on like a climber about to fall from a rock face. "Lizzy—"

"She's safe, right here. You're both safe."

From somewhere in the darkness she heard Lizzy's voice. "Is she sick? Is she going to die?"

She didn't hear his response because the sky and his

face started to spin together, and she realized with horrible clarity that she was going to pass out. And if she passed out she wouldn't be there for the child. "She can't go in the sea. She mustn't go in the sea. Promise me."

"No one is going in the sea." His voice was strong and sure. "You need to relax."

She tried to say something. Tried to tell him she couldn't relax. She wanted to warn him he needed to take care of Lizzy, but then darkness poured in where there should have been light, and the last thing she remembered were powerful arms catching her as she fell.

He'd never seen anyone so pale. Lying on the sofa back in Castaway Cottage, Emily's cheeks were as white as a Maine winter, the only color in her face the dark shadow of her lashes and the soft pink of her mouth. Still shaken by the moment she'd crumpled in front of him, Ryan reached for his phone and was about to call the medical center when she opened her eyes.

"Thank God." He put the phone down so that he could have both hands free if she passed out on him again. "You had me seriously worried." He'd handled panic attacks before, but none as acute and inexplicable as the one he'd just witnessed. He wanted to understand the cause. A glance at their surroundings had revealed nothing obvious, and gentle questioning of Lizzy had revealed no clues.

Emily struggled to sit up, but he pushed her flat and then wished he hadn't. For the first time since he'd first met her, she had left her hair loose, but even those tumbling curls failed to hide the shape of her breasts clearly visible through the fabric of her pajamas. He'd found himself wishing that whatever had triggered the panic had occurred after she'd dressed.

He wondered what it said about him that she was lying there dazed and vulnerable, and he was thinking about sex.

"Stay there." He shifted slightly, but his attempts to stop her sitting up had shifted her pajama top, giving him a perfect view of the swell and dip of her breasts. "Don't move." He spoke between his teeth, and she looked confused.

"Are you all right?" Emily asked.

"You scared the shit out of me."

Her eyes were soft and dazed. "I'm sorry."

Nowhere near as sorry as he was going to be if he didn't get himself under control. "I'm calling a doctor."

"That's not necessary."

"Emily, you passed out."

"I'm fine now."

"Has it ever happened before?"

She gave a brief shake of her head. "No."

"I'm taking you to the medical clinic." Somewhere he wouldn't be able to lay a finger on her, preferably with a large expanse of water between them. "Or maybe the mainland. You should have tests."

"I don't need tests."

"One moment you were sprinting across the sand as if you were trying to break records, and the next you collapsed."

Aware that Lizzy had been watching, scared, he'd tried to look as if this was normal behavior. As if having a panic attack on a beach was nothing out of the ordinary.

He'd held her, calmed her, breathed in the summer

scent of her and tried to forget she was built like Venus. He was fairly sure she'd forgotten she was wearing nothing but thin silk pajamas.

"Where's Lizzy?" Her voice was urgent, and he could see she was about to drag herself from the sofa and prove to herself that the child was safe.

"She's fine. She's in the garden with Cocoa."

"The front door—"

"I locked it."

"She—"

"I know. She told me she stood on the chair to get the bucket. She told me you'd forbidden her from going to the beach." And he wanted to know why. In fact, he had so many damn questions, it was a struggle to hold them back. He intended to ask them later, but first he needed to be sure she wasn't going to pass out again. "Are you feeling dizzy?"

"No. You must think I'm crazy."

"What I think," he said slowly, "is that something scared you. Do you want to tell me what?"

"I woke up and found her gone. Saw the door open. I thought—"

"What? That the press had found you? That she'd been taken? Are you worried about kidnappers?"

"No. Not that." Before she could say anything else, Lizzy came back into the room with Cocoa at her heels. She stopped in the doorway when she saw Emily sitting up.

"You're awake."

"Yeah, she's awake." Ryan rocked back on his heels, knowing that whatever it was Emily had been about to tell him was going to have to wait. "Come and say hi." He knew children denied the truth would often imagine something far worse. It was important for her to see that nothing bad had happened.

Lizzy slid onto the sofa and looked anxiously at Emily. "Are you still mad at me?"

"I was never mad at you."

"You were screaming. You squeezed me hard."

"I was scared. I was mad at myself for falling asleep and not watching you properly. I—I was worried something might happen to you—" Her throat worked as she swallowed. "I'm sorry if I scared you. We'll talk about it properly, but not right now."

"You fell and I thought you'd died."

"Oh, honey, I'm sorry I gave you a fright." The guilt in her eyes told him just how seriously she took the role of guardian.

Lizzy crawled closer. "Ryan said you weren't dead, just sleeping. I guess you were really tired."

"That's right." Her voice sounded husky. "Tired. And worried, because the door was open and you were gone."

"I wanted to dig in the sand. I wanted to use my pink bucket."

"I know. I should have done it with you, then you wouldn't have felt as if you had to do it on your own. Next time I want you to ask me." She looked exhausted, drained, and Ryan could see the effort it took her to put her own feelings second and reassure the child.

He encouraged Lizzy to go back into the garden with Cocoa. The resilience of children never ceased to amaze him. He knew it would be a long time until he forgot the raw fear in Emily's face as she'd sprinted across the sand to grab Lizzy. He could still feel the way her body had trembled against his, the way her fingers had dug into his shoulders.

Guilt chafed, like sand in a shoe. "I never should have bought that damn bucket."

"It's not your fault. It's all me."

"Tell me what happened."

"I had a bad night. Slept late." She lay against the cushions, pale and exhausted. "When I woke, the house was quiet. And then I came downstairs and saw the chair by the shelves."

"Yeah, I saw that. I assumed you'd done it."

"No. I put the bucket out of reach because I was afraid she might grab it and take it to the beach."

"And she did."

"I saw the front door open. All I saw was the sea and I thought—I thought—" Anxious, she shot to her feet and swayed. "You're *sure* the front door is locked?"

"Yes, and the key is in my pocket." He wondered if she knew her pajamas were virtually see-through when she stood in front of the light. He could see the fluid curves of her body through the thin fabric. "Sit down, Emily."

"I'm fine."

He wasn't. He wanted to peel off those pajamas and explore every inch of that creamy skin with his mouth. "Sit down before you fall."

She sank back onto the sofa and closed her eyes. "I should have hidden the key. I put her at risk."

"Risk of what?"

"She's six years old, Ryan."

"I sense this isn't a generic risk we're talking about. I'd like to understand what sent you flying across the sand like a champion sprinter."

"I was trying to reach her. Trying to stop her going in the water. It's my job to protect her."

"Why would she have gone into the water?" He cast his mind back. "She was digging. She wasn't interested in the water."

"Children love the water."

And he knew from her bloodless cheeks that the issue here wasn't the bucket or even the fact that Lizzy had left the house. It was the sea. The sea was the reason she spent her time in the kitchen. The reason she sat with her back to the water and didn't want to go out in his boat.

"Talk to me." He kept his voice gentle. "Tell me what that was all about, because we both know it wasn't about Lizzy."

She curled her legs under her. "You're right, it isn't about her. It's about me. I'm not the right person."

"The right person for what?"

"To be looking after a child."

He remembered feeling the same way, even though in his case the real burden had fallen on his grandmother. "I know all this has come as a shock to you. You haven't had time to get used to the idea that you're her guardian, but you will."

"You don't understand."

"I remember staring at my sister who was asleep in the middle of my bed, and my grandmother telling me we were all she had. I wanted to run like hell in the opposite direction before I could screw it up, because I knew I would. There were a million ways to do things wrong, and I didn't know how to do them right. Trust me when I say I know it feels like an overwhelming responsibility you're not qualified for, but you're going to be fine. You muddle through, twelve hours at a time."

"No, you really don't understand. I'm not the right person." Her fierce tone caught his attention.

"Why aren't you the right person?"

She stared at a point on his chest, her fingers clenched in her lap and then finally lifted her head and looked at him. "Because I killed my sister. She died because of me."

Seven

"She's asleep," Ryan said, standing in the doorway. He'd spent the whole day and the whole evening taking care of things, and judging from the absence of complaint from Lizzy, he'd handled bedtime with the same cool competence he'd displayed on the beach.

"I usually read to her."

"She told me. *Green Eggs and Ham*." He gave a short laugh. "It's been a while, but I'm still word perfect. And she recognized quite a few words, so whatever you've been doing has made a difference even in a short time. She's asleep now. She's exhausted."

And she knew she had him to thank for that.

He'd distracted Lizzy with a game in the garden that involved so much running with the ball and the dog she'd worn herself out. When she was almost falling asleep on the spot he'd made supper, enrolling Lizzy in helping him. He'd stood her on a chair at the scrubbed kitchen table and shown her how to break eggs into a bowl.

From her position on the sofa, Emily had watched through the open door as Lizzy had smacked each egg on the side of the bowl and paused as golden yoke and slippery white had slid and pooled in the center. There had been two accidents, and each time he'd cleaned up and let her try again. Plenty of adults would have opted to do the job themselves. Not Ryan. He'd stood, infinitely patient, and let her master the task until the carton of eggs was empty and the bowl filled with yolks that floated like small suns on the translucent liquid.

Then he'd handed Lizzy a whisk and demonstrated the movement. When it had proven too hard, he'd covered her small hand with his and did it with her until they had a frothy mixture. It didn't seem to bother him that he could have done it himself in a quarter of the time.

The part that involved heat, he'd done himself.

He'd stood in front of the stove in Kathleen's sunny kitchen, sleeves rolled back to reveal powerful forearms as he poured the mixture into a pan and produced a perfect omelet.

She'd wondered how she could be noticing he was sexy at a time like this. Apparently she was more vulnerable to the appeal of the strong protective type than she'd thought.

She felt dizzy and strange, as if a healing wound had suddenly been wrenched open, leaving her bleeding and weak. Her mind was flooded with thoughts she'd worked hard to block out for most of her life. At some point she must have slept because she woke to find herself covered with the patchwork quilt.

And now he was standing there, no doubt wondering how soon he could reasonably leave.

"I've taken up so much of your time—"

"It's my time. My choice how I spend it. How are you feeling?"

"Better. Did you leave the door open so we can hear her?"

"Cocoa is lying at the bottom of her bed. If she wakes, we'll know."

"The dog is on her bed?"

"The two of them seemed happy with that arrangement. Is it a problem?"

"No." Emily slumped back against the sofa, thinking that of all the problems she had, that one didn't even register. "I can't believe you looked after her all afternoon."

He eased himself away from the door frame and strolled into the room, a smile playing around his mouth. "You owe me. And I'll be collecting."

She didn't know whether it was his words or the look in his eyes, but something sent her pulse hammering like rain on a roof. The air simmered with a heat that made it difficult to breathe. She had no defenses against his brand of raw sexuality. She felt out of control, as if she needed to fasten a seat belt or anchor herself to an immovable object. It was like tiptoeing around the rim of an active volcano, knowing that one wrong step would send you plunging into a fiery furnace.

"What do you usually charge for babysitting services?"

"I don't offer babysitting services. This was an exclusive, one-off deal. Don't ever mention it." His eyes gleamed with humor. "I wouldn't want word to get around."

"In that case I'm especially grateful for your sacrifice."

He gave her a long look that brought the blood rushing back to her cheeks more effectively than any medical intervention. "You finally have some color."

And he was responsible for the color.

"I owe you an apology."

"For what?"

"For drowning you in emotion." Now that the sharp edge of fear had passed, she felt deeply embarrassed. First she'd had a meltdown, and then she'd spilled confidences she usually kept locked deep inside. "Most men hate emotion like they hate throw pillows and scented candles."

"I'm not a lover of throw pillows, but I'm not afraid of emotions. They tell you more about a person than hours of conversation."

"If that's true, then by now you're thinking I'm a hysterical neurotic."

"If I told you what I really thought, you'd kick me out." Leaving her to ponder on that, he walked into the kitchen and returned a moment later carrying a bottle of wine and two glasses.

She wanted to ask him what he really thought but wasn't sure she wanted to hear the answer. "Don't you have somewhere to be?"

"I'm where I want to be." He sat on the sofa next to her and put the bottle and the glasses on the floor. "Talk to me."

"Sorry?"

"Tell me what happened."

The breath left her lungs in a rush. "I don't talk about it."

"Maybe not usually, but tonight you're going to talk about it." He poured wine into a glass and handed it to her. "Tell me about your sister." Another man would have tiptoed around the subject. Not him.

"That isn't a very sensitive question."

"This morning you had a full-blown panic attack. I virtually had to peel you off the ground. It would help me to know what happened, so that I can help make sure it doesn't happen again."

"I was with Neil for three years and he never asked for the details."

Sympathy turned to incredulous disbelief. "Never?"

"He respected boundaries."

"I'm starting to understand why you don't feel the need for rebound sex. You can only rebound from something with substance. And I'm not respecting boundaries, so talk to me."

Her hand shook, and the wine almost sloshed over the top of the glass. "What do you want to know?"

"Everything." He eased the glass out of her hand and set it down on the floor. Polished floorboards gleamed in the late evening sun, and through the open window she could hear the relentless sound of the waves breaking on the shore.

"Why?"

"Because I'm absolutely sure you didn't kill her." He reached out and pulled her into the curve of his arm so that her body was pressed against the hardness of his.

She didn't consider herself a tactile person. She and Neil had often sat on separate sofas, facing each other, disconnected, as if occupying different worlds. In some ways they'd lived parallel lives.

It was true that she'd never talked to Neil about her past, but it was also true that he'd never asked. And she realized now that he hadn't wanted to know. He'd talked about respecting boundaries, but what he'd really meant was that he didn't want to deal with emotion.

If Neil had found himself in this position, he would have floundered, both with her emotions and with the child. Ryan had handled both without missing a beat.

"There isn't a happy ending to this, Ryan."

"Yeah, well, we both know life is full of messy endings. Tell me about your sister."

"I was four when she was born. My earliest memory was holding her because my mother was drunk on the sofa. I remember looking down at her and promising that I was always going to take care of her."

"Why weren't the authorities involved?"

"I don't really know. My mother was good at doing just enough, I guess. We slipped through the cracks. By the time my sister was six months old, I was doing almost everything for her. I went from being the loneliest child on the planet to the happiest. I loved her. And she loved me back. The first word she spoke was *Em*, and she used to follow me everywhere and sleep in my bed."

"Sounds like Rachel." His voice was low. "Drove me crazy. It was like trying to shake off a burr that had stuck to your clothes."

"Yes." Her whole body ached with remembering. "I loved it. I loved holding her. Most of all I loved being outdoors with her. I hated our apartment so much. It was cramped, airless, and everything bad happened there. I was the one who begged my mother to take us to the beach. We lived close, but we never went. Spent our days cooped up in one room while she drank her way through whatever money she could scrounge from men." She breathed. "She wasn't a prostitute, not officially, but she'd discovered early on that men liked her body, and sleeping with them was a useful way to get what she wanted. It took me years to see that she had a low opinion of herself. That she didn't think she had anything to offer except a pair of breasts that made men stupid."

"This is why you dress in black and wear your shirts buttoned up to the neck?"

"Sometimes my curves are all men see. Or they see them first, and make judgments. I discovered it was best to take them out of the equation."

"Honey, I hate to be the one to break this to you, but buttoning your shirt up to the neck doesn't hide the fact you have an incredible body—but we'll come to that part later." He tightened his grip on her shoulders. "Finish your story."

"On that particular day she agreed to take us. I don't know why. Parenting wasn't her thing, but it was sunny, and by then she was very pregnant with Lana. I guess she thought she could sleep on the beach as easily as she could sleep at home. I remember pulling a blanket from the bed to sit on. Katy had just started walking, and I thought the sand would be a soft landing."

"The moment we got there, my mother fell asleep." She felt his arm tighten, as if he knew she was getting to the bad part. "I was pleased. She was always angry and I thought we'd have more fun together with her asleep. Katy and I played in the sand, and then Mom woke up and went for a walk."

"She left you?"

"Technically she was never looking after us, but at least until that point she was there. I remember feeling anxious. We lived a short bus ride away, and I didn't know how to get home. And then I saw her sitting in a bar with some guy I'd never seen before. She was nine months pregnant. Can you believe that?"

"He approached her?"

"Maybe. Or maybe she saw him sitting there and thought he looked like someone she could easily part from the contents of his wallet. I carried on playing and next time I looked I couldn't see her anywhere."

His arm was still around her, and he moved his thumb up and down her arm, the gesture soothing and sympathetic. "That must have been terrifying."

"Not at first. You're forgetting, that was my normal. I was used to being unsupervised."

"Didn't anyone on the beach notice that you were on your own?"

"Yes. A woman with a child about the same age as Katy came over to me and asked if we were all right and where our mother was. I'd been watching their family, copying some of the things they were doing. The dad kept lifting the child in the air and swinging her around until she was helpless with giggles. I tried to do it with Katy, but she was too heavy and I couldn't swing her high enough to make it fun."

"Did you tell her you were on your own?"

"No. My mother had told me over and over again that if I was ever asked, I was to say everything was fine. She said that if I didn't do that, they might take Katy away."

His hand stilled. "They might have taken you away, too."

She swallowed. "I wish they had. I've thought about it over and over again. I wish I'd said to that woman, 'I don't know where my mother is.' I wish they'd taken Katy, even if it meant I never saw her again, because at least I'd know she was alive. That was the day I first realized my situation was unusual. I remember looking around the beach at the families and thinking that although those families all looked different, they had one thing in common. There was an adult in charge. Until that moment, I hadn't been aware that we weren't normal. 'Normal' is the life you're living, isn't it? This was how it was for us, so I assumed this was how it was for everyone."

"Your mother didn't come back?"

"Not right then. Katy was bored and she kept trying to eat the sand. I had to find a way of occupying her, so I carried her to the sea. I thought I'd put her toes in the water. I didn't intend to go in deeper, but she loved it so much and she was squealing and wanting more, so I carried her in until I was up to my knees."

"There were other people around you?"

"Yes. It was busy. We splashed for a while, and then we went a little deeper and—" Her heart was pumping hard. "I don't know what happened next. Maybe the beach shelved sharply, or maybe someone had dug a deep hole. Either way I stepped and there was nothing under my feet. I felt the water rush into my nose and ears, and I tried to find the bottom but it wasn't there, so then I tried to push Katy up so that she could breathe, but she was too heavy and my arms couldn't hold her." She felt it again, the rush of the water and the feeling of panic and utter helplessness. "I kicked and struggled, but I could feel the water pulling me. It was so powerful."

"You were caught in a rip current."

"I don't remember anything else until I came around on the beach. I remember being sick, and all these adults crowded around me. I looked around for Katy, but she wasn't there. I must have let go of her when I lost consciousness. They mounted a search and found her—"

She felt his arms come around her, heard him murmur *I'm so sorry,* and *you poor baby,* against her hair, while he held her tightly.

"Then my mother reappeared. She was hysterical, but looking back on it, I don't think it was because of Katy. I think it was because she was afraid she might be charged with neglect."

"Was she?"

"No. The authorities got involved, but in the end they decided it was a terrible accident. I don't know what she said to them and I think we were followed up for a while, but nothing ever happened."

"Did anyone question you?"

"They tried to, but I couldn't speak."

"You were in shock."

Emily felt the ache deep in her chest. "Katy was the only thing in my life I'd ever loved. When I realized she'd gone, nothing mattered. I didn't care what my mother did or didn't do. I was catatonic. Without Katy I didn't care about anything. Five days later my mother had Lana. She expected me to look after her the way I had for Katy, but I couldn't." She breathed, wondering how honest to be. How much to confess. "From the moment Lana was born, I didn't feel anything. I didn't want anything to do with her. My mother told me I was cold. Unfeeling."

"That's horseshit."

"She told me this was my chance to make up for having killed my sister."

"Jesus, Emily, please, tell me you knew that wasn't true."

"When you're a child you believe what grown-ups tell you."

"At least tell me you don't believe it now."

She breathed. "Part of me does, because it's true. I did take her into the water. I did let go of her."

"It was an accident. As you say, you were a child. You shouldn't have been given responsibility for her. A tragic, terrible accident, but still an accident. Did you ever talk to anyone about it?"

"Brittany and Skylar. And Kathleen. They're the only people who know. Talking about it doesn't help, and anyway, it's in the past."

"You sit with your back to the water and you don't go near the sea. I assume that's why you stayed in the cottage with Kathleen while your friends were on the beach. That sounds as if it's in your present, not your past."

"I'm scared of the water, that's true. And I'm scared of having responsibility for a child. I loved Katy with every part of me and losing her ripped my heart out from the roots. I can't love like that again. I choose not to."

His thumb moved gently on her arm. "You think love is something you can switch on and off?"

"I know it is. I don't feel deeply. That's why Neil ended it."

His thumb stopped moving. "Neil ended it because he was a dick."

Emily gave a shocked laugh. "You've never even met him."

"Thank God. I already have enough evidence to

know he's a dick. For a start, he was with you for three years and didn't once take the time to explore why you were too scared to open up to him. What the hell was wrong with the guy?"

"Not everybody wants to spill their innermost secrets."

"It's called intimacy, Emily, and it's a basic requirement for a successful, healthy relationship. What you two had sounds more like roommates or first cousins."

She flushed, because hadn't she had that same thought herself? "You can't judge a relationship from the outside. There is no right and wrong. Just what works for that couple."

"I agree, but that's not the only reason I know he's a dick."

Emily sighed. "What's the other reason?"

"He let you go."

Heat rushed through her. She was aware of his arm, locking her securely against him. Of the brush of his hard thigh against hers. "It wasn't his fault. I've shut down that part of myself. I don't want to feel anything."

"If you were mine, I would have made you feel." He spoke with quiet emphasis, his thumb moving in a gentle rhythm over her arm. "I wouldn't have let you hide away."

And that, she thought, was why being with him both excited and terrified her. "Ryan—"

"Who cared for Lana when she was born?"

"My mother had to. It helped that Lana was very pretty. My mother discovered it got her attention and she liked that. Used it. I've often wondered if her childhood contributed to the person Lana became. She was insecure. She learned early how to make her looks work for her. When Lana was about seven, my mother met someone. He was older, no kids of his own. He owned a nice house in a good neighborhood and we moved in."

Ryan stilled. "Is this going to end badly? Because if so, I might need to top up my wineglass."

"No. He was a good man. And that's the weird part because I never understood what he saw in my mother. I think it was complicated. Something to do with having lost his own daughter to drugs and wishing he'd done more. I don't know. At the time, I didn't question it. For the first time in my life I had a room of my own, plenty to eat and access to all the books I could read. Those books saved me. I spent my time lost in worlds that didn't look anything like the one I was living in. I studied hard because I didn't want a life like my mother's. It was because of him I went to college and met Brittany and Sky. When he died, he left me money. I think he knew if he didn't give it directly to me, my mother would drink her way through it."

"And Lana?"

"She was scouted on the subway one day. She worked a short time as a model, then turned to acting and loved it. I think because it gave her the perfect way of avoiding reality. Each film represented a new fake reality. That's why she fell in love with her leading men. To her it was real. And when the filming ended, so did the relationship. Every time."

"Do you think she meant to have Lizzy?"

"I doubt it. Lana wasn't the sort who would be prepared to share the stage with a child. She wanted to be the center of attention. I don't think she saw much of Lizzy."

"So in that way she was like your mother."

"I hadn't thought of it like that."

"And the two of you weren't in touch?"

"I hadn't heard from her in years. That was my fault." It was painful to admit it. "I made no effort to bond with her."

"Because you'd already lost one sister. She could have made an effort, too. She didn't have your reasons for keeping her distance." He leaned forward, picked up the bottle and filled her glass. "Drink."

"You're the one who should be drinking. I can't believe I dumped all that on you. I bet you're just dying to run screaming through that door."

He didn't budge. "Now I understand why Brittany told me you were in trouble. She was the one who suggested you come here?"

"When we were at college, we made this pact that we'd help each other if we ever needed it. My friends gave me something my family never had. A sense of security. I know that, no matter what happens, Brit and Sky will always be there for me. And I for them. When I first heard I was Lizzy's guardian, the priority was to find somewhere safe to stay. The press had been crawling all over the house. I was told that she needed to be kept away from everyone so that she could just process her grief and learn to live life a little. We talked about having security, but I couldn't see how that would do anything but draw attention. No one knew I existed, so the safest thing seemed to be for me to take her and disappear. But of course the first thing a child wants to do when they see Shell Bay is dig in the sand." She breathed. "I should have stayed in New York."

"But you wouldn't have had help in New York." He was silent for a minute. "Emily, it wouldn't take much for the press to find out Lana had a half sister."

"But if they find that out, they will also find out

Lana and I hadn't seen each other for years. They're not likely to link us."

"They could."

It wasn't what she wanted to hear, and she felt a ripple of unease. "Even if they did, they wouldn't look for me here, would they? There's no trail."

"No." He turned his head and gave her a smile that was probably meant to reassure her but didn't.

"You're speaking as if you have knowledge. Have you ever been targeted by the press?"

"No." He eased his arm away from her and rose to his feet. "But I know how they operate."

"The lawyers thought the story would probably die. That if I lie low, the journalists would get bored. I paid cash for my ferry ticket, so they shouldn't be able to trace me, and no one is going to be looking for the daughter of a movie star in rural Maine."

"That's true, and even if they come, you'll be protected. The islanders are a close community. We protect our own. If the press arrive, then we'll be ready for them." He turned to look at her. "Thank you for telling me. Now I understand why you don't feel you're the right person to care for Lizzy."

She sagged against the sofa. "You do?"

"Yes, and for the record, I think you're the perfect person."

"You're wrong. I know the same thing won't happen again because I won't let her go near the water, but this is about more than her personal safety. It's about not being able to give her what she needs. Bringing up a child requires more than just accident prevention. To flourish and grow, a child needs to be loved. They need a parent, or parent substitute, who cares about them. It was only when I saw Kathleen with Brittany that I discovered how love could look. I can't do that. I can't give her what she needs. I can't love another child. I won't."

"So why didn't you say no? She could have been put in foster care."

Emily felt something twist inside her. "I couldn't do that."

"Of course you couldn't. Because you already care, Emily. You wouldn't have taken her if you didn't care. But you're scared shitless."

"That part I'm not arguing with." She felt a stinging in her throat. "A child deserves to be loved and I can't love her. I just can't." She heard the shake in her voice and knew he heard it, too. "I won't let that happen to me again."

"And what if you can't stop it happening?"

"I can. I've been this way for so long I can't change. Neil always told me I was cold. That I needed to be 'thawed out.'"

He made a sound in his throat that resembled a growl and flexed his fingers. "Emily, honey, do me a favor— no more talk about Neil for a while."

She thought he was joking, but then she looked at his face and saw the hard set of his mouth and the icy glint in his eyes.

His gaze stayed fixed to her face for a long moment, and then he scooped up the jacket he'd thrown over the chair hours earlier. "I should go." His voice was thickened. "If you need me, call."

The abruptness of his departure shocked her. "Wait—what about Cocoa?"

"Keep her overnight. As long as you push her into

the garden by six in the morning, you shouldn't have any accidents. I'll call my grandmother and explain."

She stood up, too, and saw him straighten his shoulders as if he was warding her off. "Thank you for everything you did today. I apologize for drowning you in emotion."

"I'm not leaving because of what you told me, Emily."

"Then why are you sprinting out of the door?"

He let out a long breath. "Because I'm not Neil."

It was her turn to stare. "But—I don't understand."

"I have spent the last few hours trying manfully to ignore the fact you're wearing nothing but a pair of very sexy pajamas." His voice was husky. "I never thought I'd want to put you back into one of those shirts that button to the neck, but right now I'm thinking that would be a good choice of clothing."

"You're leaving because of my breasts?"

"No, not just because of your breasts." He gave a crooked smile. "All of you. The shape of your face, the curve of your shoulder, the dimple in the corner of your mouth—you name it, I'm noticing it. But because you've had a crappy day and you're vulnerable I am making a supreme effort to keep my hands off you and not do what I'm burning to do. Right now, that means walking out that door."

Her heart was beating so hard she thought he must be able to hear it.

She should have just nodded.

Or maybe opened the door for him.

Instead, she asked a question.

"What are you burning to do?"

Eight

This was the moment to leave.

He knew a mistake when he saw one, and he was definitely looking at one right now.

No single mothers. Wasn't that his rule?

And not only was Emily vulnerable, but there were still things about him she didn't know. Things that made it more likely she'd push him out of her house than invite him to kiss her. There was no way he was leaving her without support, and not just because Brittany would fire an arrow into his butt.

Now he knew what she was going through, he was determined to help her. And helping her didn't involve stripping off those pajamas and pinning her to the kitchen table.

"What I'm burning to do is irrelevant."

"I've been honest with you. I want you to be honest with me." Her voice was soft and smoky, and it slid into his senses like a drug.

Shit.

"Emily, I can tell you that the last thing you want right now is for me to be honest."

"Please."

The right thing would have been to make an excuse, but she was wearing those damn pajamas, a confection of silk and sin, and she was looking at him with those wide eyes, her mouth was right there and—

With a soft curse, he took her face in his hands. He felt the softness of her skin under his fingers and heard her breathing grow shallow. "You want to know what I'm burning to do? I want to strip off those pajamas and smash down every boundary you've ever created. I want to explore all those places you've never let anyone go, and I'm talking about your mind as well as your body. I'm not like Neil. I don't respect your boundaries. I want you open to me."

Her eyes widened with shock, and her lips parted. "That will never happen."

"If I wasn't about to leave, I'd make it happen." He lowered his head but kept his mouth just clear of hers. She was so close he could almost taste her, feel the short shallow breaths she snatched into her lungs.

"You wouldn't, because—" Her face suffused with color. "The truth is, I'm not that crazy about sex."

For a moment he thought he must have misheard. "You don't like sex?"

"It's fine. Nice." With a whimper of embarrassment, she eased away from him. "I can't believe we're having this conversation. You're right. You should go. And I never should have asked."

"Wait a minute—" He caught her around the waist and pulled her back to him. "Did you say 'nice'? You think sex is *'nice'*?"

Her face was on fire. "Yes. What's wrong with that?"

He drew in a deep breath. "Honey, 'nice' sex is for

people in retirement homes with dodgy hips and a heart condition. At your age you should be having clothes-ripping, mind-blowing, animal sex that leaves you unable to walk or think."

"All right, you should *definitely* go now." She was deliciously flustered, and he dragged her back to him and slid his hands into her hair, feeling it tumble and curl over his fingers in a slide of soft silk. She smelled like blossoms and sunshine. Her lips reminded him of the strawberries that grew wild in Kathleen's tumbling coastal garden.

"You have gorgeous hair. Is wearing it up part of your disguise, too?"

"I don't have a disguise. Just because I choose to dress in a certain way doesn't make it a disguise. And wearing my hair up is the practical option. It's always breezy on Puffin Island. It stops it blowing into my eyes."

"So, in New York you wore it loose?"

She hesitated. "No."

"Like I said. A disguise. You've created a persona, because you're afraid someone is going to see who you really are. But I see you, Emily Donovan. I'm standing here, looking right at you, so you can damn well stop hiding." His hand was still in her hair, his mouth a breath from hers.

"You don't see me. And I can tell you I've never had clothes-ripping, mind-blowing, animal sex. I'm not like that."

"You mean you weren't like that with *him*. You'd be like it with me, Emily."

"I don't—"

He kissed her. He parted her lips with his, licked

into her mouth and felt her go weak against him. Those full breasts pressed against his chest, and he hauled her close, holding her with the flat of his hand while the other stayed buried deep in her hair. He deepened the kiss until white heat snaked across his skin, until rampant hunger and raw sexual need tore through him. Her mouth was eager and sweet, and the softness of her breasts pushed against his chest. He'd intended the kiss to be brief, but now he'd started there was no stopping. Instead of letting her go, he backed her against the wall of Kathleen's hallway and caged her, planting an arm on either side of her and holding her there with the weight of his body. He knew he should probably say something, but he was so turned on he could barely stand upright, let alone speak, and she didn't speak, either. He felt her trembling against him, felt her fingers slide up to his shoulders and hold on as if she were afraid she might collapse without his support.

He dragged his mouth over her jaw and down to her throat, heard her soft gasp as he slid his hands down her ribs, his thumbs brushing the underside of her breasts.

The single button holding the front of her pajamas together slid out of its silky mooring, exposing luscious curves of creamy white flesh tipped with dusky pink.

Ryan had to force himself to breathe. He was so aroused he felt disoriented. Slowly, he slid his thumb over the tortured peak and heard her moan. He stroked, licked, tasted while she whimpered, squirmed and arched against him, those full lush breasts pushing into his hands.

Drunk on her body he slid his hands lower, down the silk of her back inside her pajama bottoms to cup warm, bare flesh. Everything about her was soft and inviting. He could have drowned in her and died happy.

The only sound was the soft murmurs that came from her throat and the steady thrum of his own heartbeat. The tension in the air was syrupy thick, coating both of them in a heavy, suffocating warmth. And then he took her mouth again, kissing her deeply while his fingers slid between her trembling thighs. He parted her gently and slid his finger into that slippery warmth, feeling velvety softness open for him as her body allowed him intimate access. He held still for a moment, stroked his other hand over her jaw and felt her shift against him with restless need. Gently he stroked and teased, paying attention to every gasp and murmur until he felt the pleasure roll through her. She cried out as she came, her body clamping down on his fingers so that he felt every throb, every contraction.

He held her, murmured soft words against her hair, breathed in the scent of her until the last pulse died away and she lay limp against him.

Ryan tried to steady his own breathing.

He was rock-hard. So aroused he was ready to take her there and then, but he forced himself to slowly withdraw his hand and smooth her pajamas back into place.

Her head was dipped forward, so all he could see was the shimmer of her hair and the shadow of thick, dark eyelashes.

"Emily, look at me." His voice sounded raspy and rough, but he was impressed he'd managed to form a coherent sentence, so he wasn't about to apologize for that.

Her hands were locked in the front of his shirt, as if he was the one solid, reliable thing in a collapsing world.

"This is embarrassing. You need to go now."

"Why is it embarrassing?"

"Because you—and I—damn it, Ryan, you know why. We lost control." Her voice was muffled against his chest, and he clenched his jaw.

"I didn't lose control."

Slowly, she lifted her face to his. "You didn't?"

"If I'd lost control, I would have undressed you, not dressed you. If I'd lost control, you'd be naked now and flat on your back on the sofa instead of standing there in your pajamas." And he was starting to question that decision. "You're right, I need to go, but not because this is embarrassing."

"Why, then?"

Because he wanted to undo his good work, rip off those silk pajamas, spread her legs and taste all of her, not just her mouth.

Deciding she wasn't ready to hear that, he smoothed her hair, tilting her face to his. "Because it's getting late, you had a shitty day and you need to get some sleep."

Her eyes were glazed and confused, her cheeks flushed and her mouth damp from his kisses. "I didn't—" Her voice was low and husky. "I wasn't expecting—I can't believe you did that. Or that I—I didn't know it was going to be like that."

"I did." Reluctantly, he released her. "I knew it would be exactly like that."

She stepped back, traced her lower lip with the tip of her tongue as if she couldn't believe what had just happened, and then sent him a glance that almost had him flattening her back against the wall again.

Her gaze was on his mouth. "Lizzy is upstairs. She could have woken."

"Cocoa would have barked."

She bit her lip. "I don't want her waking up to find me naked with a man. When you're six, it's unsettling."

It had obviously happened to her. Subduing the rush of anger, he focused on the practical. "Could you drop Cocoa back with my grandmother in the morning? She lives in Harbor House. It's the big white one overlooking the bay."

"Of course." She blinked, as if she'd been asleep and woken up on a different planet. "And thank you."

"For proving that a kiss can be more than nice?"

There was a long, pulsing silence. "For listening. For helping me out with Lizzy. As for the other—" her voice cracked slightly "—we won't mention it again. That's the end of it."

He watched her for a long moment and then strolled toward the door.

"It's not the end, Emily. It's the beginning."

Agnes Cooper lived a fifteen-minute walk from the harbor and the Ocean Club in a pretty white clapboard house with a shingle roof that pitched steeply at the front. Overlooking the rocks at Puffin Point and the bay beyond that, it had been built on a large plot of land and was protected by mature trees and a well-nurtured garden. Emily was immediately charmed, and the feeling stayed with her as she walked with Lizzy up to the wooden door bracketed by lanterns.

It was the sort of house she'd always pictured when she'd escaped into stories about homesteads and large happy families. The sort of house a child would have drawn, with clean lines and pleasing symmetry.

As she waited for Agnes to answer the door, she smoothed her hair and tried not to think about Ryan.

Hours had passed, and yet she could still feel the roughness of his jaw against her cheek, taste the heat of his mouth and remember the delicious explosion of pleasure he'd drawn from her with each skillful, intimate stroke of his clever fingers. Most of all she remembered the way he'd focused on her, as if she were the only thing in his world. The roof could have fallen in on the cottage, and neither of them would have noticed.

Never in her life had she felt as if she were the focus of anyone's world. In the three years she'd spent with Neil, not once had she lost control. Sex had been a choice, not a need, and it had always followed a predictable pattern. She'd always had the feeling that either of them could have walked away at any point, and it wouldn't have mattered. After Ryan had walked away, she'd felt so wound up and frustrated she'd almost chased after him and begged him to finish what he'd started.

Lizzy tugged at her arm. "Your face is red."

"It's the sun."

She was wondering how she was ever going to look Ryan in the eye again, when the door opened. Any awkwardness she might have felt from the knowledge she'd spent the previous night physically welded to this woman's grandson melted away under the warmth of the welcome.

As for Agnes and Lizzy, it was love at first sight.

Some friendships, Emily knew, were instant, and this was one of those.

Within five minutes of knocking at the door, Lizzy was sitting at the kitchen table eating freshly baked chocolate cookies as if it were something she'd done hundreds of times in her life before.

"Handsome bear." Agnes slid her glasses onto her

nose and took a closer look at the toy clutched tightly in the child's fingers. "Ryan's sister Rachel had a bear just like him. He's upstairs somewhere. I had to mend him a few times. Looks like yours could do with mending, too. Would you like me to do that for you?"

Lizzy glanced at Emily and then slid the bear across the table.

Understanding the trust implicit in that gesture, Agnes examined it carefully and then produced a sewing box from a cupboard. "It's nothing serious. Just something that happens when a bear is very loved. Emily, could you thread the needle for me, honey? My eyes aren't what they used to be."

Emily dutifully obliged and then glanced around the sunny kitchen as Agnes settled down to mend the bear. This, she thought, was how she'd imagined a kitchen should look. The countertops gleamed, pots of fresh herbs were lined up along the windowsill, and delicious smells wafted from the stove. Through the windows she could see butterflies flitting through the colorful blooms that crowded the lush, leafy sanctuary.

"You have a beautiful home."

"It's too big for one person. I rattle around like a bean in a jar." Agnes glanced up from her emergency repair and saw Emily looking at the herbs. "I love to grow my own food, but it's harder now I can't tend the garden myself. So, Ryan bought me herbs I could grow on the windowsill."

Having finished the cookie, Lizzy slid off the chair and wandered after Cocoa, leaving Emily with Agnes.

"Thank you for letting us borrow Cocoa."

"I call her my therapy dog because having her around makes everyone feel better." Agnes tilted the bear toward the light and sewed, each stitch minute and carefully aligned. "Did she make Lizzy feel better? Ryan said she hasn't been sleeping well."

"He told you that?"

"Not the detail." She glanced over the top of her glasses, and there was a sharpness to her gaze that hadn't been dimmed by failing vision. "He told me you were looking after your niece." She snipped the thread and handed the mended bear back to Emily. "It's always challenging when life sends you a responsibility you weren't expecting."

"It happened to you."

"Yes." Agnes stared at the garden for a moment, a faraway expression on her face. Then she smiled. "Why don't you make us both a cup of tea, and we'll take it through to the living room. I love early summer, and I don't want to waste a moment of the sunshine. I can't sail any longer, but I love to watch the boats. Ryan is the same. It's in his blood. His father spent every moment of his time on the water."

Suppressing an impulse to ask a million questions, Emily followed Agnes's directions and made tea, added cookies to a plate and carried it all through to the living room at the front of the house.

It was a room full of warmth and charm, flooded with natural light. A large bay window overlooked the sloping garden, and she could see a narrow path winding down to the small rocky cove below.

"This house is perfect."

Agnes gestured to the window scat. "That's my favorite spot. On a clear day you can see right across the bay to the mainland. Do you like sailing?"

Emily put the tray down on the table. "I've always

been afraid of the sea." And under that quiet, sympathetic gaze it all came tumbling out, all of it, right up to the point where Ryan had kissed her.

That small detail she omitted, although she knew that at some point she was going to have to think about it, to work out what to say next time their paths crossed.

That time arrived sooner than expected. She turned her head to take another look at the view and saw him striding toward the house, talking on the phone. He took the steps two at a time and then paused, staring across the water as he continued the conversation.

Agnes watched and then shook her head. "There are times when I could drop that phone into the cookie jar and put the lid on it. Technology has a lot to answer for. Still, I suppose it means he can join me for lunch occasionally and isn't tied to his desk."

"Lunch? Oh, my goodness, I hadn't realized it was so late." Flustered by the knowledge that her next encounter with Ryan was going to be so soon, Emily scrambled to her feet. "We just called to drop off Cocoa. We've taken up too much of your time."

"The one thing I have far too much of is time, so someone taking some of it is my idea of a good turn. I enjoyed talking to you. I hope you'll come again."

"We will. And thank you for mending Andrew." Emily glanced out of the window again and saw that Ryan was standing with his back to them. Eyeing those broad, powerful shoulders, she wondered if she could make her escape out of the back door so she didn't have to face him.

The last time she'd seen him he'd—

And she'd—

Holy crap.

Scrambling for her shoes and her purse, she called for Lizzy.

"Is there a fire?" Agnes's tone was mild. "I get the distinct impression you're not happy to see my grandson."

"He's been very kind, but he's already done enough."

More than enough. He'd made her feel things she'd never felt before, and right now she wasn't in the mood to confront that.

"Kind?" Agnes looked at her curiously. "I've heard him described as selfish, ambitious, focused and damn nosy—most frequently by his youngest sister. *Kind* isn't a word I hear too often."

She wasn't sure what word she'd use to describe the man who had been ruthlessly focused on nothing but her pleasure the night before.

Thinking about it made her cheeks heat, so that by the time Ryan strolled into the house, she looked as if she'd been sunbathing without protection.

"Ryan." Agnes brushed the crumbs from her lap. "You missed the cookies."

"My loss." He stooped to kiss his grandmother on her cheek, and Emily felt her throat close as she witnessed the genuine affection between them.

His childhood must have been hard and his loss overwhelming, but he'd grown up surrounded by this easy warmth and love.

"Lizzy and I were just leaving."

He straightened, squeezed Agnes's shoulder and turned to look at Emily. For a moment his gaze lingered on hers, and then he smiled. "I've rearranged my afternoon so I can take you out for lunch."

"Lizzy had a large breakfast, and—"

"Alone."

"Alone?"

The air was heated by a tension that was only present when he walked into a room.

"Good idea. Everyone needs a little adult time." Agnes was brisk. "Lizzy and I will sit here and sort through Rachel's old books and toys. It's a job I should have done a decade ago, but I've been putting it off."

Lizzy appeared in the doorway, Cocoa at her heels. "Can we play?"

"With the toys? Of course. You will decide what we keep and what we give away. Do you like books?"

Lizzy nodded slowly. "Emily has been reading to me."

"Good. Because I have more books than the library."

It was one thing to let Lizzy play in a different room, something else entirely to leave her alone with someone. Emily shook her head. "I can't."

"She's safe here with me." Agnes spoke quietly. "We're not going to leave the house."

Lizzy was holding Andrew tightly. "I'm not allowed to go to the beach."

Emily bit her lip. "Lizzy—"

"I'm too old for the beach," Agnes said calmly. "I'm too old to be brushing sand out of my shoes and out of the house. We are going to stay indoors and have fun. It's been a long time since I've had the pleasure of young company."

To refuse would be insulting to Agnes, but to accept would mean being alone with Ryan.

"She isn't used to strangers." She realized how ridiculous that was as an excuse, when Lizzy had virtually been raised by strangers.

Lizzy must have thought it, too, because she climbed onto the sofa next to Agnes. "I want to stay."

Deprived of excuses by the excuse herself, Emily gave a helpless shrug.

"If you're sure—"

Agnes smiled. "I can't think of anything I'd like more. Don't rush. We'll still be here when you get back, and nothing is going to happen."

Lizzy inched closer to Agnes. "Sometimes there are men with cameras."

Agnes's mouth tightened. "Not on my property, pumpkin."

As she left the house, Emily felt Ryan's hand on her back.

"You told my grandmother the truth?"

"Yes. Was that a mistake?"

"No. And you have no reason to worry about her safety. If Puffin Island were ever invaded, Agnes would lead the defense. She raised two children of her own and then took on three grandchildren. Lizzy is in good hands."

She tried to ignore the warmth of his hand. Tried to forget how those hands had felt as they'd moved over her body. "Four. You're forgetting to include yourself."

"I was part of the management team." His smile made her heart beat faster.

Her level of awareness was a constant hum beneath the anxiety about being responsible for Lizzy. "It's the first time I've left her."

"I know." He stopped and eased her to one side so that a family loaded down with beach gear could pass them. "Raising a child isn't about locking them away until they're eighteen and then pushing them out of the door. It's about giving them the tools to be independent. You should be pleased she was happy to stay with Agnes. She could have been clinging to you, especially after what happened. But we both know that this isn't all about Lizzy. You're looking for an excuse to avoid me."

"That isn't true."

"No? So look me in the eye."

"We're in public."

"I know and I promise not to rip your clothes off. Now look at me."

"What happens when people don't do what you want them to do?"

"If it's something that matters to me, I'm persistent."

Was he implying that she mattered to him? The thought of it made the blood rush from her head. Normally she was a calm, logical thinker, but whenever she was this close to him her thoughts scattered. "You have to back off, Ryan. I can't think when you say things like that."

"Good. You need to think less, not more." He took her arm and guided her across the street away from the bustle of the busy harbor, to the relative calm of Main Street with its attractive buildings and colorful storefronts. They walked past several sea and surf shops and a few high-end boutiques catering to the wealthy set who had fallen in love with the beauty and relative seclusion of Puffin Island. Emily had seen the lavish summer houses dotted around the island, from colonial homes to elaborate beach houses. Despite that, or perhaps because of it, the place had an eclectic, cosmopolitan feel.

"Where are we going?"

"I'm going to buy you an ice cream."

"A—what?"

"You said you'd eaten breakfast and didn't want lunch, so I'll buy you an ice cream instead. Simple pleasures. If you're going to teach Lizzy how to live, you need to start doing it yourself. The next thing I'm going to do is get you out of those clothes."

She felt as if she were trapped in an airless room. "You mean you don't want me to wear so much black?"

He gave her a wicked smile. "Take it any way you like." Without giving her a chance to respond, he pushed open the door of Summer Scoop and smiled at the young woman behind the counter. "Hi, Lisa, how's it going?"

"Good, thanks." The woman used that overly bright tone that people adopted when things were totally crap.

The place was empty.

"I'm treating Emily to ice cream." Ryan put his hand on the small of her back and eased her forward. "Something smooth, creamy and indulgent."

Lisa reached for the scoop. "Kirsti thinks there's an ice cream for every mood. How would you describe your mood today, Emily?"

She felt the pressure of Ryan's hand on her back. The slow deliberate stroke of his palm through the thin fabric of her shirt.

Was "sexually frustrated" a mood or a physical condition? She turned her head, saw the amused gleam in Ryan's eyes and glared at him. "I can't find the words to describe my mood."

"Then tell me your favorite flavor."

Trying to escape the dizzying, distracting stroke of his fingers, Emily stepped forward to examine the various options. "It all looks delicious. What do you recommend?" She was so hot she wanted to jump into the freezer with the ice cream.

"Children love Banana Buttermilk, but for adult first-timers I usually recommend Blueberry Booster or Smuggler's Tipple."

"Smuggler's Tipple?"

"Chocolate and rum." Lisa picked up a small pot. "I can do you a small taster?"

"No need. You said the word *blueberry*, so I'm sold."

Ryan chose Caramel Sea Salt. "Lisa moved here last summer from the mainland. She has six-year-old twins, Summer and Harry."

"Summer?" Emily glanced at the sign over the counter, but Lisa shook her head.

"Just a coincidence. Would you believe that was the name of the place?"

Ryan smiled. "Kirsti would say it was fate."

"Kirsti is an incurable optimist." Lisa's tired smile suggested she didn't suffer from the same affliction. "We arrived here last Easter for a holiday. We needed a fresh start—well, this seemed like a good place. We used to come in here for a treat, and one day the owner told us she was moving to Florida because she didn't like the winters here. My daughter decided it was named for her." She handed Emily a pretty waffle cone topped with creamy blueberry ice cream.

"Owning an ice cream business must be every child's dream."

"I wanted them to grow up surrounded by fresh air and a community of people who knew one another, so it seemed like my dream, too."

"But it isn't?"

Lisa kept her head down as she dipped into the salted

caramel ice cream. Emily could tell she was reluctant to discuss her problems with a customer.

"We're fine. But if a few more tourists chose to buy our ice cream, I wouldn't be sorry." She handed the cone to Ryan. "Eat it in the sunshine because we all know that by tomorrow the sun might have gone into hiding. Enjoy."

Emily licked around the melting edges and moaned. "This is the best thing I've ever tasted." She saw Ryan's gaze drop to her mouth. The heat in that look was enough to melt all the ice cream in Maine.

"I agree with Lisa." His voice was husky, and there was a shimmer of something dangerous in his eyes. "Let's eat this outside."

Emily left the shop, flushed from head to toe. She kept her gaze fixed on the harbor. "Lisa seems worried."

"Does she? The moment you started licking that ice cream, my mind went blank. I was thinking about your tongue and all the things I could do with that ice cream. All of them involved your naked body." He spoke in a low voice and then cleared his throat. "Good morning, Hilda. I didn't see you there."

"Ryan. Emily. It's a beautiful day. Have you caught the sun?" She peered at Emily. "You're looking red. This may not be the Caribbean, but don't make the mistake of thinking you can't burn here. Water intensifies the sun's rays."

"She has fair skin," Ryan said smoothly, "but I'll make sure she buys sunscreen later." He turned and winked at Emily who knew she was the color of a tomato.

"Sunscreen. Great idea." She tried desperately to

change the subject. "You were right about the ice cream, Hilda. It's delicious."

"Best ice cream in Maine. Breaks my heart to see the girl struggling, especially with those two young children. In my opinion it was unfair of May Newton to sell her the business in the first place." Hilda's mouth flattened into a thin line of disapproval. "She knew it was in trouble. No one can make the place pay. It's had five owners in as many years."

Emily frowned. "Five owners?"

"You can't sell enough ice cream in the summer months to keep a family going over the winter." Hilda waved at someone on the other side of the harbor. "I'll leave you two to finish your ice cream." She moved away, and Emily sagged against the wall of the shop.

"Do you think she knew?"

"That I was talking dirty to you five seconds before she arrived? Probably. She doesn't miss much."

"I'm going to have to move back to the mainland."

"Hilda had six children of her own, so I doubt that sex is a mystery to her. You have ice cream at the corner of your mouth. Am I allowed to lick it away?"

"Only if you don't mind being punched in public."

"I never object to a physical relationship, and it would do you good to rediscover some of those emotions you've been blocking out." His eyes were hooded, his voice low, and she felt her insides melt faster than the ice cream.

Flirting was as alien to her as all the other emotions swirling inside her. She tried desperately to change the subject. "Is it true that Summer Scoop is in trouble? That the place has had five owners in as many years?"

His smile told her he knew exactly what she was doing. "Yeah, that part is true."

"So you think Lisa made a mistake buying the business?"

He shrugged. "One person's mistake is another person's adventure."

She wondered if that comment was aimed at her. "But with two children to support, the stakes are different."

"True." He finished his ice cream and licked his fingers. "Children have a habit of killing adventure."

She thought of the way Lisa had talked about her kids. Even in that brief encounter, she could see they were everything to her. "I think to some people kids *are* the adventure."

"They can also be too much reality." His tone was dry. "How is your ice cream?"

"The ice cream is delicious. The place should be packed."

"It should be, but it never is. I'm probably a tiny bit to blame for that. The Ocean Club pulls in a lot of casual lunchtime and evening business."

"But it's a different market."

"Maybe, but we're all competing for the same tourist dollars."

Emily glanced at the pretty ice cream parlor. "There should be room for both of you. Do you stock her product?"

"Sorry?"

"Do you serve her products at the Ocean Club?"

"I have no idea. I don't micromanage. I leave that to the chef. I think he makes his own."

"This ice cream is good. And it's homemade on the island from the Warrens' organic dairy herd."

"How do you know that?"

"It says so on the poster. Makes me imagine green pastures and everything healthy, which is ironic given the fat content." She finished her ice cream regretfully. "That was good. It wouldn't hurt you to put in an order."

"That's what I have to do to gain approval?" There was humor in his eyes. "I'll talk to Anton."

"Anton? Seriously?" Emily laughed. "You have a chef called Anton?"

"I do."

"Is he French?"

"No. Born and bred in Maine. The things he can do with a lobster would make you cry. Can those shoes of yours cope with a walk?" He glanced down at her feet. "There's a view I want to show you."

And suddenly she realized that she was standing in the street, laughing with a man as if this was her life. As if she were free to follow her instincts and impulses.

Just for a moment, with the sun on her face and Ryan by her side, she'd forgotten everything.

"I should get back."

"Coward."

"I'm thinking of Lizzy. I haven't left her before."

"She'll be fine with my grandmother." His voice was soft. "Walk with me."

"Why?"

"Because it's midday and half the residents of Puffin Island are going about their business in Main Street. As you're keen to avoid attention, I'm suggesting we get out of here."

"You could just stop looking at me," Emily muttered. "That would do it."

"That isn't an option." He took her hand and drew her into the narrow street that ran between the bakery and the hardware store. It wound away from the main harbor area and was a shortcut to the Ocean Club.

"I might be able to help her."

"Who?"

"Lisa. I might be able to give her business advice. I'm a management consultant. It's what I do. It's what I'm good at."

They took the path that led up past the Ocean Club and turned inland. This side of the island was thickly wooded, with steep trails zigzagging through dense forest. On the other side was farmland, with rolling pastures leading down to the sea.

Shaded from sunshine, breathing in the smell of pine, Emily made a mental note to bring Lizzy here.

"It's pretty." And quiet. The only sound was the call of the birds and the snap of twigs under their feet. "I can see why Lisa would have chosen to live here."

"Here—" he handed her a bottle of insect repellent "—better use this on the areas that aren't covered. We have mosquitoes the size of small birds, and they love black. Tell me about your job."

"My expertise was strategy and operations. I worked mostly in the consumer goods industry."

"You know about ice cream?"

"Not specifically, but that doesn't matter. I'm a problem solver. I look at product, pricing, positioning, supply chains—" She broke off. "This is boring. You don't want to hear the detail."

"All those long words are turning me on, but I

confess I zoned out when you said 'positioning.'" He grinned at her. "Clearly I have a thing for management consultants. Who knew?"

"We're in a competitive market. Companies need to stay agile."

He groaned. "Honey, you are killing me. Just don't start talking about growth or I'll be arrested."

Because everything about him unsettled her, she chose to ignore the innuendo. "We apply lean principles—"

"That's going to be a challenge given the amount of fat in Summer Scoop ice cream. I assume you decided to be a management consultant because it requires not a shred of emotion."

"I like the logic and predictability of figures, that's true, but there is emotion attached to what I do. Companies expand and contract depending on the advice my company gives."

"But it isn't personal."

"No," she conceded. "It isn't personal. It suits the way my brain works."

"So, what are you going to do with that brain of yours now?"

"I don't know. I have enough money saved to support both of us for a little while, so I'm still taking it twelve hours at a time." Sun filtered through spruce and pine, and Emily realized they'd walked quite a distance from the harbor. "I never knew it was this densely wooded."

"Maine isn't called the Pine Tree State for nothing. It takes a couple of hours to walk to the top, but the views are incredible. I'll take you one day."

"And Lizzy."

His hesitation was so brief it would have been easy

to miss. "And Lizzy." His tone was deceptively light. "If that's what you want."

The way he said it left her in no doubt as to the way he saw their relationship.

For him, it was all about exploring the physical connection and nothing else.

As for her—she had no idea how she saw things.

Confused by her own feelings, she changed the subject. "Would she want help, do you think?"

"Lisa? I don't know her that well, but given that this was her dream, I'm guessing the answer to that would be yes. No one wants to give up a dream, do they? It gets a little steep here." He held out his hand, and she hesitated and then took it. Immediately those strong fingers curled around hers, and she remembered the night before, the way they'd felt locked in her hair, stroking her breasts, buried deep—

"I'm not dressed for hiking." Her face was hot, and she tried to ignore the feel of his hand on hers.

"Are you too hot? Unfasten a button on that shirt. Don't worry about insects, I'll keep my eyes on you."

"I'm cool, thank you." She sent him a look designed to wither, but he merely smiled.

"Really? I'm hot as hell, but that may be because I'm marinating in my own sinful thoughts about last night." Twigs snapped under his feet as he walked. "Have you ever had forest sex?"

Emily almost stumbled. His hand tightened on hers, and she kept her eyes on the ground, picking her way along the trail. "I've lived in cities all my life."

"You've never had outdoor sex?"

"You mean apart from all the sex I had in the middle of Times Square?" Her sarcasm drew a smile.

"You never had sex in Times Square." Swift and sure, he backed her against a tree, caged her. "You never had sex anywhere you might be caught. With you it's all locked doors and the lights off. I bet you've only ever had sex in a bed." A smile flickered at the corners of his mouth, and she felt her tummy tumble.

"You don't know that."

"I do." His gaze dropped to her mouth, and his voice was rough. "Because you've only ever had 'nice' sex. And 'nice' sex isn't the sort that happens with your back against a tree and your skirt around your waist."

"I'm not wearing a skirt, and I don't see anything exciting about bark burn."

Eyes gleaming, he lowered his head toward hers. "Want me to show you?"

Yes. She, for whom sex had been all the things he'd described. Locked door and lights out. "I have to get back to Lizzy." The only sound was the birds in the trees and the pounding of her own heart. "Seriously, Ryan." She tried to evade him, but she was trapped between the tree and the hard power of his thighs.

His hand came up to her face, his fingers gentle. "Am I scaring you?"

She didn't answer because her heart was in her mouth. Her stomach squirmed with a twist of intense desire. Even the smell of fresh air and the sound of the sea hadn't been enough to cool the memories of what he'd made her feel.

"Not scare exactly. But my life is already complicated enough."

"I'm not offering you complicated." His voice husky, he lowered his head and trailed his mouth along the line of her jaw. "In fact, right now I've been reduced to man in its most basic form. What I'm offering is simple."

"You're talking about sex." Her eyes closed and her heart raced. She felt the erotic drag of his mouth move down to her neck and linger on the pulse just above her collarbone. "Sex is never simple."

"It can be."

Dizzy with the intensity of wanting, she placed her hand on his chest "Ryan—"

"Yeah, I know." Reluctantly he eased away from her. "I'm pushing my luck for a first date."

"This isn't a date."

"Ice cream followed by a walk in the woods? On Puffin Island that counts as serious." He tucked a strand of hair behind her ear with a gentle hand. "We'll go back now. You don't have the right footwear for a long walk. If you're going to be living on Puffin Island, you might want to do something about that. Unless you have a secret stash of outdoor gear?"

"Most of my clothes are like the ones I'm wearing."

"That's what I figured. This is an outdoor paradise. We'll have you hiking, mountain biking and kayaking in no time. Better buy some equipment. We have a great selection in the Ocean Club. And I'm going to take you out on my yacht. The best way to see the island is from the sea." They started walking back down the trail, with sunlight beaming through the trees and the sounds of the forest in the background.

"I will walk in the forest, but I'm never going on a yacht."

"Penobscot Bay has some of the best sailing in the world."

"Maybe, but that doesn't mean I have to experience

it firsthand. I don't like the idea of all that water underneath me, and—" she hesitated "—I don't swim."

He stopped. "You never learned?"

"I haven't been in the water since that day."

Shock spread across his face. "I assumed—that
should have been the first thing your mother did for
you."

"She didn't, and I'm glad she didn't."

"Everyone should be able to swim."

"Not me. I don't need to because I'm never going in
the water." She tried to pull away, but he tightened his
grip and pulled her back toward him.

"I'm going to teach you."

She closed her hands over his arms to steady herself, her fingers biting into the rock-hard muscle of his
biceps. "I don't want to learn."

"I'll teach you in the Ocean Club pool. There's a
shallow end."

"I don't care if you're offering to teach me in your
tub—I'm not interested in learning to swim. I am happy
to hike and ride a mountain bike, but you will not persuade me to go on a boat of any sort, and you certainly
won't persuade me to swim."

"Not even if I promise to keep you safe?"

She looked into those eyes and felt her center of balance shift. "A woman might be many things with you,
Ryan Cooper. But I don't think 'safe' is one of them."

Nine

At Lizzy's insistence, they called at Agnes's every morning to walk Cocoa. Resigned to her new role as dog walker, Emily paid a trip to the Outdoor Store, equipped them both with hiking boots, rain slickers, insect repellent and a small rucksack, and each day they took the dog and explored a different part of the island. On the first day they followed the road out of the harbor and along the trail that wound its way through overgrown fields to the south of the island, accompanied by song sparrows and butterflies. The trail skirted the edge of the Warrens' farm, sixty-five acres of mixed hardwood, pasture and hay fields. They stopped to admire the herd of dairy cows who provided the organic milk for the ice cream at Summer Scoop, and walked on through meadows crowded with Queen Anne's lace and goldenrod.

On another day they walked the coastal path around to the east of the island. Emily chose the route that went a little way inland, rather than the path that clung to the rocks and rose up over the bluff. Here, the mossy woods crowded the shoreline, sending dark shadows across rocky coves. Gulls bobbed in the water, and seals played hide-and-seek in the surf around the rocks. Cocoa strained at her leash, desperate to explore, but the one place Emily refused to walk was on the beach itself.

She tried to retrace the walk she'd done with Ryan into the woods, but Lizzy was nervous and Emily was afraid of getting lost. She insisted Lizzy wear her hat whenever they were outdoors, but the people she passed were either tourists or locals and none of them showed any interest in a young woman and her daughter. Gradually the acute fear of discovery faded to a dull, background throb.

They returned from their walks at lunchtime, and Emily called into the delicatessen to pick up something for lunch. They then took it back to Agnes's and ate it picnic style, either on the covered porch overlooking her garden or, if mist had blown in, at her kitchen table.

Occasionally Emily left Lizzy with Agnes while she went and bought provisions, but otherwise she kept the child close.

"Do you think I'm overprotective?"

Lizzy had fallen asleep on the sofa after an exhausting morning with Cocoa, and Agnes and Emily were drinking iced tea in the light-filled living room.

"I think you had a bad experience, and you haven't had to rebuild your confidence." Agnes was sorting through another box of children's books for Lizzy. "You lived a life that didn't include the sea or young children, so you didn't have a reason to challenge your fear or push yourself out of your comfort zone. But you will, now you're living here. You can't live on Puffin Island and ignore the sea. It's essential to island life. It feeds us, and it keeps us connected to the mainland."

"I think I preferred the mainland. There was no

chance of drowning in Manhattan, and I never went near the Hudson."

"But Manhattan has other dangers."

Emily sipped her tea. "I didn't really think about them."

"That's because we're all a product of our experiences. Someone who had a bad experience in a city might think differently."

"Do you think I can change?"

"You already are. Look where you're sitting." Agnes added another book to the pile. "A week ago you sat with your back to the window, but now you're in my favorite spot on the window seat, looking at the boats on the water. It's a pretty sight, isn't it?"

Emily turned her head. "There's glass between me and the water."

"But you're looking at it. That's progress. And I've made progress, too. Lizzy and I have cleared four boxes of books this week."

"Most of them are now in Castaway Cottage. Thank you. It's generous of you. And I love books." Books were almost all she'd brought with her from her old life. Old battered copies and first editions she'd collected over the years. "Whenever I had something to celebrate, I bought a book."

"I need to reduce all the clutter, but I'm not good at parting with anything." Agnes reached for another box. "This is something else I can't bring myself to clear out."

"What is it?"

"All of Ryan's stories. Of course, a lot of it is online, but I'm not good with the internet, so he used to send me the paper versions." She opened the box, and Emily saw neatly sorted stacks of newspaper clippings.

"There were stories about him in the press?"

"He wasn't the subject of the story, he *wrote* the story. He didn't tell you that? He's so modest. He won a Pulitzer Prize, you know, for news reporting."

No, she didn't know. Emily's mouth dried. "Are you saying he's a journalist?"

"Was." Agnes leafed through the clippings, pride on her face. "The best. He had a way of getting to the emotion of a story. He's a good listener. People tell him things. Things they would never tell other people."

I'm not afraid of emotions.

Emily stood up, feeling as if she were sleepwalking. She'd told him things. Things she'd never told other people. She'd done things with him she hadn't done with anyone else. "Would you look after Lizzy for a while? There's something I need to do."

"Of course." Agnes glanced up from her news clippings. "She's perfectly safe here with me."

It took Emily less than five minutes to walk the short distance to the Ocean Club.

She strode through the door and into the crowded Bar and Grill where Kirsti was circulating.

"Hi, Emily." Kirsti gave her a friendly smile. "No Lizzy today?"

"She's with Agnes." Her voice sounded robotic. "I need to see Ryan."

"Of course you do." Kirsti behaved as if Emily's unplanned visit was the most natural thing in the world. "He's in his office. He's had a hell of a morning, so I know he's going to be pleased to see you."

No, Emily thought grimly as she walked to the back of the Ocean Club. *He most definitely wouldn't be.*

Ryan's office faced the water, and he was on the phone with his feet on the desk, when she walked in.

"He was supposed to fix the pump. I told him we'd—" He broke off as he saw Emily. "I'll call you back, Pete. Go check it out. Don't delegate this one. If necessary I'll dig out the tools and do it myself." He hung up the phone and smiled.

That assured smile was the final straw. "I need to talk to you."

"Just when I thought a bad day wasn't going to turn good, you walk in." He lifted his eyebrows as she slammed the door shut. "Is this about sex in public places? Because—"

"You lied to me." The anger was like a burning coal inside her. Later there would be other emotions, but right now fury overrode everything else. Fury and a deep sense of betrayal.

Ryan removed his feet from the desk. "Calm down."

"I'm calm. Just angry."

"I'm not sure it's possible to be calm and angry."

She paced across his office and stood in front of him. "I won't ask why you didn't tell me, because that part is obvious, but I will ask what your intentions are. I have a right to know that." She needed to know whether she was going to have to leave the island. The thought made her stomach churn because she had no idea where she'd go.

"My intentions?"

"You lied to me. You sat there and talked to me about how the press wouldn't be interested. You reassured me. You sat in my kitchen and acted as if you were my friend. As if you were someone I could trust. You bought Lizzy a *hat*, for God's sake, to hide her from prying eyes and all the time you're—you're—"

"Wait a minute. Slow down. We're talking about Lizzy? I thought you were talking about this thing we have." The look he gave her could have singed the edges of her hair. "The chemistry. I thought it unsettled you. That's why I backed off. I was giving you space."

Her gaze met his, and for a moment she was knocked off balance. "I'm talking about the fact you're a journalist, Ryan. When were you going to tell me? After a piece on Lizzy came out with your byline?"

He stilled. "How did you find out?"

"I'd like to say I looked you up on the internet because anyone in my position with a shred of common sense would have done that, but I didn't." After they'd had waffles on the deck that first morning she'd looked up the Ocean Club and spent half an hour on their slick website. She'd read his bio and been impressed. She hadn't thought to put his name alone into a search engine. "Agnes was sorting through a file of all the stories you've written. She's proud of you. She didn't seem to know you'd conveniently kept that part of your life from me."

His gaze didn't shift from hers. "Did you look at the stories?"

"No. I wasn't in the mood to mull over your career success. I was too busy wondering why you'd chosen to keep it from me. And the answer is pretty obvious."

"Emily, listen—"

"I listened when you suggested Lizzy and I join you for lunch. I listened when you said I could trust you. I told you everything. And you're such a good listener, aren't you, Ryan? So good at parting people from their secrets. For a while I thought you had a gift with people, but now I realize it's one of the tools of your trade. You even won a prize for it. Tell me, is sex another part of your superior technique to get people to tell you everything?"

His face was blank of expression. "You know it isn't."

"I don't know anything." She felt an ache deep in her gut because even now part of her wanted to believe that what had happened between them was real. "All I know is that you lied."

"I was going to tell you. I was waiting for the right moment."

"And when was that going to be? When you'd told everyone the whereabouts of Juliet Elizabeth Fox?" She saw the brief flare of anger in his eyes.

"Do you really think I would do that?" He stood up so suddenly the chair scraped on the floor. "Hell, Emily. I've been doing everything I can to make the two of you feel safe here."

"For what purpose? So that you can tip off a journalist as to exactly where Lana Fox's child is living and get the credit? Is this what you journalists call an exclusive? You deliberately withheld information about yourself. If your past had no impact on the present, then why didn't you tell me the truth? You told me about your childhood, about your brothers and sisters, your parents, Agnes—but not once did you mention that you used to be a journalist."

He swore under his breath and ran his hand over the back of his neck. "Listen—" He broke off and scowled as the door to his office opened, and Kirsti put her head around. "Not now—"

"Sorry, boss." Kirsti slunk away, closing the door behind her again, and Emily turned and walked toward it.

"You didn't need to send her away. I've said all I have to say."

"Good. So now it's my turn. Sit down."

"There is nothing you have to say that I can possibly want to hear." She reached the door at the same time he did, and he stretched past her and pushed it shut with the flat of his hand.

"Except the truth. You don't have to believe me, but you'll at least listen." He was standing so close to her she could smell that elusive male scent that made her knees weaken.

"Why are you suddenly so keen to tell me the truth?"

"Look around you, Emily. What you see is a man who has plowed every last dollar and cent into this business and this island. I'm not a journalist. I haven't worked as a journalist for four years, and even when I did I wasn't reporting the sort of story you're describing." There was a hardness to his jaw and shadows in his eyes that she hadn't seen before.

Or maybe she hadn't been looking.

"So why didn't you mention what you used to do?"

"Because it isn't part of my life now, and once I discovered why you were here, I knew I couldn't talk about it. You needed someone to trust, and if I'd told you, you wouldn't have trusted me."

"You're right, I wouldn't have. But that should have been my choice to make."

"Brittany trusts me. Isn't that enough for you?"

"She should have told me the truth instead of telling me you were a friend."

"I am a friend. And the reason she didn't tell you is because she didn't think it was relevant."

"You were a journalist! How can that not be relevant? And whatever has happened before, I need you to be honest with me now, for Lizzy's sake, if not for mine. Should I be worried? Have you told anyone she's here?"

He hesitated for a second too long. "I made one call after that day you saw the photo in the newspaper, but only to try and get a sense of how interested people were."

Her heart started to race. "You *called* someone?"

"An old friend. And he didn't know why I was calling."

"How do you know? What if he guesses? They could come here."

"The media is losing interest. Lana was the story, not her child. They're not going to come."

"If they do—if they find her and scare her—there is no quick way off the island. If they come, where do I run to?"

"You won't need to run. They won't come."

"That first day when you came knocking on my door—" it was painful to ask the question because she was afraid of the answer "—it wasn't because you were looking for Lizzy?"

"I've told you. Brittany asked me to keep an eye on you."

"Why would you agree? I've known you long enough to know you don't do anything that doesn't suit you. What is this relationship you have with Brittany that you're willing to put your life on hold to keep an eye on a stranger? What do you gain from this if it isn't a story you can sell? She told me that you owe her."

He gave a tired smile. "That's a private joke."

"I've had enough of private. Exactly *what* do you owe her?"

He turned and paced across to the window of his office to stare out over the water. "I was best man at Brittany's wedding."

Of all the things she'd expected him to say, it hadn't been that. "Her wedding? *The* wedding? So you're friends with the bastard who walked out on her at the end of their honeymoon? Oh, my God." A suspicion formed in her mind. "We saw him. He was flying the plane Skylar took last weekend. I recognized him. The first thing Brittany did when she arrived at college was pin a large photo of him on the wall to remind her never to be stupid about a man again. I stared at his face long enough to be able to recognize him when I saw him in person. Did you know he was back here?"

"Yeah, I knew. Zach is the best pilot you'll ever meet. He owns his own plane now and flies the mega-rich to their yachts and beach cottages. The rest of the time he does his own thing, and it so happens he's chosen to base himself on Puffin Island."

"He was flying for Maine Island Air."

"He helps them out sometimes. I didn't think it was something that needed mentioning as Brittany isn't here anyway, and their marriage was over before it started."

"You are the master at withholding information."

"Whereas you clearly support the principle of full disclosure, so by all means go ahead and tell her he's here if you think that's going to make her day and lift her mood."

She knew it wouldn't. "If you were best man, then you must know him well. Are you two still friends?"

"Yes." He didn't hesitate. "Friendship isn't something you throw away just because someone makes a bad decision."

"Bad decision? You don't think he should have left Brittany?" She saw tension ripple across those wide shoulders and he turned to look at her.

"What I think," he said slowly, "is that he should never have married her in the first place. That was the bad decision."

"So why does Brittany blame you?"

He gave a humorless smile. "Because I knew it was a match made in hell. He got cold feet and wanted to ditch her on her wedding day, and I drove him to the wedding instead of the airport because I knew she'd be devastated. I didn't want him to hurt her. Turned out he did that anyway, and I made it worse. Ditching her at the altar would have been a hell of a lot less complicated than ditching her at the end of the honeymoon."

It was a lot to take in.

"What about the rest of it?" She forced herself to ask one more question. "Did Brittany tell you to kiss me? Was that part of the deal?"

His eyes darkened. "You know it wasn't."

"I don't know anything, Ryan. And I don't know you." With those quiet words she turned and left the room.

He waited until he knew Lizzy would be in bed and then knocked on the door of Castaway Cottage, unsure whether she'd even open it.

The island was folded in mist and darkness, and behind him he could hear the rush of the sea against the shore. He was thinking how much courage it must have taken to choose this place as a refuge, when the door opened.

Emily's feet were bare, and her hair fell soft and loose around her face.

She didn't look pleased to see him, but he'd braced himself for that.

"I need to talk to you."

"We've said all there is to say."

"I want to show you something. Give me five minutes. If you still want me to leave after that, I'll leave." The thought of what he was about to do made him feel as shaky as an alcoholic who hadn't had a drink in a month.

She stared at the box in his arms and opened the door a little wider. "Lizzy is asleep."

"Good, because this is between us." He carried the box through to the kitchen. Given the choice, he would have destroyed it long ago, but he knew keeping it meant a lot to his grandmother.

He put it down on the table next to one of Lizzy's paintings, a classic child's drawing of a house with smoke coming from the chimney. There was a garden, drawn with careful strokes of green, and a curve of custard yellow sand next to an ocean bluer than anything he'd seen in Maine. It was obvious to him that this was his grandmother's house. The innocent charm of the picture jarred uncomfortably with the dark reality he'd placed next to it.

He stood for a moment with his hands on the box.

He'd chosen to live life looking forward, not back, and he didn't relish what he was about to do.

"That's Agnes's box." She stood next to him, waiting. "I already know what's in it."

No, he thought. *You don't.* "I want you to take a look. Read."

"I don't need to read."

"You wanted to know about my past." He felt distant and detached, as if someone else had climbed into his body. "This is my past."

"Which you try and forget. Why? Do you regret the stories you wrote?"

"No. But they stay with you." He flipped open the top and gripped the back of the chair until his knuckles were white. "Especially that one."

She stared at his face and then down at the file. In slow motion, she picked up the clipping on top. Award-Winning Photojournalist Killed in Kabul?

"We worked with a translator and a driver. Together we made two trips into Iraq and four into Afghanistan. Me as foreign correspondent, Finn as a photojournalist."

There was a long silence. "You were a war reporter?"

"I met Finn on my first day in Baghdad, and we hit it off right away. We had an ongoing argument about which was the better medium for telling a story—words or images. He said that I wrote about the truth whereas he showed it. Neither of us wanted to be embedded with the troops. We wanted to be free to tell the stories we wanted to tell. The ones other people weren't telling."

She sank down onto one of the kitchen chairs. "Ryan—"

"After a British journalist was killed, Finn decided he'd had enough. He said we'd ceased to see beauty in the world, only the bad and the ugly. Everything we saw was distorted and discolored by conflict. He wanted to take photographs that didn't involve human suffering. I talked about this place all the time, and we were always making plans. I was going to run a sailing school, and he was going to use his photographic skills to raise awareness of the importance of marine conservation. On really bad days we decided we'd open a bar together and drink our way through the profits." He stopped and heard the scrape of the chair on the floor as she rose to her feet.

A moment later a glass of water appeared by his hand.

He took a sip, embarrassed by how much his hand was shaking.

"We were about to fly home, but I wanted to do one more story, so we went with our translator and fixer to a local village. Finn was joking that he was going to sail my yacht while I did the work when our vehicle was hit." Just for a moment he felt it again, the blinding flash and then the white and the lack of sound. "We were close to a military base. A helicopter pilot risked his life to get us out of there, but it was too late for Finn. He was killed instantly."

Her hand reached across and covered his, slim warm fingers sliding between his.

"I'm sorry."

"I was the one who was sorry. If it hadn't been for me, we would have been on our way home. I was the one who pushed for one more story." Even now, four years later, the knowledge left a bitter taste in his mouth and the gnawing agony of guilt. He reached into the file and pulled out a photograph. "This was one of his last photographs."

She removed her hand from his and took the photograph. "It's very powerful." She stared at it for a long moment and then placed it carefully back in the box and closed the lid. "You were badly injured?"

"Bad enough. I had serious internal injuries and my shoulder was messed up. I was in and out of hospital for four months. I had eight rounds of surgery. And I was a difficult patient. Ask Agnes and Rachel. They took the brunt of it." He stared at the file. "Rachel was home from college for the summer and she virtually moved into my hospital room and stayed there with me until I was discharged. The first day back on the island, she forced me to get dressed, and I managed to walk as far as the harbor before having to sit down. My legs wouldn't hold me and my shoulder was agony. Every day she made me get up and walk a little farther until eventually I was walking as far as the lighthouse. I had no idea my little sister could be such a bully. When I was strong enough to walk as far as Shell Cove, she decided I should start swimming. I remember the day she and Alec forced me to go sailing. It was a perfect day, and I felt the wind fill the sails and knew this was where I wanted to stay."

"So the sea healed you."

"In a way, but I think it was more about the people. Before I left the island I couldn't wait to get away. I felt trapped, I was going crazy. I thought anywhere in the world had to be better than this place, living among people who know everything from how much you weighed when you were born to what you liked to eat for dinner. Then I discovered differently." He licked his lips, not sure whether by being economical with his words he was sparing her the detail or himself. "I guess you could say my priorities changed. An honest person would probably say it was a shame I had to be blown up to discover something I should have known all along."

"I think we don't always see things clearly when we're living in the middle of something." There was a long silence. "I owe you an apology."

"No. I'm the one who owes you an apology for not being honest, but I was afraid you wouldn't trust me. And I wanted you to trust me."

"Because you feel you owe Brittany."

He could have told her the truth. He could have told her that the reason he couldn't stay away from her had nothing to do with Brittany, but that would have led the relationship in a direction he suspected she wasn't ready for it to go. And he wasn't sure he wanted it to go there, either.

Whatever she thought about her suitability for the role of parent, she'd shown herself to be fiercely protective of Lizzy. That fact alone meant he should stay the hell away from her.

"That's right." He kept his face blank. "I owed a friend a favor."

"The other night—"

"You had a bad experience. Neither of us was thinking straight." Finding willpower he didn't known he possessed, he stepped back and reached for the file. "I should go. I have a pile of paperwork waiting for me before I turn in. If you need anything, you know where I am."

He saw something flicker in her eyes. Hurt? Confusion? Either way, he saw her register the dismissal and draw the conclusion that his attentions had all been driven by nothing more than a Good Samaritan inclination and a debt owed to a friend.

It was a measure of her inexperience that she believed his words over her own instincts.

If she'd looked into his eyes, she might have questioned it because he was pretty sure that the words coming out of his mouth were not backed up by the expression on his face.

He wanted to drive her back against the wall and kiss her until she could no longer articulate her own name. He wanted to strip off those clothes and fill his hands with those voluptuous curves.

Instead, he ground his teeth and walked to the door.

Ten

A spell of hot weather brought tourists flocking to Puffin Island. They spilled off the ferry, a riot of color and smiles, overloaded with bags, children, strollers and equipment for all weather. Some came by car, some as foot passengers, and most of them headed for the beaches close to the harbor. The waterfront was crowded, the restaurants full and the locals talked about how this was the best start to a summer season they could remember in a long time.

The bay was busy, the water dotted with boats of all shapes and sizes, from the majestic schooners that Lizzy called pirate ships to sleek racing boats and small pleasure crafts.

"Can we see the puffins?" Lizzy paused on the harbor, watching as a crowd of people queued to board one of the many trips around the island to Puffin Rock. "Ryan said he'd take us."

"He's very busy." It had been over a week since she'd seen him, and she'd been trying desperately to put him out of her mind. It was hard, just as it was hard to think up excuses to stay away from the water.

Emily looked at the boat bobbing in the waves and felt sick. She was getting a little more confident each day, but was still a long way from taking Lizzy on a boat trip. "Is there anything else you'd like to do?"

"Waffles and chocolate milk?"

Everything Lizzy suggested involved Ryan.

After he'd left that night, Emily had switched on her laptop and done what she should have done right from the start. Typed his name into the search engine.

She'd clicked on article after article, and when she'd finally shut down, hours later, her cheeks had been wet from all the tears she'd shed.

He'd told her he wasn't afraid of emotion, and that was backed up by everything she'd read. His writing was full of emotion. He didn't just report the facts, he reported the effect on those who were suffering until the reader ceased to be an outside observer and slid into the story. She'd felt the heat, tasted the dust, cried with the mother who had lost a child to a roadside bomb. And she'd read the reports written by others on the accident that had wounded him and killed his friend. And they were glowing reports. As a journalist he'd been respected both by his own profession and the military.

The explosion had been global news.

Exhausted, she'd taken herself to bed and lain awake for hours, thinking about how hard his recovery must have been. Clues to just how hard had been in everything he hadn't said.

But he'd built a new life. The life he and his friend had planned together.

And that life didn't include children. It was a responsibility he'd made it clear he didn't want.

He'd helped her because he owed Brittany. There

was nothing more to it than that, and she wasn't going to do that horribly needy thing of looking for more. A few steamy kisses didn't mean anything to a man like him. Even without knowing his background, there was a raw physicality to him that told her that a simple sexual relationship was familiar territory to him. And no doubt none of those relationships had included sex with the lights out.

She needed to move on.

Pushing it out of her mind, she dragged herself back to the present.

"How about ice cream?" Trying to do something that would reduce the likelihood of bumping into Ryan, she made an alternative suggestion. "Let's go to Summer Scoop."

Visiting the shop had become a routine, and not just because Lizzy loved the ice cream. Emily was keen to support the struggling business. She liked Lisa and sympathized with her situation.

"Chocolate is still my favorite." Five minutes later Lizzy was licking her cone, the ice cream sliding down her chin. "Can we live in a place that sells ice cream?"

Lisa handed her a napkin. "It's not the dream it seems, sugar."

Because it was Saturday, both the twins were hovering. They alternated between "helping" in the store and reading, playing or watching a DVD in the little cottage attached to the business premises while Lisa supervised through an open door.

Knowing how hard it was to keep Lizzy entertained, Emily wondered how she managed it. "It must be hard work."

Lisa pushed blueberry ice cream into a crisp waffle

cone. "The irony is that I came here because I wanted a better life for the kids. I wanted them to live close to nature. I saw us spending time together as a family. But I spend less time with them now than I did when I was living with my mother in Boston." She handed the cone to Emily. "I'm working, and they're doing their own thing through that door in the living room. At weekends they 'help' in here, but they get bored with that pretty quickly. They entertain each other, but I can't afford to close, so that I can have a day out with them."

"Could you employ someone one day a week?"

"We don't make enough money to pay anyone. One of the freezers broke last week, and that used the last chunk of my savings. You don't want to hear about this. It's boring." Lisa opened a drawer and put a fresh pile of napkins on the counter.

"It's not boring to me. I'm just sorry your dream isn't working out the way you wanted it to."

"I have no one to blame but myself. I had my head in the clouds. No one before me has been able to make this place work, but I thought I'd be different. I like to call it optimism, but my mother says it's blind stupidity." That confession came with a smile, but Emily heard the thickening in her voice.

It was that, together with the hint of weary resignation, that made up her mind.

She dropped into a crouch next to her niece. "How would you like to watch a DVD with Summer and Harry?"

Lizzy stared at her. "Now?"

"Yes. They're just through that door." She felt a flutter of anxiety and suppressed it. She reminded herself of what Ryan had said about the importance of

Lizzy becoming independent. "I'll be right here, talking to Lisa. We'll leave the door open." She could see the halo of Summer's blond hair through a crack in the door, hear laughter as the twins watched a cartoon.

Lisa looked surprised, but she pushed open the door to the cottage, and moments later Lizzy was happily settled with the twins and a bowl of popcorn.

"Have you noticed how similar Lizzy is to the twins? They could almost be triplets!"

"It's the hair." Satisfied that Lizzy was safe, Emily turned back to Lisa. "Tell me the truth. How bad is it?"

Lisa gave a tired shrug. "Bad enough to make me want to eat a vat of chocolate ice cream by myself. I stayed up most of the night looking at the numbers, but they were still the same this morning. Looking at them doesn't change the fact this dream is over for me."

"You're sure?"

"Yes. I keep hoping and putting off the decision, but I'm not going to make it through another winter. It will take me a while to sell this place, and I can't afford two places. I don't know which is worse—giving up on my dream or moving back home with my mother and hearing her say 'I told you so.' She makes me feel about the same age as the kids."

"Is there no alternative?"

"Not that I can see." Lisa's eyes filled, and she pressed her fingers to her mouth. "Sorry. I can't believe I'm telling you this. You came in for an ice cream, and instead of a blob of blueberry I give you a dollop of self-pity topped off with liquid misery. I don't charge for that, by the way. It's on the house."

"I asked the question." Emily grabbed a handful of napkins and handed them over. "Here. Blow."

"I don't want the kids to see me like this. You know what it's like." Lisa blew her nose hard. "You try and keep a bright smile on your face, no matter how bad things are. And when I tuck them in at night I realize that none of it matters really as long as I have them. They're the best thing in my life." She gave a faint smile. "Thanks for listening."

"I can do more than listen. I might be able to help, if you'd like me to." Emily glanced around the store, looking at all the unused space. "You say that no one has been able to make this business pay. Did anyone ever try doing anything different with it?"

"Different? You mean apart from sell ice cream?"

"There's more than one way of selling ice cream." Emily walked to the door and stared through the glass to the busy harbor. "There are plenty of people out there. The island is busy."

"But the tourists don't always come in here, so that doesn't help me."

Emily watched the flow of people. "Because they walk straight off the ferry and turn left to the beach."

"On a hot day, yes. And to walk past Summer Scoop, they need to turn right. They sometimes call in at Swim and Sail or visit the Lobster Hatchery, but they don't come down this far." Lisa's shoulders sagged. "I'm doomed."

"You're not doomed. Every tourist that arrives on that ferry is a potential customer. We just need to think about how to tempt people in."

"I was thinking of taking my clothes off." Lisa gave another weak smile. "Just kidding. That would scare them away. I did think of putting a sign up by the ferry if they'd let me, but then I decided it wouldn't help.

Folks just want to head to the beach. And you know what the weather is like in this place—it's sunny now, but we get our share of fog and rain, and then people are thinking about shelter, not ice cream. They want something to do with fractious children."

Still thinking, Emily turned. "Fractious children?"

"Yes. You're stuck in a rental property or a hotel watching the rain sheet down or trying to see through mist thicker than the steam from a kettle. You put on the same DVD and then the kids start fighting, and it's all *'Mom, I'm bored.'* Puffin Island is an outdoor place. There's stuff you can do in the rain, but drying clothes every day can be exhausting."

Emily strolled across the room, her mind exploring various options. Usually she worked as part of a team of people, and the businesses were large corporations. Her contribution merged with those of others, like a single drop of rain blending with the ocean, unidentifiable and yet still part of the whole. "You have plenty of space."

"It needs redecorating, but I don't have the funds for it and I can't afford to close while it's done."

"Maybe we could do something imaginative with the space. Something that encourages people to come in when it's raining. Offer something they can't get anywhere else on the island."

"I don't have the cash to invest in a new venture."

"It won't be a new venture. Just a few additions to the old one. Tell me about the business itself. Who do you rent the building from?"

"Someone who knows how to bleed a person dry."

"And how many different types of ice cream do you stock?"

"Thirty, but not all of them sell well."

"Thirty?" It sounded like a lot to Emily. Her head was crowded with ideas and questions. "We need to start at the beginning. Those figures that kept you up all night. Would you share them with me?" Back in her comfort zone, she knew what was needed. Here, finally, was something she knew how to do. "If you're willing to share it, I'd like everything you can give me on your business. Turnover, profit, loss—any information you have."

Lisa blinked. "If you give me your email address I'll send some spreadsheets to you. There isn't much profit."

"Yet." Emily scribbled down her email. "We're going to change that."

"Do you really think you might be able to help?"

"I hope so. Helping businesses used to be my job." She didn't add that most of the businesses she'd worked for had been faceless, multinational corporations.

If anything, the small, personal nature of the business made success all the more imperative.

If this business failed, it directly affected a family.

Lisa looked uncomfortable. "I can't afford to pay you, unless you call free ice cream payment."

"If it's blueberry, then the answer is yes. And no payment is necessary, but if it makes you feel more comfortable you can pay me in advice."

"Advice?"

"I have no idea how to raise a six-year-old," Emily said frankly. "You have two of them, and they seem healthy and happy, so you must be doing a lot right. And you seem to do it without turning into a ball of anxiety, so any tips would be welcome."

Lisa gave a disbelieving laugh. "Seriously? That's what you want in exchange for saving my business? You've been a mother as long as I have."

Emily hesitated. "No," she said finally, "I haven't. Lizzy is my niece." She looked around for somewhere to sit. "Do you know what you need in here? Some stools and a little bar where people can sit indoors if they want to." But in the absence of seating, she leaned against the wall, and ten minutes later she'd told Lisa an abbreviated version of the story. All she left out was Lizzy's true identity. That, she hadn't trusted to anyone except Ryan and Agnes.

"So you'd never even *met* Lizzy until a couple of weeks ago?"

"That's right. And I am messing it up."

"I'm sure you're not."

Emily thought about the incident on the beach. Of the number of times Lizzy had asked if they could go and see the puffins and she'd refused. "Trust me, I am."

Lisa was about to say something when the door opened, and Ryan strolled in.

Emily felt her legs melt beneath her. The sensation of control left her. One glance and she was like a teenager with a serious infatuation, except that she'd never felt anything as intense as this as a teenager.

It was the first time they'd seen each other since that evening at her house.

She knew she owed him an apology but had been too much of a coward to seek him out and say what needed to be said.

He paused on the threshold, his gaze locked on hers. She felt a rush of hunger, an awareness so sharp it made her stomach knot, that same white heat that came when he touched her. It felt as if they were the only two people in the room.

Except that they weren't.

"Ryan!" Lisa walked across to him, apparently oblivious to the electric atmosphere. "Emily is going to help me think of ways to boost the business."

"That's good to know." He pushed the door shut. "And it relates to why I'm here."

Emily wondered if he had the same effect on all women and then noticed Lisa's pink cheeks and decided that, yes, of course he did. Ryan Cooper was a sexy guy. No woman was likely to miss that.

She wiped her fingers on the napkin. "I'll leave the two of you to talk."

"Don't go." Ryan strolled across to the freezer and scanned the rows of ice cream. "I have a business proposition for you, Lisa. We'd like to start using your ice creams at the Ocean Club."

Emily felt a rush of gratitude. Without looking at Lisa's finances, she had a feeling that it might not make enough of a difference to keep Summer Scoop afloat, but at least it was a positive step. And he'd taken it.

Lisa's face suggested that any good news was worth celebrating. "Seriously?"

"It's good ice cream. You'll need to talk to Anton about flavors and quantities."

"I'll do that. And thank you." Lisa looked as if she was about to hug him. "Could I offer you a celebratory scoop?"

"Thanks, but after six o'clock my preference is for a cold beer. I'm meeting Alec in ten minutes at the Ocean Bar. That's not the only reason I'm here." His gaze slid to Emily. "We're having a lobster bake on South Beach next Saturday."

"I know." Lisa brightened. "I've booked tickets for the three of us. The twins really enjoyed it last year, and the weather is promising to be lovely. Emily, you should come. Lizzy will love it."

A beach party? She couldn't think of anything worse. People. Distractions. Everyone so busy having fun that they failed to notice when a young child was in trouble. "I can't. Skylar is coming for the weekend."

"Bring her, too." Ryan's tone told her he knew exactly what she was thinking, and his next words confirmed it. "We always employ a couple of lifeguards for our beach parties, and not that many people venture into the water once the sun goes down. Too cold." He and Lisa discussed a few more details, and then he gave Emily a nod and strolled out of the shop.

Lisa sighed. "With twins, aged six, I don't think about sex much, and then a guy like him walks in, and suddenly I can't help my mind from drifting."

Emily was about to say "who wouldn't" and stopped herself. There were some things she still wasn't willing to share. "I'm glad he's going to stock your ice cream."

"Me, too, although what I'd really like to do is to serve it on his naked body. Not that I want a relationship," Lisa added hastily, "but a few hours of mind-blowing sex with Ryan Cooper would make me forget my troubles."

Or add to your troubles, Emily thought.

She owed him an apology, and the longer she left it, the harder it would be.

Making a decision, she turned to Lisa. "Would you watch Lizzy for just five minutes? There's something I need to do."

Ryan had walked as far as the harbor when he heard her calling his name.

"Ryan, wait!" There was an urgency to her voice,

and he turned quickly, forgetting his intention to keep his distance. The moment he saw her he wanted to drag her against him and kiss her until both of them forgot the time of day. To make sure he didn't touch her, he thrust his hands into the pockets of his jeans.

"Is something wrong?"

"Nothing is wrong." She was slightly breathless. "I owe you an apology."

"For what?"

"For the things I said. For accusing you of deceiving me. I—I overreacted. I understand why you did what you did." She was building bridges while he was trying to widen the gulf between them.

"You were protecting your child."

"You've been nothing but kind to me since I arrived here, and I should have trusted you."

She'd asked for honesty, so he decided to give it to her. "I'm not kind, Emily. Don't make that mistake. My sister will tell you I'm a selfish, stubborn s—" He caught himself and then gave a short laugh. "I was editing it for children, and then I realized that for once we're on our own. No child."

She glanced at the hordes of tourists spilling from the ferry and gave him a hesitant smile. "Not exactly on our own."

He was grateful for the crowds. Only the knowledge that he'd be arrested for indecency stopped him doing what he wanted to do. "So you left Lizzy with the twins. Good decision. Lisa is a responsible person, and the twins are sweet kids."

"They are." Her gaze slid to his. "I didn't think you liked kids, Ryan Cooper."

"I like them when they belong to someone else."

"I was talking to Lisa about the business." She was earnest and serious, but it made no difference because he already knew how much passion was simmering beneath that modest shirt. She dressed to hide her body, but curves like hers weren't easily disguised, and he'd already discovered what was underneath her clothes. He could still feel the dip of her small waist and the fullness of her breasts. He could taste the sweet flavor of her mouth as she'd opened to him, and he wanted to taste it again. He wanted to drag her into the nearest empty side street and indulge in the sort of sex she'd never be able to describe as "nice."

Realizing she was waiting for an answer, he cleared his throat. "That was kind of you."

"Not really." She looked uncertain. "It's probably driven by a selfish need to feel competent at something I'm doing. That certainly isn't child rearing. I need a crash course."

Her insecurity tugged at him. He remembered feeling the same way a million times.

"Anyone who feels competent at child rearing is deluding themselves. If it's going well, then you'd better realize it could change at any time. Just when you think you've got something nailed, they hit another phase, and suddenly you have no idea what you're doing."

"Was that how it was with Rachel?" Her earnest gaze made him slide deeper into the hole he'd dug for himself.

"Yeah. Losing my parents coincided with a difficult phase, so we never knew whether she was exhibiting grief or whether it was just normal behavior. We stumbled through it, making it up as we went along."

"I'm worried my lack of skills might be psychologically damaging."

He was pretty sure that being the child of Lana Fox would have done far more damage psychologically, but he kept that thought to himself. "I'm sure you're doing just fine."

"I ordered a ton of books, but so far I haven't had time to read them."

He could imagine her, focused on the internet, reading all the back cover copy in an attempt to decide which book would guarantee a safe future for Lizzy. "Parents never do. They're too busy being parents. And I'm not sure what books can teach you that your instincts can't."

"I'm not sure I have the right instincts." Her eyes were wide with uncertainty. "I know I don't have the right feelings for her, but I can protect her. That's my job. I'm trying to learn what she needs."

He wondered why she didn't recognize the feelings that were so obviously spilling over inside her. She had so much love to give it was like watching a balloon ready to burst.

Yet another reason to keep his distance.

"What she needs," he said slowly, "is to have some fun and lead a normal life with you in the background to guide her. Let her do the things other kids her age are doing."

A dimple appeared in the corner of her mouth. "You're saying that because you want to recruit people for your lobster bake."

He suddenly realized how much harder the evening would be if she turned up to the lobster bake. "You're right. Forget it. I know a party on a beach would be your idea of a nightmare. You should stay away."

"We are going to the lobster bake."

Skylar glanced up from the beads she was threading with Lizzy. "Are you serious?"

"Yes." Determined to do this before she could change her mind, Emily grabbed a large beach bag and started stuffing things inside. She had no idea what was needed for a trip to the beach, so she improvised, ignoring the part of her brain that told her she should be packing re-suscitation equipment. "Get changed. Pack a sweater."

"We're going to the beach?" Lizzy erupted with excitement. "Can I take my bucket?"

Emily felt her stomach roll, but she reached for the bucket and stuffed it into the bag before she could think of all the reasons not to. "It's in. Anything else? Don't forget Andrew."

Skylar's eyebrows rose as Lizzy went running from the room. "Who is Andrew? Please, tell me he's some hot guy you have chained in your wardrobe for your nighttime pleasure."

"Andrew is the bear. He has to come everywhere." Some things she was learning.

"I don't know whether to be impressed or disap-pointed." Her friend sat back in the chair. "You are a different person."

"I learn from my mistakes. I only forget a bear once."

"I was talking about the beach."

"Oh."

"What changed your mind?"

"I realized that I have a responsibility to teach her to be safe around water, and avoiding it isn't going to achieve that." Emily added a pretty beach towel to the bag. "If I'm not careful, I'll make her scared and I don't want that."

"You're going to teach her to swim?"

"No. I can't swim myself." She thought about Ryan's offer and dismissed it. There was no way she was putting as much as a toe in the water, but she was prepared to go to a lobster bake on the beach. That would be a start.

It had been Ryan's parting remark that had been responsible for her change of heart.

A party on a beach would be your idea of a nightmare.

But not Lizzy's. And why should Lizzy be made to suffer because she was freaked out by water? The last thing she wanted to do was pass her phobia on to the child.

Lizzy came back downstairs wearing pink sparkly flip-flops. "Can we make a necklace to wear to the beach?"

"Great idea." Skylar pushed a box of beads toward her and glanced at Emily. "We're fine here if you want to go and change."

Leaving Lizzy to make jewelry with Skylar, Emily walked out of the kitchen, but her friend's voice followed her up the stairs.

"Emily? Don't wear black."

Eleven

Lobster bakes were a regular feature during the summer months. Anton, the chef from the Ocean Club, prepared the food the old-fashioned way, steamed in seaweed and cooked in wash kettles over open fires using water from the ocean. The event drew locals and tourists alike, all keen to savor the tradition and taste the very best seafood while enjoying an unparalleled view. Some did a little beachcombing, while others, the braver ones, chose to swim in the sea.

Overseeing it all, Ryan was in midconversation with Alec when he noticed Emily hovering at the edge of the beach. If it hadn't been for the fact that Lizzy and Skylar were by her side, he wasn't sure he would have recognized her. She'd swapped her usual discreet, dark colors for a dress that flowed around her curves in a swirl of purple and blue. The breeze breathed life into the fabric, playing with it so that it lifted and revealed a flash of toned leg.

Ryan lost the thread of the conversation. Hit by a punch of sexual awareness, his brain blanked.

Emily was holding Lizzy's hand firmly. That sight alone should have been enough to damp down the lust.

It didn't.

He wondered how long it had taken her to pluck up the courage to bring Lizzy to a party on a beach.

"Single mother," Alec reminded him, handing him another beer. "All your alarms should be going off right now."

"My alarm is malfunctioning."

"Then get it fixed. Last time my alarm system malfunctioned I found myself with an expensive divorce."

Ryan ignored him. "I need you to do me a favor."

"The answer is no."

"You don't know what I'm going to ask."

"Yes, I do." Alec drank. "You want me to babysit so that you can drag her back to your cave and get laid. We may have Wi-Fi and hot and cold running water, but that look on your face hasn't changed since the day man roamed the earth dressed in animal skins."

"I don't want you to babysit. I want you to be friendly to Skylar. And you can relax because I'm sure a woman as gorgeous and happy as she seems to be wouldn't need to ruin her day by getting involved with a moody bastard like you. If it helps, I think she's already in a relationship. Some guy running for senate."

"Makes sense. She seems the sort to be turned on by power."

Ryan didn't think Skylar seemed that sort at all, but he kept that thought to himself. "So, are you going to do it?"

"You do know you have a major problem, don't you?"

"You're talking about my choice of friends?"

"I'm talking about the fact that in order to get the

girl, you're going to have to deal with the child." Alec lifted his beer to his lips. "For you, that's like walking through a ring of fire."

"All I had in mind was a drink and conversation. You've gone straight from a single look to divorce in sixty seconds."

"Every divorce begins with a single look. Never forget that."

"No chance while I'm hanging around with you. When is this cynicism going to die?"

"Never. It's keeping me safe."

"It's keeping you single."

"Same thing."

Ryan shook his head. "I thought you came here to heal."

"I came here to work."

But Ryan knew that wasn't the whole story. For plenty of people, Puffin Island was a sanctuary. It was the reason Lisa had chosen to uproot two small children in an attempt to build a new life. It was the reason Brittany had offered her cottage to Emily.

It was a place where wounds could heal, bathed by the beauty of nature.

Some wounds, he thought. *Not all.*

He saw Emily tighten her grip on Lizzy's hand and linger at the edge of the beach as if she were about to step into a pit of alligators. Her anxiety was almost painful to witness. He wanted to stride across the sand, fold her into his arms and stand between her and the sea. It was as if she were frozen.

Another panic attack?

Remembering how she'd been that day Lizzy had wandered onto the beach, Ryan cursed under his breath.

"Damsel in distress," Alec said flatly, "the most dangerous kind of all. They wait for you to show your soft side, and then they go in for the kill."

Ryan didn't think there was a single part of himself that could be classed as "soft" right at that moment. And he knew that nothing his friend had said applied to Emily. "That isn't what's happening here."

The water was her phobia.

The fact that she was here, facing up to the thing she feared most, simply increased his respect for her.

Shit.

"It's my job to greet guests, so I'm going over there—"

"Of course you are. Since that was always going to be the outcome, you should have done it five minutes ago."

Ryan ground his teeth. "Next time we're out in the boat, I hope the beam cracks your skull."

"I'm not the one who needs a smack round the head."

"You can stay here growling if you like, but I'm going to be sociable."

"You mean you're going to see if there's any chance comfort could lead to grateful sex."

Ryan gave a half smile. "Brittany asked me to look out for a friend in trouble. That's what I'm doing."

Part of him recognized that he might be the one in trouble, but he decided to ignore that along with the speculative look from Alec.

He strolled across the sand, checking everyone had what they needed and that there were no problems simmering. South Beach was one of the best beaches for swimming on the island, a curve of sand where the sea shelved gently and lacked the strong undertows characteristic of other parts of the island. One end of the beach was rocky, but those large gray slabs of granite provided a perfect platform for jumping into the water. Some of the braver individuals were swimming, their shrieks cutting through the air as they dipped into the cold waters of the Atlantic. Ryan might have joined them if it hadn't been for the woman hovering on the edge of the party. He'd put two of the guys who worked behind the bar on lifeguard duty. Kirsti was handing out drinks and welcoming people with her own individual brand of warmth that involved a significant amount of matchmaking.

As Ryan walked past her, she handed him a couple of extra beers from a bucket brimming with ice and winked.

He took the beers, ignored the wink and joined Skylar and Emily.

"This is a surprise." He handed over the beers and then dropped to his haunches to greet Lizzy, noticing the bows in her hair. "Pretty necklace."

Lizzy fingered it. "I made it with Skylar."

"Emily!" Lisa arrived with the twins, holding on to each hand. "Can Lizzy join us? We're hunting for shells on the far side of the beach with Rachel."

The request seemed to stir Emily from her trance. "Rachel?"

"My sister," Ryan murmured in response to her blank expression. "Even on her day off she doesn't miss the opportunity to grab a group of young children and stimulate their minds."

Emily held tight to Lizzy's hand. "That sounds like fun." The tone she used told a different story. "I'll come, too."

Ryan understood that for Emily, being here was an

enormous step. It was too much to expect for her to leave the child in someone else's care. Blocking out Alec's comment that in order to get the girl he had to deal with the child, he swung a giggling Lizzy onto his shoulders.

"Now you have a seagull's view."

He ignored Kirsti's approving glance and strolled across the sand, wincing as Lizzy's small hands tugged at his hair.

"Hey, that's attached to me."

"I'm too high up. I don't want to fall." But she was giggling, and he saw Emily glance at the child and smile, too.

By the time he reached Rachel and the twins, his scalp was sore from being pulled, and he swung Lizzy down, forgetting to make allowances for his injury.

He said nothing, but something must have shown on his face because Emily reached out and touched his shoulder gently.

"You hurt yourself?"

"It's fine." He could feel the warmth of her hand through his shirt. He remembered those fingers sliding under his shirt and resting lightly on his back. Sliding over his jaw and into his hair. Locked with his as he'd lifted her arms above her head and plundered her mouth.

Her gaze lifted to his, and he knew she was remembering the same thing.

She withdrew her hand quickly.

"Ryan?" Rachel was glancing between them curiously, and Ryan pulled himself together and introduced Emily and Lizzy. After that, all he had to do then was stand back and watch while his sister worked her magic. Even as a child, Rachel had wanted to be a teacher. He remembered her lining up all her toys and standing up to teach the "class."

The tide was far out, exposing granite boulders crowded with rockweed, barnacles, whelks and mussel shells. Within seconds Lizzy was holding Rachel's hand and searching nearby tide pools for sea creatures while Emily stood tense as a bow.

"I should go with them."

He wondered whether it was the sexual chemistry that was responsible for her tension or the proximity of the water.

"She'll be safe with my sister." He saw Rachel point out where Lizzy should step to be safe on the rocks. "Rachel is the best teacher Puffin Elementary has ever had. She adores the kids, and she knows exactly how to handle them. And she'll be working at Camp Puffin all summer. Relax."

"We're on a beach," she muttered. "I don't think relaxing is possible."

"Try." Against his better judgment, he put a comforting hand on her back. He felt her stiffen and then relax into the reassuring pressure and draw a deep, shuddering breath through her body.

"Pathetic."

"Who is pathetic?"

"I am." She kept her eyes fixed on Lizzy the whole time, every muscle in her body tense and ready to move in an instant.

"You're here. You're standing on a beach. That's not pathetic. It's brave."

"Brave would be getting in the water."

He glanced at her profile. "One step at a time."

"They're having fun." She watched a group of mothers play with their children in the shallows, an activity punctuated by much delighted squealing.

"You sound surprised."

"I guess for me beaches are more about fear than fun."

"I didn't expect you to be here."

"Would you rather I hadn't come?"

"No." He was beginning to wonder why he was fighting it. He glanced at her, wondering if she felt it, too, but she was staring at Lizzy, her green eyes focused on the child. Emily's hair was loose and softly curling, strands of blond and caramel floating around blush-tinted ivory skin that reminded him of the strawberries-and-cream flavor Lisa served in Summer Scoop.

If she were a dessert, he would have eaten her in two mouthfuls.

She stirred, her arm brushing against his. "I came because of you."

"Me?" For a moment he thought she was propositioning him, and then he realized their minds were working along different tracks, and she was still thinking about Lizzy.

"You told me she needed to have fun and lead a normal life. On Puffin Island a beach picnic is normal. I don't want her to be afraid of the water."

"Can she swim?"

"I have no idea." She turned slightly green. "You're worried she might fall in?"

"No, but swimming is an important life skill. It will give her confidence. In the summer, the pool at the Ocean Club is closed to the public in the mornings so that Rachel can give swimming lessons to the kids as part of Camp Puffin. I'm sure she'd take Lizzy."

Emily's expression showed an agony of indecision, and then she nodded. "Yes. It's a good idea." She said it as if it were the worst idea in the world.

"Every kid should be able to swim."

"Yes." She stared straight ahead, and he knew she was wondering whether she might have been able to prevent what had happened if she'd known how to swim.

"It wouldn't have made a difference." He spoke softly, so they couldn't be overheard. "You were too little. Most grown-ups don't know what to do when they're caught in a riptide. Even if you'd been able to swim, there is no way you would have been able to save her."

"I'll never know. You're right. I'll ask Rachel if she'll teach Lizzy." She watched as Lizzy scooped water from a tide pool into her bucket. When it was too dark to play any longer, they picked their way back across the rocks, juggling children, brimming buckets and sandy feet.

Anton and his team were layering potatoes, onions and garlic on top of the lobster in four large kettles over open fires. Then came corn and hot dogs and finally the whole meal was sealed to keep in the steam. Small tables were groaning under the weight of various appetizers, freshly baked bread and mixed salads. As well as hot dogs, the menu included hamburgers for the children, and the smell of cooking scented the air, mingling with the scent of the sea.

At the far edge of the beach, the forest crowded the edge of the water, and the setting sun sent a mosaic of warm light over the treetops and the sand.

Lizzy was clutching the bucket Ryan had given her, now filled with shells and other interesting objects she'd found in the pools.

As they sat down on blankets near the fire, Emily examined the contents of the bucket.

"That's pretty." Skylar leaned across and helped herself to a piece of turquoise sea glass, the ends of her hair sweeping the sand. "Polished up, that would be gorgeous."

"Ryan, look!" Lizzy crawled over to him and dropped a shell in his lap.

He picked it up and duly admired it. It was impossible not to respond to Lizzy's enthusiasm, and he caught his sister watching him curiously.

It was obvious from her expression she was wondering what he was doing.

He was wondering the same thing.

To give himself space from Lizzy's impromptu show-and-tell, he rose to his feet and excused himself on the pretext of checking in with Anton, but Rachel reached him before he made it halfway across the beach.

"What's going on, Ryan?"

"What do you mean?"

"Oh, please—" she anchored her dark hair with her hand "—you're carrying Lizzy on your shoulders and looking at shells. Who are you and what have you done with my brother?"

"You're not funny."

"No, what isn't funny is you using a child to get access to Emily's body!"

He ground his teeth. "Do you want to speak a little louder? I don't think they heard you in Boston."

"It's not fair, Ryan."

He swore under his breath and dragged his fingers through his hair. "That isn't what I'm doing."

"Then what are you doing?"

"Honestly? I don't know."

"But you like Emily."

Like? Such an insipid word didn't even begin to describe his complex feelings. "I sympathize with her situation."

"That wasn't sympathy I saw in your eyes when you looked at her."

"Back off."

"We both know you're not interested in taking on anyone's kids long-term, so just be careful, Ryan. I'm thinking of Lizzy. She's young. Kids get attached."

"Are you lecturing me?"

"Yeah, so now you know how it feels." She punched him lightly on the arm and walked back to the group at the far side of the beach, leaving him staring after her.

She was right, of course.

He wasn't interested in taking responsibility for a child.

He thought about Lizzy's hands locked in his hair and the delicious sound of her giggle as he'd bounced her across the sand.

What the hell was he doing?

He'd told Rachel to back off, but he was the one who needed to back off.

He talked to Anton for a few minutes, exchanged small talk with a few locals and then returned to where the others were sitting.

Instantly Lizzy slid across the blanket to show him another shell, but this time he encouraged her to show Skylar instead and sat detached while they continued to sift through their personal hoard of treasure.

When the food was ready, they used rocks to crack open the lobsters and ate until they were full.

Ryan watched Emily, wondering why he'd never before seen a beach picnic as a sensual activity. There was too much licking of lips and sucking of fingers for his own personal comfort.

The twins and Lizzy, tired from so much outdoor activity, fell asleep in a heap between Rachel and Lisa who were talking about plans for the summer. Skylar was still sorting through sea glass and shells, holding up each piece to the light of the fire to take a closer look.

Emily leaned forward, too, and the soft fabric at the neckline of her dress gaped slightly, giving him an uninterrupted view of smooth, full breasts.

Remembering exactly how they looked bare and aching for his touch, Ryan felt a raging hunger that had nothing to do with food.

Lust was hot, liquid and brutal. The final straw was when he saw a couple of the male swimming instructors from the Ocean Club pool almost fall on their faces as they tried to get a better look at Emily's luxuriant curves. Ryan gave them an icy glare that had them backing away, and then sprang to his feet.

"I need to talk to Anton again."

Emily glanced up at him in surprise. "You're leaving?" Her disappointment was so obvious he almost changed his mind.

And then he saw his sister's eyes narrow and knew he was in trouble.

"I'll be back." He stumbled and planted his foot on a shell, earning his sister's wrath.

"Ryan! Get your great big feet off the blanket. Ugh. You have no idea how many of my paintings he ruined when I was little."

He turned his back on seashells, children and Emily's curves and walked across the beach.

Alec was deep in conversation with a couple of marine biologists, and Kirsti was dancing with one of the instructors from the kayak school.

Across the sand he saw Jared end a conversation with a couple of lobstermen and glance toward Rachel.

Ryan ground his teeth and carried on walking.

His sister was right, her life was her business.

He had his own problems.

His problem caught up with him as he reached the edge of the beach.

"Ryan!" She sounded breathless, and he clenched his jaw and turned.

"What?"

"I thought you were going to talk to Anton?"

"He's busy." The truth was he'd forgotten about Anton; he'd been so intent on giving himself some space.

"Is everything all right? Lizzy was all over you. I hope she didn't make you feel uncomfortable. Or irritated."

Uncomfortable, he could have handled. Irritated, he could have handled. What he couldn't handle was the fact he'd found her adorable. "She was great. Every kid loves the beach." Too late, he remembered that she hated it. "Listen, Emily—"

"It's fine. You don't have to walk on eggshells—or maybe I should say seashells." A dimple appeared at the corner of her mouth. "Can I walk with you for a minute? I could use five minutes of adult time."

Unable to find a response that wouldn't seem rude,

he nodded. "Are you cold? Do you need a wrap or something?"

"I'm fine."

It was a good job one of them was, he thought dourly, fixing his gaze on the rocks ahead. "When the tide is out you can walk right around to the next beach."

"It's pretty. I was thinking about what you said the other day," she said quickly, "about teaching me to swim. If you meant it, then I'd like to."

"You want to swim?"

She pulled a face. "No, but I think I should. It's important for Lizzy. I'm sending the message that water is scary and to be avoided, and that's not only unfair, it's dangerous. She needs to learn how to swim, and once she's learned, I need to be able to take her."

"What changed your mind?"

"Watching the kids in the water. They were having so much fun. And listening to Rachel and Lisa talking about all the summer activities they have planned at Camp Puffin. Beach camp, kayaking, sailing. I want her to be able to do those things one day. I thought maybe Agnes would be willing to watch Lizzy for an hour while you teach me. Would you do it?"

He wanted to refuse. "Are you sure you want to do this?"

Say no.

"I'm sure. What would I need to bring?"

His mouth was dry. "Just yourself and a bathing suit. But if you don't have a suit, then—"

"I have one."

He hoped to hell it hadn't been chosen by Skylar, or they would both be in serious trouble. He was tempted to suggest a wet suit but then decided that wasn't going to hide much, either. "Maybe you should wait a few weeks and—"

"I don't want to wait. Let's set a time. That way I can't change my mind."

He felt sweat bead on his forehead. "I need to look at my schedule."

"How about tomorrow? It's Sunday."

"Weekends are our busiest time at the Ocean Club. Lunches are always crazy, and we're fully booked for dinner."

"So how about five o'clock?"

They'd walked as far as the next beach where the rocks opened up into a cave. When the tide was in, it filled with water, but right now it was a moonlit, cavernous grotto.

It was a favorite tourist spot on the island.

It was also a favorite haunt for teenagers looking for somewhere to have sex.

"Ryan?"

"Yeah." His voice didn't sound like his own. He was wishing he'd walked in the opposite direction. "Five o'clock should work. But if you change your mind, just let me know."

"Don't let me change my mind, even if I go on my knees and beg you."

The thought of her on her knees almost made him stumble. "Emily—"

"Look!" She tugged her hand from his and walked toward the cave. "This place is amazing. Did you know it was here?" Her almost childlike wonder was in direct contrast to the dark, carnal thoughts that filled every inch of his brain.

"Yes." He was so aroused, it was difficult to walk.

"Be careful. The sea gets trapped in a few places and the pools can be deep."

"How far back does it go?"

"When the tide is out, you can walk through to the next beach." Or you could stop halfway and—

"Lizzy would love it."

Even the mention of a child right now seemed inappropriate given that his thoughts were definitely adult only. "It's a dangerous place. It fills up when the tide comes in. The coast guard has rescued more people from here than any other part of Puffin Island. Promise me you won't come here without someone who knows the tides."

"I promise." Her voice was soft, and she slid her arm into his. "And thank you."

"For what?"

"For not making fun of the fact I'm scared of water. For caring enough to warn me. I appreciate it."

He had a feeling she wouldn't be thanking him if she could read his mind.

The sound of music wafted on the breeze, and he knew a few people would be dancing on the beach.

"We should go back."

"In a minute. Rachel is lovely. So warm and sweet-natured. Lizzy loved her instantly."

"Yes. Fortunately she's nothing like me."

"You're kind, too."

The breath hissed through his teeth. "I've already told you, I'm not kind."

"You've been very kind to me. You stayed with me when I had a panic attack. Most men would have run. You're patient with Lizzy, even though I know you've already done all the child rearing you intend to do. And now you've offered to teach me to swim."

He must have been out of his mind. "About that—"

"Thank you." She stood on tiptoe and put her arms around him. "I'm so sorry I yelled at you."

He caught her arms in his hands. "Emily, I lied to you. You were right to yell at me. And I'm not kind."

"I think you are. And you lied because you didn't want me to freak out. It was the right decision."

"Emily—"

"I know you didn't do it for me exactly, you did it for Brittany, but that makes you a loyal friend and I respect that."

His control snapped. "You want to know how kind I am? Right now I'm thinking of all the ways I could have sex with you in this cave without one of us injuring ourselves on the rocks."

She went still. "Here? Right now?" Her voice was breathy with shock. "Someone might come."

Yeah, you, he thought, but he managed to trap the words inside his brain for once instead of letting them escape from his mouth.

"I tell you I want to have sex with you in an infinite number of positions and that's what worries you?" He waited for her to pull away but she didn't.

Instead, she looked at his mouth. "Maybe if we did it quickly, we wouldn't be caught." Her voice was a whisper, and the gleam in her eyes made everything inside him tighten.

"I'm going to pretend you didn't just say that to me."

"Have you ever had sex in this cave?"

"I'm going to pretend you didn't say that, either."

Her eyes danced. "I'm pretty sure you're not a virgin, Ryan."

And he was pretty sure she was close to being one. He wondered how many lovers she'd had before Neil and decided he didn't want to know the answer.

She was certainly an outdoor-sex virgin, and he wasn't going to be the one to do something about that.

"We should go back."

"Not yet." She rested her hand on his chest, her features indistinct in the moonlit cave. "I've been thinking a lot about that kiss. I wondered if you'd thought about it, too."

He'd been trying not to. "We should definitely go back."

"There's something I want to do first." She stood on tiptoe again and brushed her mouth over his, and his grip on control unraveled like the chain of an anchor that had been tossed overboard. When her tongue licked into his mouth, he could no longer remember why he was fighting this.

Forgetting Rachel, Lizzy and all the obstacles he'd been trying to keep in the foreground of his brain, he buried his hands in her hair, angled his mouth over hers and kissed her back, opening her mouth with his, exploring those sweet depths with skilled, ruthless strokes of his tongue.

He tasted the delicious sweetness of her and buried his hands in that glorious hair. She smelled of summer blossoms and rose petals, everything about her silky smooth and feminine. She pressed her luscious curves against him, winding around him like a delicate plant growing up a rough rock face.

He felt her tug at his shirt and then slide her hands

over his skin, and the feel of her brought him to his senses.

The cave magnified sound. Her gasps blended with soft echoes and the hollow drip of water sliding off rock. From beyond the cave came the faint rush of moonlit waves hitting the sand and the distant sound of laughter.

It was the laughter that penetrated his desire-clouded brain.

He eased his mouth from hers and heard her moan a protest.

"Ryan—" She breathed his name and opened her eyes reluctantly. "I want—"

"I know what you want." Despite the dim light, he could see the dark streaks of color on her cheeks.

"But you don't want the same thing. You're not interested."

He wondered how the hell she could think he wasn't interested, given that seconds ago she'd been welded against a part of him that should have told her exactly how he felt on that subject.

He thought about what Rachel had said. He thought about Lizzy. "We should get back. People will wonder where we are."

She registered the rejection. "You're right, we should get back." She stepped away unsteadily, like someone absorbing a punch. "It was unfair of me to ask you to teach me to swim when you're so busy. I'll book with one of the swimming instructors."

He thought about the two swimming instructors who worked at the Ocean Club, both of who had almost fallen on their faces trying to look down Emily's dress.

"I'll do it."

"That isn't necessary. I can—"

"I said, I'll do it."

"In that case, I'll see you at the pool tomorrow." The exchange was awkward and stilted.

"Sounds good."

It didn't sound good at all.

Twelve

Emily stood by the entrance of the Ocean Club pool, shivering.

If someone had told her a month ago she'd be dancing at a beach barbecue and learning to swim, she would have called them deluded.

But here she was, with a bathing suit tight and uncomfortable under her clothes.

When she'd first noticed it in the bag of clothes Skylar had delivered, she'd ignored it, thinking she'd have no possible use for it. As a result, she hadn't taken a close look until five minutes before she was ready to leave the cottage.

She'd always assumed one-piece bathing suits were less revealing than bikinis, but not this one. Or maybe it was just that her shape wasn't designed for it. And instead of sober black, the color that denoted seriousness in all things, it was red.

Red for danger, Emily thought, which pretty much described her situation right now. Not just because of the water, but because of the man. Still, Ryan had made it clear he didn't want to take their relationship further, so she didn't need to worry about how she looked in the damn swimsuit. She could focus on the water itself.

Fighting the urge to change her mind, she undressed in the changing room, pushed her clothes into a locker and wrapped herself in a towel.

Ryan was alone in the pool, cutting through the water with powerful strokes that suggested an above-average athletic ability.

Remembering what he'd told her about his shoulder, she wondered if he'd used the pool as part of his recovery from his injuries.

When he reached the edge, he pulled himself out of the water in a lithe, fluid movement. His muscles bunched, and water streamed off those broad shoulders, droplets clinging to the dark hair that shadowed his chest. He was all sleek planes and streamlined power. Dazed by the vision of raw male strength, Emily blinked, reflecting on the unsettling discovery that apparently the mere sight of a man's half-naked body could turn a thinking woman stupid. Everything around them faded, and she could see nothing except the glitter of his eyes as he scanned her from head to foot.

Mouth dry, she tightened her grip on the towel.

Her physical awareness was so acute she wondered how on earth she was supposed to concentrate on swimming with him in the pool.

Even without her fear issues, she'd drown.

"Hi." He barely glanced at her before turning to pick up a towel from the bench near the water. In that moment she saw the vicious scars that curved over his shoulder and down his back. It looked as if he'd been mauled by a tiger.

Those scars told her everything he hadn't and filled

in details he'd omitted in his sparse recounting of the incident that had killed his friend and left him severely injured.

She wanted to ask him about it, but he'd already made it clear the subject was off-limits, so she stayed silent while he wiped his face and looped the towel around his neck. Leaning forward, he picked up a long float shaped like a fat piece of spaghetti and bent it in half.

"We're going to put this around your middle until you're confident."

She was pretty sure that was going to be never, but she kept that thought to herself.

"All right."

He strolled across to her. "You're planning on swimming in a towel?"

If it had been an option, then she would have taken it. He might be unselfconscious about his body, but she wasn't. She wished now she'd just walked out of the changing room in the suit, instead of drawing attention to herself. Better still, she wished she'd picked out a suit herself. Surf and Swim in the harbor would probably have stocked at least ten swimsuits more suitable than this one. Something actually designed for swimming. This one looked as if she was trying to seduce him.

Knowing that the longer she left it, the worse it would be, she let the towel fall.

Face burning, she met his gaze. "You're thinking I should have worn a more serious swimsuit, but I don't really have the shape for any sort of suit, and Skylar bought me this one—" Her voice tailed off, and her cheeks grew redder by the second. "Do you want me in the water?" *Oh, God, why had she phrased it that way?* Now it sounded as if she were propositioning him.

"That would help." His voice was roughened and raw, and he flung the towel back on the bench and slid back into the water himself.

Dying of embarrassment, Emily sat on the side and dangled her legs in the water. Staring down into the blue depths, embarrassment gave way to another emotion. A hollow pit of fear sat where her stomach was supposed to be.

Through the spangled surface of the pool she could see the bottom, but sliding into water seemed like the most unnatural thing in the world.

She probably would have sat there forever had Ryan not moved in front of her.

"Are you sure you want to do this?"

No. "Yes."

"In that case, put your hands on my shoulders." His firm command cut through her building panic.

"You want me to slide in?"

"Yes. You're going to be fine."

"Lizzy had her first lesson with Rachel this morning. She can't stop talking about it."

"Emily." His voice softened a little. "Put your hands on my shoulders. I won't let you fall, and I won't let you go under the water."

Unable to postpone the moment any longer, she steeled herself and put her hands on his shoulders. Her palms made contact with hard, unyielding muscle.

"I don't want to hurt your shoulder."

"You're not hurting me."

"You're gritting your teeth."

"That's not—" He closed his eyes briefly and shook

his head. "Never mind. Just do this. Every moment you hesitate makes this harder."

Taking a deep breath, she slid into the water. It was deliciously cool against her heated skin, and that might have been a relief if it hadn't been for the fact that the movement of sliding in brought her body in close contact with his.

Her thigh brushed against the hardness of his, and she heard him curse softly.

"Sorry—" Anxiety made her clumsy, and she gripped his shoulders with her hands, then realized she might be hurting him and forced herself to relax her grip.

"You're doing fine." He put the float around her, demonstrating how it would support her weight, showing her how to move her limbs.

"For now, get used to being in the water. You won't go under the surface because you have the float and you have me. We'll stay in the shallow end."

For a man whose defining characteristic was restless impatience, he was a remarkably patient teacher.

An hour later she swam the width of the pool with just the float, and he complimented her on her style.

Her confidence rose. "Can I try it without the float?"

"I think you've done enough for one day."

"I think it would help my confidence to try."

"It won't help your confidence if you go under and never want to get back in the water again."

"You could stay close by. Grab me if I look as if I'm going under."

If other people could swim without a float, then so could she.

Determined to do this, she put her float on the edge of the pool.

She pushed forward, and instantly her body felt heavy and strange. Without the float she no longer felt buoyant. Starting to sink, panic fluttered inside her, and then she felt his hand on her stomach, lifting her, giving her that extra support.

"You're doing fine." His voice was calm. "It feels different without the float, but the movements are the same. Keep kicking. Keep using your arms. You won't go under, I promise. I won't let you."

And suddenly instead of thinking about drowning, she was thinking about that hand on her stomach. About how it would feel if he moved it a little lower. It made her feel safe from drowning but unsafe in every other way.

She didn't dare look at him, so she focused on the side of the pool instead, kicked and used her arms, and suddenly she was swimming, really swimming, not elegantly but staying afloat without help. She kept kicking and moving her arms, spurred on by his encouragement, until finally she reached the side and grabbed it.

"Good job." Ryan was right next to her, and at last, now that the possibility of drowning seemed to have passed, she allowed herself to look at him.

His dark hair was slick, and droplets of water clung to the powerful muscles of his shoulders.

He was the sexiest man she'd laid eyes on.

And he wasn't interested in her.

She gave a bright smile. "Thank you. That was brilliant."

He didn't smile back. Instead, he eyed the changing room door, as if judging how fast he could get out of here. "You did well. Do you always work that hard at things?"

"If it's something important."

His gaze slid back to hers. "I think that's enough for one day. I need to get back to work."

"Of course. Thank you for taking the time to teach me. I can do it by myself from now on."

He frowned. "You can't do that."

"I'll stay in the shallow end, but I need to practice."

"Tell me when you're going to practice. I'll make sure I'm here."

"You're busy. You don't want to—"

"Damn it, Emily! The purpose of this exercise is to increase your confidence around water, and that's not going to happen if you're on your own, so just say yes."

"Yes. Tomorrow," she murmured. "Same time. But you don't seem very happy about it."

"I'm happy."

"Ryan, you're speaking through your teeth, and you can't wait to get out of this pool."

"Because you're standing next to me in a swimsuit that looks like something from a porn movie."

She stared at him, her heart pounding. "You said— I thought—"

"What did you think?"

"That you weren't interested. That this was all too complicated for you. That—" she hesitated "—that I'm not your type. I don't know enough about sex. I—I'm not exciting enough."

There was a long pause.

The only sound was the soft lap of water against the side of the pool and her own breathing.

"If you were any more exciting I'd need medical attention."

Her stomach dropped, but this time the feeling had nothing to do with fear.

The air was punctuated by a tension as unfamiliar and alien to her as the swimming.

"I thought… Then why—"

"Because you don't want what I'm offering."

"How can you possibly know what I want when you haven't asked me?"

His gaze held hers, and in that single moment the world consisted of the two of them and nothing else.

How could a single look be so arousing?

How could he do this to her?

"Emily—" He cradled the side of her face in his hand, stroking her cheek with his thumb as he looked down at her as if he was making a decision about something.

She was terrified he was going to change his mind. Walk away as he had the night before.

Instead, he lowered his head with a slow inevitability that made her wonder if anyone had ever died of anticipation.

His mouth brushed over hers with unhurried, skilled deliberation, the gentleness at odds with the leashed strength of his body. His eyes looked darker than usual, almost drowsy, clouded with emotions she found impossible to read.

And then the kiss altered. Instead of a lazy, exploratory brush of his mouth, it became hungry and urgent, and she felt the strength in his hands as he cupped her bottom and pulled her hard against him, the movement bold and blatantly sexual. She felt the hard, thick ridge of his erection through the thin fabric of her suit and the slick stroke of his tongue against hers as he slanted his mouth over hers and kissed her deeply.

Her hands gripped the brutal swell of his biceps and then slid upward over his wide shoulders and into the thickness of his hair.

He held her hard against him and kissed her with skill and purpose, the cool of the water contrasting with the heat of his mouth and the burning fire that blazed inside her. She was weightless in the water, slippery as a sea creature, and they kissed like demons, locked together and frantic.

He made a sound deep in his throat and then buried his mouth in her neck, and she tipped her head back, eyes closed, shaken and aroused as sensation ripped through her.

He backed her against the side of the pool and trapped her there. "I want you," he growled the words against her mouth. "Can you feel how much I want you?"

Yes, she could feel it. The hard, intimate pressure of his body against hers. The rough demands of his hands and mouth.

She drove her fingers into his hair, her mouth colliding with his in a kiss that stripped away reservations and inhibitions. "I want you, too." She felt his hand slide upward and cup the weight of her breast. Then his thumb made a slow slide over her nipple, teasing it into an aching peak until she squirmed against him, engulfed in exquisite sensation and delicious anticipation.

Her mind shut down. All of her senses were focused on him, on his hands, his mouth, on the dangerous heat that burned through her body.

She hadn't known it was possible to want someone this much.

They were doing everything except having sex, and just when she was hoping he'd cross that line sometime very soon, there was the sound of a door in the distance, and he released her.

"We've got company." His voice was husky and uneven, and he kept his hand on her waist until he was sure she was steady on her feet.

Emily looked at him dizzily, thinking that it was a good thing her feet could touch the floor of the pool; otherwise she definitely would have drowned.

Gradually it dawned on her that they were in a semi-public place.

One of them needed to say something, and she decided that since he'd taken the lead on everything else, she'd do that part. "If I'd known swimming was this much fun, I would have done it years ago."

He made a sound that was half laugh, half groan and brought his mouth back to hers. "Leave Lizzy with Agnes tonight. We can watch the sunset from my bed."

She eased away, feeling the pull of regret. "I can't."

"Why not? She'd be safe."

Lizzy would be, but what about her? Up until the past few weeks, she'd never thought of herself as particularly sexual. What if they got as far as bed and she disappointed him? This was a small island. She could be committing herself to a summer of awkward encounters.

Her nerve fled. "I'll get changed and we'll forget it ever happened."

"Sure. That should work, as long as no one looks at the surveillance footage."

She glanced up and saw a camera focused on the pool. "There are cameras?"

"Yeah, we just starred in our own private movie."

Emily gave an embarrassed laugh. "Well, hopefully no one will ever have reason to examine the footage." She didn't trust her arms to be able to haul herself out of the pool the way he did, so to avoid a potentially ungainly accident, she chose to use the steps. She could feel him watching her every step of the way from the pool to the changing room.

"Emily—"

She turned her head. "Yes?"

"If you change your mind, you know where I live."

After that swimming lesson, everything changed.

Or maybe the change had been happening gradually, and he hadn't noticed it.

Either way, Emily went from hiding away in Castaway Cottage to being a visible part of the Puffin Island community.

She and Lizzy visited Agnes every morning to walk Cocoa, only now whenever Ryan called on his grandmother, he noticed small gifts on the kitchen table. Gifts that revealed exactly how Emily was spending her time with her niece. A bowl heaped with blueberries picked fresh from the bush. A plate of home-baked cookies and a picture of a boat bobbing on the waves painted by Lizzy.

"I think that girl is enjoying doing things she's never done before," was all that Agnes would say when he questioned her about the gifts that kept appearing.

"Lizzy?"

"I meant Emily, but that statement is probably true of both of them."

Judging from the interesting shape of the cookies, Emily was as experienced a cook as she was a swimmer, but he wasn't about to diminish her attempts to entertain the child and become part of the local island community at the same time.

A week after the first swimming lesson, he walked in to find Agnes wearing a necklace of glittery pink beads.

Recognizing Lizzy's signature color, Ryan refrained from reaching for his sunglasses. "Nice necklace."

"Lizzy made this with Emily. The child has an eye for anything that sparkles. I guess she inherited that from her mother."

"Does she talk about her mother?"

"A little, to Emily. They've made a scrapbook together, with pictures and news stories." His grandmother gave a faint smile. "Positive ones."

Aware of the rumors that had surrounded Lana Fox's colorful love life, Ryan wondered how long Emily had toiled to find material suitable for young eyes. He could imagine her, those green eyes serious as she'd searched for images to keep Lana's memory alive for her daughter.

"I came to see if any of your group need a ride to your book club meeting tonight, apart from Hilda."

"Emily is picking Hilda up. She offered to take me, too, but I didn't want to stop giving you a reason to call by."

"I don't need a reason to call by." Ryan frowned. "Emily is making the trip specially?"

"She's a kind girl. She and Lizzy have baked a blueberry pie for our meeting. But, no, she isn't making the trip just for that. Once she's dropped Hilda off, she's going around to Lisa's to talk business. She's put together a plan to save Summer Scoop." Agnes said it as if it were a sure thing, and Ryan felt a flicker of unease.

"She's not a magician."

"No, she's something better." Agnes glanced at him over the top of her glasses. "She's a management consultant. We've never had one of those on the island before."

Ryan refrained from pointing out there wasn't much of a demand for management consultants on Puffin Island.

Much as he admired Emily's generosity in offering to help, he was more circumspect about her chances of being able to do anything that would substantially boost the profits of a business that had been struggling from the outset.

"I hope she comes up with a plan."

"She will." His grandmother sounded sure. "Emily is a smart young woman, and she is determined to help make the business work. Lisa has a smile on her face for the first time in months. It broke my heart when I heard she'd bought the place, a widow with two young children. Summer Scoop has been struggling to survive since Doris Payne first opened it forty years ago. The whole community has been trying to find ways to help the girl, but there's only so much ice cream a person can consume without their arteries exploding. If Emily can find a way to sell more of it to the summer crowd, then we'll all be in her debt. How is the swimming going? That's assuming 'swimming' is all you're doing in that hour and a half you spend together every night." She picked up her purse and her keys and took his arm as they walked to the car.

Ryan kept his expression blank. "It's all we're doing."

"Shame." His grandmother gave him a look. "She's perfect for you."

"You've been talking to Kirsti."

"Rachel. And I have eyes. Don't make that mistake of thinking age means I don't see."

"You wear glasses."

"Which make my vision near perfect. That girl is longing for a family and a home."

"Maybe those glasses of yours need changing because she's been running from both those things most of her life."

"Sometimes you run from the things you want most, because those are the things that scare you." His grandmother looked at him pointedly, but Ryan chose not to engage in that particular conversation.

He wasn't scared. He just didn't want that.

After that first session in the pool, he'd made a point of not touching her, choosing instead to stay close enough to help if she found herself in trouble, but far enough away to ensure they focused on her swimming and not the sexual heat that underpinned every encounter.

Having made the decision to conquer her fear of water, she refused to let anything stand in her way. Not her own nerves or even an incident when she'd slid on the side of the pool and plunged into the deep end. She'd come up spluttering, wild-eyed, but had rejected his offer of assistance and instead choked and splashed her way to the side of the pool without help.

He suspected she'd lowered the water level by swallowing half of the pool, but he respected her determination to do it by herself.

He dropped his grandmother at her book group, but instead of driving back to the Ocean Club, he parked outside Summer Scoop.

The store was closed, and Lisa answered the door with a glass of wine in her hand. "Ryan!" She opened the door to let him in. "Emily is here. We're having a Save Summer Scoop meeting."

He looked at the wine. "That involves wine?"

"It definitely does. Emily brought it. It's delicious. Come and join us."

He followed Lisa into the small kitchen, noticing the toys piled hastily into a box in the corner. Emily had papers spread all over the kitchen table and her laptop open.

This was an Emily he hadn't seen before.

She was dressed in skinny jeans and a turquoise T-shirt that hugged her curves. Distracted by those curves, Ryan lost orientation and banged into the door frame. Pain exploded through his shoulder, and he decided life had been more comfortable when she'd worn black, voluminous tops.

He thought back to a disturbingly frank conversation they'd had the day before when she'd told him how hard it was to find clothes when you were big breasted. She'd explained that cute underwear was hopeless and that bras needed serious engineering to have any hope of offering support, and that when she exercised she had to wear two support bras. She'd explained that shirts that buttoned down the front were no good because they always gaped and that she couldn't wear long necklaces because they dangled off her breasts.

By the time she'd finished talking, he'd been relieved he wasn't a woman.

As he waited for the pain in his shoulder to die down, she lifted her head from the laptop and flashed him a smile.

"Hi, Ryan." She was keying numbers into a spreadsheet, her fingers swift. An untouched glass of wine sat by her elbow.

"So—" dragging his gaze from her hair, he eyed the papers spread across the table "—you're finding ways to attract tourists and put me out of business?"

"Competition is healthy, Ryan." Emily hit Save. "It will be good for you."

He was fairly sure that what would be good for him was a few hours with her naked in an oversize bed, but he kept that thought to himself. "I had no idea you had such a ruthless streak."

Lisa handed him a glass of wine. "She's amazing. We've been looking at ways to reduce costs. Emily thinks I should talk to Doug Mitchell about the rent on this place."

Ryan thought about Doug, who never gave anyone anything for free if he could charge for it. "Doug isn't known for his financial generosity or his gentle heart. Don't get your hopes up."

"He's a businessman." Emily printed out a document. "He's charging almost twice what he should, and if Summer Scoop closes, he won't be getting any rent at all."

"Unless he finds another dreamer like me." Lisa topped up her own wineglass.

"You're going to speak to him tomorrow." Emily rescued the pages from the printer, clipped them together and slipped them into a file. "Show him these numbers."

"Can I do it on the phone with a script?"

"It's harder to say no to someone face-to-face. We can rehearse it, if it would make you feel better."

Lisa looked gloomily at Ryan. "I had no idea she could be this scary."

He didn't answer. There was plenty about Emily he found scary, the biggest thing being just how much he wanted to drag her back to his place. "If it persuades Doug to reduce the rent, it will be worth it."

"If he does, then there might be some hope for me. Look at all these ideas." Perking up, Lisa picked up a sheaf of papers. "Scoop of the Day. Every day we pick a different flavor and promote it. Happy Hour—half-price ice cream between 3:00 p.m. and 4:00 p.m. every day. Name an ice cream—every time you buy an ice cream, you enter into a competition to have an ice cream named after you."

Ryan wondered if anyone would buy an ice cream called "Hot and Desperate."

To distract himself, he glanced over Emily's shoulder at the spreadsheet, and immediately her scent wrapped itself around him. "How will discounting increase profits?"

"Because we're going to drive more traffic toward the store." Emily pushed a piece of paper toward him. "We're going to ask the town council for permission to put a sign up next to the place where the ferry docks. Also to put some pretty tables and chairs outside, so that people can sit for a while and watch the boats."

Ryan refrained from pointing out that they could sit and watch the boats from the deck of the Ocean Club. "And when the fog rolls in and folks are trapped indoors?"

"They can be trapped indoors here." Visibly excited,

Lisa started sketching out ideas using the twins' art materials. "We're going to paint the place and put tables and chairs inside. We're going to have things for the kids to do, like coloring and jewelry making."

"Won't that have a significant cost implication?"

"It shouldn't." Emily made a note to herself. "Skylar knows plenty of suppliers."

"I thought her work was high end."

"It is now, but before she started designing jewelry for the rich and famous, she used to do the occasional children's party. She's very creative."

Lisa snapped the top off a blue pen. "And Emily's biggest idea? A stand on the waterfront just beyond the harbor and near the beach."

Emily pushed a sketch toward him. "If they won't come to the ice cream, then we'll take the ice cream to them. What do you think?"

It was so obvious Ryan wondered why no one had thought of it before. "You'll need a food truck license."

The anxiety was back on Lisa's face. "Will that be hard? Would they refuse me?"

"I don't see why, when everyone is so keen to see Summer Scoop work. And they gave a license to Chas when he wanted to serve gourmet burgers. Seems to me that gourmet ice cream right next door would make perfect sense. He might even be prepared to lease you the stand next to his. He owns both of them." Ryan caught Emily's eye. "Let me speak to a few people. Assuming there is no problem with the license and Chas is willing to help, who would run it? You don't have the budget to employ anyone, do you?"

Emily finished her wine. "Lisa could run it at lunchtimes and weekends when the island is at its busiest.

I've been going through the numbers, and her quietest time here in the store is lunchtime—I guess because people are either already on the beach or they're in one of the restaurants or cafés. If we get the go-ahead with the license, we're going to try it for a month. See what happens."

"Leave it with me." Ryan put the papers back on the table, and Lisa passed the wine across to him.

"Drink. You've earned it. You're now officially part of the rescue team. I'm especially grateful since I know we're in competition."

"I can stand a little competition."

"In that case, next time you hold a lobster picnic on the beach, Lisa is going to provide the ice cream." Emily pushed the laptop toward him. "Take a look at these numbers, and tell me if you can see anything I've missed."

He couldn't see anything except those smoky green eyes and that soft mouth, but he forced himself to look at the screen. "Seems to me you've pretty much covered everything." Up until now he'd only ever seen her out of her depth, literally and figuratively. It was interesting seeing her comfortable and confident. "Where's Lizzy tonight?"

"Snuggled in the twins' bedroom." Lisa topped up all the glasses. "Hard to know which of them is more excited. Lizzy looks so much like them, they could be triplets."

"She's staying the night?"

"No, I'll scoop her up when we're ready to go home." Emily shut down the spreadsheet and closed the laptop. "Which I guess is now."

"You could leave her here and pick her up in the morning." Lisa said it casually, but Emily shook her head.

"We're taking this a step at a time."

"You mean you're taking it a step at a time."

She smiled. "You're right, that's what I mean. Letting Lizzy sleep over is a step I haven't reached yet."

"Think what you'd be able to do with a whole night off." Lisa grinned at her. "Adult company. Sleeping in."

"I have to go." Trying not to think of what he'd do with Emily if he had her in his bed for a night, Ryan stood up. "I need to work late to make sure you're not going to put me out of business."

Lisa laughed and walked him to the door.

"It's a crime that a man with a body like that should be allowed to wear clothes." Lisa sat back down at the table. "That's the worst thing about being a widow. No sex. Actually, it's not the worst thing. The worst thing are the rules you don't even know exist."

Emily slid her laptop back into her bag. Having Ryan there had seriously disturbed her concentration. "Rules?"

"I call them Rules for Widows. Society has unwritten rules about when it's decent to start seeing other men. The problem is that none of those rules take into account the quality of the relationship."

"You were unhappy?"

Lisa stood up and walked to the bottom of the stairs, checking there was no sound from the bedroom. Then she closed the kitchen door carefully so there was no chance they could be overheard. "Miserable. My husband had three affairs that I know about, one when I was pregnant with the twins. There were plenty of times when I could have killed the bastard myself, so it makes no sense that I got lumbered with all this guilt when he died. Why should I feel guilty? I want to smack it out of myself."

"Oh, Lisa—"

"Hey, life doesn't always send us what we want, as we both know."

A month ago Emily would have agreed wholeheartedly. Now she didn't even know what she wanted. The feeling of panic that had been her constant companion when she'd first arrived had receded to manageable levels. She and Lizzy had found an easy rhythm that was unexpected. But most unexpected of all was how much she enjoyed her swimming lessons with Ryan. Not just being with him, but the actual swimming. It gave her a feeling of strength to have overcome a fear that had been part of her life for so long.

"Why did you choose Puffin Island?"

"Because it had happy memories for me." A dreamy look crossed Lisa's face. "My parents brought me every summer. Dad was a marine biologist, and he worked at the university, so we used to come for the whole vacation. We hired a cottage near South Beach and did all the usual beach-based things. Poking around in tide pools, kayaking—I loved it. I spent a couple of summers at Camp Puffin, but the happiest one was when I turned seventeen."

"You met someone?"

"Took me five minutes to fall in love." She reached for her wine. "Do you remember that exciting feeling of discovering your own sexuality as a teenager?"

For Emily, it hadn't happened as a teenager, it had happened a few weeks before when she'd first met Ryan.

And the discovery process was ongoing. She was beginning to think she didn't know herself at all. "What happened?"

"I met him a week before we were due to go back to Boston. Something clicked between us. I'd never met anyone I could talk to the way I could talk to him. We spent every moment together." Lisa gave a humorless laugh. "I often wonder if that's been the root of my problems. That one perfect week ruined me for anything afterward."

"You didn't stay in touch?"

"I tried. I sent him emails, but they bounced so I guess he gave me an email that didn't work." Lisa shrugged. "I thought about him all the time, but then I met Mike. I've often wondered if it was my fault he had all those affairs. Because I was too closed off. My heart hurt, and I didn't want it to hurt again. Does that make any sense?"

Emily thought about the way she'd protected herself after her sister had died. "Perfect sense."

"Maybe Mike knew there was a tiny part of me I kept from him."

"Or maybe that had nothing to do with it. Did you think about leaving him?"

"All the time, but I didn't want my babies to grow up without a father, and he was a good dad. If he'd been a terrible father I could have left for their sakes, but leaving for my own sake felt like the ultimate in selfishness."

"Is it selfish to want a good life for yourself?"

"He was with one of his lovers when he died." Lisa blurted the words out. "They had to cut both of them out of the car. I'm worried that one day the kids will look up the press coverage and find out the truth."

"Oh, Lisa—" Emily reached across and took her hand.

"I just want to protect my babies." Lisa's eyes filled, and she groped for a tissue. "I want to stop anything bad happening to them. Isn't that ridiculous?"

Emily's mouth was dry as sand. "Why is it ridiculous?"

"Because you can't control everything. It took me a long time to see that and realize there wasn't anything I could have done. I couldn't stop their father having an affair. I couldn't stop him dying with his latest girlfriend in the car. I couldn't stop the press finding out. All I could do was teach them to cope with whatever life threw at them. That's the best lesson of all, isn't it? I wanted to make sure they grew up strong and able to look after themselves. I didn't want to fill their heads with my baggage because, life being what it is, I knew they'd probably pick up plenty of their own."

"Don't talk to me about baggage." Emily sat back in her chair. "I suspect Lizzy and I could fill a cargo plane with no space left over."

"But you have skills. You're supporting yourself and Lizzy. I brought the twins here because I thought hard work and a dream would be enough. I wanted to get away from the sympathy and the pitying looks and live in a place where people didn't know my rat bastard cheating husband had died in a car with his skinny lover." She sniffed. "I wanted to show the twins I was strong, but all I've done is show them I have bad judgment. I've failed."

"What you've shown them is that you're not afraid

to go after what you want. And if it doesn't work out, then you'll find a way to pick yourself up, and that's a good lesson for any child because life is about falling and then getting up again. But it's going to work out. You're not going to fall. Not this time."

"You don't know that."

"Yes, I do." Now that she knew the full story, she was even more determined to do what she could, even if she had to eat all the ice cream herself. "Providing Doug drops the rent and we can reduce some of your other costs, you'll make enough to keep going. But we're aiming for better than that. The boy you met that summer—you haven't seen him since you've been back on the island?"

Lisa shook her head. "No. And he isn't a boy now. Late twenties, I guess."

"What did he look like?"

"Tall and dark. A bit like Ryan. He likes you, by the way."

"Ryan?" Emily didn't think "like" described what was going on between them. "He was Brittany's best man. He's keeping an eye on me because she threatened to kill him if he doesn't."

Lisa laughed. "Somehow I don't think that's what's going on here. Are you interested?"

Emily thought about the slow kisses and the wild heat.

She was interested. And scared. The greater the emotion, the greater the capacity for hurt, and she knew this relationship could go nowhere.

"I have Lizzy. That's more than enough to adjust to for now. And children are the perfect contraception."

"True. On the other hand I might be able to help with that. Would you trust me with Lizzy?"

"I have trusted you with Lizzy. She's sleeping upstairs with your kids."

"I mean overnight. I swear if a photographer knocks on the door, I'll kill him with my bare hands. Even if I didn't already hate them after everything they printed about Mike's accident, I wouldn't let anything happen to Lizzy. I already love her."

"I trust you, Lisa. It isn't you, it's me. I have a problem with letting go." Over a glass of wine, she'd told Lisa the truth about Lizzy's identity, but she hadn't shared the story about Katy. "I want to be there the whole time to protect her."

"Are you really worried the photographers will come here?"

"Every day that passes makes it less likely. Ryan thinks the trail will have gone cold. That they've lost interest."

"So leave her with me," Lisa urged. "Go on a date. Have a night of wild sex. Believe me, if that is ever an option for me, I'll be dropping the twins with you!"

A wild night of sex.

Was she the only person in the world for whom sex had never been wild?

Feeling inadequate, Emily shook her head. "That isn't going to happen."

Thirteen

Two days later Ryan was on his way to deal with a problem at the marina when he saw Emily walking hand in hand with Lizzy toward the section of the harbor reserved for the boat tours. The child was talking nonstop, and Emily was listening attentively, occasionally nodding and interjecting.

He compared it to the first day when she'd sat in the Ocean Club staring at Lizzy as if she were a bomb that might detonate at any moment.

Instead of using the path down to the marina, Ryan diverted and joined them on the waterfront. "Taking a trip?"

"Yes." Lizzy was so excited she was almost dancing. "We're going on the boat. I swam on my own yesterday for the first time, and now Emily is taking me to see the puffins before they fly away for the winter."

It was impossible not to respond to that excitement. Also impossible not to wonder how much of a treat it would be for Emily.

"Sounds like fun." He cast a look at Emily and saw shades of pale under the bright smile. It was her skin color that made up his mind. "Why don't I take you myself?"

Emily shook her head. "That's not necessary. I know you're busy."

Ryan thought about the meeting he had scheduled with the multimillionaire yacht owner who wanted to negotiate the fee for using the Ocean Club facilities. He'd been looking forward to the cut and thrust of a negotiation that would end in him taking a generous chunk of the guy's money, but the anticipation was clouded by the thought of what might happen if Emily had a panic attack while Doug was in the middle of the bay. "Doug crams as many people on the boat as he can to make money. Sometimes the kids can't even see properly. You'd be more comfortable with me."

"There isn't—"

"I want to go with Ryan! Please?" Lizzy was visibly excited at the proposed change of plan, and Ryan drew Emily aside. He breathed in the scent of blossoms and lemons and wondered why he was doing this to himself.

"Are you sure this is a good idea?"

"A boat trip? Yes. I promised."

And she would never break a promise, he knew that. "Then let me take you."

"No, but thank you for offering."

"Are you refusing because of what happened in the pool?"

Her gaze skidded to his and away again. "I'm refusing because this is a child-centered day, and you have better things to do with your time."

He certainly had other things to do with his time. Whether they were better or not, he wasn't sure. "I can manage one boat trip, Emily. I'll make sure you're both safe, and you can wear life jackets the whole time. You'll be happier, I promise." He saw her gaze flicker to the tourist boat where Doug was taking money from people as they boarded. The boat was filling up, and he knew that it was going to be at full capacity. "With me, if you discover you hate it, or if she hates it, we can turn around any time and come back to the harbor. You can't do that with Doug."

"I thought you sailed a flashy racing boat."

"I do, but I'll borrow Alec's sloop. It's a traditional wooden boat. You'll love it."

Her expression told him she didn't think there was anything to love about boats. "Lizzy isn't too young for that type of boat?"

"I took Rachel sailing for the first time when she was four. Spent a whole summer teaching her knots. Bowlines, hitches, figure of eights. By the time she was eight she was sailing a Sunfish by herself."

"I don't even know what that is."

"It's a dinghy. It has a habit of capsizing." Remembering made him smile and then he saw she'd turned green. "Alec's boat is stable."

"It doesn't need a crew to sail it?"

"I can sail it alone. And I'd be happy to take a couple of passengers." He saw her glance from Lizzy to the now heaving boat in the harbor.

"Well—if you're sure. Thank you."

Ryan glanced at his watch. "Can you give me an hour? I'll meet you at the marina." He figured that would give him time to part the multimillionaire from enough of his cash to ensure the Ocean Club had a good summer.

* * *

An hour later Emily stood nervously at the marina, listening to the clink and creak of masts and the shriek of seagulls.

Was she crazy?

Learning to swim had given her a confidence boost, but not for a moment did she kid herself that swimming in a calm pool under Ryan's watchful gaze would be anything like swimming in the choppy waters of Penobscot Bay. If Lizzy fell overboard, she doubted her ability to save her.

The only thing stopping her from backing out was the knowledge that this was her problem, not Lizzy's.

Emily had spoken to the grief counselor regularly and been advised that outdoor activities were to be encouraged. Since Lizzy had started her swimming lessons with Rachel, there had been no more bad dreams, and she was sleeping in her own bed.

"There's Ryan! And he brought Cocoa." She sprinted toward him before Emily could stop her.

"Lizzy!" Her heart rate doubled, but she saw Ryan lengthen his stride and scoop the child into the safety of his arms.

"No running by the water. You might fall."

"Yes, Captain Ryan." Lizzy was grinning and wriggling like a fish in a net. As soon as Ryan put her down, Cocoa was in her arms.

Emily watched as dog and child greeted each other with mutual adoration. "The dog has her own life jacket?"

"Everyone does. Let's start with Lizzy." Once Lizzy was wearing a life jacket, he turned to Emily. "You're going to wear this the whole time, and if you don't feel safe or you want me to turn back, tell me." He secured the jacket with strong, sure hands, and she thought to herself that feeling safe had more to do with the way he made her feel than a flotation device.

"If Lizzy falls in—"

"She's not going to fall in." His hands were firm on her waist, his gaze holding hers. "Do you trust me?"

It was hard to focus on anything when he was standing this close to her. She dropped her gaze, but that move gave her an eyeful of his chest and biceps.

"Yes, but even you can't control the sea."

"But I can ensure Lizzy's safety." He tightened the life jacket "And yours."

"You have to sail the boat, and if she falls in—"

"No one is going to fall in. Unless you're planning on stripping down to that red swimsuit, in which case it will be a case of man overboard, and you'll be rescuing me." Beneath the mild humor, she heard male appreciation and felt her stomach drop.

He was the only man who had ever made her feel this way, and she had no idea how to handle her feelings.

He whistled to Cocoa who clearly recognized it as some sort of signal because she wagged her tail enthusiastically and sprang onto the boat.

Next he scooped up Lizzy and put her safely on the deck with instructions to sit down and not move until he told her what to do, and finally he held out his hand to Emily.

The rise and fall of the boat mirrored the feeling in her stomach. "I could have spent the afternoon painting or making jewelry."

"Which would have been a thousand times more boring than going to see seals and puffins." Letting go of

her hand, Ryan picked up a short length of rope from a
bag he'd put on the deck.

"We're going to see puffins!" Lizzy was finding it
hard to keep her bottom on the seat.

"Yes, but first you're going to learn to tie a knot, because all good sailors learn knots." He squatted down
in front of the child with the rope in his hands. "Watch
closely. First you make a rabbit hole—" he formed a
loop with the rope "—out comes the rabbit, around the
tree, back down the hole." He showed her again and
then handed the length of rope to Lizzy, who copied
it perfectly.

"Like that?"

"Great job." He stood up. "Keep practicing."

He maneuvered the boat skillfully out of the marina,
guided it through the markers and out into the bay. He
stood easily on the deck, loose-limbed and relaxed as
he absorbed the rise and fall of the boat. As they left
the sheltered harbor of the island, Emily felt the wind
pick up and gripped the seat, but there was something
undeniably magical about being out on the water with
the sunlight dancing over the surface of the sea.

She decided that if he was relaxed, then maybe she
could be, too. She forced the tension from her muscles
and took a few breaths.

Ryan pointed the boat into the wind, and it rocked
gently while he hauled up the sails, first one, then
another. Then he returned to the wheel, adjusted the
angle and worked the lines until the wind filled the
sails, and the boat seemed to come alive in the water.
And then they were moving, skimming the surface
of the water at a speed that took her breath away. It
felt like flying, and Emily felt a sharp stab of anxi-

ety. Then he turned his head and shot her a smile, and anxiety gave way to exhilaration. The wind whipped at her hair, and the spray of the sea showered her skin, and in that brief moment she understood why so many considered sailing to be the ultimate adventure. There was a rhythm to it that she hadn't expected, a beauty to the curve of the sails and the gleam of sunshine on the polished wooden deck.

Ryan stood at the wheel, legs apart and braced against the rise and fall of the boat as he judged tide and wind. He sailed along the rocky coast of Puffin Island, past the lighthouse that guarded the rocks by Shipwreck Cove, and across the inlet. They saw large houses tucked along the shoreline, children exploring the mysteries of the tide pools. From here she could see where the forest touched the sea and rocky outcrops that provided home to a variety of nesting seabirds.

It was a clear day, with not a hint of the fog that had a habit of shrouding the sea in the summer months.

As they sailed away from the island toward Puffin Rock he pointed out Castaway Cottage and Shell Bay.

He allowed Lizzy to steer the boat, an offer that resurrected Emily's anxiety until she saw him put the little girl between himself and the wheel and cover her hands with his.

They dropped anchor in a little cove, and Ryan pointed out a seal pup and its mother lying on a sunny ledge.

"Take a look at the puffins." He helped Lizzy adjust binoculars. "Puffins only come on land when they're breeding."

"They live on the sea?"

"Yes. They're skilled divers, and, here's the coolest

thing of all—" he crouched down behind her, helping her focus in the right place "—when they're flying, they beat their wings up to four hundred times a minute and reach speeds of around fifty miles an hour."

"How do you know?"

"Because biologists study them." Ryan took the binoculars from her, and Lizzy peered over the side of the boat.

"My mom said I should be an actor or a ballerina, but I think I might want to be a biologist or the captain of a boat and do this every day. Can women be captains?"

"Women can be anything they want to be." Ryan handed the binoculars back to her, and Emily thought again that for a man who didn't want the responsibility of children, he was remarkably good with them.

Ryan opened the cooler, and they ate a picnic of delicious sandwiches he'd ordered from the kitchen of the Ocean Club, and then sailed the boat farther out into the bay before giving both of them a brief lesson on tacking.

It made her happy to see how much Lizzy was enjoying herself. She was swift and nimble in the boat and a fast learner.

Emily found it more exciting than she would ever have imagined. It was impossible to picture anything bad happening while Ryan was in charge, so she closed her eyes and enjoyed the feel of spray on her face, the warmth of the sun and the smell of the sea. By the time they arrived back at the marina, she'd decided that maybe, just maybe, she didn't want to move to Wyoming.

Ryan sprang off the boat, secured it and then reached for Lizzy. "How does pizza sound?"

"I'm going for a sleepover."

"It's the twins' birthday," Emily explained as he glanced at her in surprise, "and she really wanted to." And she was trying hard not to show how nervous she was about it. One of the hardest things about parenthood, she was discovering, was not transferring her own hang-ups to Lizzy.

"You're not meant to call them 'the twins.'" Lizzy grabbed Cocoa. "They're separate people."

"You're right. Thank you for reminding me. It's just that 'twins' is so much quicker to say than 'Summer and Harry.'"

"We're going to eat pizza, birthday cake and then watch a movie in our pajamas."

"Sounds like a perfect evening." Ryan strolled across to Emily and took her hand as she stepped off the boat. "So, you're on your own tonight." The way he said it made her heart beat faster.

"Yes."

"Have dinner with me." He spoke quietly, checking that Lizzy was still occupied with Cocoa. "I'll book a table at The Galleon. Fine dining. Candles. Lobster. Adult company."

The invitation took her breath away.

The three years she'd spent with Neil hadn't prepared her for the intensity of feelings, and she wasn't naive enough to think that an evening with Ryan would end with dinner.

"You wouldn't be able to get a table at this short notice in the summer."

"Are you looking for an excuse to say no?"

"No, but people book months in advance, the moment they know they're coming on holiday."

He simply smiled. "So, is that a yes?"

"I'm covered in sea spray and I'm a mess."

His gaze traveled slowly from her hair to her mouth. "Option one," he murmured, "is for you to shower at my place."

Her breath caught in her throat. "Ryan—"

"Option two is that you go back to the cottage and change."

"Or there's option three," she croaked, "which is that I stay home alone."

His eyes were hooded. "I didn't give you an option three."

They'd reached a crossroads. A point where a decision had to be made.

Feeling as if she were plunging into the deep end of the swimming pool, she took a deep breath. "I'll take option two."

As she dropped Lizzy off with Lisa and the twins, she felt like a teenager on her first date, and the nerves increased as she drove back to the cottage to shower and change. By the time she walked up the steps to Ryan's apartment, she felt slightly sick, and the feeling intensified as he opened the door.

This wasn't an afternoon with Lizzy as the focus. It wasn't a swimming lesson where the objective was improving her stroke and confidence in water. This was a date. Just the two of them. Man and woman.

Amusement flickered in his eyes. "Don't tell me—you've spent the last two hours thinking of all the reasons you shouldn't be doing this."

"Maybe it's a mistake."

"Maybe." He stood to one side to let her in. "But most mistakes don't smell the way you do, so I'm willing to take that chance. I have champagne in the fridge. Hopefully that will numb your panic."

Was it panic? She wasn't sure. It felt more like excitement with a heavy dose of nerves. It was the first time she'd been in his home, and it took her breath away. Acres of glass offered spectacular views over the bay, and the setting sun sent slivers of gold across the darkening ocean. The place was designed to make you feel as if you were part of the scenery, not just an observer. You could almost smell the sea and feel the wind in your hair. It should have unsettled her, but didn't. Maybe it was because she was slowly getting used to the sea, or maybe it was because from up here it felt as if they were suspended above it, safe from the dangerous lash of the waves.

As for the apartment, the decor was exactly as she would have predicted: sophisticated, minimalist and masculine, everything chosen for its clean lines and simplicity. The kitchen area was a gleaming run of polished steel, sleek and practical. The walls that weren't glass were lined with bookcases, and in one corner a spiral staircase wound its way up to a sleeping shelf.

"What's up there? Your bedroom?"

"No. An obscenely large TV and my state-of-the-art sound system."

She laughed. "It's amazing." It was also the least child-friendly apartment she'd ever seen. "It has the feel of a loft. This will probably surprise you, but I could sit and look at this view all day."

"Me, too. Sometimes I'm tempted to do just that. Then I remind myself that if I don't get off my butt and earn money, I won't be able to afford to look at the view." He stood next to her, his shoulder brushing against hers. "When I was in the hospital, I thought about this place all the time. Even as a kid I knew these buildings had potential. I used to lie there, planning what I'd do with it. It took my mind off the pain."

"You've built a successful business."

"Winters are still lean, but even they are picking up since we started to pull in the winter outdoor crowd. And a few artists have shown interest in renting these apartments for the winter months. North light. I'm lucky to be able to build a life here." He strolled across to the fridge, removed a bottle and scooped two slender stemmed glasses from one of the cabinets.

"What are we celebrating?"

"The fact that you've learned to swim? Your first boat trip? Your first night without a six-year-old sleeping in the room next door? Adult time? The list of possibilities is endless." Under his gentle persuasion the cork came free with a gentle pop, and he poured the champagne and handed her a glass. "Or maybe we should drink to courage."

"Courage?"

"Swimming, sailing and sleepover. Knowing how hard all of those things must have been for you, I think it's an appropriate toast."

Remembering the vicious scars on his shoulder she decided he wasn't low on courage himself. "I loved the sailing. And you were so patient with Lizzy."

"She's a great kid. Gutsy, funny—she reminds me a little of Rachel at the same age. Were you scared to let her go tonight?"

"Yes. But she wanted to do it so badly, and I trust Lisa."

"Does she know the truth?"

"About Lizzy's identity, yes. She had a bad experience with journalists herself, so she was sympathetic." She wondered if she'd been tactless given his past profession, but he shook his head, reading her mind.

"I'm not about to defend the actions of the guy you told me about."

"It's been almost a month. Do you think they could still come?"

"It's less likely with every day that passes."

She stared down into her glass, watching the bubbles rise. "It's weird. This is the first time I've been on my own for a month, and instead of feeling free, I miss her."

"Kids have a habit of sneaking up on you. Before you know it, they've hooked you and you can't get free." He finished his champagne. "We should leave. They're holding our table."

The Galleon restaurant was situated a short walk from the harbor, with views over the ocean and the passing yachts. Despite the island location, or perhaps because of it, they'd managed to secure themselves a reputation as one of the top restaurants in Maine. They operated six months of the year, and during the winter months the owner and chef, Sallyanne Fisher, spent time traveling the world on the hunt for new recipes. As a result the menu was eclectic and interesting.

Sallyanne herself greeted Ryan with a kiss and showed them to a secluded table in the corner of the restaurant with a view over the water.

"Who did she have to disappoint to give you this table?" Emily slid into the chair with the view, noticing that they were partially hidden from their neighbors.

Ryan smiled. "I fixed her boat last summer. She's been grateful ever since. And on an island this small it's impossible not to know your neighbors and your competition."

"It doesn't bother you?"

"Why would it? The quality of the food here is attracting foodies from everywhere. It's good for all of us."

It certainly was good.

They ate sautéed jumbo shrimp with roasted garlic and baby spinach, followed by fresh Maine lobster washed down with a Californian white that was cool and so delicious, Emily drank more than she'd intended to.

They finished off by sharing a blueberry cheesecake. As she took the last mouthful, Emily moaned and closed her eyes. "This is so good. I'm going to tell Lisa to find a way to make this into an ice cream."

"It's generous of you to help her."

"I'm doing it for selfish reasons. After everything that has happened lately, I need to feel competent at something."

He picked up his glass. "You're competent at a lot of things."

"Not swimming or parenting."

"There's nothing wrong with your parenting skills. Just your confidence. But you're pushing yourself out of your comfort zone on a daily basis. And you're loving it."

She put down her glass. "How do you know that?"

"It shows on your face." He glanced at the dress. "It shows in everything."

"It isn't just about Lizzy. It's about me. I never did these things. I never sat on a beach and tried to eat ice cream before it melted over my fingers, I never pushed my fingers into a heap of flour and made my own pizza base, I never made necklaces out of flowers. Lisa showed me how to make the perfect pirate map. You soak paper in tea, dry it out and then burn the edges."

He smiled. "So ballerina is definitely off her list."

"Seems that way." She put her spoon down. "The thing about kids is that they make you pay attention to the small things. Things that as an adult you rush past on your way to something else."

"That's exactly what drove me crazy as a teenager. I wanted to rush past it on my way to something else."

She nodded. "You were at an age when everything was changing radically. You were trying to work out who you were, and suddenly you were expected to be responsible for other people. That's scary, but also rewarding. Lizzy's reading is coming on so fast. Agnes has been reading to her, too. She gave us lots of Rachel's old books."

He sat back in his chair, studying her across the table. "Still worried you can't love her?"

"She's very easy to love."

"And that scares you."

"Yes, but lately I'm doing everything that scares me, so I guess this is just one more thing."

"You're an impressive person, Emily Donovan. You took on a child you'd never even met and agreed to live a life you didn't think you wanted. Most people in your position would have put her in foster care."

"I don't think so." She took a deep breath. "I think most people would have done what I did. Spending time with Lizzy makes me wish I'd tried harder to have a relationship with Lana. I blame myself for that."

"How was that your fault?"

"I keep wondering whether if the accident hadn't happened, or if I hadn't reacted so badly to it, maybe things would have been different. Maybe we would have been closer."

"Or maybe she was never going to be the sort of person who wanted that."

Emily thought about her half sister and the uncomfortable similarities to her mother. "She was so beautiful, and yet she seemed to need to have that confirmed all the time. Maybe that was my mother's fault because looks were the only thing she valued."

Maybe it was because he was such a good listener, but suddenly she was telling him everything, about how she'd been teased in school about her body, how she'd tried to disguise her shape, how she'd mistrusted relationships.

The conversation wasn't all one-sided. He talked a little about how he'd felt stifled by looking after his younger siblings and about how guilty he'd felt leaving his grandmother to cope when he'd taken up a place at college.

"She wanted that for you."

"Didn't stop me feeling guilty."

"But by then the children were older. And the fact that you wanted to leave doesn't change the fact that you loved them."

"Like the fact that wearing black doesn't disguise the fact you're the sexiest woman alive."

The shift in the atmosphere rocked her off balance, and she felt her pulse quicken. "How much of that wine have you drunk? Your brain is malfunctioning."

"My brain has been malfunctioning since you wore those pajamas."

She stared at him across the table. He was sensationally attractive, those eyes dark as flint in a face where every line and angle spoke of strength and masculinity. The air was alive with a tension she had only ever experienced around this man.

The sexual energy was palpable, and by the time they returned to his apartment, she was feeling lightheaded from a heady mixture of wine and anticipation.

He found his keys, opened the door and flicked a switch that turned on a couple of lamps and sent a warm glow over the spacious room.

"It's late," she murmured. "I should probably go home." Because she was nervous, she walked to the window, and he threw his keys down on a small table near the door and followed her.

"Is that what you want?" He stood behind her, and his hands closed over her arms.

She closed her eyes. "It would be sensible."

"And do you always do what's sensible?"

"Always. I like order and predictability. I'm only interested in things I can control." She kept her eyes forward, staring into the darkness of the bay. Lights from boats sent a warm glow flickering across the water. "With you, I feel out of control. As if I've lost my balance."

"Good." He moved her hair aside gently, and she could feel the warmth of his breath on the back of her neck. "I'm pleased I unbalance you."

"I'm worried the reality will be a letdown."

"It won't be." He turned her to face him. His gaze was slumberous, and all she saw in his eyes was liquid desire that mirrored hers. "Are you nervous?"

"Yes. I don't feel any of the right things when I'm

in bed with a man. It's as if something inside me isn't switched on."

His smile was slow and sure. "Maybe it's a question of knowing where to find the switch. Why don't you leave that part to me?"

"I think there might be something wrong with me."

"Honey, there's nothing wrong with you. I have surveillance footage that proves it."

She thought about that night in the pool and leaned her forehead against his chest. "I thought you said it would be wiped."

"After sixty days." His fingers gently massaged her hair. "So for the next few weeks I have visual evidence that you're not who you think you are. Or we could try a different way to prove the same thing."

Her heart was pounding so fast she felt sure he must be able to feel it. "Are you always so sure about everything?"

"Not everything." He lowered his head so that his mouth was a breath away from hers. "But this I'm sure about." His hand slid to the nape of her neck, and he held her head while he kissed her slowly, taking his time as he explored her mouth, her jaw, the hollow of her neck until the urgency inside her was a primal, desperate beat.

She wrapped her arms around him, felt him haul her close so that she was anchored against hardness and strength. And still he kissed her, his mouth exploring hers with leisurely skill until all she could hear was the soft thrumming of her own pulse in her ears and his murmured words of encouragement. If he hadn't been holding her, she would have sunk to the floor in a pool of molten desire. She was dizzy with it. Disoriented.

All she knew was that of all the things that had happened over the past month, this felt the most right. Her hands were in his hair, her mouth responding to the erotic rhythm of his kiss.

She slid her hands down his back and tugged at his shirt.

She pressed against him, feeling the rigid thickness through the thin fabric of her dress.

"Steady." He whispered the words against her mouth. "We have all night."

She wanted to tell him that she wasn't going to last five minutes, let alone all night, but at that moment his hand slid from her hip to her rib cage, and she felt his fingers brush the underside of her breast. It was such a relief that she moaned, but then he drew his hand away and smoothed her back instead, leaving her body vibrating with frustration.

"Ryan—" She'd never felt this desperate for anything in her life before, but even her pleading didn't persuade him to alter his pace.

He continued to kiss her, long and deep, until she was trembling and shivering, until thick syrupy pleasure spread through her body. She was wondering what would happen when he finally touched her, when he slid the zipper on her dress and she felt his fingers slowly trace the length of her spine. His hands moved to her shoulders, and the dress slithered onto the wooden floor in a whisper of silk, leaving her standing in her underwear.

He eased her away from him, and the look he gave her from under those thick, dark lashes sent a lick of fire burning across her skin.

She trembled with arousal. "I wish—"

"You wish?" His voice was husky and deep, and she lifted her hands to the front of his shirt and started undoing the buttons. Because she was shaking, she fumbled, but he didn't help her, just stood and waited, holding himself still while she struggled to get him naked.

In the end she gave up and ripped at the last few, sending buttons bouncing across the floor.

She heard him laugh, and then he scooped her into his arms as if she weighed nothing and carried her across the room, through slivers of dark and moonlight, to his bedroom. She saw briefly that it had the same incredible view, the same canvas of sea and stars, and then he was lowering her onto the bed, the muscles of his shoulders bunched as he supported her weight.

Clumsy, she fumbled with his belt, but her fingers were useless, and instead she gave up, frustrated, and covered him with the flat of her hand. He made a sound somewhere between a groan and a laugh and finished what she'd started. She stroked her hands over his powerful shoulders, lingered on the rough texture of his scar and slid lower. She felt the roughness of his thigh brush against the softness of hers, and then he shifted, giving himself full access to her body.

She started to remove her underwear, but he stopped her, pressing her flat to the bed with a wicked smile.

"That's my job."

"But—"

"Be patient." He kissed her throat, and then his mouth moved lower to the full swell of her breasts, now pushing hard against the supportive fabric of her bra. His fingers brushed against the thrusting tip, and liquid heat pooled deep in her pelvis. For a moment she wondered whether his patience and control signified a lack of desire, but then she saw the dangerous glitter in his eyes and knew he was balanced on the edge, just as she was.

And then he was kissing her again, and she felt him remove her bra, leaving her breasts full and exposed.

"With a body like yours it's a sin to wear clothes—ever."

Her hips shifted against the softness of his sheets, her body arched, and still he explored, tasted, teased until she was sobbing his name, her fingers digging hard into the powerful muscles of his shoulders.

"Ryan—"

"Not yet." But his hand finally moved between her thighs, lingered there, stroked through the sheer fabric of her panties and then slid inside, parting delicate folds until she was gasping. When she didn't think she could stand it any longer, he stripped off the last of her underwear, and his fingers explored her with slow, skillful strokes and then slid deep, touching her in a way that was new to her until sensation built with suffocating intensity. She felt the first flutters of her body, but instead of finishing what he'd started, he moved down her body, kissing her stomach and lower until he was settled between her thighs.

Desperation gave way to acute shyness. This was something she'd never done with Neil, and she tried to wriggle away, but Ryan held her firmly, urging her to relax, to just breathe, to trust him, and then she felt the silky stroke of his tongue and the warmth of his breath against exposed, slippery flesh. He held her there, trapped and helpless, while he explored and exposed all of her body's secrets, until she could no longer keep still. Finally, when she was sobbing and desperate, she felt him pause and reach for something from the nightstand and then he shifted over her, hard and heavy.

"Look at me." His soft command penetrated her clouded brain, and she opened her eyes, met the burning intensity of his and then moaned as she felt him enter her with a series of slow, deliberate thrusts. She felt her body yield to the invasion of his, felt her muscles ripple against the swollen thickness and moaned his name.

"Am I hurting you?"

She was drowning in pleasure. "No! I just—I need—"

"I know what you need." His voice thickened, he lowered his mouth to hers and rocked into her, deeper, harder, until each stroke, each driving relentless thrust propelled her closer to ecstasy.

Inhibition fled. Her only fear was that he might stop, that he might once again delay the pleasure. But not this time. Instead, he shifted the angle so that the combination of masculine thrust and delicious friction finally opened the gate to that elusive peak.

Pleasure rushed at her like a wave, slamming into her, the intensity of her climax catching her by surprise. She heard him groan her name, and then he was kissing her, stealing every sob, every cry with his mouth as the ripples of her body tipped him into his own shuddering release.

Afterward she lay, eyes closed, shaken by the depth of her own feelings. He gathered her close, soothing her with gentle hands and soft words, and then she was dimly aware of him leaving the bed. In the distance she heard the sound of water coming from the bathroom, and then he returned to the bedroom, scooped her boneless, pliant body easily into his arms and carried her through to the steamy, scented heaven.

"I never take baths, just showers." She slid into the water with a groan. "I might drown. I need a life jacket."

"You're not going to drown."

She heard the smile in his voice and opened her eyes. Confronted by the hard planes of his body, her gaze lingered on the dip and swell of muscle, the strength of those shoulders, the board-flat abdomen and the hair-roughened length of his thighs.

Catching her looking at him, he raised one eyebrow questioningly, as unselfconscious as she was anxious and unsure.

"You cannot possibly be shy after what we just did." His voice was deep pitched, roughened by desire, and she discovered that far from being sated, it was as if her body had woken from a deep sleep.

"Maybe. You could turn the lights off if you like."

"Honey, your body is so perfect anything less than a spotlight is a waste." He slid into the water next to her, and she silenced the voice that questioned why he'd installed a tub big enough for two.

Her hair hung damp and curling in the steam, the ends heavy and wet as they clung to her neck. He pushed it aside and brought his mouth down on hers.

"You're beautiful."

She straddled him, her skin sliding against his, the warmth of the water mingling with the heat of his skin. She pressed her mouth to the rough texture of his jaw, felt the rhythm of his breathing change as her hands moved down his body.

By the time morning came they'd done everything except sleep.

They lay, wrapped up in each other, watching dawn break over an ocean as smooth and still as glass.

"I've never had a date like this one." Her voice broke the sleepy silence, and she felt him stir and tighten his grip.

"It's good to try new things." His voice was husky, and he shifted her under him and looked down at her through lowered lids. "Still think there's something wrong with you?"

"No." She slid her arms around his neck. "You obviously have special powers."

He lowered his mouth to hers, smiling against her lips. "Sweetheart, I haven't even started. Any time you want another display of my special powers, let me know."

She felt the weight of him on her, dominating and unbelievably arousing. "It's dawn. I'm picking up Lizzy in three hours, and the thing about having children is that there isn't a whole lot of opportunity for sleeping in the day."

"True. Sleepless nights suck. Unless the reason for it is sex." He rolled on to his back, but he kept hold of her, locking her body against his. "I want to know more about you. Tell me something. Anything. Did you like school?"

"Mostly, yes. I liked the learning and the routine. There was a consistency that wasn't ever present at home. Once I walked through those gates, I knew what was going to happen. The people behaved in a predictable way. I was never going to walk in and find them drunk or naked with a guy I'd never met before."

"I've heard a lot of reasons for enjoying school but never that one."

"Was there a teacher that stood out for you? For me it was Mrs. White. We used to wonder if she'd had her hair dyed to match her name, but she was the best math teacher. I was good at numbers. There was a beauty to it, a logic, that wasn't present in anything else in my life. I had a gift, I think, and she saw it. She took me under her wing. I don't know if she guessed what was happening at home, or whether she was just one of those people who are really good at bringing out the best in every child. Either way, she helped me. I was always the last kid in the building."

"You didn't want to go home."

"To begin with that was the reason, but after a few years it was because I didn't want to leave. School was a place full of possibilities. Mrs. White made me believe education was the key to another world. I wanted that key so badly. For the first time ever, the future looked exciting. I made it into college because of her. Every night when I left she gave me a new book to read, and every morning I gave it back and exchanged it for a different one."

"You read a book a night?"

"I read from the moment I arrived home until I fell asleep. If the book was good, I didn't sleep much. Sometimes I'd talk about the books with my stepfather, but mostly I just lived in my own world, and he respected that."

"And your mom?"

"She didn't care what I was doing." She ran her hand

over his shoulder, feeling the uneven texture of his skin under her fingers. "Does it hurt? And don't lie to me."

"It's worse when the weather is cold and occasionally when I use it without thinking. But I don't mind." He hesitated. "At the beginning when I was going through the endless surgery and rehabilitation and taking the pain and frustration out on my family, I kept thinking of Finn. Every time I was tempted to feel sorry for myself, I thought about him. And the pain reminds me to live in the moment."

"I wish I was more like that. I spend half my life—no, more than half my life—" she corrected herself "—worrying about stuff that hasn't happened yet."

"You're not alone. Most of us go through life thinking about tomorrow, and we miss today. That was one of the things that made Finn such a great companion on our trips into dangerous territory. He noticed the small things that other people missed. It was also what made him a great photographer."

"You don't talk about him much. You don't talk about any of it much."

His fingers moved slowly up and down her arm. "The past is useful if it teaches you something about how you should be living in the present. Other than that, it's just the past."

Emily thought about her sister. "I think I've been living my whole life governed by the past. I didn't think about it and didn't talk about it, but it was there in everything I did. Skylar said that to me once and she was right. If it hadn't been for Lizzy, I probably would have stayed that way forever."

"And now?"

"Children have a way of making you live in the present. She doesn't see further than the next meal or the next activity." But she knew it wasn't just Lizzy who was responsible for the change in her. It was Ryan.

He turned his head to hers, the gleam in his eyes telling her he knew what she was thinking. "If you need a suggestion for what the next activity could be, just ask."

Fourteen

She left before Ryan woke, tiptoeing out of his apartment as sunlight shimmered through the wall of glass.

The trail of clothes strewn around the room told the story of the night before, and she gathered them up, dressed swiftly and quietly closed the door behind her.

As she walked down the steps that led from his apartment, she wished she'd thought to bring something else to wear.

She was acutely conscious, not only of the dress that announced to the entire island where she'd spent the night, but of the small things. The slight whisker burns on the sensitive skin of her neck and the fact that her body ached in unusual places. And then there were the other things. Emotions she didn't recognize. Feelings that were unfamiliar.

It was as if she'd gone to sleep as one person and woken as another.

She arrived to pick up Lizzy and was grateful that Lisa said nothing about the fact Emily was overdressed. Instead, she supplied a strong cup of coffee and proceeded to make small talk about her plans for the make-over of Summer Scoop.

On the drive home Lizzy talked nonstop about her sleepover, an evening apparently bursting with pizza and popcorn.

Emily parked outside the cottage and stared at Shell Bay.

Had Ryan woken up?

Maybe she should have left a note, but what would she have said?

Thanks for the best sex of my life.

"Can we dig in the sand?" Lizzy sounded hopeful, and Emily turned to look at her, wondering why everything felt different.

"Yes. Let's do it. Right now." Before this new version of herself vanished. Before she went back to being the person she'd been the day before.

They both changed into swimming things and pulled on shorts and T-shirts. Then Emily gathered up a blanket along with the bucket and spade and walked along the short sandy path that led directly to the beach.

Most of the tourists chose to stay on the beaches close to the harbor, and there was only one other family on Shell Bay.

Emily put the blanket down, and Lizzy stripped down to her swimsuit and started digging. "Can we build a boat?"

Emily would have preferred something a little less challenging for her first sand sculpture, but she gamely set her mind to scooping out the hull of a boat, using her hands to fashion seats and a prow while Lizzy filled and refilled the bucket.

They dug together for half an hour, and then Emily

straightened and stripped off her shorts and tee. She dug her hand into her bag and surreptitiously checked her phone, but there were no messages.

Disappointment hovered like a cloud over her happiness.

Lizzy glanced up at her. "Skylar says red is your color."

"Does she? And what's your color? Pink?"

Lizzy shook her head and patted down the sand. "Turquoise. Like the sea."

Close by, the other family was playing a ball game, and when the ball came flying in their direction, Emily caught it and threw it back.

She hadn't intended to walk to the water's edge, but somehow that was where she ended up, and she stood with her toes curling into the damp sand, feeling the lick of the tide on her ankles. Ahead of her lay the vastness of the ocean, an infinity of blue merging with the summer sky on a horizon so straight it could have been drawn by a child with a ruler.

The expanse of water made her catch her breath, and she turned her head, needing to see land, and there right behind her was Castaway Cottage, looking over the beach like a benevolent friend. It was impossible to believe anything bad could happen within sight of the cottage and easy to see why Kathleen had bought it all those years ago. It was the perfect Maine beach house, a retreat that most people could only dream of owning.

Lizzy dropped the bucket and ran to her side. "Are you going in the sea?"

"Yes." Up until that point, she hadn't realized that had always been her intention. "I am."

"Can I come? I haven't swum in the sea yet, but Rachel said I was ready."

She wanted to refuse. She still wasn't sure she was ready to do it herself, let alone take someone else with her.

On the other hand, if this was a test, then she might as well make it the ultimate test.

"I want you to use your float."

Lizzy ran off and returned moments later carrying it.

Maybe she should have waited for Ryan. He would have come with her, she knew, but she also knew this was something she had to do by herself. It was her fear to conquer, and no one could do that for her. It felt as if she'd climbed almost to the top of Everest and was only a few steps from the summit. She didn't have to do this, but she knew she would never feel whole until she did.

She told herself that she knew this beach, that she'd watched the ebb and flow of the tide enough times to know how the beach shelved. Here, in the perfect curve of Shell Cove, there were no dangerous currents, no riptides. The safety of the swimming was one of the many reasons Brittany was constantly being bothered by people wanting to buy the land. There was surely no more perfect spot in the whole of Maine.

She took a single step forward, and Lizzy took her hand, dancing over the small waves without fear.

"It's freezing!" She squealed and laughed, while Emily watched, entertained and a little envious.

Had she ever been that carefree?

Had there ever been a time when she enjoyed the moment without worrying that something bad was about to happen? *Had she ever lived without protecting herself?*

"Aunt Emily—" Lizzy tugged her hand impatiently "—come *on*!"

And she realized that living in the moment was a choice, and she stepped forward and kept walking until the water was above her knees.

Another family joined them in the water, the children squealing as the father swung them high into the air.

Reassured by their presence, Emily scooped Lizzy into her arms and held her out of reach of the waves.

The water was midthigh, and she knew she didn't need to go any deeper. This was enough for now. The ocean stretched ahead of her, calm today, sleeping in the warm afternoon sunshine. The surface sparkled, inviting, and Emily knew that it had to be now. It was the perfect time.

"Are you ready?" Steeling herself, she lowered Lizzy to the water and watched her kick out, confident as she started to swim. "Swim parallel to the shore. Stay in line with the beach. That's it."

Without allowing herself to think too much, Emily slid forward into the water, gasping as the coldness closed over her shoulders. Immediately she had the urge to stand up, to feel the reassuring pressure of the sand beneath her feet, but she fought the panic and forced herself to breathe and move her arms and legs in the same rhythmic strokes she'd used in the pool. She felt the gentle lift and fall of the water as she swam, felt the sea lick at the edges of her hair and her face, playful, not threatening.

Panic was replaced by calm and then by pleasure and no small degree of pride. She was swimming, really swimming. She'd learned a new skill. The sea was in control, she knew that. But if she was careful, they could coexist.

Next to her Lizzy splashed and swam, chin raised like a dog out of the water, and Emily murmured words of encouragement, telling her to keep going, keep kicking, and she wasn't sure if she was saying the words to herself or the child.

They swam halfway along the cove before Lizzy declared that her arms were too tired, and Emily stood up, feeling the reassuring pressure of the sand beneath her feet. The water was still at midthigh but too deep for Lizzy, and she scooped her up and held her tightly, safely out of reach of the water.

"You swam so well."

She felt Lizzy's arms creep around her neck and the softness of her curls brush against her chin. She breathed in the smell of salt and sea and closed her eyes, rocked by the tight squeeze of those skinny arms and the priceless gift of trust. Something inside her that she'd thought had died sprang to life and bloomed. She wasn't sure how it happened or even why, but at some point holding turned to hugging. The deep chill that had become part of her slowly thawed as they stood, tangled together, intertwined and close.

"I like living here." Lizzy's voice was soft, and Emily felt her eyes sting.

"I like living here, too."

"Can we have a puppy?"

Eyes stinging, Emily started to laugh. "Let's take this a step at a time, shall we?"

"A puppy would be the best thing ever. I love Cocoa, but she's Agnes's best friend, so we can't have her."

"No, we can't." A puppy. Realizing she was actually considering it, Emily shook her head in disbelief. "Let's go indoors and wash off all this sand." Holding Lizzy on her hip, she waded back to shore. "Oh, wait, let's finish our sand yacht."

By the time they'd finished their impressive structure, the sun was dipping down below the horizon and clouds were gathering.

They ran indoors trailing sand and laughter into the house, showered, changed and then picked blueberries from the bushes in the garden and made a pie.

"Push your hands into the flour—" Emily stood Lizzy on a chair, and together they weighed and stirred and mixed while outside the sky darkened and thunder rumbled.

"Will we live here forever?" Lizzy had somehow managed to cover every available surface and herself with flour.

Emily poured the blueberries into the pie dish. "Castaway Cottage isn't ours. It belongs to Brittany, my friend."

"If she comes home, where will we live?"

Emily paused, understanding the child's need for security in a world that had crumbled around her. "We'd stay here until we found somewhere perfect for us." She sent mental thanks to her friend and the pact they'd made all those years before.

"Will we stay on Puffin Island?"

It was something she hadn't considered until the past few days. "That's something we'll have to talk about."

"I want to live here. I don't want to leave Cocoa. Or the puffins. I like swimming. Rachel says if I'm still here when school starts after the summer, she'd be my teacher."

Emily leaned across and wiped the flour from her mouth. "You'd have to call her Miss Cooper."

Lizzy grinned. "I'd be with Summer and Harry."

"That sounds like fun. Are you done making pastry? I'll finish off and then we can clean up and read a book while our pie is cooking."

She heard the front door open and then the sound of paws on the floor as Cocoa sprinted into the kitchen.

"Cocoa!" Abandoning her duties as pastry maker, Lizzy jumped off the chair and hugged the dog, spreading flour and goodwill in equal measure.

Emily's heart lifted as Ryan walked into the room, wiping droplets of rain from his face. "She's learned *sit*, but *stay* is still giving us a problem."

His gaze connected with hers briefly, and the look he gave her sent heat rushing to her cheeks.

"Would you like to stay for dinner? It's Lizzy's favorite gourmet treat. Mac and cheese followed by blueberry pie."

"That sounds like the best invitation I've had in a long time." He hunkered down next to Lizzy. "I saw a boat on the beach. A boat that is even better than mine. No idea how something that spectacular could have just shown up on the sand like that. Any ideas?"

Lizzy was giggling, her hands full of Cocoa. "Emily and I made it. We copied yours."

"It's a better-looking boat than mine. Any time you want to build me a proper boat, go right ahead." He rose to his feet. "So, you played in the sand."

"And the sea. I swam."

His eyebrows rose. "With Rachel?"

"With Emily."

"Emily swam in the sea?" There was a strange note to his voice, and Emily slid the pie into the oven.

"I remembered everything you taught me."

"You should have told me you wanted to do that. I would have come with you."

"It wasn't something I planned. And I needed to do it by myself."

He nodded slowly. "And how did it feel?"

She thought about the sensation of the water on her limbs, the terror of feeling the waves tug at her and the satisfaction of having confronted something that frightened her so badly. "It felt good. I don't think I'll be swimming to the mainland anytime soon, but it was a start."

Lizzy scrambled to her feet. "Ryan, will you read a story?"

"Sure." He lifted her into his arms. "What's it to be? *Green Eggs and Ham*?"

Knowing how badly Lizzy needed to be wrapped in that security blanket right now, Emily sent him a grateful look. "I'll fetch the book."

"Not that one." Lizzy's arms were around his neck. "I want the one in your head. The one you told me that time Emily was sick, about Abbie, the lighthouse keeper's daughter who kept the lights burning when her father couldn't get back to the island."

Ryan sat down at the table with Lizzy on his lap and started telling the story while Emily made sauce for the mac and cheese. Thunder boomed outside the cottage, and Lizzy flinched against Ryan, who carried on telling the story in his calm, steady voice.

"It was one of the worse storms ever—"

"Worse than this one?"

"Much worse than this one..."

Lizzy kept interrupting, asking questions. Did Ryan think Abbie had been afraid? Why hadn't she used a boat to escape? Could the waves have covered the lighthouse?

He answered everything with the same quiet patience, returning each time to the story until another clap of thunder came from overhead. This one was so loud even Emily flinched, and Lizzy hid her face in Ryan's chest and clutched his shirt.

"I don't like storms."

"Plenty of people feel the same way." His hand smoothed her spine, gentle and reassuring. "Rachel was the same, but don't tell her I told you."

"But she's big and brave."

"Yeah, but she doesn't like storms. Everyone is afraid of something."

He'd used the same calm tone with her, Emily remembered. On the day of her meltdown, it had been his voice as much as his presence that had calmed her. When Ryan spoke, it was impossible to believe anything bad could happen, that the world could be anything other than a safe place.

Lizzy relaxed her hold on his shirt. "Are you afraid of storms?"

"Not storms, but there are plenty of other things that scare me."

"Like what?"

He hesitated. "I don't like hospitals. I don't like the way they smell or sound. I'll do just about anything to avoid going into one."

Lizzy pondered. "But what if the doctor said you had to go to the hospital?"

"Then I'd go." His hand stroked her hair. "Being afraid doesn't mean you don't do something, it just means it isn't easy and you have to try a little harder than other people."

"Aunt Emily?" Lizzy was looking at her. "What scares you?"

Loving and losing.

And she hadn't faced that fear. Instead, she'd done everything she possibly could to live her life in a way that meant she could avoid it.

Emily stirred the sauce in a mindless, rhythmic movement that required no attention.

The only sound in the kitchen was the faint simmer of liquid and the heavy patter of rain against the window.

"Aunt Emily?"

"The sea," she croaked. "Until today I was afraid of the sea. You have to let Ryan finish the story."

His eyes fixed on hers, he carried on with the story, his tone and the words he used making it all too easy to picture Abbie's struggle during that terrible storm.

As the rain sheeted down the windows, Emily found herself picturing the girl trying to keep the lamps burning in the lighthouse and take care of her three sisters and sick mother, while the sea boiled and lashed at her home.

Lizzy listened, absorbed. "What do you think Abbie was afraid of?"

"I don't know. Whatever it was, she didn't let it stop her keeping those lamps alight and protecting the shipping in that terrible storm."

"I want to hear the part where she rescues the hens—"

He'd already told that part of the story, but Ryan repeated it, and Emily sent him a grateful look. There was something intimate about sharing a thought that came with no words, and her chest warmed as she turned back to her sauce. She could feel his eyes on her, feel him watching every movement as she stirred the sauce until it was smooth and perfect.

"I love the sound of the rain on the roof," she said. "Close your eyes and listen."

Lizzy closed her eyes. "It sounds like an army with heavy boots."

Emily smiled. "It does." She looked at Ryan. His jaw was dark with stubble, his hair curling slightly from the rain. She wanted so badly to touch it, to slide her fingers into it and drag his mouth down to hers as she had the night before. The atmosphere was heavy, filled with unspoken need, the silence eloquent. His smile was intimate and deeply personal, and her response to that smile was so powerful it was hard to breathe through it.

She'd never realized that not touching could be so arousing.

He must have felt the same way because he shifted slightly in his seat.

Lizzy opened her eyes and tightened her grip like a monkey. "I don't want you to go."

"I'm not going anywhere." His voice was husky. "But I need to help Emily, so will you cuddle Cocoa? She hates storms, too."

Distracted by this new responsibility, Lizzy scrambled under the table with Cocoa.

Emily's heart rate quickened as Ryan stood next to her. He covered her hand with his and stirred the sauce, his mouth close to her ear.

"I'm hungry."

She didn't dare look at him. "The food won't be long."

"That isn't going to help me." His voice shimmered with wry humor.

The urge to kiss him was almost unbearable, and she wondered how she was going to make it through an evening without being allowed to touch him.

"Ryan?" Lizzy's voice came from under the table, making them both jump.

He kept his eyes on Emily's face. "Yeah?"

"You should hug Emily, too, in case she's scared."

"Oh!" Flustered, Emily almost dropped the spoon. "There isn't any need—"

"Great idea." Ryan removed the spoon from her hand, slid his arm around her and pulled her against him. "Are you scared, Emily?"

She placed her hand on his chest, intending to make a flippant remark and push him away, but she could feel the steady beat of his heart against her palm, and instead of pulling back she curved her hand up to his shoulder.

"I'm not afraid of storms," she said quietly.

"But you're afraid of other things." His voice was low, and she knew this conversation was no longer for Lizzy's benefit.

She was afraid. Not of the storm and not of him, but of her own feelings.

His cheek brushed against her hair, and she could feel the warmth of his hand low on her spine. She was pressed against thick, hard masculine pressure, and desire blurred her vision and her thoughts. It was obvious that his frustration matched hers. She wanted his mouth on hers so badly she almost dragged his head to hers right there and then.

The effort of holding back simply increased the erotic intensity of the moment.

Every sense was exaggerated. She could hear the relentless patter of rain on the roof and the soft bubbling of the sauce on the stove. She felt the warmth of his breath on her neck and the slow stroke of his fingers on her spine.

His hand cupped her cheek, and when she looked into his eyes she saw heat and raw desire.

She'd never wanted anything or anyone as badly as she wanted him.

Her stomach tightened.

His mouth was so close to hers he was almost touching her.

"Emily?" Lizzy's voice came from under the table where she was still playing with Cocoa. "I can smell burning."

The moment was broken.

They rescued the sauce, and later, much later, after a supper of mac and cheese followed by blueberry pie, Emily tucked Lizzy into bed.

The thunder had moved on, leaving only the rain, and Emily flicked on the tiny lamp by Lizzy's bed. "I'm going to leave the door open, so if you want me you just have to call out."

"Will you be downstairs?"

"The whole time. I'll be able to hear you."

"Will Ryan be there, too?"

"For a while, but then he'll be going home."

"I like it when he's here. I wish he could stay."

I wish he could stay, too.

"He has to go home." Emily tucked the patchwork

quilt around the little girl and the bear. "And you need to go to sleep."

"Maybe he could do a sleepover one night, like I did with Summer and Harry."

Emily felt her tummy tighten. "We'll talk about that another time."

"Can Cocoa sleep on my bed tonight in case the storm comes back?"

"I'll ask Ryan."

"Can we swim in the sea again tomorrow?"

The questions were endless, a ruse to postpone the moment when Emily left the room.

"It depends on the weather." She sat on the edge of the bed and stroked Lizzy's hair. "Are you still scared? I could sit with you if you like."

"No." Lizzy's eyes were drifting shut. "I'm going to think about Abbie in the storm. She was brave."

"She was."

"Emily?"

She paused, waiting for another question. "Yes?"

"I love you."

Caught off guard, Emily felt her heart miss a beat and the breath jam in her throat.

It hadn't been a question, but still a declaration like that demanded a response and how was she going to respond?

Of all the things that scared her in life, this scared her the most.

More even than walking into the sea and swimming.

She thought of what Ryan had said about fear. She thought of Abbie keeping the lamps burning in the storm.

And then she closed her eyes and took the leap. "I love you, too."

* * *

"Is she asleep?" Ryan offered her a beer, but Emily shook her head and walked to the window, her expression dazed. "What's wrong?"

"Everything." She wrapped her arms around herself, staring straight ahead. "I've lived my whole life trying to stop this happening."

Ryan put his hands on her shoulders and turned her to face him. "What?"

"She told me she loved me." Her voice shook slightly, and he saw emotion shimmer in those green eyes, along with something else.

"And that scared the hell out of you."

"Yes." She took a deep breath. "I can't do this, Ryan. I don't want this."

"You don't want her to love you? You're scared because she's putting all her trust in you, depending on you?"

There was a long silence, and then she lifted her face to his. "No, I'm scared because I love her back."

"Emily—"

"She's been with me for a matter of weeks, and I was so sure I had this under control."

"Feelings are the hardest thing in life to control."

She raked shaking fingers through her hair. "What am I going to do?"

"Same thing everyone else does. You're going to take life a day at a time, enjoy the good parts and deal with the bad."

"The bad broke me."

"You were a child and you were alone. You're not alone now." He pulled her against him and lowered his mouth to hers. "Tell me why you ran out on me this morning."

"I needed to pick up Lizzy."

"Next time, wake me." He kissed her and heard her moan softly. "How soon do you think Lizzy will want to go for another sleepover?"

"Not for a while."

"In that case I am going to be taking a lot of cold swims in the sea." He lifted his head and smoothed her hair back, searching her face. "Do you regret it?"

She shook her head. "Do you?"

It had been the best sex of his life. "No." He could feel her curves against him and had to use all his will-power not to strip her naked and press her back against the sofa. "But Kirsti saw you leaving, and I had to endure half an hour of questions, none of which I answered."

"Oops. Awkward."

"Not really. I'm immune to Kirsti. Let me know when you and Lizzy want to go out on the boat again."

"You'd take her again?"

"Of course. Why wouldn't I?"

She gave him a long look. "I guess I'm a little surprised. You make no secret of the fact your preference is for a child-free life."

"I'm suggesting a boat trip, not inviting her to move in. I like Lizzy. She's been through a trauma, and I know how that feels. And it's the only way I can spend time with you."

There was nothing more to it than that.

He had no idea why people insisted on making things more complicated than they were.

Fifteen

The regeneration of Summer Scoop took place the following weekend.

Lisa had bought the paint and supplies, and Ryan had managed to enlist an army of volunteers from the students who frequented the island over the summer months. They arrived in a minivan emblazoned with the logo of the Marine Center, ready to pitch in for the reward of free ice cream.

Skylar, who had flown in for the weekend, put herself in charge of the interior. She'd discarded the option of plain walls in favor of a mural. She and Lisa had pored over designs, before finally agreeing on an ocean theme.

"It needs puffins," Lizzy had announced firmly, and so puffins had been added to the design.

Skylar had given all three children paintbrushes and small pots of paint, and put them in charge of painting the sand under her strict supervision.

"She should be a teacher," Rachel murmured as she joined the group outside, painting the exterior. "I'm going to try and tempt her to do a few weeks at Camp Puffin next summer."

Years of weathering and chipped paint vanished under several coats of glossy blue that added cheer to the front of Summer Scoop.

Lisa had bought wrought-iron bistro tables and chairs from an online auction site and was busy cleaning them up. "I bought them from a lady in Bar Harbor who is moving to live with her daughter in Canada."

"They're fantastic." Emily watched with half an eye as Lizzy painstakingly added to the sand. "Did you talk to Doug about lowering the rent?"

"Yes. I said exactly what you said I should say and he agreed."

"I thought he might."

"I can't thank you enough." Lisa wiped her forehead on her forearm. "Finally, I feel as if there might be hope. Without you I think I would have given up."

"You wouldn't have."

"I certainly wouldn't have thought of all this. And I wouldn't have been able to persuade everyone to help."

"That was Ryan. He always says that islanders can be the most irritating people alive until you're in need, and then they're the best."

"He's right. And your friend Skylar is a talented artist."

Emily glanced across to Skylar who was painting a puffin on the rock. "Yes. Her career is taking off. She has an exhibition in London in December."

"Jewelry?"

"Among other things. She's produced some stunning glass sculptures inspired by photos a colleague of Brittany's sent her from Greece. Lily is an expert in Minoan ceramics, and Sky has been working with her. This new collection will be a modern take on ancient artifacts or something. The colors were inspired by Greek islands so lots of swirling blue and white. She's calling it *Ocean Blue*."

"Does she have a studio?"

"She rents space in another artist's studio. He's a glass artist."

Her friend had confided that Richard hadn't seemed pleased either with the amount of time Skylar was spending in the studio, or her growing success.

Emily wished they'd had more time to talk about that, but in between entertaining Lizzy and giving Summer Scoop a face-lift, there hadn't been time to explore the personal.

They worked through the day, pausing just long enough to eat the pizzas Ryan ordered from the Ocean Club.

While Lisa supervised the children, Emily sat on one of the chairs next to Ryan.

"Why is it that whenever I see you there are a million people around?" He spoke in an undertone, and she glanced at the small crowd who were transforming Summer Scoop.

"They're working miracles."

"Leave Lizzy with Lisa, come back to my place and I'll work some miracles of my own."

She felt her cheeks warm. "I'm helping the community."

"I'm a member of the community, too." He pushed the pizza toward her. "And talking of that, an oceanfront cottage has come up at the Puffin Retirement Community."

She paused, a slice of pizza in her hand. "Are you thinking about Agnes?"

"I'm not thinking about it—she is. She's struggling to cope in Harbor House. The truth is the house is too big for her, and it's hard for her to see her friends. She's been thinking about next steps. She's asked me to take her to see it on Monday."

"Doesn't Hilda already live there?"

"Yes. That's part of the reason Gran wants to move. To be closer to her friends."

"And you don't want her to go? It upsets you that she is thinking of leaving the house. You feel you should be able to do something to keep her there."

"She's lived there most of her life."

"But people's lives change, their needs change. What was right for a person five years ago or even a year ago, might not be right now." She realized that she could have been talking about herself.

"She loves that house. Even on days when her arthritis is bad, she loves sitting and watching the boats and the people coming and going on the ferry. I'm worried she's thinking of leaving because she doesn't want to be a burden to me."

"Have you tried asking her what she really wants?"

"She wouldn't give me a straight answer."

"She might if you were honest with her. I think you should take her to see it. I think you should keep your mouth zipped, let her look around and do what she needs to do to make a decision. Then you should talk. This isn't about you, Ryan. It's not about what you're doing or not doing. It's about what she needs and wants."

They returned to the painting, and finally, as the

sun was dipping down over the horizon, they finished. Lisa stood back and admired the freshly painted frontage with the new sign and the beautiful mural visible through the large window.

"I love it. I might cry."

"Don't cry," Ryan drawled. "I hate bawling women."

Emily noticed his eyes narrow slightly as Jared looped his arm around Rachel's shoulders and kissed her on the head. "She's an adult now," she said quietly, and he pulled a face.

"I know. I still want to kick his ass for kissing my sister."

"She looks happy."

"She's too trusting. And if he breaks her heart I *will* kick his ass." He frowned. "Oops. Lizzy is crying. Someone is tired. Do you want me to—?"

"No. I'll go to her." Concerned, Emily scooped up Lizzy and knew immediately something wasn't right. She put her hand on the child's forehead and frowned. "You're burning up. Are you not feeling well? Lisa, I'm sorry, I'm going to have to take her home."

"Of course. Thank you for everything. Do you have medicine? It's probably just a cold or something. Give me a call later and let me know how she is."

Ryan walked with Emily to the car. "I guess we'll have to postpone that romantic night."

"She was fine when she woke up, and she was painting happily all day. It's come on very suddenly." She pressed her hand to Lizzy's forehead again and felt a flash of unease. She was relieved Skylar was staying another night. It would be moral support.

"Give her lots of fluids." Ryan opened the car door

for her. "Don't let her overheat, and if you're worried get in touch with the medical clinic. You have the number?"

"Stuck to the fridge."

"If you're worried, call me. I'd come back with you, but we have a wedding at the Ocean Club tomorrow and things are a little crazy."

"We're fine, Ryan." She strapped Lizzy into her seat. "I should go."

She closed the door, and Ryan put an arm on either side of her, caging her. "As soon as Lizzy is better, we need to arrange another sleepover."

For a moment she thought he was going to kiss her right there in public, but then he pulled away and she saw Skylar walking toward them, loaded down with art materials.

"Have I kept you waiting? I was taking photographs of the mural for my website. How's poor Lizzy?"

"Feverish." Emily knew she was going to be answering a hundred questions from her friend the moment they were on their own. "I'm going to get her home."

"Keep her cool," Ryan advised. "Don't let her overheat." He stood back so that Emily could slide into the driver's seat. "I'm sure she'll be better tomorrow."

Tomorrow came and Lizzy was worse. She was restless and fractious all morning, and by the time Emily dropped Skylar at the airport at lunchtime her temperature was high.

Skylar stared up at the sky. "Storm blowing in. I wish I could stay, but I have a meeting with the gallery. They've sold some of my pieces and need more, and I really have to do some work on my collection for the exhibition in December."

"Of course you can't stay. We'll be fine. It's just a cold, I'm sure." She ignored the uneasy twinge in her stomach that told her it was something more.

She was a worrier, so she had to counteract that by forcing herself to be rational.

All the same she was up all night, checking Lizzy and keeping her cool. By morning, Lizzy was worse, not better. It was when Emily was changing her soaked T-shirt for the second time that she noticed the rash.

Icy calm, shaking, she bundled her into the car along with Andrew and drove her to the medical clinic, telling herself that it was probably just a virus, that kids got sick all the time and then got better again. Taking no chances, she called ahead to warn the clinic that she was coming.

She badly wanted to call Ryan, but she knew he'd spent his formative years dealing with this sort of thing and now avoided it. And anyway, today was the day he was taking Agnes to see the retirement home. He already had enough demands on his time.

The threatened storm had been building for days, and huge angry clouds hovered above them. Out in the bay the sea bounced and foamed with anger. By the time Emily reached the medical clinic, fat raindrops were pelting the car.

The nurse practitioner was busy, but one of the physicians who covered the clinic on a periodic basis was available.

Emily almost stumbled as she gave Lizzy's full name, reluctant to disclose her identity even to a medical professional bound to keep such details confidential.

If the doctor was surprised to find the daughter of

Lana Fox on a remote island in Maine, she kept the thought to herself.

It took her less than five minutes to decide Lizzy should be transferred to the hospital on the mainland.

"My instinct is that it's just a virus. Her throat is clear, her ears look fine, and normally I'd suggest waiting a few hours. But we have bad weather coming in, and I don't want you trapped here with no access to a higher level of medical care if she gets worse, especially as I can't find an obvious source for the infection."

Emily felt her stomach lurch. The fact that the doctor was sufficiently concerned to suggest a transfer to the mainland snapped the leash on her anxiety.

She wished she'd had the foresight to pack a bag.

And she wished yet again that Ryan were here.

While Lizzy lay, eyes closed, Emily pulled the doctor to one side. "I'm worried that it could be meningitis. Please, tell me I'm overreacting."

The doctor hesitated a few seconds longer than was reassuring. "That's just one of the options on the list. There are many others. I think it's unlikely, but she has a high temperature and a rash so I have to treat it as a possibility until we've ruled it out. I'm going to give her an injection. The hospital will be able to do more tests. Try not to worry."

Emily wondered why doctors said that when it was clearly asking the impossible. "What can I do?"

"Stay here while I call them. You'll be more comfortable here than in the waiting room, and you're my last patient."

As the door closed behind her, Emily was engulfed by silence.

Looking at Lizzy's listless form, anxiety overwhelmed her. Her heart, protected for so long, was exposed and vulnerable.

Desperate to hear Ryan's voice, she pulled her phone out of her bag and was dialing his number when the doctor walked back into the room.

The phone slipped back into her bag, forgotten.

"I've spoken to the pediatric department on the mainland, and, given the weather forecast and the lack of facilities here on the island, they want you to come in. They're expecting you."

Emily stood up, on legs that felt more like water than flesh and bone. "I'll take the ferry."

"The last ferry left early because of the storm. There won't be another crossing today."

"Can we fly out?"

"Island Air has grounded all flights." The doctor hesitated. "There is a private pilot willing to take you, but it's your decision."

In Emily's mind there was no decision to be made. "Where can I find him?"

"Up at the airfield, but you need to hurry. The winds are increasing. Is there anything you need before you go? Anyone you want to call to be with you?"

She thought about Ryan, taking Agnes to the home. She thought about Skylar, back in Manhattan and Brittany digging somewhere in Crete.

She was on her own with this.

Emily looked at the bear in Lizzy's arms. "We have the essential items."

The doctor handed Emily a letter. "Give this to the doctors. My number is on there, so they can call me. The pilot's name is Zachary Flynn."

Zach.

The man who had broken Brittany's heart.

The man whose photo had been stuck on Brittany's wall for those first few months of college, so that they could all draw on it.

A million objections crowded her brain, and in among them was the fact that Zach was a man not known for being reliable.

Why was he prepared to fly when no one else was?

The doctor was still talking. "I'll arrange for an ambulance to meet you when you land and transfer you to the hospital."

Despite her panic, Emily forced herself to drive carefully on the slick roads. The filthy weather had driven the tourists indoors, so she encountered very little traffic on her way to the airfield on the north of the island.

Glancing in her rearview mirror, she checked on Lizzy who was lying with her eyes closed, her face flushed with fever.

The wind buffeted her car, and rain almost obscured her view. What if even Zach decided it was too dangerous to fly? What if the weather transpired against them and trapped them here?

Creating disaster in her head, she parked, grabbed her bag and scooped Lizzy out of her seat, knowing that every second she waited increased the risk that Zach would decide he didn't need to risk his neck for a woman and a child that weren't his responsibility.

From what Brittany had told them, he wasn't big on responsibility or social conscience.

The plane sat on the runway, small and insignificant compared to the driving force of the weather.

Emily glanced at the wild, foaming fury of the sea, so different now from the still calm that had allowed her to swim with Lizzy only days before. Struggling to walk against the wind, she realized how tired she was. After two nights with virtually no sleep, her legs threatened to give way.

"I've got her." She heard a deep, male voice through the relentless howl of the wind and felt strong arms lift Lizzy from her.

Only when they were safely inside did she allow herself to look at the man she was entrusting with their lives, and decided that the photo Brittany had pinned to the wall all those years ago hadn't done him justice. Years had passed, of course, but muscles and maturity had only improved Zachary Flynn.

There was a daredevil gleam in his eyes that she would have expected to see in a man who had tempted her friend to throw away everything for love. There was also hardness, a toughness that suggested he knew more about life than most people ever would. Brittany had told them his childhood had been bad, but they'd all agreed that nothing excused the way he'd treated Brittany.

And now here was Emily, needing him, relying on him.

She felt like a traitor.

"Strap in," he ordered. "It's going to be rough up there."

Reciting apologies to Brittany in her head, she did as he ordered. "But visibility is good?"

"Yeah. That's because we have a hell of a crosswind. Wind gives great visibility."

Digesting the news that the visibility was bad news, not good, Emily sank back in her seat. "But you're confident? You think it's safe to fly?"

His gaze flickered to Lizzy. "I'll get you there safely, but you're going to be shaken up some."

She sensed from his low drawl that it was an understatement and took her eyes off Lizzy long enough to glare at him.

"I just hope you're a better pilot than you were a husband." The words left her mouth before she could debate the wisdom of antagonizing the man responsible for their lives.

He gave her a long, steady look and then turned back to the controls without comment.

Emily breathed deeply, hoping this wasn't going to turn out to be the worst decision of her life.

She heard him talking over the radio, but she had no anxiety to spare for the pilot or the fate of the plane. Everything was focused on Lizzy who lay with her eyes still closed.

She felt another lurch of fear.

Was it going to happen again?

Was she going to love, only to have the person she loved ripped away from her?

She barely noticed the plane lifting off, gave no thought to the yawning expanse of the bay or the hungry bite of the wind, both ready to consume a small plane in a moment if the pilot made any mistakes.

Zach made no mistakes.

The flight was bumpy, but Emily was too occupied with Lizzy to dwell on the possibility of plummeting into the ocean. If she hadn't been so worried, she would have thanked him for what she was sure was flawless and courageous flying. But there was no room for anything in her head but the panic.

They landed smoothly, and from there it was a short

transfer by ambulance to the medical center where the pediatric team was waiting.

Lying in the room, surrounded by medical equipment, Lizzy opened her eyes. She looked ridiculously small and vulnerable. "Are you going to leave me here?"

"No." Emily was appalled she would even think it. "I'm not going anywhere."

"My mom always left if I was sick. She didn't want to catch anything. She said being ill made her ugly."

"I'm right here and I'm staying right here." Emily felt an ache in her chest, and she took the little girl's hand. "I won't leave you."

"Where's Ryan? I want Ryan."

The pitiful plea shot straight through Emily's heart, and her only thought was *me, too*.

"He can't be here, sweetie."

It shocked her just how badly she wanted him to be.

The doctor wrote something on a chart. "Is there someone you need us to call? If you give us this Ryan's number we can contact him."

"No. He's—" How to describe their relationship? "He's just a friend." A friend with other commitments. Other priorities. "There's no one."

The doctor accepted that and then sat down to take a medical history.

Emily realized how impossible this was. How had she ever thought Lizzy's past could be kept a secret? "I don't know much about her history," she admitted. Left with no choice, she briefly told the doctor all she knew.

"So you don't know the identity of Juliet's father?"

"No. And I know nothing about her health as a child, although the lawyers did give me details on her vaccinations."

"Do you have those?"

Emily pulled the papers out of her bag, telling herself that it was ridiculous to be concerned that they knew Lizzy's identity. The medical team had to know. And everything here was confidential, wasn't it?

"We need to take blood, Miss Donovan. If you'd rather wait outside—"

"I'm staying." She didn't even let him finish the suggestion. "You can work around me." She kept hold of Lizzy's hand, talking to her about the puffins, Ryan and the twins, anything to distract her while the medical team worked.

The next few hours were a blur of tests, bright lights and beeping machines. Of needles, sterility and stress.

Lizzy barely reacted, her eyes closed, the blotches on her skin vivid against the white background.

The walls were covered in a mural, a farm scene, and Emily stared blankly at brightly colored fields until the white dollops of paint started to look more like clouds with legs than sheep.

Her eyes were gritty and her head throbbed.

Staff came and went. Emily desperately wanted reassurance, but no one had answers for her questions.

At one point a nurse dimmed the lights, gave Emily a blanket and advised her to sleep, but she was too afraid to close her eyes, so she curled up in the chair, holding Lizzy's hand in hers.

Outside the wind howled and whipped the rain against the window, and she recited *Green Eggs and Ham* quietly, wondering how her life could have changed so much in less than a month.

She thought about the night she'd arrived, and how much she'd wanted to return to the safe, predictable life she'd carefully constructed for herself. She'd struggled against it, but gradually her new life had peeled away the layers of protection she'd worn for so long.

She'd believed that having Lizzy was the worst thing that could have happened to her, but it had turned out to be the best.

Despite her attempts to stay awake, she must have dozed for a little while, and when she opened her eyes Lizzy was looking at her.

"Why are you sleeping in a chair?"

"I didn't want to leave you." Groggy, Emily shook off the fog of sleep and felt Lizzy's chest. Her skin was cool to touch, and the rush of relief was so acute her eyes stung with tears. "How are you feeling?"

"I had a bad dream."

"Oh, baby—" Emily scooped her into her arms and held her. "You're safe. I'm here. I'll always be here."

"Why doesn't Ryan come? I love Ryan."

Emily held her tightly. Cold spread across her skin and penetrated her heart, and she realized with a rush of alarm that she'd made a mistake letting Ryan become so closely entangled in their lives. She'd only thought about herself, not Lizzy. Their relationship was fun, but she knew that for him it ended there. He didn't want the responsibility of anything more.

"I know you like Ryan a lot."

"I don't like him, I love him. And he loves me. He reads to me, and he takes me to see the puffins. He taught me knots. He's going to teach me to sail this summer. He promised."

Guilt sucked her down like water in a whirlpool. How did you explain to a child of six that a man had other things to do with his time?

She stroked the child's hair, trying to calm her. "There are lots of people on the island who can teach you to sail. Rachel, for instance."

"I want Ryan to do it. I love Ryan and so do you."

"That's not true." How could the words of a child cause this sudden feeling of panic? "I like Ryan a lot, but I don't love him."

"Yes, you do. He makes you smile. That day on the beach when you were sick, he took care of you. And he taught you to swim. You wanted him to do it and no one else."

"I—"

"Rachel says it's because you trust him. And that's why you wanted him to take us in his boat."

"Trust, yes. But not love." Emily's mouth was dry. She told herself children said things they didn't understand. "I don't love him."

"Why doesn't he come?"

"Because he doesn't know you're in the hospital."

"He'd want to know." She said it firmly, and Emily forced herself to breathe slowly.

"It's complicated, Lizzy. When you're older, I'll explain it to you."

"I already know why."

"You do?"

"Yes. It's because he's scared of hospitals. He said so."

"That isn't why. We're his friends, Lizzy, but we're not his family. He doesn't love us in that way."

"Skylar says friends can be better than family. She says you, she and Brittany are like sisters."

"That's true, we are, but—" How did you explain this to a child? "That isn't the way it is with Ryan. He has other people in his life to think about. He's taking his grandmother to look at somewhere new to live today. She'll be able to tell us all about it when we see her next."

"I already know. She wants a house that isn't so big." Lizzy's face crumpled. "I want Ryan. I want him to tell me the story about Abbie and the hens."

"As soon as we're back home, I'll ask him to come and tell you the story." She stroked Lizzy's hair and then looked up as a nurse came into the room. "She just woke up. She feels cooler."

The nurse checked the reading. "Her temperature is down. That's a good sign."

Emily was willing to grab any piece of good news. "What happens now?"

"We wait for these results, but she seems to have turned a corner."

Emily discovered she wasn't good at waiting.

While Lizzy slept and nurses walked in and out of the room checking her temperature and the rate of the IV, she sat there thinking about Ryan and everything Lizzy had said.

It was true that she'd asked him to teach her to swim and take them out on the boat, but that was because he understood her situation.

And the sex had been incredible, but it was still just sex, and she wasn't going to make the mistake of thinking it meant more than it did.

The door opened, and Emily glanced up, expecting it to be one of the doctors, but it was Ryan who stood in the doorway. His hair was sleek from the rain, his shirt clinging to his broad shoulders.

Seeing him there brought a rush of pure emotion.

Elation. Relief. And something far deeper and infinitely more terrifying. She could hear Lizzy's words in her head.

You love him. You love Ryan.

Heart pounding, she managed to speak. "What are you doing here?"

He strode into the room scattering droplets of rain. "You're in the hospital. Where did you think I'd be? How sick is she?"

"Ryan!" Disturbed by the noise, Lizzy opened her eyes and her face brightened. "You came."

"I would have come sooner if I'd known." He walked straight to the bed, put down the large bag he was carrying and sat next to Lizzy. "Hi, tiger. What have you been doing to yourself?"

"I'm sick."

"I can see that." He picked up the bear. "And how is Andrew? Did he get sick on the flight over?"

Lizzy managed her first smile for days. "I held him all the way."

"You need to get well fast because the puffins miss you. And talking of puffins—" he reached into the bag and pulled out a stuffed puffin, complete with brightly colored felt beak "—I thought Andrew might like company." He snuggled it next to her as the door opened and a nurse walked in.

She frowned when she saw Ryan. "Relatives only."

"I'm a relative." Cool and self-assured, Ryan didn't budge, and the nurse looked at him curiously.

"Are you Ryan by any chance?" Her severe expression softened when he nodded. "She's been asking for you. Maybe now you're here you can persuade Emily to go and eat something. She hasn't left the room since she arrived."

"I didn't want to." Emily stayed firmly in the chair, trying to understand what was going on. He claimed not to want the attachment of a family, and yet he'd flown through filthy weather to get here.

She tried to work it out, but her brain wasn't functioning properly. She was so tired she wondered if she'd even have the ability to stand up when the moment came. Her short nap in the chair had made her feel worse, not better, as if the taste of sleep had reminded her brain what she'd been missing. Now that the danger had passed, the adrenaline that had kept her going vanished, taking energy with it.

"I wanted you to come," Lizzy said sleepily, "but Emily said you wouldn't because you don't love us the way we love you."

Oh, crap.

Meeting Ryan's questioning gaze, Emily felt herself turn scarlet. "The fever has made her very confused."

"I'm not confused," Lizzy murmured. "Do you love us, Ryan?"

Emily held her breath. How on earth was he going to deal with a question like that?

"Of course I love you." He didn't miss a beat. "You think I'd endure a ride in that bumpy plane if I didn't love you?"

"You see?" A satisfied smile curved at the corners of Lizzy's mouth. "I told you."

Emily felt a wash of cold spread over her skin. His answer was designed to soothe but he was making things worse, not better. He was using words like a comfort blanket, wrapping them around a sick child.

What would happen when the blanket was ripped away and the child was left freezing and shivering? "Lizzy—"

"Are you scared?" Lizzy was still looking at Ryan.

"Scared?"

"You said you were scared of hospitals." Her eyes closed. "You can hold my hand. I'm not scared of hospitals, only storms. I'm glad you're here. I wanted you to tell me about Abbie and the hens." But she was already asleep, and Emily sat, thinking about the way she'd felt when Ryan had walked into the room.

It was as if the sun had come out in her life.

The nurse put her hand on her shoulder. "She's going to be fine. The doctor will be here in an hour to talk to you. Why don't you go and get a cup of coffee? I'll be right here, and if she wakes, I'll call you. There's no need to look so anxious."

Yes, there was, because Lizzy was right.

She was in love with Ryan.

Sixteen

It was true that he hated hospitals. He hated them so much he could hardly bring himself to walk into one. Something about the paint and the clinical smell took him right back to those months after his injury. As soon as he stepped through the door it came rushing back. The white light of the explosion, the pain and the sick empty feeling that came from knowing Finn wasn't in the hospital with him. Normally he blocked it out, but not today. Today the memories were playing like a movie in his head. The pitch-black of the helicopter, the rattle and sway, the bouncing beam of light from the headlamp of the flight medic. And the pain. Unimaginable pain.

Hoping they discharged Lizzy fast, he coaxed two cups of coffee from a temperamental machine and took them back to the waiting room.

Emily was standing in front of the window, staring into space.

Shock, he thought. Shock and exhaustion.

"Here—" He handed her the coffee. Remembering

the last time she'd keeled over, he put his own down on the table. "Why the hell didn't you call me?"

She looked at him blankly, like someone emerging from a long coma, seeing the world for the first time. "It wasn't your responsibility."

He remembered the sharp kick of fear he'd felt when he'd heard about their white-knuckle flight across the bay to the hospital, about the sleepless night he'd had waiting for the wind to die down sufficiently for him to make the crossing to the mainland. His mind had conjured a dozen nightmare scenarios, all of which involved Emily coping alone with a steadily deteriorating Lizzy. By the time he'd arrived at the hospital he'd almost caused casualties in his haste to reach her bedside.

Only when he'd seen Lizzy, awake and improving, did his own feelings about hospitals resurrect themselves.

He picked up his coffee, noticing with a twinge of wry humor that his hands were shaking.

Jesus, he couldn't even walk into a hospital without falling apart. He was meant to be supporting Emily, and he was in a worse state than she was.

What a hero.

Her silence was starting to disturb him. Retrieving his journalistic skills, he tried to think like her. Tried to get into her head. She'd be scared. Scared of losing another child. Of letting her down. "You're doing a brilliant job, Emily. You're taking good care of her."

Still there was no reaction, and he wondered if she'd even heard him.

"You're not going to lose her, Emily. She's going to be just fine. Kids get sick fast, and then they recover fast. The same thing happened when Rachel was young. You don't need to panic."

But she didn't seem to be panicking. She looked numb. Catatonic.

"It was Zach who called me." He ignored the fact that he seemed to be having a conversation with himself, and finally she stirred.

"Why would he call you?"

He couldn't believe she'd asked that question. "I guess he heard the rumor that you'd left my apartment wearing the same dress you'd worn to dinner and thought I might like to know." If she'd picked up on the dig that she should have been the one to call him, there were no visible signs of it.

"He was brave. Please, thank him from me."

"He's a gifted pilot."

She didn't argue. "Does Brittany know that he's back on the island yet?"

"I don't know. I still haven't told her. Who knows how long he'll stay, and she isn't here anyway, so why bring it up?" The last time he'd interfered with their relationship he'd made things worse. "Why the hell are we talking about Zach and Brittany? They're both old enough to sort out their own relationship. The fact that they don't is their business, not ours. Are you going to drink that coffee?"

She sipped mindlessly and pulled a face. "You put sugar in it?"

"You need the energy, and this stuff tastes disgusting with or without sugar. When did you last eat?"

"I'm not hungry."

He was willing to bet she hadn't slept, either. Looking at the dark shadows under her eyes, he decided she was too tired to be able to decide whether to move forward or backward.

She'd been going through torture, and she'd been going through it alone.

Anger and frustration simmered beneath his own layers of tension. "Hell, Emily, why didn't you call me? We're friends."

Her gaze flickered to his and away again. "We are friends. And as a friend, I respect your boundaries."

"Boundaries?" He lowered his voice. "You talk to me about boundaries after what we did in bed together the other night?"

"That's different. This was a problem, and it wasn't yours to deal with."

She was the one who was different, and he had no idea why. Was it tiredness? The stress and anxiety of coping alone? Worry about Lizzy?

He decided the hospital was driving them both crazy, and the sooner he got them both home to Puffin Island, the better.

They kept Lizzy in the hospital for another twenty-four hours.

Despite Emily's protestations, Ryan insisted on returning the following morning to drive them back to the island.

She'd suffered another sleepless night, but this time her concerns were for herself as well as Lizzy. How had she managed to fall in love? She didn't understand how it had happened. All she knew was that she had to reverse the feeling fast. She had to fall out of love with him, and, more important, she had to help Lizzy fall out of love with him, too.

"So, the final verdict was a virus?" He slid behind the wheel. "*Virus* is a word doctors use when they don't have a clue what's going on."

Exhausted, Emily fought the urge to rest her throbbing head against those wide shoulders.

"They don't really know what it was, but it wasn't meningitis, and she's on the mend, so that's all that matters."

Now that the immediate panic about Lizzy had passed, she knew she had to think about the future. She'd woken up to the mistakes she'd made. Her mind was trying to make sense of it all, but the stress of the past few days caught up with her, and the smooth purr of the engine rocked her to sleep.

She woke as they drove off the ferry along with carloads of summer visitors.

John, the harbormaster, waved them over, and Ryan pulled up.

"She's doing fine, John."

"Good to know." Needing to check for himself, John stepped forward and looked at Lizzy. The smile spread along his weathered face. "We missed you, pumpkin. Ryan has been keeping us updated. Wait there. I have something for you." He vanished into his hut and emerged moments later holding a miniature version of the ferry, handmade and beautifully carved. "I've called her the *Captain Lizzy*. I made it in my workshop."

"For me?" Lizzy reached for it, enchanted. "It's like the *Captain Hook*. Does it float?"

"Should do. You'll have to take it down to the beach and test it. Let me know."

"Will you come?"

"To the beach?" John scratched his beard. "Maybe

I will. Dora and I enjoy a walk on the sand. I appreciate the invitation."

"Look." Lizzy leaned forward to show Emily, and she examined the boat, marveling at the detail. There was a ramp that lifted and lowered and a little chain that fastened across the back.

"It's perfect. Thank you, John." She admired the craftsmanship, touched by the sentiment as much as the hours he'd obviously spent. She remembered how afraid of him she, Sky and Brittany had been.

As Ryan drove away, she mentioned it to him. "We used to be scared of him."

"Plenty of folk are. It's a trick he uses to stop people messing around near the ferry."

"I thought Lizzy had driven him crazy asking questions."

"John loves anyone who shows interest in the *Captain Hook*." He eased the car along the crowded roads. "And you're an honorary islander."

"Because I'm staying in Brittany's cottage?"

"Not just because of that. You've contributed to the community. Not only have you earned Hilda's approval, but Summer Scoop's business has doubled in the past few days. And all the islanders were worried about Lizzy. I couldn't walk down the street without being accosted for information, so in the end I had Kirsti put out a tweet on the Ocean Club Twitter account. Hope you don't mind." He slowed for a group of tourists who were loaded down with beach bags and coolers. "It's the silly season."

"This is why the business has doubled. It's the summer crowd."

"Not true. You had some great ideas."

"What's it like on the island in winter?"

"Quiet. I love it, although obviously the weather can be brutal. It can also be fun. I'll take you snowmobiling."

He was making the assumption she'd still be here in the winter.

Realizing they were leaving the harbor, Emily reached for her purse. "Could you take me via the airfield? I need to pick up my car."

"Jared drove it home for you yesterday."

"Jared?"

"The guy who is dating my sister. The guy I'm trying not to punch."

"But I've never even met him. Why would he help me? And where did he get the keys?"

Ryan glanced at her. "You left them in the car. I guess you had other things on your mind."

"I—" She'd left them in the car? "That doesn't explain why he'd help me, a stranger."

"Apart from the fact he can't keep his hands off my sister, he's a decent guy. And as I said, you're an honorary islander." Ryan took the coast road, and Emily looked out of the window at the islands dotted around the bay.

An honorary islander.

A month ago she hadn't been able to imagine living here. Now she couldn't imagine leaving.

When she'd arrived on that first night, she would have turned around and left again had there been some way of getting across the water; but at some point leaving had ceased to be a priority. The charm of the island had sneaked up on her, like the slow merging of the seasons.

The contrast to the night of the storm was incredible. The rain had stopped, the sky had cleared and visibility was perfect. It was as if it had never happened.

When they reached Castaway Cottage, she stepped out of the car and felt the breeze on her face. The scent of salt and sea expunged the last memories of clinical sterility. Shell Cove lay in front of her, a perfect crescent of golden tones, and she wondered why she'd wasted all those summers keeping her back to the water.

She realized she didn't feel trapped or scared, she felt free. For the first time in her life, she felt as if she'd come home.

Turning back to the car, she bumped into Ryan.

"Sorry—" He put his hands on her arms to steady her, and she stood for a few seconds, disoriented by his closeness and the terrifying depths of her feelings. Her eyes were level with the tanned skin at the base of his throat and the dark stubble that shaded his jaw.

Scooping up Lizzy, she carried her to the cottage and waited while Ryan unlocked the door.

"I should have asked you to stop at the harbor so we could pick some things up."

"You won't need anything." He walked through to the kitchen, and she saw the table was heaped high with bags and parcels.

"What's all this?"

"This," Ryan said dryly, "is all courtesy of your neighbors. Welcome to Puffin Island, where everyone knows what you like to eat for dinner. And if you're in trouble, they provide it." There was humor in his eyes as he pulled open the fridge and stepped to one side, so that she could see the contents.

Emily gaped and Lizzy wriggled out of her arms.

"There's so much food!"

"There is." Emily felt weak. "Was this you? Did you do this?"

"It was everyone. The town council sent out an email to everyone and coordinated people's contributions. They thought you wouldn't want to be thinking of food for a few days while you settle back in."

"The town council emailed?"

"That's nothing. If you stay here much longer you'll be expected to give them your phone number. Then you'll get a call or a text in an emergency."

Still looking at the food in disbelief, Emily shook her head. "What sort of emergency?"

"Well, let's see—" he leaned back against the counter "—there was the time two years ago when the Ratners' barn caught fire, and they needed as many people as possible to help. Then there was the time when the power went out last January, and they needed volunteers to check on the elderly and vulnerable. It's a good way of communicating to a wide number of people in the shortest space of time."

"I'm really touched." She opened one of the bags and pulled out a doll and a pile of books for Lizzy. "That's so thoughtful." Tears thickened her throat, and she realized with a flash of horror that she was going to cry.

Tired, she thought. She was just tired, that was all.

"I need to get Lizzy to bed." Forcing herself to keep moving, she carried Lizzy up to her bedroom and tucked her in.

"Will you open the window? I want to listen to the sea."

Emily opened the window, realizing that she no longer shrank from the sound. "Better?"

"Can Ryan read me a story?"

"I think you need to sleep."

"But could I have a story first?"

Ryan, Ryan, Ryan.

"It's my turn to read to you." She sat on the edge of the bed, picked a story and started to read. Lizzy was asleep by the end of the first page.

Emily stayed for a few minutes, staring down at tumbled blond hair and vulnerability.

She'd been almost the same age when she'd lost her sister.

She'd been alone with her feelings. There had been no one to comfort her. No one to protect her.

Reaching out, she stroked the curls away from Lizzy's face and bent to kiss her.

Lizzy wasn't alone, and she was going to do her best to protect her. A few weeks earlier the responsibility had almost sent her running. Not now. Now, the fierceness, the desire to protect came not from duty but from somewhere deep inside. A place she hadn't accessed for a long time. And finally she knew what she had to do.

Ryan was in the kitchen with his back to her, staring out of the window to the garden. He turned when he heard her walk in. "The storm flattened some of the plants."

"I'll deal with it tomorrow." She looked at those broad shoulders, at his handsome face, *at the man she loved.* "Thank you for what you did. Coming to see us. Bringing us home. All this—" She glanced at the surfaces, covered in gifts and donations of food. "I'm grateful."

"I didn't do it for your gratitude." His eyes darkened. "I missed you."

Her heart bumped against her chest. "Ryan—we can't do this—"

"I know that. You're exhausted."

"I don't mean now. I mean ever. Whatever there was between us, it has to stop."

There was a long, pulsing silence. "Because you don't want a relationship?"

It was a fair question. She hadn't thought anyone would break through the layers of protection she'd woven around herself, but Ryan Cooper had managed it.

"Because *you* don't. And it isn't fair to Lizzy."

Those dark brows met in a frown. "What's between us has nothing to do with Lizzy."

"How can it have nothing to do with Lizzy? She's part of my life, Ryan. She was asking for you just now. She wanted you to read to her."

"You should have called me. I would have been happy to read to her."

"This time." Her mouth felt as if she'd swallowed sand. "She's growing too attached to you. She asks for you all the time. Every other word is *Ryan*. In the hospital she was crying for you—"

A muscle flickered in his cheek. "You should have called me—"

"Why? You don't want that level of attachment. She's starting to expect things, and you don't want anyone to expect things from you. You've told me that often enough."

"So you're going to tell her I won't read her a story? Is that fair?"

The words goaded her temper. She thought back to the hospital, with Lizzy sick and missing him. "What's not fair is you telling her you love her. Behaving as if she's important in your life."

"She's a sweet kid, and—"

"Yes, she's a sweet kid, but we both know you're not interested in kids, Ryan, no matter how sweet they are. You've made that perfectly clear, and I respect that, but then you confuse everything by saying you love her!"

"You're overreacting. She was sick. She needed reassurance and I gave it. It's as simple as that."

"It's not simple. Thanks to you, it's complicated! And she didn't need lies! What happens when she's well, Ryan? Have you thought about that?"

"We'll handle that when she's well."

"*I'll* be the one who has to handle it. I'll be the one who will have to answer questions about where you are and why you don't want to spend time with her. I'll be the one who has to handle a child who feels miserable and let down, who has expectations that are never met." Her voice rose. "We both know this relationship of ours is just for fun, but that isn't how she sees it. What's going to happen when you've had enough of teaching her knots and taking her to see the puffins? She's a child. She doesn't understand the complexity of adult relationships. Children need consistency. They need to know where they stand. Love can't be given and then withdrawn. It doesn't come and go like the tide. I appreciate you bringing us home. It was kind of you, but now it's over."

But instead of walking away, Ryan strode across the room and took her face in his hands. "And what about us?" His eyes demanded all the answers she wasn't voicing. "You've talked a lot about Lizzy, but what about us?"

Dreams flitted into her head, and she pushed them brutally aside.

"There is no us." She fought the temptation to slide her arms around his neck and bring her mouth to his. "I love living here. I never thought I'd feel this way about living on a small island surrounded by water, but I do. I know we can't stay in this cottage forever, but whatever we do, I don't want to leave the island. I want us to stay. I want to build a life here. I don't want things to feel awkward between us." She stared up at him, rocked by the emotion in his eyes.

"So, you're ending this because of Lizzy. What about you?"

What about her? Despite having protected herself fiercely, she'd managed to fall in love twice. First with Lizzy and then with him.

Being with him had taught her she still had the ability to love deeply, but now she had to learn to switch it off again.

"I won't compromise Lizzy's happiness for sex. Even clothes-ripping, mind-blowing, wild animal sex."

"That's what it was to you?"

"Of course."

For a moment she thought he was going to say something else, but then he stepped back, his face expressionless.

"In that case there's nothing more to say. Call me if you need anything. Puffin Island is a small community. We look out for each other."

Because she didn't trust herself not to cave in and chase after him, she turned away, watching the last drips of sunlight bathe the garden, listening to his footsteps as he walked to the door.

As it closed behind him, she flinched. And remembered exactly why she'd spent all those years making sure she didn't love.

Seventeen

❧━⟳⟲⟳━❧

"There's not enough storage space." Ryan slammed one door shut and dragged open another. "Murph Compton should be shot. He expects everyone to live in a damn rabbit warren, so that he can live in a mansion."

"You're describing my future home," his grandmother said mildly, "and the storage space is perfect for my needs, providing you don't break the doors before I move in."

Ryan strode moodily across the small sunny kitchen and opened another door. *What the hell had Emily meant when she'd said he'd confused Lizzy?* "The contents of one of your kitchen cupboards would fill this whole place."

"I've been clearing out. It's called downsizing."

"There's no room for a toaster on that counter."

"I didn't realize you had such an emotional connection with my toaster, but if its welfare is that important to you, then, please, consider it a gift." Agnes sighed. "What's wrong, Ryan?"

"Nothing is wrong. I just can't understand why you want to live here, that's all." He strode back through to the airy living room and tried to forget about the confrontation with Emily. The whole "cottage" would have fit into half the downstairs space at Harbor House. "Where are you going to store everything?"

"I don't intend to store anything. I intend to declutter my life. Does the thought of that make you angry?"

He looked at her blankly. "What?"

"You're angry."

"No. Yes." He thumped his fist against the wall. "She's cut me out. She doesn't want to see me again."

Agnes eyed the wall and then her grandson. "I assume we're talking about Emily."

"She says it's confusing for Lizzy. That she's getting too attached."

"I see."

"Do you? Because I don't." It had been stewing inside him since the conversation a few days earlier. "Can you believe she didn't call me when she was in the hospital?"

"I expect she didn't want to bother you. You're a busy man. A busy, *single* man."

"You could have said that without the emphasis and the look."

"Everyone has the right to make their own choices in life. You've made yours. You need to allow Emily to make hers. She's a smart woman."

Smart and sexy. "Damn it, she was on her own there. It must have half killed her to have Lizzy in the hospital and she didn't call me."

"Perhaps she didn't feel that was the nature of your relationship."

He eyed his grandmother, wondering exactly how

much she knew about their relationship. "Lizzy was asking for me."

"Was she?" His grandmother looked thoughtful. "That explains a great deal."

"Does it?"

"She's afraid the child will look forward to seeing you, and the next step on from that is *expecting* to see you, and you don't want that, do you? It's one thing to take a little girl on a boat trip when it fits into your day, but you don't want to feel pressure to do it. Same goes for swimming, sailing, walking Cocoa and all those other things." Agnes opened one of the windows to let air into the room. "Better not to do them at all. That way you can be sure of protecting your personal space and making sure you live life alone, the way you prefer it. No one is ever going to want anything, expect anything or demand anything of you. You're free to go wherever the wind blows you."

Ryan looked at his grandmother in exasperation. "You're a conniving, manipulative—"

"I'm describing your life, Ryan. That's all. The life you chose. The life you want. I don't see how that makes me conniving or manipulative."

"You're trying to make me question my choices."

"If it's the right choice, then no one can make you waver. Take me as an example—" she stood back and looked around her "—you can tell me I'm making the wrong decision as many times as you like, but I'm not going to doubt myself even for a second."

"Are we talking about my life or the house? Because if it's the house, my opinion is that it's a big step. You should take some time to think about it."

"When you reach my age, you don't waste precious

time letting your brain talk you out of something your heart already knows is right."

Ryan stared at her. "She made it sound as if I didn't care. As if Lizzy doesn't matter to me."

"And does she?"

"Of course! I was as worried about Lizzy as she was. And I was worried about her." And the thought of her, anxious and alone in the hospital with no one to support her, had driven him demented when he'd been trapped. "I thought I'd proved that by flying through a storm to get to the hospital—a place, I might add, that makes me want to swallow alcohol in large quantities." He paced to the other side of the room which, given the distance, didn't do anything to relieve his tension. "Can we talk about something else?"

"You can talk about anything you like. I believe you were expressing your opinion on my new home." The words were infused with patience and love, and Ryan felt a rush of guilt.

"I'm sorry." He pressed his fingers to the bridge of his nose and sent her an apologetic look. "It's been a stressful few days. First, Lizzy being sick—"

"Yes, that was a worrying time for the whole island. I know people were very relieved when Kirsti put that message up at the Ocean Club."

"She had people asking her every two minutes." His insides felt ripped and raw. He wondered if it was the hospital visit that had affected his mood so profoundly. "I guess I thought Emily and I were friends."

"I'm sure you are. But Emily has been thrown into the role of mother and she's trying to protect Lizzy."

He knew how important that was to her, but he hated to think she saw him as a threat to Lizzy's happiness.

"I don't see why I'm such a threat. Emily is planning on staying on the island, and I'm not going anywhere."

"I think she's more concerned about your emotional presence than your geographical location." His grandmother removed her glasses and tucked them into her purse. "Whereas you seem very concerned about my geographical location. Does it bother you where I live?"

"I guess I find it hard to imagine you living anywhere but Harbor House. You've lived there since—" He broke off, and she nodded slowly.

"Since your parents died. I know how long I've lived there, Ryan. My brain is perfectly fine. It's my joints that aren't behaving themselves. I moved in to that big old house because I had my four wonderful grandchildren to care for. You'd lost your parents, and I didn't want you to lose your home, too. But things change. Needs change. This will be better for me. I can walk as far as Hilda's cottage, and I know most of the people living here. I won't have to rely on you and Rachel for lifts."

"We don't mind."

"I mind. I already made you take too much responsibility in your life. I see that now. I made mistakes."

"That's not true."

"It is true. You'd lost your parents. Your life changed overnight, and suddenly instead of riding your bike and your skateboard, you were reading bedtime stories and learning how to braid hair. And you did a fine job. It's because of you that Rachel has kept her sweet, generous nature. You gave her the security she'd lost. You were there when she needed you, but you were a child, too, and you shouldn't have had to take that on."

Thinking of Rachel raised his stress levels. "She's seeing Jared."

"I know."

"He's a decade older than her."

"I know that, too." His grandmother straightened, rubbing her hand over her back. "She's grown up, and you have to let her make her own decisions, even if some of those decisions aren't the ones you would have made. Do you think I wanted to see you fly off to dangerous places? No." It was the first time she'd ever voiced her feelings on the subject, and he realized how selfish he'd been back then, his one and only thought to get away and live his life.

"You never said anything."

"Because it wasn't about what I wanted, it was about what you wanted. And you wanted to see the world with nothing and no one holding you back. You had so much hunger inside you. There were so many things you wanted to do. When you left this island, there was a time when I wondered if we'd see you again. You were desperate for an adventure."

"That didn't end the way I thought it would." He thought about Finn, who right at the end had decided the next adventure in his life was going to be home and family.

"When I visited you in that hospital I wished you'd chosen a different path. I went back home at night and cried, but then I pulled out every piece you ever wrote and reminded myself how important those stories were, and I realized that if people like you weren't telling them, the rest of us wouldn't know what was happening in the world. I'm proud of you. I probably don't say that enough. You made the decision that was right for you."

"Is this your way of telling me to butt out of your decision to sell the house?"

"Who said anything about selling the house?" Agnes walked to the window and stared over the sea. "Moving feels right. Selling doesn't, and I'm in the lucky position not to have to take that step. I'm not selling Harbor House, I'm giving it to you."

Ryan couldn't have been more surprised if she'd told him she was taking up Zumba. "Me?"

"It's a family house and I rattle around. And before you say anything, I've discussed it with the twins and Rachel. They all agree this should be yours. I've never been afraid of moving on, Ryan. You shouldn't be afraid, either."

"I'm not afraid."

"No? I shouldn't be interfering when I've just told you Rachel is a grown-up who can make her own decisions, but I'm going to anyway, because the truth is, I feel responsible."

"Responsible for what?"

"For the fact that you don't have a family."

Ryan straightened his shoulders. "How can you be responsible? That's my choice."

"Do you think I don't know why you've chosen to live your life free of commitment? Do you think I don't know how it was for you? You were helping me at an age when you shouldn't have had a care in the world."

"Teenagers always have cares."

"But they are different cares. What you want to do with your future, whether you'll ever date that cool brunette in your class, whether you'll be tall enough, smart enough—"

"In other words, selfish cares."

"Normal cares. Your cares were deeper and heavier and most of the time didn't include you. You felt as if you had a leash tied to you, and it grew tighter every year. Because of that, you saw family as something that holds you back. You've been avoiding it ever since."

"I've been living my life."

His grandmother smiled. "Having a family doesn't stop you living your life, although I can see why you would think that way after what happened. I treated you like an adult, but you were still a child. You were still working out what sort of place the world was and how you fit into it."

"It probably did me good. I needed to think about someone other than myself." And he realized he needed to do that now. "If you love this place, then that's all I need to hear. Tell me how I can help."

"I have one remaining box of Rachel's old books and toys you can take over to Emily."

He knew he wouldn't be welcome. "Just leave a message on Emily's phone. She can pick them up when she's next in town."

"She may not be in town for a while. She'll want to keep Lizzy at home until she's back on her feet. I'd like you to take it over for me. I remember when Rachel was sick, she loved having something new to play with and read."

"I can't do that." He paced to the window, staring out over the ocean as he replayed the conversation. "She's shut me out. I was going to offer to take Lizzy on the boat again. She's showing all the signs of being a natural sailor. I enjoyed teaching her."

"Help out at Camp Puffin if you want to do those things with children."

"I don't." He wanted to do them with Lizzy. He remembered the look of concentration on her face when she'd mastered her first knot, the excited gasp the first time the wind had snapped the sails tight. Most of all, he remembered her look of happiness when he'd walked into the room at the hospital.

"I don't understand why this bothers you. You love your freedom, Ryan. I would have thought you'd be feeling relieved not to be towing a little girl out to see puffins and digging in the sand."

He realized that those moments had been the happiest he'd had in a long time. Those moments, and the ones he'd spent with Emily.

"Has it occurred to you that this isn't all about me? Emily is in this relationship, too. And it's a casual relationship. She doesn't want it to be more than that. She isn't interested."

His grandmother looked at him for a long moment. "You're many things, but I never thought you were a fool, Ryan. Can you lend me your phone? I want to call Murph and tell him I'll pick up the keys tomorrow."

"You can't pick up the keys until you own the place."

"I do own the place."

Ryan stared at her. "It only came on the market recently. You only just saw it."

"Murph called me the instant it happened, and he drove me over to take a look."

Ryan digested that. "And you didn't tell me?"

"You had a lot on your mind." She patted him on the arm. "Now, take me home and help me pack up some boxes."

It was their first trip to the harbor since they'd come back from the hospital, and they could barely take a step without being accosted by well-wishers.

Emily kept a close eye on Lizzy and tried not to fuss. "What would you most like to do?"

"Can we have waffles and chocolate milk?"

She'd been steeling herself for that inevitable request. Waffles and chocolate milk would mean visiting the Ocean Club and possibly bumping into Ryan. She'd discovered that asking him to keep his distance hadn't stopped her from thinking about him, nor had it stopped Lizzy talking about him. She'd reached the stage where she was ready to scream and cover her ears and had distracted herself by making endless collages with seashells found on the beach outside the door. But that pastime had only held Lizzy's attention for a short time. She'd discovered that a recovering Lizzy was harder to handle than a sick Lizzy. She wanted to be out on the water, swimming, seeing the puffins, anything other than staying trapped indoors.

Emily had suggested a trip to Summer Scoop, but it was clear that no activity was going to match the awesome experience of waffles and chocolate milk, so she surrendered to the inevitable. Why not? If they were staying on the island, then they were going to bump into Ryan sooner or later.

Lizzy insisted on taking both Andrew and her new puffin, and they were met by a smiling Kirsti, who showed them to their usual table.

Once again a large crowd of students had the table next to them, but this time Emily barely spared them a glance.

"One extra-chocolatey chocolate milk for an extra special guest." Kirsti placed the tall glass in front of Lizzy with a flourish and did the same with Emily's coffee. "Can I get you anything else?"

Lizzy looked around hopefully. "Is Ryan here?"

"No." Kirsti gave her a sympathetic look. "We haven't seen him this morning. He's dealing with some business down at the marina. Some guy whose ego is bigger than his yacht, and that's saying something." She walked off with a wink and a smile to serve another table of customers, and Lizzy's shoulders drooped.

She clutched the puffin in both hands, Andrew lying forgotten on one of the vacant chairs. "Why don't we see Ryan anymore?"

"He's busy, honey." It horrified her how badly she wanted to see him.

Was she really going to be able to live in such close proximity, or was she fooling herself?

Misery was a cold hard lump inside her. It was impossible not to second-guess herself. Maybe she should have let the relationship take its course. But how would that have worked? Eventually he would have moved on, and that would have made the situation even more awkward.

The best option would have been not to fall in love with him in the first place, but it was too late for that.

Lizzy put the puffin down carefully and reached for her milk. "He said he loved us."

"He does love us in his own way, but he has a job to do and his own life."

And that life wasn't going to include them.

She couldn't wallow in self-pity; she had to move on. She had to keep Lizzy busy and introduce new people into her life.

Lizzy stared miserably across the restaurant, and then the chocolate milk slipped from her hands and spilled across the table, splattering Emily.

With lightning reflexes, she rescued puffin and Andrew, but before she could speak, Lizzy shrank down in her chair.

"He's here."

Emily was busy trying to stem the flood with a couple of napkins. "Ryan?"

"The man with the camera. The one who climbed into the house."

It took a few seconds for the words to sink in, and when they did, Emily dropped the napkins and slowly turned her head. The man was standing between her and the door, blocking the only exit. He scanned the restaurant as if searching for someone, and, after a few moments, he approached a couple at the table nearest to him and showed them a photograph. Heart thumping, Emily pushed both toys into Lizzy's hands. "Get under the table, sweetheart."

"But—"

"Get under the table, and whatever happens, don't move." She positioned herself with her back to the restaurant, hoping to block the man's view.

She was thinking hard about her options when she heard Ryan's deep voice behind her.

"We're busy today. I'm going to have to ask if you mind sharing your table."

Melting with relief, Emily turned her head to warn him, but he put his hand on her shoulder and gave it a firm squeeze.

"I've got this. Just crowd around and pull up a few extra chairs." He smiled at the students at the table next door, and they swiftly decamped to Emily's table, laughing, chatting and crowding around as he'd instructed. "Anna, give Emily your hat. She's in full sun there."

The girl next to her slid her hat from her head and passed it to Emily.

She glanced down and saw the words Marine Center embroidered on the front.

"Put it on," Ryan said softly. "Keep your back to the room and leave the rest to me."

"Here—" Anna pushed a copy of *Marine Biology* into her hand. "Get stuck into that. Don't look so panicked. Ryan has got this. We've all got this."

Two bulky guys with windswept hair sat either side of her, and one of them put his backpack carefully on the floor in front of Lizzy. With so many legs and backpacks, it would be next to impossible for anyone to see her.

Even so, Emily's heart was thudding as he approached the table.

"Hi." His smile was warm and friendly. "You guys live on the island?"

Anna smiled back. "During the summer. You?"

"Sadly, mine is a short visit. I wondered if you'd seen this little girl around." He handed a photo of Lizzy to Anna, who studied it carefully, shook her head and then passed it across the table to another girl.

Their eyes locked, their fingers brushed, and the photo fell into a sticky pool of chocolate milk.

Anna tutted. "Rita, you are so clumsy." She made a fuss of wiping it and tore the edge. "Oh, no! Now I'm the clumsy one."

The man gritted his teeth as he took it back. "I thought you might have seen her? She's traveling with her mother, a woman called Emily."

"Your wife and child?"

"My sister and her little girl. There are marital problems. I promised I'd help her."

"Your niece?" Anna took another look at the photo. "She doesn't look anything like you. But, no, I don't remember seeing her."

"The address is Castaway Cottage, but it's not listed anywhere, and no one I ask seems to know where it is."

"Castaway Cottage?" Anna looked vague. "Never heard of it, and this is my third summer on the island. You could try asking Pete—he drives the island cab."

"I did. He said there is no Castaway Cottage." The man looked frustrated. "But I know that's the address."

"Not on this island. Let me see that photo." Ryan took it from the man. "She looks like Summer. Her mother owns Summer Scoop just along Main Street. Or maybe not. It's not a great picture."

"If you wanted to rent somewhere out of the way on this island where no one would look for you, where would you stay?"

Ryan didn't hesitate. "White Pine House. But there's no way she'd stay there."

"Why?"

"Because getting there is a nightmare. It's in the middle of the island at the top of a trail that is impassable in bad weather. I wouldn't even try it if I were you."

"Can you give me directions?"

Ryan shrugged. "They're your tires. Do you have a map? I can show you." He was polite and friendly as he took the map of the island from the man's hand. "You want to take a right at the forest trail. It's a pretty rough road, but it's the only way up to Heron Pond. Be careful as you take Pond Bridge. There was some structural damage over the winter, and repairs haven't been finished yet. You might want to park and walk."

The guy stepped away with a nod of thanks.

"What a douche," Anna muttered as he walked away. "Please tell me he's going to blow out his tires on the way to the pond."

"He will." Ryan was calm. "And if by chance he makes it as far as the bridge, he'll probably take a swim."

"He's going to be calling for help," Anna said happily, and Ryan smiled back.

"He'll try. There is no cell phone coverage by the pond. He's going to have a long, tiring walk back down to the road."

Emily wasn't so easily reassured. "He knows about Castaway Cottage. He must have gotten the details from the hospital." She was sickened by it. "What if someone tells him where it is?"

"How can they, when none of us has ever heard of Castaway Cottage?" Ryan winked at her and then called Kirsti over. "Is it done?"

"It was done twenty seconds after you gave me the nod. Check your phone. And for those who don't text, we've been calling around leaving messages."

Ryan pulled his phone out of his pocket, smiled and handed it to Emily. There on the screen was a text warning the islanders about the journalist, complete with a photograph.

"How did you take that without him noticing?"

Kirsti smiled. "I'm sneaky."

Emily couldn't relax that easily. "What if he comes back?"

"I guarantee you by the time he leaves the island,

he won't want to come back in a hurry." Ryan dropped to his haunches and grinned at Lizzy. "Hi there, tiger. Time to come out."

"Ryan!" Lizzy wriggled through legs and backpacks and launched herself into his arms. "It was him."

"I know, honey, but he'll be leaving again soon. In the meantime, how do you feel about spending the day at Harbor House with Agnes? She really needs your help with Cocoa while she packs boxes." He stroked her back gently, and Lizzy wrapped her arms and legs around him like a monkey.

"Will you be there, too?"

Across the top of Lizzy's head, Ryan's gaze met Emily's. She saw something flicker in the depths of his eyes, and then he set the child down, peeling her arms from around his neck.

"Later." His voice was husky. "First, I'm going to make sure Mr. Photographer never bothers you again." He turned to Emily. "Don't leave until I text you. John Harris is going to let me know as soon as he's safely on the ferry."

She nodded. Without his quick thinking, Lizzy's presence would have been exposed, and she wanted to express her gratitude. She wanted to pull back all the things she'd said, but then she saw Lizzy slide her arms around his legs and cling, and knew she had to stand firm.

"Thank you." She told herself it was the overwhelming gesture of warmth from the community that made her feel like sitting down and sobbing her heart out. For her whole life she'd felt like a small piece of a jigsaw puzzle that had been dropped on the floor and lost, fitting nowhere. Now she felt as if she'd found her place.

A small piece, fitting perfectly into a bigger picture. For the first time in her life, she felt as if she belonged. There were people looking out for her.

The price she had to pay for that was not being with Ryan. She'd thought that was the simple option.

Now she was wondering if it might kill her.

Emily spent the rest of the day packing boxes with Agnes and picking up texts from various islanders determined to give her a nonstop commentary on what was happening. She was grateful for any activity that stopped her thinking about Ryan.

"The journalist got the car stuck on Pond Bridge and had to walk back down to the harbor." She gave Agnes an update. "He called a cab."

Agnes looked interested. "And how did that turn out for him?"

Emily scrolled through her texts. "Not well. Peter told him his cab had been booked all day by a family from Boston, so he tried Larry, but his cab was in the garage having the brakes fixed."

"It's a terrible thing that island transport is so bad."

"Before he left, he went into Summer Scoop and showed Lisa the photograph."

"Did she bury it deep in vanilla ice cream?"

"No, she said the little girl in the picture looked like Summer. Then she asked if she could keep the photograph because she objected to people taking pictures of her daughter without permission."

Agnes laughed as she wrapped up two candlesticks. "That was smart of her. And there is just enough of a resemblance between Summer and Lizzy that he might believe it."

"He asked the Realtor on Main Street if he'd ever heard of Castaway Cottage, and she suggested he try Bar Harbor."

"That will be Tilly Hobson. She believes houses choose people, not the other way around." Agnes sealed the box, and Emily scrambled to her feet.

"Don't lift that. I'll do it. I've met Tilly. I spoke to her a few days ago."

"You're looking for property?"

"Yes. It was kind of Brittany to let us use Castaway Cottage, but we can't stay there forever. We need somewhere of our own, but houses don't come up that often on Puffin Island." She lifted the box and stacked it with the others and then heard her phone beep. "That will be Ryan with another update."

But it turned out to be a text from Brittany, and when Emily read it she sat down on the chair with a thump.

Agnes paused with a stack of table mats in her hand. "Another update?"

"No. This time it's Brittany. She fell on the archaeological dig in Greece. She's broken her wrist." She pulled a face and sent a text back. "Poor Brit. You know how active she is—she'll go crazy with her right hand out of use."

"What's her plan?"

"To come home while she heals and then make some life decisions. Her postgraduate work at Oxford University has finished. This dig was something she was doing for fun while she decided what to do next." Emily absorbed the implications of that. "Looks like I might have need of Tilly's services sooner than expected."

"Brittany wouldn't want you to move out. I wouldn't

rush into anything." Agnes looked vague. "Something might turn up."

Emily, who believed in structuring her life as much as she could, wasn't reassured. "I'm sure we can stay with Brittany for a while, but I feel, for Lizzy's sake, it's time we found somewhere that's ours. I want her to have security." She wanted Lizzy to have everything she'd never had herself. "I've enrolled her in school for September. She might even have Rachel as her teacher."

Agnes's face softened. "Lucky Lizzy. That girl has the sweetest nature. When Ryan was injured I couldn't drag Rachel from the hospital. Those two are very close. For weeks, she slept in the chair, and when he started the long rehabilitation process, she was the one bullying him into doing those exercises and pushing a little harder each day."

"He's very protective of her."

"Always has been. He took some serious teasing in school for looking out for his little sister. I remember one time the class had to take the thing they loved most into school for show-and-tell. It was meant to be a toy or a book. Rachel insisted on taking Ryan. They had to excuse him from math so he could sit on the mat with her. His friends gave him hell over that one, but he showed up, anyway." Agnes's eyes misted. "Oh, that little girl loved her big brother. He was a hero to her, and I've never seen anyone so patient as he was with his sister."

The lump in Emily's throat made it difficult to swallow. "He's been great with Lizzy. That day we went sailing, he was so patient with her." And she had to keep reminding herself that it had been a happy afternoon, that was all. Just because he was good with Lizzy, didn't mean he wanted to do it more often.

There was no room in life for dreaming.

She picked up a painting from the floor and paused, scanning the beautiful beach scene. "Is this one of Skylar's?"

"It's a watercolor she did when she was eighteen. She gave it to Kathleen as a thank-you for having her to stay. I admired it, and Kathleen left it to me. I love the colors. It's like bringing part of the beach indoors."

"Sky would be proud to know you love it enough to hang it on your wall." Emily wrapped it carefully. "I know it meant a lot that Kathleen believed in her. Whenever we stayed, she made sure Sky had a place to paint. Her own parents didn't do that for her. They thought her artistic talents detracted from what was important in life." She slid the painting carefully into the box. "She comes from a family of lawyers, and they wanted her to be a lawyer, too."

Agnes handed her a piece of tape. "The job of a parent is to nurture and guide, not kill dreams. What about you? What was your dream?"

"There wasn't any room in my life for dreams."

"And now?"

Something in the way Agnes was looking at her made her wonder if she'd guessed.

"I find it safer to focus on reality." Emily kept her eyes down, closed the box and secured it with tape. "I'm going to find a house that will be a good home for us. Then think about work. There's a property vacant on Harbor Road, not far from Summer Scoop. I'm thinking of maybe opening a boutique gift shop with a beach theme." The idea had come to her in the night, and she'd felt a rush of excitement and anticipation. Instead of helping with other people's businesses, why not start her own? "I want to sell everything from jewelry to shells and maybe small pieces for the home. I have to run some numbers. Ask a few questions. Do you think it's a crazy idea?"

"I think it's a good idea." Agnes pushed another empty box toward her, and together they filled it while Emily waited for another text from Ryan telling them it was safe to go home. It never came. Instead, he came himself, taking the steps to Harbor House two at a time as the last ferry of the day sailed out into the bay on its journey across to the mainland.

Emily watched his approach from the large bay window and wondered if there was ever going to be a time when she could look at him and not want him.

Seeing him made her light-headed, as if she'd walked from darkness into the full glare of sunlight.

Fortunately she had herself under control by the time he walked into the room, and he answered her question before she asked it.

"He's headed home. He won't be bothering us again. Good thing he isn't a travel journalist, or Puffin Island would be in for some seriously negative publicity about the state of our roads and the clueless nature of its inhabitants. He was persistent, I'll give him that. He must have questioned every damn person on the island, even Hilda."

"Hilda?" Emily put down the painting she'd been wrapping. "What did poor Hilda say?"

"She pretended to be deaf. She made him shout so loudly he had an audience stretching from the harbor to Puffin Point."

Agnes laughed and walked to the door. "Talking of Lizzy, I'm going to see how she's getting on with that doll's house of Rachel's." She walked out of the room, leaving them alone, and Emily wondered how it was possible to feel self-conscious and awkward after everything they'd done together.

"I can't believe everyone did that for Lizzy."

"And you." His voice softened. "They did it for you, too. It can take a long time for mainlanders to be accepted here, but you've thrown yourself into island life and you've been officially adopted."

"Oh—" Her eyes filled, and she realized how ridiculous it was to feel like crying over something she should be celebrating.

And she knew her tears had nothing to do with her status as an islander, and everything to do with the way she felt about him.

In the past few weeks, she'd learned so many things and faced things she'd buried for most of her life. Now, instead of protecting herself from emotion, she was flooded by it.

She was starting to wonder if the dream of living here was really going to work.

Now she'd started feeling again, she didn't want to stop. And she wasn't sure she could hide it.

"Thank you. I don't even want to think about how that might have turned out if you hadn't done what you did. All of you. And please thank the group from the marine center." She scrambled to her feet. "Lizzy and I will come back tomorrow and help Agnes finish up."

"Why would you leave?"

"Because in a minute Lizzy will come downstairs and see you, and then she won't want to let you go." Avoiding his gaze, she stacked the last of the boxes by the door. "The ones with the black mark can be recycled. The red mark means they can go to the charity store. The green means Agnes is taking it when she moves."

There was a tense silence.

"What if I don't want to let her go? What if I don't want to let *you* go?"

"I'm taking the box by the door over to Lisa because there are some toys that Summer and Harry might—" She broke off and stared at him. "What did you just say?"

"What if I don't want to let you go?"

There was a clatter and thump from upstairs, but for once Emily didn't rush to investigate. She trusted Agnes, and anyway, her feet were glued to the floor. "I don't know what you mean."

He closed the door, giving them privacy. "I want to talk about us."

Us.

Such a small, simple word to hold such deep significance. "There can't be an us, Ryan."

"There already is." He crossed the room to her and took her face in his hands. "There's been an 'us' from the first day you opened the door to me. There was an 'us' when you trusted me with your secret, when you asked me to teach you to swim, when you let me take you out in a boat and when you let me take you to bed. There was an 'us' when I came to the hospital, and when you told me you didn't want me in your life. If there hadn't been an 'us,' you wouldn't have felt the need to say that."

"I said it because Lizzy fell in love with you. I'm protecting her feelings."

"And what about you?" His voice was soft, his gaze holding hers. "What about your feelings?"

"How I feel doesn't matter. I can't let it matter. There's too much at stake." She felt as if she were teetering on the edge of a crumbling cliff with everything secure about to disintegrate beneath her feet.

"Do you know what I think, Emily Donovan?" His voice was husky and warm. "I think you're using Lizzy as an excuse. I think the reason you can't let it matter isn't because you're afraid for Lizzy, but because you're afraid for yourself. I think what's at stake isn't Lizzy's heart, but your own. You're scared. You've gone through life avoiding anything that threatens your emotions and that included picking men who wouldn't make you feel deeply."

She swallowed hard. "What does that say about me?"

"That you were scared. Love scares you, so you stayed in the shallow end of the relationship pool, picking guys who could never put your heart in danger. But I taught you to swim, Emily." He ran his thumb gently over her cheek. "I taught you how to kick and stay afloat. I taught you what to do when a riptide grabs you. It's important to make good decisions, but you don't have to let fear hold you back, sweetheart."

The endearment ripped at her. "Are we talking about love or swimming?"

"Both. Loving Lizzy has been hard for you, and I think it's scary for you to admit you love me, too."

Her heart skipped a beat. The fact that he knew left her feeling raw and exposed, like a sea creature left stranded on the beach when the tide retreated. "Aren't you a little sure of yourself?"

His mouth tilted into a crooked smile. "Honey, I

wasn't sure at all. I was upset that you'd pushed me away. I thought you weren't interested. It was Agnes who made me see the truth. You associate love with being hurt, and you're afraid I'll hurt you. You're protecting yourself."

Why would she deny the truth? If she was honest, maybe he'd respect her wishes and stay away, instead of making things harder. "Yes."

"You've lived your life doing that, caring for yourself, protecting yourself. You learned how to heal yourself, nurture yourself, and part of the way you did that was to cut out the things that threatened you. Children. Love."

"It worked better for me that way. But Lizzy is my family now. I had no choice about that, but now I wouldn't have it any other way. Skylar was right that sometimes the worst things can turn out to be the best. When the time is right, I'm going to formally adopt her."

"It never crossed my mind you'd do anything else. What would you say if I told you what I want is to spend the rest of my life trying to stop anything from hurting you and Lizzy? What would you say if I told you I want you both in my life?"

She took a few unsettled breaths, trying to listen to her head and not her heart. Trying to use reason and not emotion. "You value your independence. The ability to come and go as you please. You told me you didn't plan on giving that up anytime soon. This relationship can't be a revolving door, Ryan. You can't come and go as it suits you." Because she didn't trust emotion not to defeat reason, she pulled away from him and started to walk across the room, but he caught her arm and hauled her back to him.

"Damn it, Emily, I don't want a revolving door. I want to walk through it and stay. I want to lock it and throw away the key. I'm telling you I want to be with you. Both of you. I'm telling you I love you."

At first the words floated on the surface of her brain without penetrating. Then she assumed she'd misheard. "I—what?" She wondered if wishful thinking had conjured the words in her head. Had he really said that aloud?

"I love you."

"No, you don't. You love your freedom. You love being able to go with the wind and the tide."

"Yes. But there comes a time when what feels right is to drop anchor and stay a while in the same place. For me, that time is now."

She looked at him and saw her feelings mirrored in his eyes. "Ryan—"

"If this new, fledgling family of yours is looking for extra members, I thought I might apply. I can give you my résumé if you like, but you'll find I'm well qualified in certain aspects of child care including, but not limited to, rescuing soft toys from dangerous circumstances."

In all her life she'd never known a feeling like this one. She didn't know how to express everything in her head and her heart.

"I— Ryan— I don't know what to say."

"I want you to say yes to my question."

"Did you ask me a question?"

"Not yet, but I'm about to." He pulled his hand out of his pocket and handed her a box. "Will you marry me?"

Emotion swelled inside her, and her eyes filled. She opened the box and stared down at the sparkling diamond through eyes misted with tears.

"Ryan—"

"Will you trust me with Lizzy? Will you trust me with your heart? Can you do that?"

The cliff gave way beneath her feet, but instead of falling she was flying. "Yes." The word was almost inaudible, so she said it again. "Yes. Oh, yes."

And then he was kissing her, his mouth hard and demanding, his hands possessive and protective. Somewhere through the mists of passion, she heard the door opening, and she pulled away to see Lizzy peeping around the door with Agnes behind her.

"Can we come in, Ryan? Have you done it?"

Her hand still locked in the front of his shirt, Emily glanced up at him. "You told her to stay away?"

"I told her I had something important to ask you."

"He said it was private." Lizzy skipped across the room, and he scooped her up.

Watching the two of them together, Emily felt her heart flutter.

"Lizzy, we have something to tell you."

"I already know." She leaned her head against Ryan's shoulder, blond curls brushing against dark. "Ryan loves us. I told you that in the hospital, but you didn't believe me. Can we go and see the puffins again soon? Can we go sailing and eat waffles?"

"Yes." Emily's voice was muffled as Ryan pulled her close with his other arm. "Yes, we can do all those things."

Agnes walked into the room, a smile on her face. "Tilly is on the phone. You called her about a rental, but I told her it was a mistake."

Emily eased away from Ryan's grip, wondering how she was supposed to focus on the practical when her head was spinning. "But Brittany is coming home, and I still need to find somewhere to live."

She saw Ryan exchange a look with Agnes and smile.

"You don't need to find somewhere to live." He lowered Lizzy to the window seat that overlooked the harbor. "I happen to know of a large family home with a sea view that's not even on the market yet. It will be perfect for us."

* * * * *

Acknowledgments

Without my brilliant editor, Flo Nicoll, writing would be nowhere near as much fun or as productive. I'm grateful for her wise comments and the insight she offers on each book.

I'm thankful to my agent, Susan Ginsburg, and the team at Writers House who continue to be a wonderful source of support and encouragement in my career, and to the fantastic teams at Harlequin UK and HQN in the US who work so hard to put my books into the hands of readers.

Thanks to my husband for answering my questions on sailing, for not drowning me whenever he's taken me out on the water and for not rolling his eyes when I hung over the side moaning like a drama queen.

Developing a new series is always fun and exciting. I'm grateful to fellow author and friend Nicola Cornick for always being on the end of the phone when I hit a plot problem and to Andrew Cornick for generously allowing me to use his beautiful photographs of puffins on my website.

My two sons bought me a colony of soft toy puffins

to act as inspiration on my desk, thus providing further proof of my family's support of my unusual profession.

My final thanks go to my readers, who cheer me daily with their kind emails, Tweets and Facebook comments. Thank you for buying my books. You're the best.

Sarah
xxx

Join #1 *New York Times* bestselling author

SUSAN WIGGS

on the shores of Willow Lake with this story of uncovering the past and finding somewhere to belong.

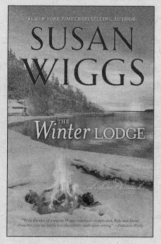

When Jenny Majesky loses everything in a devastating house fire, the last thing she expects is to find an unusual treasure hidden amid her grandfather's belongings—one that starts her on a search for a truth she never knew. The Winter Lodge, a remote cabin owned by her half sister on the shores of Willow Lake, becomes a safe refuge for Jenny, where she and local police chief Rourke McKnight try to sort out the mysteries revealed by the fire.

But when a blizzard traps them together, Jenny, accustomed to the safe predictability of running the family bakery, suddenly doesn't feel so secure. For even as Rourke shelters her from the storm outside, she knows her heart is at risk. Now following her dreams might mean walking away from her one chance at love.

Available now, wherever books are sold!

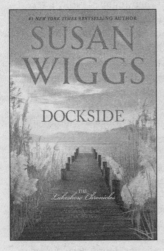

#1 *New York Times* Bestselling Author

SUSAN WIGGS

Revisit the tranquil shores of Willow Lake in this heartwarming tale about the loves that fill a woman's life.

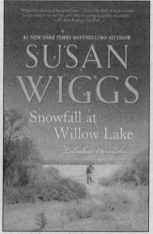

International lawyer Sophie Bellamy has dedicated her life to helping people in war-torn countries. But when she survives a hostage situation, she remembers what matters most—the children she loves back home. Haunted by regrets, she returns to the idyllic Catskills village of Avalon on the shores of Willow Lake, determined to repair the bonds with her family.

There Sophie discovers the surprising rewards of small-town life—including an unexpected passion for Noah Shepherd, the local veterinarian. Noah has a healing touch for anything with four legs, but he's never had any luck with women—until Sophie. But Sophie's heart needs healing...and both she and Noah need a chance at happiness.

Available October 24, wherever books are sold!

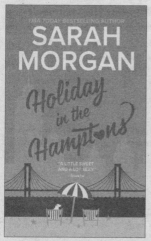